# THEIRS TO CHERISH

---

QUINTESSENCE

SERENA AKEROYD

# THEIRS TO CHERISH

Triggers:

- General violence,
- Miscarriage,
- Torture,
- Kidnapping,
- Gun violence

SAWYER

# ONE

THE MUSIC WAS sultry and sexy.

The beat throbbed around them, turbocharging it with a storm of sensation that seemed to power the air itself. The heat was oppressive in the tight confines of the bar, and her skin was slick with it, her hair clinging in unfurling tendrils to her throat, her skin-tight dress hugged her in places she didn't even want to think about—but she didn't care.

Nothing mattered.

Sandwiched between Devon Jerome and Sawyer Bennett, Sascha Dubois was in her element.

If a person had more than one element, she'd found it.

Not only was she the stuffing in a genius sandwich, she was also on the dancefloor, wriggling, writhing, and generally strutting her stuff as they danced to a beat that was most definitely of their own making. Tango, of course, was not known for requiring three dance partners to move together. She and her guys had improvised and created something that made her feel like she was having sex on the dance floor.

Behind her, Sawyer bumped and ground into her. His hands were on her hips, and each time he rippled with a new move, stepping in a perfect rhythm with her and Devon that was years in the making, his cock dug deep into her butt. She loved that feeling. *Loved* it. Wanted to roll around in it like a kid intent on diving into a new mound of fresh snow, with snow angels at the top of their to-do list.

Devon moved like a pro.

*She* was the crappiest dancer among them, but being in the middle had its benefits. She didn't have to move all that much, just had to roll her hips and sway and wriggle against them, letting her guys do the work.

The thought had laughter rippling from her, and she let her head fall back against Sawyer's shoulders, not surprised when he leaned down to nip her ear and growl, "What are you laughing at?"

The 'you' came out more as a 'yoo' and the 'are' had such a roll on the letter 'r' that her pussy spasmed in response. His Scottish brogue felt like a sensory firework display on most days, but when they were so close to having sex? It was like the start of a detonation sequence that ended with her coming all over his face.

Because, Sascha knew, there was no way today was ending any way other than with her spit roasted between them.

Tango led to sex.

It was her incentive to remember the steps.

Devon had told her so.

Her lips curved in a smile at that particular memory; Devon's incentivizing strategy had been born out of her inability to put the steps together. With his usual problem-solving brain, he'd decided that orgasms were the solution.

He hadn't been wrong. Now, she could remember the steps, but she wasn't any good at them.

Positive reinforcement didn't a dancer make.

"I'm just thinking," she half-shouted, loud enough to be heard over the music.

"Always dangerous," Sawyer grumbled, but she heard the amusement in his tone.

She looked over at Devon whose focus was on her tits. Since they'd found out she was pregnant, he was monitoring the stages of pregnancy through her breasts—at least, that's what she told herself.

Could she help it that they'd doubled?

Carrying her son, Valentin, had proven that! Now, Devon's already bizarre hyper focus had been captured by her cleavage, which meant she was used to speaking to him with his eyes anywhere but on hers.

There was something sexy about his intensity though.

The way he looked at her made her feel primal and raw, and no matter how *round* she got, or how huge she felt, his desire for her never lessened. If anything, his sexual appetite seemed to increase.

And she wasn't about to complain on that score.

Like her, his hair was mussed and sweaty. Though Glasgow was freezing—and boy, that was no understatement—inside the tango club it was sweltering hot, the temperature close to tropical. Which meant his face was as slick as hers, the cowlick that made her heart melt had wilted, and, though his hair was closely shorn, it had still slipped down to cover his forehead. His face, so beautiful with his firm lips, strong jaw, wide brow, and eyes so blue she felt she could dive into them, was set in stern lines as he split his focus between her breasts and the moves he'd learned years before—and still had to teach her from time to time.

He'd made the dance into some kind of math exercise. She had no idea how he did it, no idea how he'd used that to teach Sawyer the steps, but either way, she was monkey in the middle and she sucked at it. But she'd carry on sucking, just because it made him look at her like *that.*

He was leading them, making sure they moved in a pattern that followed the tango steps. He was the driving force behind the dance and when his mouth was set, his brow furrowed, and his eyes burned, Sascha could drop to her knees and just...

She groaned inwardly.

Thoughts of tasting his cock, of having Sawyer's in her fist, plagued her. Yes, *plagued*, because there was no way, when he still looked so focused, that they were getting out of here any time soon.

"You getting wet, lass?"

The words were a rumble along her nerve endings, an added sensation she didn't need in her already overwhelmed system. She'd thought she'd hidden her groan, but she must have made a sound. Sometimes, being the center of their attention was a nuisance.

They missed nothing, because her men were, in every way, shape, and form, unlike the rest of the male population.

She cut her hair? They noticed, and would demand she account for every lost inch—not because they were controlling, but because most of them had a 'thing' about her bright auburn locks. Devon especially. He liked it when she wrapped it around his cock as she sucked him off. She couldn't do that after a haircut. And Devon didn't accept 'split ends' as a justifiable excuse. Even Kurt, the most chilled of her men, would stare at the shorter length with disappointment in his gaze—reminding her of Tin when she informed him it was time for bed.

Sawyer's chin scraped against hers, nudging her thoughts to the issue at hand, and she licked her lips as his words hit home. Was she wet? Yes! She tilted her face to slide her sweaty forehead against Sawyer's equally slick throat. She felt the faint burn as the tender skin of her temple rubbed lightly over his five o'clock shadow, but she didn't stop. The sensation grounded her, and she seriously needed to be grounded.

"Yes," she whispered, softly enough she couldn't be heard over the music.

Still, he laughed, the sound so cocksure and satisfied she wanted to throat punch him then kiss it better. He rocked his pelvis forward, nudging her with his thickness again—God, they were all so big. It drove her fucking wild. "No chance we're getting out of here for another hour, at least," Sawyer said directly into her ear, having read Devon's intent look with an accuracy that made her want to groan because it confirmed her own. "Torture."

Licking her lips again, she tried to speak but words failed her, so she just nodded.

"Unless..." His statement trailed off and her eyes flared wide as he reached up, moving his hands from her waist to curve them over her tits. She moaned a little, their sensitivity making her freeze in Devon's grasp. Her sudden lack of motion had broken that hyper focus of his, *or* given it a new target—Sascha figured that was more accurate.

His head tilted to the side, and his brow puckered. "What's wrong?"

His voice was barely audible over the music. A sudden guitar solo pierced the dark nightclub. It was close to pitch black with only a rosy red light shimmering over the packed floor. Dancers were crammed together, uncaring of the close quarters, just loving the opportunity to revel in the freedom that came with this sexy tangle of arms and legs, the vibrant delight of being in a lover's arms.

The wraparound dress she wore was skin-tight, hugging her belly and her ass, cupping her breasts in a firm hold. She felt sassy and sultry, but under Devon's deep stare?

She felt like a Queen.

*He* made her feel like that.

This man. This brilliant, gifted man, who could and *had* solved mathematical mysteries that had confounded a whole generation of mathematicians, looked at her as though she were his be-all and end-all.

As if without her in his life, he had no reason to live.

Under that heady appraisal, she was about to speak when Sawyer leaned forward, pushing Sascha with him, and urging her closer to Devon's chest where her tits connected with his pecs. The move brought him closer to his best friend of three decades, as he'd sandwiched her even more deeply between them, and he hollered, "Sascha's ready for bed."

She had to hide a grin at that clever wording—you had to be smart where Devon was concerned. He had the brain of a lawyer with the disinterest of a zit-pocked adolescent in doing chores. So, sure, she *was* ready for bed. Just not for sleep.

"You are? What's wrong?" It was like Sawyer hadn't spoken, his focus on her was absolute.

"Just ready to get off my feet," she said, aiming for airy, and unsure if she hit the target. At her back, she could feel Sawyer shake with laughter, but he grabbed her elbow before she could nudge him in his belly.

Devon scowled. "I knew we shouldn't have taken her dancing," he grumbled, scowling at Sawyer. "But you said she'd be fine."

"She *is* fine, ain't you, lass?" Sawyer purred, and the double entendre had her snickering.

Finally, Devon seemed to get with the program. "What's going on?" he demanded, pulling away to plant his hands on his hips.

She reached for him with a welcoming smile, then when he neared, she slipped her hand down his front. The black tee was stuck to him, clinging to his taut abs in a way that let her feel his muscles, before she reached his cock and cupped him over his jeans. "I'm hungry," she told him, looking up into his eyes, wishing she could see the true blue of them, but in this light it was impossible.

He clucked his tongue. "First you're sleepy, now you're hungry? Make up your mind, Sascha."

"How about she's horny?" Sawyer grunted, his patience gone now.

"Why didn't you just say so?" Devon groused in return, and just like that, he grabbed the hand that was holding his cock, and tugged her off the dancefloor.

One thing that could be said for tunnel vision, it moved mountains.

Within seconds, she was away from the writhing bodies who

were making a frantic kind of love to the rhythmic Hispanic beats, and was heading for the exit.

Sawyer disappeared at her back, and she knew he was heading for the seats they'd claimed as their own a while ago. Whether their coats would still be hanging on the backs of their chairs, she wasn't sure, but she hoped so. It was going to be freezing outside, or as Sawyer's mom, Jacinta, called it, "A wee bit nippy."

"Nippy, my ass," she grumbled under her breath.

Nippy?

Definitely *nipply*. Her tits felt bright pink from the cold, and her nipples were beaded to a prominence that bordered on the ridiculous —another sin to lay at Valentin's door. Her tits had never been the same after breastfeeding him.

This was the kind of cold that made your bones freeze.

Yet Jacinta considered these temperatures to be quite mild. And considering there was no snow, Sascha guessed she wasn't wrong.

Thankfully, they'd yet to stay in Scotland when the weather was so inclement, and if she had her way, she would live without that particular experience.

It certainly wasn't on her bucket list. Glasgow rocked, but if they could just raise the temperature a few degrees? She'd be happier than a camel on Wednesday.

She clenched her fingers around Devon's as he moved them toward the vestibule. This was her surprise; they'd only arrived last night, and she'd spent most of the day sleeping because this baby made her want to live during the night and pass out through the day. This was her witching hour, and the first thing they'd done was bring her here.

It was a new club, Devon had told her. Looking proud as punch to have used the wonderful invention that was something called 'Google.' He'd told her about the new search engine, declaring it would change the world.

Like it hadn't been around for a decade or more.

Yeah, living with Devon presented certain *issues*.

Certain she'd seen Devon on the internet, and even surer he'd had to have used it at some point to search for *something*, she'd asked Sawyer about Devon's sudden discovery of Google, and Sawyer had merely said, "Bing."

Like no further words were required.

Which took her into a labyrinth of questions like exactly how Devon had avoided Google for so long? She knew for a fact he didn't live in a cave...

Seriously, though, what woman had the time to figure out why her savant partner worked the way he did?

So, while the man could recite complex economical and mathematical theories in his sleep, he barely remembered to brush his teeth and hair without setting alarms for everything on his phone—or Sawyer setting those alarms. Even she'd started doing it.

Shit, it was the only way to get anything done where Devon was concerned, and even then, if he was totally focused on work, there was no guarantee he'd even *hear* the alarm.

That's why she'd started setting five or six at a time.

A woman had to have some wiles on her side, didn't she?

When a hand cupped her shoulder, she smiled up at Sawyer. He'd shoved their coats at Devon while holding onto hers. Wrapping the quilted down around her, he tucked her up tight then draped her scarf across her shoulders. After Devon gave Sawyer his jacket, they both dressed against the cold weather and pulled on gloves. She found a pair of her own in her pocket.

The slinky black dress certainly hadn't been made for the Scottish midwinter, even if the peacoat Devon had bought for her at the same time was cozier than a quilt.

"She'll freeze her tatties off," Jacinta had declared earlier after giving her the once over.

Devon had sniffed and tucked her into the rather marvelous down-stuffed coat he'd also bought her.

"That's more like it," Jacinta had told him, her approval evident, then she'd beamed at her. "You look bonnier than I can tell ye, Sascha."

Now, surrounded by the enveloping folds, she wanted nothing more than to be surrounded by him. *Them*. Screw the coat.

A wicked thought came to her as they walked out into the cold night air. Lips curving, she asked, "Know what I want to do now?"

Sawyer choked out a laugh. "Go to McDonald's like last night?"

She snorted. "I was desperate and pregnant. What's a girl to do?"

"Wait the twenty minute ride to Jacinta's house?" Devon asked, his tone caustic.

Since they'd found out she was pregnant again, he'd turned into a health nut. Two in the house were way too many.

"I was starving," she grumbled. "And no, this has nothing to do with French fries." Although, the more she thought about it, the more she actually did want a burger.

Fuck.

Ooh, and fries to dip into a chocolate milkshake.

*Epic*.

Scrunching her nose as she nixed the idea, she mumbled, "You just spoiled my suggestion."

Sawyer tugged her into his side and he curled his arm over her shoulder. He nipped at her ear. "Spit it out, lass."

But she pouted. "No. You spoiled it."

Sawyer stilled. "Wait a minute. Was it a sex thing?"

"It totally was."

He groaned. "But you're always hungry at this time."

"Well, I was hungry for something else."

Devon, brows high and his expression hopeful under the amber streetlamps, asked, "For cock?"

Sawyer muttered an expletive. "Yes, Devon. What the fuck else would she be hungry for if it wasn't a burger and it was sex-related?"

Devon shrugged, jostling those super broad shoulders under his silk and wool blend Epsom coat. Jeez, he looked fine. The dark navy complimented his thick black hair and made his creamy skin look more olive—she'd wanted to jump him the minute he'd stepped out of the bathroom three hours ago.

In her opinion, she'd been patient for waiting *this* long.

And Sawyer? Who, unlike Devon in jeans and a tee, was in a dove gray button-down and black slacks, looked formal and sexy as fuck.

Or was that sexy enough *to* fuck? Sascha thought, hiding a wicked grin.

"I just wanted to make sure we were on the same page," was Devon's lofty retort.

"That's the perfect tense. *Were*," she said on a sniff. "My suggestion can just fall into obscurity seeing as you're both mean to me and my burger cravings."

"You know they're not good for you, lass," Sawyer immediately countered, his hand sliding around her waist so he could pat her belly. "If you'd just waited, we'd have made you a nice one. With ground steak instead of that processed shit."

She grimaced. Gah, they totally didn't get it. "Don't you sometimes just crave the processed shit?"

Devon heaved a sigh. "That's the American in you."

"Yeah? Well, I was hoping to have some English and some Scot in me, but we can't have everything, can we?"

Sawyer groaned. "Lass!"

She chuckled, deciding he'd suffered enough. Not Devon, though. He looked as oblivious as ever.

"Do you have like a lovers' hill or something?"

"A hill for lovers?" Devon asked, brow puckering. "The Scots aren't the most romantic of people, Sascha."

"Yeah, bud," she said drily. "You keep telling yourself that when Sawyer's the one who brings me flowers and chocolates, and you're the one who forgets our anniversaries unless you have four alarms set."

He scowled. "I remember."

"Since when?" It was Sawyer's turn to butt in, and he did so with a snort.

"Since the day you arrived. I remembered to set the alarms, so that has to be worth something. I just forget that I haven't wished you 'happy anniversary.'"

Despite herself, she had to giggle. "You're a nut, Devon," she told him, entwining her arm through his and rubbing her nose against it.

"No, Sascha, I'm not a nut," he said, his tone patient. "I'm Homo sapiens."

Sawyer groaned. "Sascha, you had to see that one coming?"

Her giggle morphed into a belly laugh. She dragged them to a halt as she bent over at the waist trying, and failing, to touch her knees, she used Sawyer as support instead.

"What's wrong with her?" Devon asked, clueless to a fault. His ability to concentrate was so intense in some matters, but on others? He might as well *be* a walnut.

"She's laughing at you."

"That isn't very nice," Devon said with a tut.

"Can't. Help. It," she gasped out, then using Sawyer to straighten up, she fanned her hands in front of her to cool down. "Your face," she bleated, then repeated with a snort. "*I'm Homo sapiens*. Priceless. Remind me to tell Sean that one. He'll laugh."

Devon pouted, but he didn't complain when she patted his chest then tilted her head back in preparation for a kiss from him. His six-feet plus height didn't present that much of a problem when she wasn't hefting another human around inside her, but now? There was no way her center of gravity was up for the challenge of standing on tiptoes.

He ducked down so he could press a kiss to her lips. It was just a peck... until she curled her arms around his neck and clung tightly to him. When he speared his tongue in her mouth with very little prompting, she gasped and waded into the fight. She jolted when Sawyer slapped her ass and grumbled, "We're in the middle of

Argyle Street, if you want to have an audience, we're in the best place."

Grumbling, she pulled back. "Lover's hill?" she repeated breathily.

Sawyer slapped her ass again. "If there was one, I'd be the one to know, provided I knew what it was for."

She twisted back to look up at him. "You park up there and neck, you know?"

"We can just go on one of the council estates for that. I'm sure the residents of Carntyne would get a kick out of watching that," Sawyer said drily. "But we'd also lose our hubcaps and our license plates."

"Oh. No fun." But her eyes twinkled at his joke. Even if it was at her expense.

"No, but you want to get down and dirty in the car, do you?" he asked, his brogue suddenly thick.

"Aye." She grinned when he rolled his eyes.

"It's far more comfortable at home, Sascha," Devon told her. "Nice and warm too. No fear of our hubcaps being stolen or of being arrested. That sounds like fun to me."

"I know, love, but that's beside the point."

He scowled. "You mean, you want to be uncomfortable?"

Her nostrils flared with amusement. "No. Not particularly, but I want you. *Now*. And I don't want to wait for the ride home."

He came to a halt. "You mean you *can't* wait five minutes?"

At his aghast expression, she nodded sagely. "I can't wait even five minutes."

His mouth rounded, then he cut Sawyer a worried glance. "We need to get to the car. Now."

She had to bite back a smile at the sudden urgency in his tone—and what she loved most was the fact that urgency was for her, not him.

"She's not going to explode," Sawyer groused, not as taken in by her plea.

"She can't wait five minutes, Sawyer. That means she's desperate," Devon retorted, grabbing her hand and half-dragging her down the street toward the lot where they'd parked their car. But she let herself be caught up in the whirlwind that was her math genius because he didn't move too fast for her ambling gait, and he was so fucking cute sometimes, she just wanted to melt.

Overhead, the streetlights only highlighted how grim the night was. The amber glow enhanced a cold that was fiery somehow, making her feel even more frigid. Everything was slick with rain, and the bitter chill in the air was only exacerbated by a nasty wind that howled down the narrow streets.

It was cold, wet, and miserable. No reason whatsoever to be happy. But being hustled towards their car for the orgasms Devon would give her because he thought she was so desperate for sex, she couldn't even bear to wait the short ride to Jacinta and Hamish's home, put a smile on her face.

How she contained her laughter, Sascha would never know. But she wouldn't laugh. If she did, he'd know she was teasing him. And that meant a delay on a Devon-gasm and those were eye-poppingly good. No way was she going to miss out on that.

Sometimes, she felt sure Devon thought she was some kind of nymphomaniac. Then, she'd ask herself if she was, because she could keep up with five guys no problem.

As Jacinta had called one of the celebrities on the TV last night, Sascha had to wonder if she too was a bit of a 'goer.' Not that she cared either way, she was just grateful she had the sex drive to satisfy her quintet of lovers.

The Mercedes gleamed under the grim amber puddle of light, and she shivered with relief at its proximity. More because she was cold, not starving for cock, though Devon's concerned glance told her he thought it was the latter, not the former.

But his concern wasn't founded on a throwaway sentence from her.

It had been established during her first pregnancy, and had been further cemented in this one.

The truth was: a pregnant Sascha was a horny Sascha.

And a horny Sascha was an aggressive Sascha.

Most of her guys were used to it now, but Devon still stared at her like she'd grown two heads because he wasn't used to being slammed against a wall so she could drop to her knees and suck his cock. And his perplexity only soared when he had to help her to her knees to facilitate said hunger.

Two days ago, when she'd turned into the aggressor on him, he'd stared at her in complete bewilderment, even as he was hissing as she swallowed him down whole.

His unique brain didn't seem to grasp the changes in her, and the way her hormones would fluctuate. Devon just knew he had to deal with them, and that he had to keep her happy.

Because she liked that he kept her happy, she'd decided not to change his opinion of her—the one that had her painted as a cock-hungry pregnant lady in his mind. Better that, in her eyes, than a fuddy-duddy.

Fuddy-duddies didn't have much sex appeal, and she loved that they saw her as a sexual being. It was the most empowered she'd ever felt in her life.

Hiding a smirk, she ducked into the front seat of the car when Sawyer opened the door for her. Devon climbed into the back as their Scot rounded the front of the vehicle and hopped in behind the wheel.

Devon didn't drive, even though he had a license, Sawyer was the one who drove them anywhere. Not that that happened much in London, but they did go out quite often here. The Merc, however, screamed Devon not Sawyer. So, while the Mercedes was a present from Devon for Sawyer's birthday, in her opinion, that was debatable.

Sawyer was a Porsche kind of guy. Sleek, low-riders that would have done a number on the small of her back. Devon? Not so much. He'd opted for a mini-tank, and the sedan was far too sedate for Sawyer's tastes. Although, Sawyer couldn't really complain—the custom-built birthday present had cost close to three-hundred thousand pounds. Sascha knew because she'd seen the money slide out of their checking account.

It stank of new car smell, and though that was usually a really nice scent, in her pregnant state, it was repugnant. Combined with the leather seats, it was working her over. So, even though it was cold, she opened the window a sliver to let some fresh air in to wash away the stench.

"Where are you taking me then?" she asked, after she clipped her belt into place and he'd started the engine.

"Don't you worry about it, lass. It's not far from here." Then, he blew her mind. Slinging an arm behind her seat, he looked over his shoulder and reversed. He moved the car like it was an extension of himself, and he looked so fucking sexy just reversing, she had to act.

"Good," she told him on a purr, and with that in mind, lifted the hem of her dress and dragged it over her thighs and up to the crease of her hip.

Sliding her hand underneath her panties, she felt how wet she was already and bit back a moan as she spread her legs and began to touch her clit.

"Lass?" The husky endearment sounded even huskier when he repeated it.

"Yes," she said on a breathy moan.

"What are you doing?"

"Tiding myself over."

He snorted at that, but it was Devon who said, "Are you sure those folic acid pills aren't actually Viagra?"

"Viagra doesn't work on women," she told him drily.

"Well, the female equivalent then," he said, sounding perplexed.

"Is that a complaint?" she gasped as she strummed her clit with one hand and slid two fingers from her other into her pussy.

"No, not at all, I just... I'm concerned for you."

She was touched, but she was too horny to care. "You can't expect to dance with me for hours, have your cocks nudging into me the whole time, and not think I'm going to want to screw your brains out, Devon."

He clucked his tongue. "You had sex with both of us this morning. And then again with Sawyer before we left."

"Can't keep up with me?" she jibed, but a breathy laugh escaped her at that. Her men were always hard for her.

*Always.*

Even when she'd been eight and a half months pregnant with Tin, they'd wanted her.

And God, she'd wanted them.

She'd always thought it was bullshit made up in stories that a woman could be horny when she was pregnant. How could anyone feel sexy when they were carrying around a bowling ball that constantly sat on your bladder, took away your ability to give yourself a pedi, and made your back ache like you'd been driven over by a truck?

And yet, she'd felt sexy.

And needy.

And hungry.

God, the hunger.

It was fucking with her again. She hated it and loved it equally.

Especially when she had five men who fed that love.

Sawyer had taught her a phrase yesterday: happier than a pig in shit.

It was fucking gross beyond compare, but hell. She totally got it. She was that pig. In shit.

Yeah, ew, but so true.

She plunged two fingers deep into her core and bit back a moan as the slender digits didn't even come close to soothing the agony of being so empty.

Devon gritted out, "Pull over, Sawyer."

*Yes!*

Devon's voice was husky with need and so damn deep she wanted to dive in it.

"I can't, man," was their Scot's retort. He sounded grumpy about it too. "Look around you. Where the fuck can I pull over?"

She wrinkled her nose, seeing his point. They were deep in the city, no parking on either side that wouldn't catch the police's attention because all the spaces were signposted as 'no waiting.' Plus, there were streetlamps everywhere, and it wasn't exactly a quiet part of town.

She scissored her fingers and rolled her hips down. The pleasure that zigzagged through her had her blurting out, "Oh fuck!"

"She's killing me," Devon murmured, and she almost congratulated him on that—he was finally understanding the concept of saying something without meaning it.

It had just taken forty years to accomplish it, she thought on an eye roll that was interrupted by a wave of pleasure that had her closing her eyelids mid-roll and relishing the sparks of pleasure igniting within her belly.

"Oh God, please," she pleaded, her words a chant as she said them over and over again.

"Fuck," Sawyer bit off, sounding utterly harassed.

With her eyes closed, she felt the sudden change in brightness. Before, there'd been the faint glow of the street lighting that had disturbed the intense darkness outside. Now? No. It was gone.

She blinked her eyes open, and saw the lights were spaced further out as they headed away from the city, deeper into a more rural part near where Jacinta and Hamish lived.

The farther they went—at quite a pace too considering Sawyer was intent on breaking land speed records—the asphalt roads with shops at either side morphed into ones lined with hand-built walls. The thick stones were craggy and green with tufted moss that seemed like they had been there since the time of Hadrian.

With her other hand, she rubbed her clit the moment she spotted a tiny rest area—*success*. "There," she whispered.

"Yeah. There." Devon was starting to sound desperate.

Sawyer grunted. "If we get in trouble for soliciting, I'm blaming you. And you can be the ones to call my Ma and explain why she needs to get us out of jail."

"Why would we be arrested for soliciting? Sascha isn't a prostitute."

She blinked. "No, I'm damn well not!" Her cheeks turned pink as she pulled her fingers from her sex and slapped Sawyer's arm with it. "Why would they think I'm a prostitute? What kind of hookers do you know who turn tricks when they've a belly a few months away from being bigger than a basketball?"

Sawyer didn't answer, but he grabbed her wrist and dragged her fingers to his nose. She swallowed when he sucked in a sharp breath and hummed. "You smell delicious."

"She tastes better," Devon purred.

She loved the way they desired her. It ramped her up, made her feel so fucking powerful because this need was mutual.

And she wouldn't have it any other way.

The car braked to a halt with a squeal, and within a second, Sascha had the door open. She groaned as she tried to climb out of the deep bucket seat by herself, but life wasn't being kind to her. Her baby bump was just too big for the angle of the seat, which made lowdown seem waist-height.

Grumbling, she turned her legs out and waited for one of them to help her. Sawyer was laughing as he walked around the hood. He stopped a foot away, just far enough out of reach for her to pout.

"Need some help there, lass?"

"Yes," she snapped. "Your spawn seriously gets in the way of my sex life."

"Only frogs have spawn," Devon told her from the backseat.

"Exactly. You're all frogs. Even the ones in London."

"That's not fair," Devon argued.

"No? Well, neither is not being able to climb out of the damn car by myself because I'm too big to move in my second trimester."

Sawyer's nostrils flared as he finally stopped laughing—but they were proof that he wasn't taking her seriously. "What will change the spawn back to a beautiful baby?"

She pouted. "Sucking my clit."

He flung back his head and laughed. But it was Devon who spoke first, "You're a brat, Sascha."

"You carry a baby, and see if you're not a brat."

"Men aren't capable of carrying babies. That's not a fair comparison."

She rolled her eyes. "No shit, Devon. Sometimes, men just don't have it fair, do they?"

"You're not wrong actually. There's a serious lack of balance in certain aspects of society..."

Sawyer grunted. "Dev, shut the fuck up, lad. Our Sascha doesnae want a lecture on the sociological aspects of the male versus female imbalance. She wants to be fucked. By us."

Sascha started nodding, her eagerness making Sawyer's lips curve wider—and he'd started talking with a really thick Scottish accent. That made her ears very happy bunnies.

She held out her hands. "Please," she pleaded.

He cocked a brow at her. "Now, that's a nice word. What more are you capable of?"

The sudden drop in his pitch set fire to her belly. Any nerves or agitation were lost in the inferno that his inference meant.

Sawyer was... well, it was difficult to say. She wasn't sure what he was. Was he dominant? Was he just a bossy Alpha? She thought it was both, but...

Gah, none of her men fit a label, so why should they sexually?

But still, she wished she knew, because it would prepare her for the times when they stunned the hell out of her by pulling another set of magic tricks out of their version of Pandora's box.

"I-I don't know. What do you want?" She hated that she was almost mewling, but it was that tone of voice. It triggered it in her.

"I think you should suck my cock. Don't you agree, Devon?"

"I don't want to suck your cock."

Sawyer gritted his teeth. "I didn't mean for you to do it, arsehole. I meant for Sascha to."

"Oh. Yes. I think she should," he agreed.

Sawyer just huffed. "Glad we're on the same page."

Sascha licked her lips as need overwhelmed her. She changed the angle of her fingers, changed them into a 'beckoning' motion. "Gimme," she said, and it was her turn to purr now.

"I don't know, Sascha. I think you should ask kindly for it."

Her eyes widened. "Ask kindly?"

"Aye." He smiled at her, and it reminded her of the kind of smile a principal at school gave to parents at a PTA meeting.

It was bland and empty.

Not loaded with the need he'd stirred in her, not burning with the heat she knew he had to be feeling.

*Damnit.*

It was too dark out. She couldn't see his bulge. Not in the faint light from the dash, and the car's interior light had turned off after being inactive for so long.

She sucked in a sharp breath. "Please, Sawyer. I want to taste you."

"There's that word again." Sawyer smirked. "*Please.* A powerful word, lass."

"Please, *please,*" she begged, her voice getting breathy now. "I want your cock in my mouth. I want to make you feel on fire."

"That doesn't sound very pleasant."

Sascha almost screamed at Devon's pedestrian tone.

"Just you wait," she grumbled under her breath. Devon was a different kind of lover. They played, and there was no better way of describing it.

Sure, she usually lost. But really, there was no losing when you had multiple orgasms, was there?

Deciding to fight dirty, she tugged down the sharp V-neck of her dress and moved her hand into the gap she'd just made. Cupping a breast and shifting her fingers to fondle one of her nipples, she slid the other between her legs. When she released a breathy moan, Sawyer demanded, "What are you doing?"

"I need you," she said softly. "Need you so badly."

He made an explosive noise and took the step toward her she'd wanted him to make. The minute he was close enough, she wasted no time. He was the kind of prick who'd take a step back just to make her wait, and that wasn't what she needed right now.

Fuck no.

She grabbed a hold of his fly, lowered it, and then moaned when the thick bulbous tip popped out. She could scent the pre-cum, could scent his need for her, and it set her alight.

She reached into the folds and held his shaft at the base, after carefully pulling it out from between the tines of the zipper. When he was free, she dragged the tip around the curve of her lips, painting his pre-cum over the Cupid's bow like it was an expensive lip gloss.

He sucked down a sharp breath. "You're a canny lass," he told her, his voice rumbling with his need.

"I try," she murmured, then she slipped the tip in and sucked. Hard.

He let out a wild cry that sent shockwaves through her, and stumbled forward until he used the roof of the car to prop him up. She heard the dull thud of his fists hitting the expensive curved metal and had to hide her grin—if she smiled during a BJ, he'd fuck her so hard she'd scream.

Then, she thought about that.

Really thought about that.

And grinned.

A growl sounded from overhead, and it thrilled her to think that he was standing outside the car, his eyes looking out into the distance of his homeland, all while she was sucking him off. In the back of the car, she could hear the slow whap-whap as Devon jacked off. She wasn't sure how he could see, just knew he could and what he was looking at turned him the fuck on.

The car was overloaded with their pheromones. Theirs and hers.

The cocktail was potent and the need rampaging around her system was enough to make her want to throw back her head with the glory of it.

Except, if she did that, then she'd be screwing herself, because that meant no more Sawyer between her lips.

She began to suck him off in earnest at that thought. Needing him to be riled up enough to take her, needing him to fuck her until she *did* scream.

She felt the saliva gathering about her lips and spilling down her chin. It gathered in strings that she collected with her fingers and used to lubricate the jacking motion she made with her hand.

He grunted at the dual touch of tongue and hand, and she loved it.

She fucking loved it.

He muttered, "No more. I need in you, lass."

She whimpered in agreement. He pulled back, reached down, then bridged his fingers with hers. Tugging her up and onto her feet, with a gentleness that surprised her because his need had literally just been in her mouth, tears pricked her eyes. The care he showed her as he made sure she didn't feel dizzy or lightheaded at the sudden change in position was proof positive of his love for her.

He supported her against his body for a second, and as she settled into him, she pressed her forehead against his chest. "I love you, Sawyer."

"I love you, lass," he rumbled out, the brogue thicker, denser in contrast to the soft words.

God, this man.

These *men*.

She shivered, then pressed her lips to his shirt-clad pec. "Fuck me, please?"

He laughed. "Because you asked so nicely, aye, lass. I will."

Was she surprised when he hauled her up, his hands clutching her ass as he hefted her the two steps toward the hood?

Not really.

Was it fucking freezing out here?

Yes.

And did she give a damn?

No.

She'd have frostbitten nipples for the night if it meant having him inside her at last.

A moan escaped her as the heat from the hood warmed her butt when he dropped her on there. It was surprisingly pleasant, and she'd forgotten about that little fact in her dazed state. Grateful for the source of heat, she grabbed his shirt front and dragged him toward her.

"In. Me."

He grinned. "Aye, lass." He cupped her chin, tilted her head to the side, and whispered, "You want to live dangerously?"

Her eyes flared wide. "As long as you're there to catch me, I'm safe."

He let out a shaky breath. "Thank you, lass."

And that was it. The remnants of his control seemed to have been blown apart as he reached for the skirt of her dress and tugged it up. He slid his palms along her inner thighs until he hit pay dirt. She moaned as he used his thumb to drag the taut fabric over her pussy, and her hips rocked, need careening through her as he scraped it over her clit too.

She sucked down a sharp breath. "Now, Sawyer. Please, baby."

His chuckle was devious. "I thought you wanted me to suck your clit?"

"Later," she said impatiently, forgetting everything that had happened inside the car. What was going down now was all that counted.

He nudged her clit again. But this time, he'd stepped deeper between her spread legs. She moaned, knowing it was his cock that touched her clit. She fell back on her elbows. There was a dull thud as the sharp-edged joint connected with the hood, but she didn't even have it in her for her funny bones to protest. She was focused on him and her. Them.

She shuddered as he grabbed the gusset and tugged it aside. When his cock touched her bare pussy, *at fucking last*, she shuddered again, her head falling back, her neck totally unable to sustain its weight.

"Oh God, that feels so good," she said on a whimper as he repeated the same path his thumb had made—his cock sliding through her folds, touching all the good spots, but leaving the emptiest of them all weeping for him.

When he finally notched the tip in her entrance, her eyes clenched down so hard, they started to ache. But she didn't really notice. He lodged the glans inside, spreading her wider apart as he began to thrust his thick shaft into her. She shivered as he sparked every nerve ending in her pussy to life, and only when he was home, could she breathe properly.

It was always unnerving having them thrust into her. She'd not only hit the jackpot with her sexy geniuses' character and smarts-wise. She'd hit it looks and cock-wise too!

She was a supremely lucky chick.

A moan escaped her as he pumped his cock into her, nudging deep in her core where her G-spot was centered. He had the faintest curve and that always worked against her, drove her to a height that was unique to him.

She heard the sound of a door opening, and knew it was Devon climbing out of the vehicle. On any other stretch of land, she'd have been frozen with fear of being caught, but they were in the middle of the frigid nowhere. No one in their right mind would be out in this.

Except a very horny pregnant woman with her two delicious lovers, that is.

"Devon, grab my purse," she managed to bite off, before Sawyer loomed over her. With her head still flung back, he had perfect access to her throat, and he nibbled and bit, teasing her every inch of the way.

"Why do you want your purse?" Sawyer growled in her ear as his cock sped up. "If you can think about your purse, then I'm not doing that grand a job, lass."

She whimpered. "No. It's perfect. You're perfect. Lube," she whimpered. "Lube."

Like that said it all.

He snorted, stopping his hard thrusts as the snort morphed into a laugh. "Devon, it seems we're that sure of a game, she brought lube with her."

Devon wasn't amused. He was deadly serious. "Sascha is always prepared for every eventuality."

The faith imbued in that statement didn't go unnoticed. Even as Sawyer was eight inches deep inside her.

Devon's faith was a terrifying thing. It was a burden in a way. She feared there might be a day she let him down, but knew she'd do everything in her power to make sure that never happened. Still, she was no angel—angels couldn't handle as much cock as she had in her life.

But now wasn't the time to think of such matters. They'd been together nearly four years. She hadn't let him down in all that time and she would never tag on the word *yet*.

It was asking for disaster to strike.

She heard the pop of a button being opened and then a squeezing sound, liquid falling, and knew he was prepping his cock.

The very idea of being fucked out here, in the middle of nowhere, out in the fucking freezing night, shouldn't have thrilled her. But it did.

They were both going to take her, and she couldn't damn well wait.

She felt herself being gathered against Sawyer's chest as he hauled her up. Her knees were against his hips and his hands cupped her hips to balance them both. With her in that position, gravity worked a number on her and she felt his cock impaling her. Sliding impossibly deeper.

Her cunt rippled around him in waves that had him groaning with delight. "I love how you milk my cock, lass," he whispered, making her smile as she tucked her face in his throat. He was thick anyway, but in this position? It was a lot to process.

Breathing through the change in position and angle, she just let him rearrange her how he wanted. When she felt him settle against the hood, she had to bite back a laugh when he jerked upward. "Shit, that's hot."

"It is if you put your bare arse on it," Devon told him drily. "Here." He must have shoved something underneath Sawyer because their Scot mumbled:

"Cheers, mate."

Despite herself, she laughed. "My ass must be made of tougher stuff than yours."

"I think it's more like your new coat and the dress saved you," Devon told her, his tone studious.

She rolled her eyes, then murmured, "Do I get to ride you now?"

"No. I get to fuck you." The satisfaction lacing Devon's tone made a purr rumble deep inside her.

God, he got her. He knew what to say, even the simplest of things, to make her melt for him.

Sometimes, it wasn't the words but the timing, and that was Devon's power.

For a man who could be so oblivious, it astonished her he was capable of such attention to detail. But, it also made her feel privileged. Because this crazy genius of hers thought she was worthy of being the center of his focus.

"Oh, she likes that, Dev," Sawyer informed them both. "Her pussy just did the salsa on my cock."

Dev hummed. "I like the sound of that too." The sound of his feet crunching on frozen grass came loud and clear as he approached them. She felt hands cup her ass and smooth over the curves. Another sound of immense satisfaction erupted from him as he sighed with delight... a sigh he followed up by kissing the creamy skin of her butt.

"Please, Dev," she said with a little mewl. Sawyer wasn't moving, and he was so damn thick she wasn't sure if she could stand him just being in there, so deep inside her, without any relief at all.

He hummed again, damn his hide, and she moaned as finally, she felt the slick kiss of his cock against her skin. It was lube, but she knew it was also pre-cum. No way he'd been jacking off for as long as he had without feeling the effects of arousal.

Pressing her forehead against Sawyer's throat, she began to rock her hips in nervous agitation. The move did nothing to relieve the sensation of fullness she felt deep inside, but she just had to be patient. That was all.

Not a lot to ask, was it?

Yeah. It was every-fucking-thing.

Devon was a tease. She wasn't even sure if he meant to be, he just was. He seemed to have perfected it over the years too. Making the simplest of things so complex, that his calculations seemed ripe with promise now.

He was calculating something at that moment.

She just knew it.

She didn't know what, but that didn't matter. She rarely knew where his mind went.

"I think I want a tattoo."

Okay, so that was out there.

Sawyer heaved a breath. "Another time, Dev? When her pussy isn't strangling my cock?"

Another hum. "Sorry." Then, with that apology having been uttered, he pressed the thick tip to her rosette, and began to spear home.

She was used to anal sex now. Used to it, and loved it. It was the one way to make her body detonate, and she craved it as much as she did regular sex. But when two of her men took her?

Nothing compared.

Seriously. Nothing. And they were surprisingly stingy with their little forays into this kink. She wasn't sure whether that was to keep her on her toes or what.

Then, she remembered why these two didn't do this often.

"I can feel your balls, Dev," Sawyer gritted out.

Devon just huffed. "What do you want me to do with them? Chop them off?"

Sascha groaned. "Not this again." She blew out a breath as she reared up a little to glower down at Sawyer. The huff of air had her hair blowing an inch or two off her forehead. "How many times do we have to go over this? Just because they touch you, doesn't mean anything."

"I don't like it."

"Then, I'm not doing something right," she countered as he had and did her damnedest to make him forget about another's man's meat and two veg being anywhere near him. She clenched her muscles around him and he let out a satisfyingly hoarse shout. "Sweet Jesus."

The words seemed to echo around the tiny rest area, and they fueled her, lit her up with the huge break in his control. She pulsed the muscles, focusing on teasing him out of his funk, and then, behind her, she heard Devon growl.

Ha.

Talk about 'buy one, get one.'

They both seemed to take her movements as a declaration of war because after that, it was game over for her.

They fucked her. There was no kinder way to phrase it, and she loved every minute of it.

For those moments, they forgot about her delicate condition, they forgot she was their baby maker, and forgot she was anything other than theirs. Their woman. Their sexy lover who could take them to the moon and back while they took her to the stars.

She loved that she could make them forget, and she loved how their groans and grunts filled the air around her just as powerfully as their scents.

She was surrounded by them, and she knew there was nowhere else she could ever want to be.

Devon was harder, faster. He worked her over like a pro. Sawyer could only lift his hips, but it was enough to create a delicious amount of friction. And then she felt fingers delving in between them, felt the tips seeking out and finding her clit.

And boom.

Like that, she was done for.

Out for the count.

They hit a home run as the sparks of sensation fired through her veins, imploding and exploding in equal turns as they reminded her, for the millionth time since the first time Andrei had claimed her on all their behalf, that she was irrevocably theirs.

# TWO

WAS it embarrassing to have cum leaking out of both orifices 'down below' as she walked up the front steps to Jacinta and Hamish's home?

Nope.

Well, yeah. Okay, so it definitely was, but at the same time, after you gave birth, some things just didn't seem as important. Her guys had seen way too much stuff that no one with a penis should ever see, in her opinion. Only the fact they'd wanted to be there, had wanted to *see* Tin being brought into this world had stopped her from having the midwife usher everyone out of the room.

Plus, she'd been half covered with the water from the birthing pool. That had helped. She hadn't had her bits out, ready and waiting for them all to see.

Still, when you gave life to someone? Yeah, your world view changed. At least, hers had. So what she was 'leaking.' Was it gross? Yeah. But would it kill her? No, it wouldn't. And if she regretted it, that meant regretting what had just happened, and that she'd *never* do.

She'd be walking a little tenderly in the morning, which meant it was the best night ever!

She loved when they double teamed her.

Her grin was wide as she knocked on the door. She had a key, but she hated using it, especially when the downstairs lights were on, indicating that Sawyer's parents were still awake.

With some of the money from Devon's 'P vs NP' solution, he'd constructed Jacinta and Hamish a house from scratch. In the wilds of the countryside just outside of the city limits, where they'd been born and bred, the house was the size of a small mansion. And it was pretty awesome. It looked like a castle because Devon had had the architect mimic a ruin that wasn't too far from here, and now, Jacinta and Hamish were Lord and Lady of the Manor.

It was a really nice thing for Devon to have done, but she was wise to his game now. He'd done it because he loved Sawyer's mother and father, Jacinta and Hamish, who were like foster parents to him, and Sascha knew he loved them more than he'd ever loved his own. Neither of his folks liked visiting London, so they tried to visit Glasgow at least once or twice a quarter so the older couple could get to know Tin and vice versa.

Their old home had been small. Not small by most people's standards, but Devon wasn't most people. The reason he'd built them a castle from scratch was because Hamish loved history and, being the clever monkey he was, he'd constructed an adjoining building to the property at the same time.

An annex that would have made a city stockbroker weep in envy. She knew the first time she'd seen it, she'd been both astonished and overjoyed at the prospect of spending time there. It was like if a pool house back home was the size of an eight-bedroom house. Yeah. 'Annex,' her ass.

It had its own separate entrance, its own drive too. The only link was the land both properties sat on and the covered pool they shared.

The castle-like property was old-fashioned and traditional. It even had moss on it, and all kinds of ivy growing down its front facade as though the building hadn't been completed two years before.

Inside, Devon had let Jacinta have full sway and it was traditional to a tee, with Sascha's favorite room being the library, which came complete with an authentic Adam fireplace and four, yes, *four* Chesterfield sofas around it.

That was where Hamish usually sat. With a book on his lap, his reading glasses perching and almost toppling off the end of his nose, and a tumbler of whiskey at his side. Jacinta, the complete opposite of her husband, preferred soaps. She had the TV on twenty-four hours a day, even when she slept, and unlike Hamish who preferred whiskey, she had a preference for sweets.

Of all variations.

From candy to cakes.

She was going to be the death of Sawyer, who was as anti-sugar now as he'd been all those years ago when Sascha had first entered the men's lives.

Her lips curved at the thought as she pressed the doorbell this time, fearing her mother-in-law hadn't heard her knock. When, seconds later the door opened, she saw Jacinta's concerned face and frowned. "What's wrong? Did Tin have a nightmare?"

When they stayed in Glasgow, they often went out on an evening, leaving Tin with his grandmother. There'd never been a problem before, but the worry in Jacinta's eyes had Sascha's heart rate soaring.

"Cinta? What's wrong?"

With her thumb she beckoned behind her, the older woman, with her hair as bright red as it had been when she was a young lass—because of a bottle of dye Devon had assured her, not by the grace of God as Cinta swore—whispered, "Not Tin. Sean."

"Sean?" Sascha blinked. "*Sean*? He's here?"

Sawyer's mother nodded. "Aye. Arrived about an hour after you three left, and could I get any of you on those damn phones you carry about? Could I? Hell!"

Sawyer's brogue was thick, but after years of living down in England, and of being in a household of Southerners, it had worn down a tad. All these years later, Sascha still needed Sawyer to translate for her when Jacinta was feeling particularly heated.

Which was, unfortunately, now.

Tugging at her ear, Sascha asked, "What?"

Cinta snorted then grabbed her arm. "Come and see to him."

"But Sawyer and Devon are in the car."

"They'll figure out that they need to come in when you don't make an appearance." Cinta cackled. "They're supposed to be bloody geniuses, aren't they?"

"I guess. But..." Allowing herself to be dragged forward, Sascha's earlier laissez-faire attitude about walking to the front entrance of Cinta's home with Sawyer and Devon's cum still very much present in her body disappeared.

She could feel it. Slipping down to the top of her thighs, and walking in heels while trying to keep her thighs pressed tightly together...? Yeah, that took some maneuvering.

When Cinta carried on dragging her down the hall toward the back of the house where the kitchen was located, Sascha tugged back. "Wait a minute," she pleaded, then when the older woman stopped, looking harried, she hopped out of her heels and grabbed them in her hand. "That's better. I can walk faster now."

"Good! The boy's looking worse for the wear."

Sascha frowned. "What on earth's happened?"

"I don't know. He won't say. Just arrived, took up a spot at my kitchen table, ate the stew I served him, and had too much of the whiskey Hamish offered him." She tutted. "He'll have a right head in the morning."

Sascha winced—Sean never drank. Like, ever. Not even wine at their evening meal anymore, not since Tin's birth anyway. He'd done it out of solidarity. They all enjoyed a glass of fine wine with dinner, but when she'd learned she was pregnant, and after Valentin's birth, had breastfed, he'd carried on not drinking. The habit had stuck.

As far as she was aware, he didn't even drink at business meetings, so that meant he was drinking now for the first time in close to thirty months.

Racking her brain for what could have happened, she followed Jacinta, but then the doorbell rang. She tutted. "Why none of you won't use yer keys I'll never know," she grumbled. "It would save this woman's feet the trouble if you just used the damn things."

"We don't want to impose," Sascha said softly.

"Well, you're imposing by not using them. This house is tae big and my legs tae old to be wandering the halls like this." Cinta gestured toward the kitchen. "Right. I'll go let the boy geniuses in, and you go and see to Sean. I dinnae like the look of him. He looks wrecked. It hurts me heart tae see," she said gruffly, and without waiting for a reply from her, retreated to the front door to let Sawyer and Devon in.

Even concerned for Sean, Sascha's lips twitched, for, only Cinta, would call them 'boy geniuses.' Both were very much in their forties, the men having left boyhood behind a long time ago.

*And thank Christ for that,* she thought, with no small sense of satisfaction.

A contented smile tried to curve her lips, but it was destroyed by the fact Sean was here. In Glasgow.

Not that she didn't want to see him. On the contrary. She hated being away from any of her men when she visited Cinta and Hamish. But it was rare that all five of them could get away with her, and it was usually Sawyer with one of the others who would come up with Tin and her for the visit.

To have three of them around was a luxury. Well, it would have been were it not for the fact that something was obviously wrong with Sean.

Her eyes were pinched as she hurried down the thickly carpeted hallway and headed into a large kitchen.

Devon, knowing Cinta's love for cooking, had dedicated a large chunk of space to this room. There was an Aga stove that ran the full length of the back wall, and the rest of the country kitchen was designed with her in mind.

The length of the scrubbed oak countertops were loaded with gadgets and gizmos that Cinta had purchased on television programs —they were her true vice. She spent a fortune on them, and because Sawyer had a fortune to waste on such trite crap, since nothing was ever said, Cinta spent to her heart's content.

*It was a shame most of them were dust gatherers*, Sascha thought wryly as she looked at a cake pop machine and a spiralizer that were plunked next to each other.

There was also a fireplace, with two armchairs in front of it. They were spindly and old-fashioned, but they were a great place to enjoy hot chocolate. That was where she found Sean. His arms hung over the armrests, and he was slouched over.

Drunk?

Well, Cinta had claimed as much.

In a creased suit, with his hair a mess, and his chin brushing his chest, he still somehow managed to look gorgeous. With those piercing blue eyes of his closed, his impressiveness was hindered, but he was a beautiful man. As beautiful to her as he'd been that first day when she'd walked up the steps to the Kensington house and had met him on the front doorstep.

At the sounds of her padding feet, Sean tilted his head a bare half-inch to the side. "Sascha? Knew you'd come." He didn't look at her, just said the words on a low sigh. As she approached, she saw his eyes were still closed, and he didn't open them. "Wanted Tin," he said, the words slurring even more. "But Cinta said he was sleeping. Plus, he doesn't need to see his fuck up of a father." He raised his tumbler for another sip, the amber liquid sloshed against the sides and the ice cubes within tinkled in a pleasing way.

She cocked her head to the side and looked at him as she took a seat in the armchair opposite. The minute she did, she did a kind of grimace and sigh combo. The grimace because cold semen never felt good against your butt, and the sigh because damn, it felt good to sit down.

"Since when are you a fuck up of a father?" she asked him after she'd gotten over the relief of being off her feet after a long night on them, but her tone was cool. Mostly because, well, the last thing he would ever be was a fuck up, and there was no way she was going to let him waddle through the quagmire that this pity party was centered around.

If anyone was doing any waddling, it was her. Not her guys, who were great dads. The men all brought something to the paternal role. None of them were perfect, and she wouldn't have wanted them to be. None of them were, in any way, terrible either. They were exactly what Tin needed. Each one providing something the other couldn't.

It didn't matter that, biologically, Andrei was the dad—and there was no disputing it thanks to the little boy's coloring—they were all his fathers.

And that was exactly how she wanted it to be.

"I messed up, Sascha. Badly." His face crumpled, but she only caught a glimpse before it was hidden behind the double-size tumbler he raised to his lips.

Grimacing at how much whiskey he must have downed, she wondered how she could get the tumbler away from him. First things first. "How?" she crossed her legs, grimacing again at the slickness between her thighs as it made itself known. God, she really hadn't been ready for a discussion of any level of severity tonight.

She was tired and sleepy. She'd wanted nothing more than to grab Tin, tuck him into his bed in his room at the annex, then snuggle down between Devon and Sawyer to sleep for ten hours straight.

Sean's problems were her priority, but she just wasn't prepared for him to have a problem. Sean never had a problem.

It was the way he was.

Because of that, she hated that she wasn't in her best form for him. It was for that reason, with no real prior experience to guide her in problem solving for him, she hefted her fat ass out of the armchair and took the few steps over to him. When he didn't look at her, she just sat on his knee and tilted herself back against his chest.

Not saying a word, he wrapped his arms around her belly and instantly tucked his face into her throat.

He was hiding again.

Sean never hid.

Frowning harder at the fire Hamish must have lit for Sean's benefit, as they never used the kitchen after dinner, she raised a hand and began to stroke his head, letting her fingers drift through the undercut, then glide over the brutally shorn sides. He shivered a little, then pressed deeper into her.

A faint noise came from the hallway, and she saw Sawyer and Devon elbowing each other in their haste to get into the kitchen. She rolled her eyes at them, but knew that their need to get in here was for Sean's benefit.

Sean was, to put it frankly, the spine of the household.

It might sound nuts, or a little exaggerated, but that was the way of it.

He was the one person who everyone went to when they had an issue. His office was where they congregated when they needed to work or to hash out a problem. He was their backbone. And when that backbone was sloshing around drunk, well, that tilted the balance.

Not in their favor.

Devon was scowling, and she could tell, because she knew him so damn well, that his eyes were worried.

Thanks to Vasily, Andrei's grandfather, Sascha had spent a fair bit of time around horses. Whenever they visited, he insisted that she visit his stable and have a few lessons so that she could learn to ride. He said that in his family, all the men had to ride.

"I'm not a man," she told him with a huff when the learner horse, Daisy, had bitten her, and she'd tried to refuse to go on another lesson.

"No, but Tin will be, and one day, he will see his mother and be ashamed that she cannot ride as well as he can."

That logic had made no sense then, and it made no sense now, but a snickering Andrei hadn't backed her up and Vasily hadn't once been a Pakhan of the Bratva for no reason at all. The man's glower could pack a punch.

She'd seen a horse in full panic. The eyes that practically rolled and the sweat that came from their hides... Devon's baby blues reminded her of that. Without the stink that came with it.

It was cold. Cinta wasn't frivolous with the central heating, and they'd just walked in from the outside. There was no reason at all for him to be sweating, but she knew that was because Sawyer's mother had told both men about Sean's presence and condition. His eyes were wide, flared with tension as concern about Sean overwhelmed him, and the gleam on his skin spoke of a terror that was born in his emotions.

Devon couldn't be overwhelmed.

He was too fractious, his mental health too unstable even as, in many ways, he was one of the strongest men she knew. Yet another dichotomy that made no sense where he was concerned, yet, made absolute sense too.

Knowing he needed her, but that Sean did too and that he wasn't about to let go of her anyway, she held out her hand to him and he rushed over like a piranha was attempting to bite his ass. The minute her fingers enfolded his, he sank low onto his knees at their side. She winced because the stone floor was not only cold, it wasn't exactly comfortable.

"What is it? What's wrong?" he demanded, his gaze raking over the seated pair.

Sawyer walked a little more leisurely towards them. That wasn't to say he wasn't as concerned, but he didn't crowd. That wasn't in his nature. He took the armchair Sascha had just departed and sank back against the spindles which made up the backrest.

"Sean needed a drink or two."

"Or six," he gurgled against her throat. The words and the vibration made her smile a little as the sensation tickled.

"Or eight?" she teased back.

He nodded. "Needed it."

"You just never said why."

"I did." He heaved a deep breath. "Told you. I'm a fuck up of a father. Tin shouldn't have a man like me in his life."

Sawyer reared back at that. "What the hell, mon?"

Devon scowled. "What could possibly have made you think that?"

"He was only three. So close to Tin's age, and with his hair too. So goddamn white. Like a cherub, but with a naughty smile too."

"Who was?" Sascha insisted, concerned now.

There was no answer though. Sean began rubbing his forehead against her throat, and then she felt it.

It.

*The wetness.*

Tears?

Sean was crying?

Her own eyes flared wide with distress now.

"Sean, you're starting to scare me, baby," she told him, her voice shaky. And she spoke no word of a lie.

He was freaking her out.

"The third one, and I was too late."

"The third one what?" Sawyer snapped, his tone not as careful as hers.

"The third child snatched!" he snarled, and pulling his face away from her throat, he growled at Sawyer. "The third child I failed!" His eyes sparked with a fire, burning them all with his rage at the unjust world they lived in.

Even as he pulled away to glower at Sawyer, his arms curved around her belly tighter, and she didn't protest even though she felt a little squashed.

"Why would that make you a bad father?" Sawyer was calm in the face of Sean's rage.

"I let them down. What if I let Tin down? This baby down?"

Devon shook his head. "You're not making any sense, Sean."

Trust Devon to be the voice of reason, Sascha thought on a sob as she pressed her face to Sean's hair and let her own tears fall amid the messy dark locks.

"Sweetheart, you always do everything you can. We know that. You have to know that too. You didn't hurt those little boys. Some sick bastard did. It isn't your fault."

"I was too late. *Too* late, and I told them. *I* told *them* he'd strike quickly if they let the parents do a news interview," he repeated, his voice turning to a whisper.

"I'm so sorry, darling," she told him, squeezing him gently, needing him to feel her acceptance, needing him to understand that she didn't blame him, that she'd never, *ever* blame him.

He wasn't perfect, and he made mistakes, but more often than not, it wasn't his fault. It truly wasn't. The police didn't always listen. Some wanker detective didn't want some fancy criminologist stepping in on their territory.

It was easier in the big cities. Sean had made a reputation for himself, one that preceded him, and over the years, he'd made friends with a lot of people. With a lot of great detectives and policemen and women. But, when he had to work with new people, it never boded well.

Not for the victims, their families, or Sean himself.

With every victim that was lost, Sean took it to heart, and sometimes, she'd forget that. Because he kept it hidden deep inside. Why was it that she only just now saw how bad that was?

Not just for him, but for them? For their family?

What else was he keeping inside? And was this the first time he'd used alcohol to drown his sorrows? Or was it the first time she'd simply caught him in the act?

"You know you're being irrational, right?"

He swallowed. "If you'd seen what I saw, you'd be irrational too."

That had her wincing. He usually hid his white boards from her, turning them away so she wouldn't see the details of any files. As far as she was aware, he didn't do the same for the guys, so the special treatment was just where she was concerned. It was chivalry on his part. So even though she wanted to tell him she wasn't fainthearted, the way he was trying to protect her was sweet enough for her never to have pushed it in the past.

She was only just seeing how that might have been a bad thing.

"Why would you think you're a bad father?"

"I'm never there for Tin. I should be around more. T-The boy... his father was working on the computer when he was snatched from his backyard. I mean, that could have happened to us."

Considering their backyard was walled in, and the alarm system they had was beyond ridiculous, she doubted that. Rubbing his temple with her forehead, she murmured, "That's highly unlikely. And you give him plenty of your time. You're not always working cases. Being busy does not make you a bad father." She pulled away from him at that, needing to look him in the eye so he could see she was resolute in that. "You're a great dad. You all are."

His mouth tightened. "You can't understand, Sascha."

"No? Well, explain it to me."

Her simple words had him stiffening, and he shook his head, hiding from her like Tin hid from the monsters in his closet—only God knew how he'd found out about such things at his age, she'd figured that was a six-year-old's fear, not a two-year-old's.

Realizing she wasn't going to get anywhere, she guessed that he needed sleep more than he needed a lecture on why he was a great father. Pressing her lips to his temple, she said softly, "I think we should go to bed."

Sawyer murmured, "I'll grab Tin."

She nodded, watching as her large Scot got to his feet, leaving Devon behind. The worry on his face had her wishing she could hug them both equally, and it was then, she knew, her bed was going to be very full tonight.

"You sleeping with me and Sean, bud?" she asked Devon.

He stared blankly at Sean a second. "Do you mind, Sean?"

"'Course not," came his reply. "More the merrier."

"You say that now," Sascha retorted. "Wait until Tin climbs in with us in the morning."

He snorted, and the sound snuffled against her throat in a pleasant tickle. "I hope he does. I've missed him. We've all missed him. The house is so fucking quiet without him. It's horrible." His hand came out to pat her stomach. "God, when this one comes along, the house will be so much busier." He swallowed. "We need that. It brings life to the place."

He sounded so happy about that, which, truth be told, was surprising. The men were all serious, and utterly studious when it came to their work. And their work was at home.

That meant they required a *lot* of quiet time.

And yeah, you didn't get so much of that with a toddler in the throes of the terrible twos.

She always tried to keep him entertained, but he was Andrei's child.

Andrei.

The economist.

The one who wrote economic manifestos for fun, and actually worked as a hobby. He'd made several fortunes over the course of his lifetime, and had no need to work at all now.

A man like that didn't breed a child who found crayoning fun. He'd already started tinkling with the piano in the salon at the Kensington house, Andrei teaching him a few choice notes that no two-year-old should have been able to retain so young.

Was it horrible that she really hoped this baby was Kurt's?

Of them all, he was the most restful. Devon's baby might be a potential nightmare. Two of them in the household? Jesus, they'd never get anything done, and the Nobel committee might as well just camp out in her kitchen waiting for the next miracle to drop.

Of course, she mused, Devon's unusual brain wasn't something their baby was guaranteed to receive, but Sascha just knew she was destined to be surrounded by men for the rest of her life. Not just any men, but *brainy* men. Guys with IQs who made her own substantial one look subpar.

Not that they made her feel that way, but still, it was hard not to feel like a dumbass when the guys discussed quantum mechanics for fun at the breakfast table.

Her lips curved at the thought. Maybe another woman would have been intimidated by that, but she wasn't. She never had been. It wasn't about taking it all in stride, it was simply about loving them all.

Being loved by them.

It just worked.

She knew it always would too, so long as they fought for that love, and she couldn't imagine a day where that didn't happen.

With that thought in mind, she pressed another kiss to Sean's head when she saw Sawyer was hovering in the doorway. He had a slumped-over Tin in his arms, the baby's head was lolling on his shoulder, and his little body, which was usually worse than a wriggling puppy from fidgeting, was still as he slumbered.

It was amazing how one little terror could be so restful while he slept. It was unnerving, actually.

"They're here, baby," she told Sean. "We can go to the annex."

He nodded, but didn't move his face. She smiled though, and when Devon levered to his feet and held out his hands for hers, she let him maneuver her off Sean's lap.

With a grunt, she righted herself. Tonight had been a lot more energetic than she was used to, and she'd definitely be feeling the burn in her ass and thighs tomorrow.

Likely her lower back as well.

Oh the joys of mid-term pregnancy.

"Come on, baby," she prompted Sean. "Let's get some sleep."

Though he was a bit zombie-like, he did as requested and, with Devon's help, righted himself. His staggering gait spoke of how much he'd drunk, even if she hadn't seen the evidence for herself in a bottle.

What had he said?

The police hadn't listened? They'd let the parents of the child who'd perished hold a press conference?

A knot formed in her throat as she thought of all the trauma they must be going through tonight. God, was it any wonder Sean needed to see Tin? Needed to hold him and reaffirm that he was well?

And how hard was it going to be on him? The knowledge that if the police had just listened, that small child might still be with his parents, alive.

She wasn't a watering pot. Not even during her pregnancy, but now, tears blurred her vision as she empathized not only for the parents, but for Sean who would hold onto this guilt for an eternity.

When he stumbled, almost falling into the cabinet where a lot of Jacinta's dinnerware rattled with the jolt, Devon hauled Sean's arm over his shoulder. Keeping him propped up as they walked out of the kitchen, back down the hall, meeting a hovering Cinta, they managed not to do too much damage to any of Sawyer's mother's fancy porcelain.

Cinta, standing at the front door, was wringing her hands in concern as she watched Devon and Sean stagger down the corridor, and when her eyes caught on Sascha, she jerked her chin up. "He okay?" she mouthed.

Sascha shook her head, and mouthed back, "Work."

Cinta's lips pinched but she nodded. She reached up to press a kiss to Tin's limp hand—in his father's arms he was a good two feet higher than Cinta was at her tiny four feet-eleven inches, so there was no way she'd reach Tin's forehead.

Where Sawyer had come from, Sascha didn't know. Hamish, at only five-eight, wasn't tall. Yet they'd produced a son over six-feet tall, who'd make Mel Gibson in Braveheart look scrawny.

Eying her man, who looked a thousand times more delicious with Tin in his arms, because that was their child, and he was a hands-on dad who felt no shame in being his kid's impromptu mattress—hell, he didn't even mind being Tin's drawing pad! No, Sawyer was sexy, but when he was in dad mode, she could almost forget about what had just happened in that rest area.

Shoving her thoughts of that aside, because hell, Sean was feeling like crap, and they'd definitely all be passing out once they climbed under the sheets, she pressed a kiss to Jacinta's cheek, touched at the concern in her eyes, and murmured, "Tomorrow," before all five of them headed out into the cold, directly to their annex.

Sascha knew sleep was in their future, but she prayed Sean's wasn't loaded with nightmares.

Though she wanted to go harpy on whichever detective had ignored Sean's advice, she couldn't. There was nothing she could do except be there for her man, be there to hold him, to ease his internal agony over today's misery.

He needed rest, and when he woke, she just hoped a few days in the Scottish countryside would be what he needed to find some semblance of peace.

# THREE

"WHAT ARE YE DOING, MON?" Sawyer bellowed when he found Devon peering at him from the side of his bed.

"Waiting for you to wake up," was the reply from the man who was like a brother to him.

"I told you not to watch me sleep," he grumbled, squinting as he ran a hand over his face.

God, he was tired.

And that had nothing to do with the hours of dancing last night, the impromptu threesome on his car, or the late hour they'd gone to bed.

It was Sean.

Sean, who'd driven hours to hit Glasgow, because his need to be with his family had reached a fever pitch.

Sawyer had fallen into bed, but he had lain awake for hours. Sean had kept the details of the case he was working on from Sascha, but Sawyer knew. As did Kurt and Andrei. Only Devon didn't, and only because he hadn't spent much time in Sean's office. When they worked in there, sometimes there was no avoiding the white board that held the details of the cases Sean worked on. Even when he'd been taking pains to hide them from Sascha.

When Devon's face didn't even twitch with regret, Sawyer said with a huff, "I told you. It creeps me out!"

Devon shrugged, but Sawyer stared at the coffee mug in his hand with greedy eyes. "I wasn't watching you, per se. Just watching your chest."

Grunting, Sawyer pulled a face. "That just sounds even worse, ya perv."

"Why would it? If you were Sascha, then it would make sense. I'd be eying up your tits. You don't have any. There's nothing interesting to look at."

"Apparently there was enough of a show to warrant you sitting there with some damn coffee!" Sawyer argued, then he beckoned with his hand. "Give me some."

"It's mine. It's the stuff Sascha makes for me," Devon countered, hugging the mug to his chest.

"Tough shite. You woke me, you have to pay the price." He motioned again with his fingers, and with a huff of his own, Devon complied, handing over the mug as though he were handing over priceless jewels. He took a deep sip of the brew, relieved to note it was hot— an indicator Devon hadn't been perving over him for very long. Pulling a face at the taste of the decaffeinated shite in his hand, he murmured, "What's wrong?"

"Nothing," Devon replied. Quickly. Too fucking quickly.

He cocked a brow as he took another sip of the noxious brew. "How long have I known you, Dev?" Before he could answer, Sawyer gritted out, "Too fucking long to not know when you're lying. What's. Wrong?"

"Why was Sean drinking?"

"You heard him. A bad case. He was too late to help that little boy." Sawyer stared down at the mug in his hand; better that than stare Devon in the eye. The man's brain chose inopportune moments to discern truth from fiction.

"He mentioned Tin though."

"Aye. He said the bairn looked like Tin."

"But he *wasn't* Tin. So why was he so upset?"

Times like this, it was like talking to Bender from *Futurama*. Except Devon didn't fart fire or drink beer.

God help them all if he ever drank beer.

That being said, there were times when Bender was more empathetic. In his own way, when it didn't concern the people he considered his, Devon was surprisingly cold.

"We're parents, Dev. Aren't we?"

Devon frowned, apparently unsure where Sawyer was going with this. "Yes."

"How would you feel if Tin was snatched from us?"

"He wouldn't be."

The confident answer had Sawyer hiding a small smile behind Devon's coffee cup. "How do you know?"

"Because I'd kill the bastard who tried to take him." Devon's response didn't altogether come as a surprise, but the lack of tone *did*.

He meant it.

One hundred percent.

Devon would kill to protect Tin.

When Sascha had given birth, he'd been terrified Devon's quirks would manifest in such a way that he couldn't show the boy any love and affection. But Sawyer's fears had been for nothing.

In his own way, Devon was more dedicated to Tin than the rest of them.

Tin always sat on Dev's knee whenever they were together, which was a lot. The boy was glued to him unless one of his other fathers demanded cuddles. And hell, Sawyer wasn't even ashamed to admit that.

He'd never wanted fucking cuddles in his life. But when it came down to his boy? He never got enough.

"I'm sure that's how the parents of the little boy who died felt."

The words tasted wrong, but he needed to make a point. “I’m sure they thought they’d kill to save their child.”

Devon pulled a face, his brow scrunching in contemplation. "People are funny about life."

"Narrow it down for me, Dev." He waved a hand. "I mean, give me specifics. Funny—ha-ha or funny—weird?"

"Funny weird," he replied after a second's thought.

"Okay, in what way?"

"To protect you, or Sascha, or Tin, or Kurt, Andrei, and Sean. Jacinta and Hamish too... I'd kill someone. In a heartbeat. I wouldn’t care if I went to prison." He paused. “I’m sure they’d still let me do math, so I’d be okay in there, and I’d know you were safe. I wouldn’t care that I’d killed someone. Not if they were trying to hurt you, anyway.”

"It's easy to say that now, when you're safe. When we're all safe."

But Devon was shaking his head. "No. I mean it. I would." He narrowed his eyes at him. "I know you think I walk around with my head in the clouds, and I do for the most part. Not much goes on that interests me. But you interest me. You all do. That means I protect you." He scratched at his stubbled jaw. “That’s what the money’s for. I don’t want it. I’d open source most of the stuff we work on, but the money?” He shook his head. “That will protect you. Even if we don’t need it so much because of Sascha’s inheritance, it’s always better to have too much, than not enough.”

He was so staunch about it, Sawyer had to punch him in the arm. "You don't have to protect us. We can protect ourselves. And hell, we have fortunes of our own." They weren’t exactly poor. Although, admittedly, Devon and Sascha were technically the richest in the household.

That didn’t seem to faze Devon though, because he simply shrugged. "I know you can. Doesn’t mean I don’t need to make certain of that though." Even as Sawyer frowned at him, surprised by this admission, Devon pursed his lips as he eyed the mug. "Are you done with that? You’re not even enjoying it. It's completely wasted on you."

Like he hadn't just been discussing murder, the topic changed direction entirely.

Sawyer handed it back then he scraped his hand over his jaw—if he wanted anywhere near Sascha today, and he did—he'd need to shave. She liked him with a bit of stubble, but not broken glass as she considered this current level of 'fuzz.' And it itched like a bastard too.

"Sean's okay," he said, his tone contemplative. "You know what he's like when he has to deal with cases where kids are snatched. And the last one was before we had Tin. Now, it's different."

"Why is it though?"

"He can empathize."

"In what way?"

"He can understand what those parents are going through." Sawyer regarded him with calm eyes. "Can't you?" He pursued the topic, even though he knew it could spell disaster for the day. "Think about if someone took Tin. How would you feel?"

"I already told you. Murderous."

Sawyer cocked a brow, surprised by the sustained control in his voice. Devon didn't handle trauma well. He shut down. He closed up. He locked the world out. He didn't get angry.

Not at anyone save himself.

Contemplating his best friend, and the usual conundrum that was a part and parcel of being the idiot's companion, he murmured, "Okay, so, you'd feel murderous. Sean, well, he doesnae feel that way. He feels sad. He feels he let the family down."

Well accustomed to Sawyer's 'doesnae's or doesn'ts in regular English, Devon didn't bat an eyelid.

"But he didn't. He didn't take the child," Devon argued, his chin setting in a way that Sawyer recognized he was in for the long haul—great, just what he needed at four AM. At least, that's what a quick glance at his alarm clock informed him.

*Wait a second.*

**Four AM?**

Wanting to complain, but knowing it was pointless because

Devon had obviously been thinking about this for a while, he murmured, "Why couldn't you sleep?"

"I was worried about Sean."

"Why were you?" he asked, knowing he wasn't speaking emotionally because Devon, at times, could be pretty robotic.

"I thought he might throw up and choke on his vomit."

Sawyer's eyes widened. That was pretty detailed—he narrowed his eyes. "Have you been watching that stupid show with Sascha again?"

Devon scowled down at his mug, reminding Sawyer way too much of Tin when he'd been caught in the act of doing something he'd been expressly forbidden from doing—like another Sudoku. "No."

"You liar," Sawyer retorted. "You have. I told you to stop watching that."

Devon hated TV, but he'd started watching it because he liked sitting next to Sascha in their lounge. He said it was because watching her crochet comforted him, but Sawyer knew the truth.

Sascha's tits were epic. Seriously. They were porn worthy.

But when she was pregnant?

Sweet Jesus, they were even more astonishing. And with the way Devon sat, he had a perfect view down her blouse.

"You're such a pervert," Sawyer snapped at him.

"Why? She doesn't mind," Devon answered, apparently knowing where Sawyer was heading with that argument. "You said it was weird, so I decided to get consent."

Sawyer pinched the bridge of his nose. "That's something, I guess."

"And anyway, you check out her arse and feel it up when Tin isn't looking. You don't get consent for that," he retorted on a huff. "So, who's the pervert now?"

For a second, his mouth worked as he processed that particularly *correct* logic.

Fuck!

"She checks out my ass too," was all he could think to say. "And she grabs my cock under the table."

Devon pursed his lips. "I need to have a word with her about consent too then."

"I think I should be around for this conversation," he said, striving to keep his tone bland, when, inwardly, he was snickering at the prospect of Sascha being lectured by Devon of all people on informed consent.

Jesus, it was enough to make a man cackle.

"Of course. It's good for everyone to have a refresher. I mean, no means no, right?"

Instead of chuckling like he wanted, he coughed. "Indeed it does. But, there's the issue. When does Sascha ever say no?"

That had Devon blinking. "Huh. She doesn't, does she?"

"No. She's on us like butter on bread." Sawyer wasn't ashamed at the level of satisfaction in his voice. Their woman might be far-too-many-years-than-Sawyer-wanted-to-count younger than them, but the age difference didn't seem to deter her.

Sascha was the bee to their nectar, and he was pretty damn smug about that.

Devon beamed at him. "She likes us."

"Only just figuring that one out, bud?" he asked, amused.

"No. But, it's nice to know we still have her interested. It's been almost four years, Sawyer," came his serious retort. "We don't want her getting bored."

Though he wasn't wrong, Devon's earnestness was cuter than a man in his forties had any right to be. Because that wasn't a line of thought he wanted to continue, not when Dev was a bigger pain in the arse than Sascha would be with a strap-on, he grunted, "You want to work?"

"When don't I?" Devon countered.

"This is also true." He heaved a pained sigh as he clambered out of bed. With his feet on the thick rug, he stretched and blindly sought out the lamp switch on the table at his bedside.

When the light came on, he squinted then grunted as he reached for his robe and covered up.

"You still working on that problem Andrei sent?"

Andrei had taken to consulting for the Veronian embassy ever since an old friend of his grandfather's had hooked him up with the King of the country.

It was strange to think his prick of a housemate had a King's telephone number, and hell, Sawyer had no intention of helping Andrei's head get any bigger.

"Yeah. It's interesting."

Sawyer cocked a brow, then he ruined it by yawning. "It is?" Not much interested Devon, after all. Not unless it was truly complex.

"They shouldn't be suffering such high inflation. Yet they are." Devon shrugged. "It's something to think about." He cut Sawyer a look as he stood too. "I could use your input actually. I think it's something the DIVA program could help with, and I know you're more up to date with that than I am."

The Diva program had been Sawyer's baby. It stood for '**DI**scounted Cashflow – **VA**lue at risk,' the two major economic terms the program helped formulate. It was what had won them their Nobel Prize. Though Devon insisted Sawyer had been the driving force behind it, Sawyer knew that without Devon, it wouldn't exist. Though most of the initial ideas had been from his end, Devon's wild brain had taken the program and made it his bitch.

"If you think it will help, I'll take a look at the information Andrei sent over," he confirmed, then he grimaced as his brain sorted through the day's events and hit a snafu. "Shit, we're supposed go out with Sascha today."

"Shopping," Devon confirmed.

"You remembered?"

Devon huffed. "When do I forget?"

When it came to Sascha, that was true, Devon had the memory of an elephant. If that elephant also got waylaid with math problems.

"I need more sleep to deal with that particular torture though," he groused, running a hand through his already mussed hair.

"You can nap later."

"I hate napping."

Devon just grinned. "You'll forgive me when I show you the papers I've been working on."

Though he really did just want to crawl back into bed, that grin intrigued him. *Shite.* Devon knew how to twist him around his little bluidy finger just like Tin could Sascha!

Really grumbling now, he rounded the super king bed. When he was a foot away, he punched Devon in the arm again. "You're a gobshite."

"I have it on good authority that I'm actually rather tasty." Sawyer rolled his eyes. Then, before he could mock, Devon carried on, "And I'm not talking about cannibalism, either. Sascha isn't into that." He paused a second. "I asked her for verification."

"No, she's just into us," Sawyer said drily, then slugging an arm over Devon's shoulder, he dragged him out of the bedroom.

Work wasn't what he wanted to be doing right about now, but he'd deal with it. As he'd done a million times in the past, and as he'd do a million times in the future, he'd sacrifice sleep for his best friend.

Even if that best friend was, truthfully, a gobshite.

---

THE HIGH STREET, as they were known in Britain, was cold.

Really cold.

She didn't know why she was out here, it was that frigid. But it was early October, she'd needed to buy some gifts, get a head start on Christmas shopping, had craved a burger badly enough to venture out, and going into Glasgow was a hell of a lot less hassle than going into London would be.

London was life. She knew that sounded crazy, but it was true. There was a flow, an energy that was unlike anywhere else. Even when Kurt and Andrei had taken her to New York City, where she'd never been before, it wasn't like this.

New York City was special, sure.

And it had been awesome to be home in the States again, but London? It was in her veins.

That didn't mean she liked shopping on Regents Street.

She'd tried to get over the traumatic event that had happened there all those years ago, and for the most part, it had worked. But not there. She hated going. And even when she went to Bond Street or any of the other shopping hotspots in the capital, she felt uneasy. Like she could be targeted again.

Petticoat Lane Market was cool, but the gifts she had to buy had to be top end, because the people she was buying for were snobs.

Kurt and Sean's parents were difficult. They'd never accepted her. Had never even made it known they were *aware* of her, and yet, the distant relationships they had with their sons made her unhappy.

Having Tin had made her see how easy it was for the parent-child bond to break down, and that hurt her because the notion of him not talking to them when he was older, and all because of some silly life choices, made her both mad and sad.

She'd never reject him if he turned out to be gay, or even if he turned out to have a foot fetish! Why their life choices bothered Kurt's and Sean's folks, she'd never know, but it did, and it had caused a deeper chasm between the families. Though a gift was in no way a decent patch, it was something.

An olive branch.

She'd bought Margritte a silk scarf from Hermes, and Deidre, Sean's mother, was going to receive a rather nice gold bracelet—thank God for Frasers! For the two fathers, she'd settled on expensive Scotch whisky, knowing that was the easiest route. Even if they didn't enjoy it, it was something to have on their drink trays, and both families were definitely the kind to have those.

Before she'd started working as a housekeeper in London, she hadn't realized drink trays were still used.

Not outside of James Bond movies and *Downton Abbey* that is.

Most people, herself included, had a cabinet in the kitchen that they stored the liquor in. Simple. Same in the USA. But in the la-dee-dah houses—as Sawyer called them—they tended to have small trays with decanters on them. Well, the richer folk of a certain age and a certain class did. Which was why Sean had one in his office, she thought, with no small amount of amusement.

It seemed surreal to think that you could judge a person's social standing on whether they decanted their booze. But it was a thing in the UK, and who was she to judge?

She was from a world of beer-pong and margarita bowls.

That was more her style.

Even if she'd been born into a different life, the one she'd led had forged her, and she wouldn't change it. Even if her beginnings did cause her some sadness.

Overhead, the sky was gray. The road was too, and the pavement under her feet—the sidewalk—was also murky. A part of her knew she should have dragged Sawyer and Devon out for the ride, especially as the drive over had been a-migraine-in-the-making torturous, but they'd been working and she'd really just wanted to head out alone. It had been snowing off and on, and while she wore sturdy boots, she'd already slipped once. That had been enough to prompt her to go back to the car but Tin who was chortling at her side—he was the only man in her life who enjoyed shopping—had insisted on heading for McDonald's.

Like mother, like son, she feared, her lips twitching.

Sawyer hated that Tin ate Happy Meals, but hell, it was once in a blue moon! And Sascha was a firm believer that having a 'little bit of what you craved' did you good.

That was why she had five men.

Outright grinning at that as she peered into a store front, she eyed the sweaters, and wondered if Vasily would like one of them. He was approaching ninety-three, was moody with it, and often lamented Andrei's infrequent visits to Moscow, even though Andrei had flown over there more since Sascha's entry into their world than he had since he'd left for Oxford university decades earlier.

The sweater was in a traditional tartan, and though Vasily was a proud Muscovite, she thought he'd get a kick out of the sweater. Especially as it was from Scotland itself.

"Baby, let's go in here."

Though she loved Buchanan Street with its Victorian architecture and its upmarket shops, she also liked how there was half a mile's worth of shopping to be had. Most of it varied.

"But McDonald's! You said so."

Tin's whine had her rolling her eyes. But she couldn't stop herself from smiling. She knew she spoiled him because he was Andrei's spitting image. It wasn't fair, not to him or to her, but whenever he crumpled his brow and pouted, it was so beyond adorable she just melted. And then there were the times when he actually managed to look regal. *Regal!* How an almost three-year-old managed that, she wasn't sure. Andrei claimed it was the Russian in him, which only made her heart melt even more when he pulled that particular look.

"It's only eleven in the morning," she countered, trying hard not to laugh at him. That only encouraged him. "Who eats lunch now?"

"Happy Meal," he argued back. "Happy Meal!"

She winced at his chanting, which gathered the attention of a couple of Japanese tourists who twittered as they moved on. Tin, with his mop of bright golden curls, often garnered attention. He looked like a little angel; only his family knew he was more devil.

"After we go into this store," she negotiated, well aware that it was ridiculous to be negotiating with her toddler.

His lower lip popped out in mulish annoyance with her.

Just like his father in manner as well as looks. Tin's thought processes were already revealing themselves to be unique.

If she said they were going to McDonald's, that meant immediately in his eyes. And, sadly for her, she'd used McDonald's as a prompt to get him to try on some clothes twenty minutes ago.

It would have figured that with Devon around, she'd be used to phrasing things 'just so' but she was having to learn a different method with her son.

He was direct to a fault. And he was so cute with it that she often let him get away with murder, even though she'd pay for it in the end. If she'd had any uncertainty with the timing of things, there was no doubt in regards to it in Tin's face.

He was a walking, talking, mini Andrei.

It was weird.

Even weirder when he'd been a little baby.

Not that Vasily had thought that. He'd crowed when they'd hauled ass over to visit him, the baby in tow.

She smirked at the memory and tugged at Tin's hand—loving the days when she'd just lugged him wherever she went, his will be damned.

Only trouble was, as she went forward, he pulled back, and even though he was small, that gentle force on the slick pavement had her wobbling in place for a few terrifying moments. Then he compounded it by letting go entirely so he could ball his little hands into fists and stomp his foot.

For a few endless seconds, she was suspended in air. It was bizarre. She'd had zero traction on the ground, and she was both motionless and utterly out of control. Time was frozen. Just like the paving beneath her feet. Then, it crashed, just as she did. Her feet slid from under her and she, with her fucked up center of gravity, tilted forwards.

She tried to break her fall, but it was too fast. She didn't have time. Not even enough to put her hands in front of her. She went down. Hard. Her belly took the brunt of the fall as it was closest to the ground, and the moment she felt her bump connect with the concrete, Sascha released a scream.

It pierced her own ear drums, shattered her own thoughts.

Agony tunneled through her. Pummeling her senses. But what was worse was the terror.

For what seemed like hours, she just lay there. Winded. Unable to move, unable to function. Then, Tin's tantrum-in-the-making was put on permanent hiatus as he broke into terrified sobs at the sight of her on the ground.

She didn't really know what to do with herself as she lay there, an oversized lump on the ground. She was in pain, unable to twist, unable to take the pressure off her stomach. Her back ached, her knees pounded with a dull thud, and her skin felt frozen as the cold, wet ground bled through her coat and started to bite into her skin. But none of that mattered. None of it.

Deep inside, she felt it.

Something was wrong.

Her eyes prickled with tears, and the wind chill just made them sting all the more as she tried and failed to lift shaky fingers to rub at her eyes, then she felt them. Hands. Several pairs.

Before she realized what was happening, a small gathering had collected around her and they were helping to turn her over. As she was finally moved off her belly, a man dropped to his knees, "Are you all right?"

His voice was kind, kind enough to make her eyes burn a little more. She wanted to nod, but her head felt like it had been rattled. Her brain felt like it had been shaken better than one of Bond's Martinis. Instead of nodding, she whispered, "I don't think so."

"The bairn?" The man jerked his chin at her prominent bulge.

She pressed her hand to it. "I-I..." Her mouth quivered. What could she say?

No.

Nothing felt right.

Seconds before, all had been well. But now? It *hurt*. Like, maybe, she'd torn something inside.

Sucking in a breath, she finally managed to tilt her head to the side, and as she did, she saw Tin was on his little knees, his eyes pink and his cheeks raw from crying. She hadn't realized he was clutching at her arm through her thick down coat, and that gave her some hope

—if the bulky fabric cushioned his pinkies from her, maybe it would have cushioned her fall?

But that pain!

God, it was like nothing else she'd ever felt.

"We need to call an ambulance," the stranger was saying, and the small crowd of four or five nodded in agreement, their murmurs of 'ayes' blending in amongst them.

She wanted to argue; she wanted nothing more than to go home, but she couldn't. Home wouldn't hold any of the answers.

"Could you help me up, please?" she asked, and her voice was a little rusty. She didn't want to sit up, but the cold of the ground and the ache in her back made laying down even more agonizing.

"O' course," came the man's concerned reply, and she placed her hand on the slick concrete while reaching up to grab his as he levered her into a sitting position.

She winced as her bones settled, and the pressure on her stomach increased. It was compounded by glass tearing through her glove and she hissed out a long breath even as she leaned back, trying to ease the heavy sensation in her stomach.

Over eight hundred pounds of whisky lay in shards around her, and it was such a perfect representation of how she felt at that moment, she knew she could start sobbing.

She took off her glove and was relieved to note that the thick fabric had taken the brunt of the cut. There was some blood, but not much.

"I'm sorry, lass. I didn't realize there was glass. I wasn't looking," he admitted, and she shot him a wan smile.

"Don't be silly. I really appreciate you stopping to help me out," she whispered, her voice small when Tin began wailing at her side as he saw the cut on her palm. She quietened him with a shushing noise and turned in his direction but the movement had her cringing. Something was definitely not right.

Deep inside.

There was no avoiding it, no ignoring it even if she wanted to.

Biting her lip, she told her son, "Darling, it's okay. Mommy is fine."

It didn't work.

The tears fell from his eyes as freely as the snot did from his nose, and she had to sigh at the sight. God, even with a snotty snitch, as Cinta called it, he was cute as hell.

This time, however, she didn't even have to resist the urge to reach for a handkerchief to wipe his nose. She didn't have it in her to do much else than murmur, "We'll be fine, Tin."

Apparently, her tone wasn't enough to inspire confidence in him because, once again, it didn't work. One of the crowd broke away, revealing an older woman with graying hair, a red beanie on her head. Her thick woolen coat parted as she squatted at Tin's side.

"Come now, laddy, your mummy's okay. We just need to get her seen to, and when we do, then she'll be right as rain."

The woman said 'right' as 'reet,' and Tin's eyes widened. Jacinta hadn't introduced him to that particular phrase, it seemed.

"Reet as rain," he murmured, repeating the phrase with her accent too.

The woman laughed. "Aye." She cut Sascha a look. "Be honest. The hospital?"

Sascha licked her lips, then she nodded. There was no ignoring the strange sensations fluttering away inside her.

The man at her side reached into his suit coat. It was only then she absentmindedly realized how handsome he was. A silver fox, his outfit spoke not only of wealth, but of exquisite taste. The label was definitely Armani, and underneath, it was perfectly tailored to his form. She wasn't interested in checking him out, but he seemed to shine. In the dull light of a bleak morning, with the pain intruding on everything else, he might as well have started glowing. The phone in hand, he connected the call and she realized he was ringing an ambulance.

The next twenty minutes passed in a blur as they waited for it, and as each minute passed, the sense that... Her throat felt constricted from everything she was trying to repress. All the emotions and the fear. She needed to control it not just for Tin's sake, but for herself. She was terrified, and she felt so alone. So so alone. Why hadn't she gone with Sawyer and Devon like they'd planned?

Why had she snuck out without disturbing them from their work?

Tin was rambunctious and stubborn enough to be strong on occasion. With the icy floor? She'd been stupid, no, *reckless* to come out.

Hating herself, fearing the worst as the pain deepened into a blackness that bordered on labor pains, she felt rigid, frozen with fright.

As the crowd dispersed, the woman stayed as did the man. She spoke with Tin, soothing him as she informed them both she was called Martha. And the man told Sascha his name was Joseph.

"That's a real shame about all that whisky," he murmured when the gathering had dispersed, and though she'd told him he didn't have to wait, he'd dismissed the offer without even commenting—as though her words were too ridiculous to even remark upon.

She focused her splintered wits on the broken bottles beside her. "I don't drink the stuff, but even I can mourn twenty-five-year-old liquor."

He gasped as he turned over the shard with the label on. "MacAllan?"

"Yes."

"That's some gift. For your husband?"

"No. His parents," she replied, her cheeks flushing as he tilted his head to the side. Something in his gaze telling her he was asking with an ulterior motive in mind.

Considering she had a son and a baby belly, well, his interest was, in her opinion, a little unusual. Who hit on a pregnant mother?

Frowning a little, she pleated the hem of her coat between her fingers. "I wonder how long the ambulance will take," she murmured, more to herself than to him as she tried to contain, and failed, a sudden wave of agony that shattered along her side.

"You know what traffic is like at this time of the day."

She shook her head. "No, not really. I don't know the city that well." She didn't think eleven AM was exactly a busy time.

He shot her a look. "Well, it's close to twelve, so the offices will be emptying in time for lunch."

"It's nearly twelve?" Where the hell had an hour gone?

She winced, then realized she hadn't called Sawyer or Devon. What the hell was she thinking?

"I didn't realize so much time had passed," she admitted. "You really should go and get some lunch. I'm sorry for taking up so much of your break."

"I'm the boss," he informed her drily. "I can take as much of a break as I want."

She flushed again at the interest sparkling in his eyes—why did he keep looking at her like that?

Ducking her head, with the need for her men suddenly as ardent as the pain making her stomach throb, she reached for her purse only to see it wasn't there. She let out a hard sigh. "Just what I need."

"What is it?" Martha asked.

"I think one of the crowd took my purse."

Joseph swore. "That's bang out of order," he growled, leaping up to his feet as he stared down Buchanan Street, which was, as predicted, slowly filling up. "I can't believe someone took advantage of your fall."

She rubbed her forehead. "It's okay. I just..." She grimaced. "My phone."

Panic filled her. How was she supposed to get in touch with them?

The whole point of a phone was not having to remember everyone else's number, and when her baby brain was in full effect, that became more of an issue than usual.

It might have seemed crazy, but that was literally what broke her control.

The pain, she could deal with. It wasn't labor; that was more painful than even the car crash she'd been involved in years ago. It was this. Tin was here, scared, he needed his daddies. *She* needed his daddies, too. Jesus. She needed them more than Tin did at that moment, but she couldn't have them because she didn't know their damn numbers! Her bubbling fright she'd been managing to temper, but the prospect of not being able to contact her men?

It was just too much.

She began to cry, trying and failing to think up a solution, coming up short each time. The more panicked she felt, the harder it became to concentrate on those eleven digits of Sawyer's number. And the six digits of the house phone at Cinta's? They swirled around her, confusing her as they made her terror surge.

The man, Joseph, squatted at her side again. "Can you remember a phone number?"

Sascha shook her head. "N-No."

He reached for her hand and squeezed it. "It's okay. We'll work it out."

She looked into his handsome face, saw the earnestness there, and didn't know whether to be relieved or perturbed.

He was so genuine.

Was he really just a charitable man? A kind man who'd seen a pregnant woman fall, with her little boy sobbing at the sight of her on the ground?

Or was she so suspicious of people now that she couldn't trust any act of kindness that didn't come from her men?

She didn't suspect Martha, so why did she feel more uneasy about Joseph's presence than the other woman?

"T-Thank you," she released on a breath, and with that shaky breath, she heard it.

In the distance.

The wail of an ambulance.

Tin heard it too. He'd been playing with something Martha had handed him—a fidget spinner that was attached to her key ring. His head popped up as he heard the noise and his pink cheeks, flushed from the cold, blanched.

"It's okay, baby. It's okay," she tried to soothe, hoping like hell it would be.

She was cold and sore and in a bizarre pain that she really didn't know how to describe. Not only that, but she was in another country, by herself, with no way of contacting her men.

She had five of them, and not one of them could be here for her.

It seemed so wrong to ask this stranger for his help, so wrong when he watched the paramedics help her off the ground and onto a stretcher.

And it felt weirder still when he climbed into the ambulance, helped her wave Martha off, and sat talking to Tin the whole way to the hospital. But she was grateful.

She wasn't alone, and she wasn't about to face a team of doctors without someone at her side. Joseph wasn't one of her quintet, but at that moment, she just didn't want to be alone.

For that, she'd forever be grateful to the stranger.

# FOUR

"WHAT IS IT?"

"Now, lad, there's no need to be panicking."

Sawyer lifted his head at his mother's quiet words.

Quiet because Devon was at the other end of the room working.

He recognized that volume. It was a 'let's not freak Devon out' pitch, not a 'let's not worry Sawyer' pitch.

Scowling at his mother, he scrubbed his hand over his head as he demanded, "What is it?"

She winced, her shock of red hair was as bright against her pale skin as it had been when he was a boy. The only difference being the many lines that now creased her face. For all that, she was still the bonny lass he remembered, but the worry on her features made his own nerves start to fray. "Andrei just called."

Unable to discern why that would have her as white as a sheet, he realized Andrei calling heralded something else. Something bad.

Sawyer, only by the grace of God, didn't jump up and slam his chair back, as, Cinta's earlier prediction coming true, panic filled him. "What's wrong?" he insisted, trying to control his tone even as he glanced over at Devon to make sure his brother from another mother was still focused on work.

"Sascha called him because she—"

"Sascha called Andrei?" He scowled at her. "Well, what's wrong with that, Ma?"

She scowled back at him. "If you'd let me finish, son, I'd explain. She's had a fall." She whispered the word. "And someone stole her purse after she fell. She couldn't get in touch with you because she couldn't remember anyone's numbers." Jacinta grimaced, her cheeks flushing as bright as her hair. "It happened six hours ago. I was starting to get worried, but you and Devon were so busy..." She shrugged her shoulders. "I thought you knew she'd be out a long time. I thought she'd told you about it."

For a second, he couldn't process what she'd said. Then, when he could, he jumped to his feet, agitation making it impossible for him to sit down.

His woman had fallen *six* hours ago and they'd only just now found out?

Worse still, she'd had to contact the house in Kensington rather than them because she didn't know their numbers?

As horrified as he was, blackness seemed to bleed over everything else. She'd fallen, and his mother was looking like she could burst into tears at any moment.

His throat felt too clogged full of emotions as he turned to Devon. Not only was his best friend not going to take this well, he knew there was more.

More.

His mouth fucking trembled as he turned back to Cinta. "The baby?" he asked her quietly, their eyes locking.

She shook her head. "They..." She swallowed, the noise audible in the quietness of the study. "No."

Agony whipped through him like a hurricane. It left devastation in its wake, but the shame and the rage and the fear all coalesced because, as bad as he was feeling, it was nothing to what was about to happen to Devon.

And then, he felt angrier because what about his own grief? His own horror?

For a second, just a split second, he hated that he always had to think of the other man first. But, this wasn't just about him. Nor was it just about Devon.

It was about Sascha.

His throat choked again and he had to take a moment to clear it.

For a second, he stared blankly around the office, trying to process what his mother had just told him. Trying to figure out how this morning, everything had been well, save for Sean's abrupt appearance in his mother's home... Now?

Everything was turned on its head.

"Does Sean know?"

Jacinta shook her head. "He's still sleeping."

Sawyer's eyes widened. "That must be some hangover."

"Your father poured whisky down him like he was at one of those frat parties." She pursed her lips in disapproval. "I'll be surprised if the man will be able to see straight when he wakes up."

He didn't even have it in him to question how the hell she knew what a frat party was. No, he couldn't think straight, couldn't breathe right, not when their woman was in a fucking hospital. With miles and miles between them. Scared. Alone. In pain. Grieving.

He felt the soft, dry palm rake against his own, calluses that had been born from years of hard work, as they scraped against his fingers. Cinta squeezed. "Son? You need to go to her."

"Of course I do," he said on a growl, and realized he'd just been standing there.

Hovering. Dithering.

Uncertain. Unsure.

Fucking lost.

He shook his head, reached up to rub his eyes, then whispered, "Go and wake Sean, please, Ma?"

She nodded. "What should I tell him?"

"Nothing. Just... Leave it to me."

Another nod and she traipsed off, after giving his fingers one last squeeze.

Sawyer turned and looked at the large office that was twice the size of the master bedroom in the home annexed to his parent's place.

It was as manic and chaotic as their office in London, with papers everywhere, as well as little origami shapes, from cranes to roses, perched on different books and shelves where Devon had discarded them after he'd created them.

But for a second, he didn't see the sea of paper and leather, wood and tweed. He didn't see the large fireplace with its fire that had died down hours ago or the green Chesterfield armchairs before them.

He just saw Devon.

Then, he saw Sascha, laying in a hospital room, alone with Tin, and having to deal with...

The breath was torn from his lungs as he folded over, his hands coming to his knees as he propped himself up.

The storm swirled through him again, and this time, the tears that fell were honest and true. Nothing less than the wee bairn they'd had for too short a time deserved.

As the rage of emotion passed, he knew he had to move. Sascha needed him. *Them.* He didn't have time to deal with his own emotions, not when she'd been dealing with her grief without her partners at her side all day long. Feeling like an old man, he straightened up and when he did, he saw Devon was staring at him, wide-eyed.

The panic in his eyes hit Sawyer in the gut. It was an emotion that Devon felt too often and too swiftly. The chaos of the world was just something that could hit him and decimate him.

Reaching up to rub the back of his neck, he whispered, "We need to go out, Devon."

"Go out where?" His best friend's voice was hollow.

"To the hospital. Sascha's had an accident."

Devon sat up so quickly his chair tipped back—the desk behind him saved it, but Devon didn't care.

Hell, Sawyer didn't care either.

This whole room could fucking burn and he wouldn't give a shit.

"Why?" Devon demanded.

"S-She's lost the baby, mate," he told him, having to choke the words out.

"Lost?" Devon shook his head. "She can't lose the baby. He's inside her."

For a second, Sawyer didn't have a clue what Devon was talking about, then, when he realized Devon had taken him literally, he wanted to sob again.

Shaking his head, and feeling the burden of guilt load down his shoulders, he whispered, "The bairn's gone, man. He... She died." They'd wanted to wait to know the sex, and didn't even know what gender the child was.

"B-But, no." Devon's head whipped from side to side. "No. That can't be."

It could be. It was.

Sawyer didn't say that though, he just strode over to Devon, gripped his shoulder even as he grabbed a firm hold of Dev's chin. Forcing the man to look him in the eye, he murmured, "I know. You're scared. You're panicking. I feel it too, Dev. I feel it too. But... Sascha needs us." His tongue felt heavy, too thick to move as he tried to form the words that would stop Devon from breaking down. "We need to get to Sascha."

Devon's blue eyes were so wide, he could see the whites around them.

"Devon, please, mon. Please. Help me help her." He closed his eyes, unable to look into the endless bottomless pits of confusion and loss that Devon was staring back at him with.

He'd known too much loss. Too much death.

Sawyer wanted to rage even as he knew there was no point. Life just threw this kind of shite at some people.

Others had it easy. *He'd* had it easy. Poor, but loving parents had brought him into this world. They'd given him everything they could, had worked hard, harder than they should to get him the help he needed when his talents with math had revealed themselves.

It was through that talent that his parents had helped forge, with extra schooling and tutors they couldn't afford, that he'd met this man. And that was when all their lives had changed.

For the better. Always that. But still, life opened up after Dev. Sawyer realized how lucky he'd had it in the face of what Devon had endured over the years. It was why Sawyer was Devon's self-appointed protector, but now, he couldn't be. He had to be Sascha's.

She needed him.

*Them.*

And he'd already let her down.

*They* already had.

He gripped Devon's shoulder tighter and made sure, even when he tried to pull away, that Dev had no other alternative but to look him square in the eye. Sawyer, who knew his friend's capabilities, wondered why Devon hadn't realized Sascha had been gone for so long. But it wasn't fair to shove that blame on his shoulders. Sawyer had lost himself in his work too, and he knew they'd both bear the guilt of that forever.

"I know you want to break down. I know you do. But not now. I need you to think of her. I need you to focus on the woman who loves you. Who sneakily brews your coffee so you can have some without my telling you off. Who makes sure your drawers are all in perfect order so you know what to wear." He sucked in a sharp breath. "Think of her, Dev. Please."

It seemed to take a lifetime for that to hit home, too long in the face of Sascha being alone in a hospital ward somewhere, but when Devon nodded, Sawyer felt his knees turn to mush.

That had been both harder and easier than he'd ever imagined.

"I-I need to see her."

"Of course," Sawyer whispered, his voice cracking too much to even speak at a decent volume. "We're going now."

Devon nodded again and jerking back from Sawyer, rushed off and away from him. With his back to the door, he heard Devon head out, and alone, he let himself crumble once more.

These few moments were his and his alone. His brief time to mourn the child that would never be, and to allow himself to feel the misery of the moment.

It would never be enough, but it was what he deserved after failing Sascha so horrifically.

---

THE HOSPITAL WAS OVERFLOWING with people.

Wherever he turned, there were people, and at his side, Devon was barely holding it together and Sean looked like he was about to puke. Sawyer wasn't sure if that was from his hangover, or the news they'd broken to him before they'd driven like bats out of hell to the hospital, where Sascha had told Andrei she was being treated.

The more people there were, the more likely it was that Devon would freak out. He was strung tighter than piano wire, and barely keeping it together.

Sawyer knew it was a testament to how far Devon had come since Sascha had appeared in their lives. Before, he'd have been a wreck. Now? He was still a wreck, but he was coping, internalizing it all.

Sawyer didn't doubt it would come out at another point. That this crisis was contained only as they located Sascha and got to her, but that was something else to worry about at another time.

There was enough to handle without adding more troubles to their worries.

As they approached the reception desk, he had to clear his throat twice to ask, "Sascha Dubois. She's a patient. We're..." He broke off. Not only as Sascha's surname suddenly resonated with him, but, how did he explain their being here?

One man was acceptable.

But *three*?

And five when Kurt and Andrei landed at the airport?

Sean, seeming to sense Sawyer's bewilderment, murmured, "We're her family."

The woman raked her glance over them. Sawyer stiffened and felt Devon do so too at her appreciative stare. When she just looked at them, gaping, not glancing at the computer once, Sean growled, "Sascha Dubois? We need to see her."

The receptionist, in her early thirties, blushed. Her cheeks pinkening as she ducked her head and finally stared down at the computer.

"S-Sorry," she mumbled stiffly, before imparting information about the ward Sascha was on. "But visiting hours are over," the woman said to their backs as they headed out, ignoring her and her stupid remark.

If the hospital thought they could keep them from Sascha, well, they could think again, Sawyer thought grimly.

Following the sign-posted directions, he let Sean take charge of leading as he trudged along in their wake while he grabbed his phone. He should have thought to do this on their way over but he'd still been in a daze. Better late than never, though.

Scrolling through the contacts, he found the number he wanted and before he dialed it, murmured, "Devon? I need you to speak with John Ashton."

Devon turned to glower at him. "Why?"

Sawyer knew it was taking all of his immeasurable focus to stay on track, to stay calm, and this was a breach of focus the other man didn't need, but this wasn't about Devon.

It was about Sascha.

"I need you to pull strings."

"Which strings?"

Sawyer closed his eyes, seeking patience. "I need you to make the head of the NHS foundation help us out," he clarified.

"Why?"

"Because they're not going to let us in to visit her otherwise. And I want her in a private ward. You heard the receptionist, visiting hours are over."

Sean cleared his throat, but it didn't ease the rasp there. "Devon, call Ashton. We need to make Sascha comfortable."

Sawyer didn't even have it in him to be irritated that, as per fucking usual, Devon responded to the authority in Sean's tone. Instead, he chose to be grateful and he handed over his cell as they rounded another corner, ignoring Devon's awkward one-sided conversation with John Ashton. The linoleum beneath their feet was squeaky and the ivory walls were dingy, not easing Sawyer's already grim mood as they trekked across the hospital.

By the time they'd followed the many signs, they found themselves outside a ward that had Sawyer frowning.

It was private.

How…?

Even as he was scowling around at the closed doors shielding private patients, a nurse approached them.

Her scrubs were green and wrinkled. Her brow was etched with the same creases, and her fatigue was evident.

"Can I help you? Visiting hours aren't for another…"

Before she could finish speaking, a call sounded from the desk five feet away.

Her mouth opened, but she held up a hand. "One minute, please."

Sawyer nodded, but Devon didn't. When she turned her back, he strode down the corridor, peering into the windowed doors as he hunted Sascha down.

"Sir!" the nurse called out, but then whoever was on the line—John Ashton, no doubt—took her attention.

Following Devon, Sawyer watched as his best friend jolted to a startled halt. Before he could ask what had surprised him, Devon had pulled open the door.

"Who the hell are you?"

His growl had Sawyer shooting Sean a quick glance. Then, as he entered Sascha's ward, he saw a stranger seated beside the bed. He was in an armchair that NHS hospitals seemed to specialize in. That weird blue vinyl that squeaked whenever you took a seat.

But Sawyer wasn't looking at the blue vinyl or the other crimes against esthetics.

He was looking at the stranger who had Tin on his lap, who was holding Sascha's hand in his like...

Sawyer's mouth firmed then he released his clenched jaw and, like Devon, demanded, "Who the hell *are* you?"

# FIVE

THE RASPY VOICE penetrated the fog of her brain. But she knew it.

She knew it well.

A dopey smile curved her lips at the brogue that made her have eargasms on a regular basis, but when it hurt to open her eyes, she felt her brow pucker.

Why wasn't it easy to open her eyes?

The ache in her head and her body made itself known and she wondered how much white wine she'd drunk the night before to feel as shitty as this.

Then, when the memory of what had happened hit home, she tore her eyes open.

When she saw Sawyer, Sean, and Devon looming over Joseph like avenging angels, she released a sharp cry. One loaded with equal parts relief, misery, and grief.

Their attention swerved from the man in the armchair, the man who'd been there all day and night, God bless him, and over to her.

The devastation on their faces floored her. She felt it herself, but it was so perfectly reflected in their features, she felt her own crumple and the tears begin to fall.

She opened her arms and whimpered, "I'm so sorry."

Sawyer's eyes flashed as he swooped in. Before she knew what was happening, her IV lines had been shifted around and she was suddenly lying in his lap.

He threaded his arms around her waist and hauled her against him. "God, lass. What do ye have tae be sorry about?" His accent was so thick, she wanted to drown in it.

Maybe that would take this fucking agony in her heart away.

"I-I didn't keep our baby safe!" The cry was torn from her, and it was a thousand times worse for her having to repress it all day long.

Tin was such a deep sleeper that she didn't have to worry about him waking up. He'd slept through a gale once; one-hundred and twenty mile-an-hour gusts had whipped through the streets, and he hadn't made a peep.

After his own traumatic and tearful day, he'd be down for the count, and she was relying on that.

She heard a voice clearing, and behind her, Sean asked, "Who are you?"

She ignored the conversation. It was mean letting Joseph fend for himself after he'd been so kind, but she wasn't up to anything other than accepting the comfort that Sawyer's strong arms provided.

"I'm Joseph Santorini," was her savior's reply. He sounded calm, totally at ease. If she'd been on the receiving end of those grim looks her men had cast his way, she wasn't sure if she'd have felt so easy.

Sawyer, especially, looked like a bruiser. And over the years, he hadn't softened up, if anything, he'd gotten harder. His biceps and thighs were huge.

She squeezed the former as she nuzzled deeper into his embrace. He scented of leather and another scent she'd only ever smelled when they took her deep into the Scottish countryside, heather—she knew because it was his soap, the one she'd bought him for Christmas two years ago, and the one he'd used ever since. He was warm and comforting, and she was safe in his arms even if he was brimming with tension.

She pressed her forehead into his throat and repeated, "I'm sorry."

"She has no reason to be sorry." It was Joseph who spoke, and his voice ratcheted up the strain that was already throbbing through Sawyer's tense form.

She hated that he was upset, hated that they were all upset. And all because she'd been thoughtless, a reckless idiot.

"She fell. There was a big patch of black ice outside one of the stores she was going into. She went down, and..." Joseph's sigh was heavy enough to echo around the tiny private room. "Her stomach took the brunt of the fall."

She blinked, because the whole experience was just a blur of pain. What she did know was her baby's heartbeat hadn't been there when they'd checked her over. Then, words like 'placental abruption,' 'firm abdomen,' and worst of all, 'stillbirth' floated around her, and the nightmare she'd only just dipped her toes into, became fully formed.

Just like that, her child's life had been snuffed out. Simply because she'd been stupid and just *had* to go out even though it was cold as fuck today.

More tears gathered and fell. They burned as they forged a path along her eyeline, and then they drenched Sawyer's shirt front.

"We should have been with you."

*Devon.*

The agony in his voice tore at her heart.

There was a welter of pain in the depths, and that pain spoke to her on such a visceral level, she moved away from Sawyer to turn to Dev.

Opening her arms, she whispered, "It's okay."

"No. It's not okay," he replied, but his tone was wooden. "It's the exact opposite of okay, Sascha."

Stung, but knowing he was right, she buried her face in her hands.

"Thank you for staying with her for so long," Sean said, the words flying over her head as they'd done all day when Sawyer wrapped his arm around her and tugged her close once more. "If you don't mind giving us some privacy though?"

"Of course," Joseph replied, and the sounds of the vinyl seat creaking were loud as he climbed to his feet. "He's fast asleep," he continued with a little chuckle. "I've never known such a heavy sleeper."

"Thank God he was," Sean said, his voice heartfelt. She dropped her hands, knowing she had to thank Joseph, and hating that she'd be doing so with her face tear stained.

As she did, she watched Joseph pass the limp little boy in his arms over to Sean. Tin settled like he'd been born to be there, which she guessed he had. Nuzzling immediately into him as Sean shook Joseph's hand and retreated to the armchair, taking up the space the stranger had taken all day and for most of the evening as well.

As he approached the bed, she held out her hands, wincing at the wetness of her tears on them as she whispered, "I'll never be able to thank you enough for being here for me. For us." She cut Tin a glance. "You helped us both, so much." Her smile was wan as she asked, "That bottle of '85?"

Joseph tilted his head to the side. "What about it?"

"I think you've earned one. Please, leave your card?"

"That's not necessary," he protested with a genuine smile. "But, look, I'll be on my way. I'm just happy I was able to help."

She smiled at him, trying to control the quiver in her lips, as he waved awkwardly at the four of them before grabbing his coat, which he'd dumped at the foot of the bed, and headed out the door.

For a second, there was nothing but quiet, then Devon, his tone colder than she'd ever heard from him, snarled, "I don't trust him."

The coldness hit her hard. "What about him do you have to trust? He didn't have to stay with me, Devon. But he did. And he was there for me. For us." She didn't say 'when you weren't' because it wasn't their fault they hadn't been there. It had been hers. Not only for being unable to remember their fucking numbers, but for sneaking out without them. But Joseph had stayed when he could have just left her.

He'd taken being a good Samaritan to a level she'd thought was a thing of the past.

Dev's mouth firmed into a mutinous line but he didn't maintain the topic, dropping himself down onto the foot of the bed and pressing his hand to her ankle instead. "How are you?"

"How do you think I am?" She pressed her lips together a second, clenched her eyes shut, then managed to gasp out, "I lost the baby, Dev. I lost—"

But he shook his head. "I didn't ask about the baby. I asked about you."

She blinked at him, shut her eyes once more, and turned to burrow into Sawyer again. "Tired. Hurting." She gnawed at her bottom lip. "Regretful." Resentful. Guilty.

*Ashamed.*

She quieted those words before they could escape her lips though. They didn't need to hear that. Didn't need to know she'd...

Sascha pulled back from Sawyer's arms and asked, "When will Andrei and Kurt get here?" She didn't have a doubt in her mind that they'd have dropped everything to be here for her.

"In three hours." Sean spoke, but his gaze was trained on Tin. "They'd be here sooner but there were no seats remaining on the earlier flights."

She nodded, aware that it would have been too much to ask from the fates after such a shitty day.

"What happened, Sascha?" Sawyer asked, his voice a rumble.

"N-Nothing. It was just like Joseph said." She bit the inside of her cheek, hating that they were going to say, 'I told you so.' "I was holding Tin's hand and he pulled me one way and I intended to go the other. It was just a stupid accident. If that ice hadn't been there,

there'd have been no problem. But it was slippery, and I just...I lost my balance.

"It just hurt. Hurt so badly. Deep inside." She pressed her hands to her stomach, remembering the pain like it had happened moments before.

"I'm so sorry you had to go through that alone," Sean whispered, and when he turned to look at her, his eyes were as bleak as winter. He leaned forward and pressed his hand to her thigh.

"It was an accident," she repeated. "When I fell, Joseph, and this lady, Martha, came to help, but I'd attracted a small crowd. One of them took advantage, stole my purse. I couldn't remember your numbers. None of them." She closed her eyes. "Not a single one. It took five hours for me to remember the London house's."

She had to bite back the cry as she realized she wouldn't be worrying about the brain fog that came with pregnancy anymore. Oh Christ, what she'd give to be back in that fog. What she'd give for this to be yesterday, or for it to be tomorrow. For this fucking day to be over.

"Have the police been?"

She nodded. "Joseph dealt with them. Said he didn't see who took my bag, and that he wasn't looking at the crowd so he didn't have a clue who could have taken it either." She swallowed. "I'm sorry it took me so long to remember. You should have been here."

Sean whispered, "Stop saying 'sorry.'" He pressed a gentle kiss to Tin's head, reminding her of yesterday's scare on his part. "We're the ones who should be apologizing."

When he turned to look at her, she wanted to wince at the guilt in his eyes. Immediately shaking her head at him, she murmured, "No, Sean. No."

"Yes. Sean's right," Sawyer growled. "We should have been with you. Tin's getting strong. It's been freezing... the streets were bound to be dangerous. We should have been with you," he repeated, as though saying it twice would make it hit home harder.

"Do you want me to be angry at you?" she asked quietly.

Devon shifted on the bed. "You should be. I'm angry at me. It's my fault. Sawyer said you were supposed to go shopping." He stared at her, and in those blue eyes, she saw a chasm that had never been there before. It wasn't between him and her, it was between him and the world—and that scared the crap out of her. "We were working."

They had been. When she'd popped her head around the door, they'd been so busy, and she'd thought nothing of it. She was used to them working all sorts of hours, and it wasn't like she'd needed her hand held while she shopped for gifts they weren't interested in.

Except, this time, she *had* needed her hand holding.

"Will they kick you out? I don't think I'm supposed to have visitors. They only let Joseph stay because of Tin. Because I needed help and didn't know who to call on."

"The police should have come to my mother's."

Her voice was small as she murmured, "I could only remember her old address. It was like my brain turned to mush."

"Oh sweetheart, I'm so very sorry," he replied, and she heard the remorse in his tone, a deep welter of pain that she hadn't meant to stir.

Amid the day's panic had been the terror of not being able to remember any of their details, then, when the doctors had left her, sobbing quietly in her bed after the silence of the birth, and Tin had been returned to her with Joseph holding his hand, she'd remembered the London house's landline number.

That had felt like a gift from God.

"Hush, lass," he told her, seeming to sense the ramble that were her thoughts. "Tomorrow's another day."

Releasing a trembling breath, and fully aware of the fact that she couldn't think about any of this without wanting to cry, she nodded and whispered, "I want to sleep. I need this day to be over with."

"O' course, lass." Sawyer helped settle her down, and she was about to ask him to stay, fearful he'd, *they'd* leave, when he settled behind her and slid a hand over her stomach. The hand he pressed there made her eyes burn with unshed tears. "I-I'm sorry, lass. I wish we'd known the person they'd become, and I'm sorry you had to go through everything that happened today without us at your side." He pressed his nose into the slight cavern of her throat, and she felt the welcome warmth of his breath brushing her tender skin.

"She, Sawyer. She was a little girl. And she was perfect." So perfect, Sascha still didn't know what had happened. How things had gone so wrong.

His breath whooshed out from his lungs, making it sound as though he'd been punched in the gut. "How do you know that?"

She tensed. "She was... I had to deliver her." Hadn't he known that?

He went silent, and the rest of the room did too, telling her she had spoken loud enough for Devon and Sean to overhear her whispered words. Sawyer pressed his face to her shoulder, hiding from the world, and then for the second time in as many days, she felt the wet kiss as one of her men cried, and hid his tears from the rest of the world in her nape.

---

WHEN JACINTA WALKED through the door, Sascha started crying, and with his mother's tears too, Sawyer felt like he was drowning.

Sascha wasn't the kind of woman who cried a lot. If she had PMS, she got angry. She'd rage and seemed to feel no fear at butting heads with any of the men in the house.

She wasn't weepy. Didn't even cry at the sappy movies she watched sometimes. But, to see her shed tears now? It made his own heart feel decimated in the face of her grief.

And his shame stemmed from the fact that he shared that grief, he even matched it, but, more than anything was his horror at having left her to shop by herself. At his having been too busy to notice she'd been gone for all those hours without even thinking about where she was.

This wasn't just anyone. It was Sascha.

*Sascha.*

The woman who was their fucking world.

He had three responsibilities in his life. Three. And two of them had walked out that door in cold weather. He shouldn't have even let them drive. Not when he knew the route from his mother and father's place could be a nightmare in the weather they'd been having.

She should never have gone out at all, and that she had was because he'd been working, because he and Devon had gotten caught up in the files Andrei had sent them about the state of the Veronian economy. And Sawyer loved working with the DIVA program so much, he'd fallen into his tests with zeal.

Sascha had always been strong, but over these last few years, since having Tin and discovering the truth of her heritage and having inherited a fortune, she'd grown even stronger.

She could be like a bull in a china shop.

He knew her. Knew her so well that he could imagine her looking at the weather, peering at the roads, and thinking, "I've got this." Never fearing they'd be slick with ice, or that out in the city, it could be equally as dangerous.

Buchanan Street, where she'd been shopping, was on a damn hill. She knew that. She'd been there countless times before. Everyone knew it was a bit treacherous in the winter. When the ice was out, the ground was like it had been greased up!

Still, she'd gone there because he hadn't been paying attention.

He watched his mother wrap her arms around Sascha, tears drenching her eyes and curling over her cheeks, as she rocked his woman as though she were a baby.

Tin had clambered toward Hamish, and was settling in his lap now that Sawyer's father had taken a heavy seat in one of the questionably sanitary armchairs that had acted as their bed throughout the night.

They'd taken turns climbing in behind her, each of them needing to feel her close. When Andrei and Kurt had strode in, grief written all over their faces, fatigue in their eyes, and their desperate need to hold Sascha strumming through their bodies, they'd done so without waking her up by some miracle. With all her men around her, Sascha seemed to be brighter today, but when compared to the darkness that brimmed in her eyes, that brightness was just a drop in the ocean.

He knew she was putting on a brave face for them, and he wanted to tell her it wasn't necessary, that she should be herself when she was with them, but he knew to tell her that would be cruel.

Because the brave face was for Tin too.

Hell, for him more than any of them.

Tin hadn't pushed his mother over, but he was an ebullient little boy—all he knew was he'd been holding his mother's hand, had tugged one way, and she'd come tumbling down.

Was it any wonder he spent most of the time curled up close to Sascha? Except when he wanted to sleep, then he'd climb onto one of their laps and promptly pass out.

"When's the doctor due in?" Cinta asked. "I want to get you out of this place. I hate damn hospitals."

"Another half-hour. But she'll probably have to stay in." Sean's voice was weighed down with his own particular misery.

They were all feeling it.

Cinta squeezed Sascha's arm. "It will be all right, lass. Might not feel like it now, but it will." His mother licked her lips and murmured, "I lost my first. Stillborn as well." Her head bobbed as her throat worked. "The pain never leaves, lass, and the memory will always be wi' ye, but ye move on, and that little mon o'er there will help wi' that."

Sascha just nodded, but he could see she didn't agree, and anyone with eyes could see that too.

Who could blame her?

Time might heal all wounds, but this particular wound wasn't something they were ever likely to forget.

She'd given birth.

Why hadn't he realized that?

Why hadn't he thought about it?

He'd just thought she'd bleed. That's what happened in the movies, didn't it? They didn't give birth, and they didn't get to look at the baby.

He closed his eyes at the thought. The nurses had already been in, offering the da' the chance to see the bairn. The nursing staff had looked around, trying to guess which man was the father, and they'd been unable to say, 'all of them.'

The prospect of *that* though wasn't something he felt he could bear. Sascha said she'd taken pictures. But, Sawyer wasn't sure he could... He cut his thoughts off that track.

Kurt would go with her.

He was the one who was most in touch with his feelings, and he always seemed to understand Sascha. Always seemed to know what she needed. He'd go and do that for her benefit.

Well, either him or Sean.

It wasn't fair to offload that onto either of his friends but Sawyer knew, point blank, he wouldn't be able to look at that tiny person and not feel like dying himself.

He sucked in a breath when a knock sounded at the door. More nurses swarmed in, and as they'd done for most of their time here, looked disapprovingly at the cluster of folk as they went about their business.

He had no doubt that John Ashton had told the staff to treat them like VIPs, which meant seeing to Sascha's needs even when the room contained a crowd.

Devon's charitable foundation had funded a wing at this particular hospital. Sawyer's sister had died of ovarian cancer eight years ago, and Devon and Sheila had always been close. It had been his idea to construct the special wing dedicated to cancer treatment, and he'd maintained a close working relationship with the management.

Well, Sawyer had.

Devon never really got close to anyone.

Save for the people in this room, that is.

Everyone was under the impression that it was Devon behind the emails and letters, but it was Sawyer, even if his brother had fronted the large sum of money the wing had necessitated.

Devon moved away from the bed where he'd been leaning and came to stand next to his side at the back wall. Kurt and Andrei had to move away too, but they stayed close, their hands hovering a second before they settled on Sascha's knee and calf while the nurse took some more blood after doing a basic vitals check.

As they watched, Devon murmured, "I don't trust that guy."

Sawyer frowned, the nurse was a woman. "Which guy?"

"Joseph Santorini," he murmured, saying the name like it was poison-strewn.

"Joseph?" He blinked, and it took a second to remember the name. "Sascha's right, Devon. He was there for her when we weren't." He didn't want to hammer that home, but he didn't have a choice if Devon was going to fixate on the man who'd saved Sascha from more grief. "Let's just be grateful he was here when we couldn't be."

"Yes. He was. That's my fault, I know. But I'm telling you. Something was off about that guy."

Sawyer cringed. The trouble was, Devon's instincts were usually right on target where things like this were concerned.

Raising a hand, he dragged it down his nose before he pinched the bridge. "What was it?" Devon had the irritating knack of being able to discern shit about other people that few else could. His brain, as weird and wonderful as it was, saw things most missed. Which meant Sawyer couldn't dismiss his concerns as being out of hand or irrational.

"I don't know."

His impatience levels soaring, Sawyer closed his eyes. "Devon, is now really the best time?"

The other man wriggled his shoulders. "You know I wouldn't say anything about it if I didn't feel something was wrong."

Because he *did* know that, Sawyer felt like screaming. "You have to narrow it down, Devon."

"He was lying."

The simple statement had Sawyer's brow puckering. "What the hell do you mean?" What did a stranger have to lie about to another stranger?

"What do you mean 'what do I mean?'" Devon grumbled. "The clue's in the title, isn't it?"

Sawyer rubbed his chin. "Yeah. But I want specifics. You can't just tell me that he was lying and not tell me what he was lying about."

Devon considered that a second, then he nodded. "He wasn't working in town. Out on a lunch break," he clarified.

"What was he doing then?"

Devon huffed, but his already pale face, lined with the grief and the anger he was fighting to control, seemed to whiten even more. Unlike most of them who were struggling with their grief and how to handle Sascha, Devon was raging. Sawyer had never seen it before, and he wasn't sure he liked it. "How the hell do I know?" he snapped. "I just know he was lying about it."

"So what if he was? What does it matter? We'll never see the man again, Dev. Look, this isn't the thing to be focused on. I know what you're doing. You're feeling guilty. One of us should have been with her and instead, we were working. But shifting the blame onto a guy who really helped us out when we couldn't be there for..." His nostrils flared as the words choked him. "I mean, she has *five* men, Devon. Five. And not one of us were there for her. Fuck."

Devon's jaw tightened, but he didn't say anything, just stared straight ahead, watching as the nurse finished up.

"Look, shifting that blame is natural. But, we messed up. We did. We fucked up and by him being there for our woman, she's here today. We need to own that, Devon. We need to make sure it never happens again. We need to make sure she's so fucking safe from now on, that she gets sick of us asking how she's doing, because I refuse for her to ever be in a situation like this again."

"What are you two whispering about?"

Sascha's voice jolted Sawyer from the intense conversation he was having with his best friend. He reared back, hard enough for his shoulders to connect with the wall with a dull thud.

"Nothing."

She narrowed her eyes. "Oh yeah?"

"Yeah."

"You can't, technically, have a conversation about nothing."

Devon's statement had Sawyer heaving a sigh. "No? Well, we just did. So miracles truly can happen."

On the brink of arguing, Sawyer elbowed Devon before he could open his mouth. He knew him well enough to know that Dev wouldn't bring up the topic in front of his mother; he wouldn't want to upset her, even though Jacinta had been raised on Breardon estate and had moved to an equally as impoverished estate after she'd wed his father.

If there was one thing his mother wasn't, it was a weakling.

She was tough as leather and, in her heyday, had the ability to make grown men cry.

No, Jacinta certainly didn't need coddling, but he never discouraged Devon because his mother thought it was sweet, and she, in return, babied Dev.

If there'd been anyone in need of coddling when Sawyer had first come to know the army brat, it was Devon, and Jacinta had more love than a teenaged Sawyer had known how to handle, so splitting the load between Sheila and Dev had been a relief.

Stepping over to the foot of the bed, he grabbed the rail and squeezed—better that than Devon's throat. The man could be so fucking obtuse sometimes.

Finding a reason to dislike Joseph, a man who'd helped their woman out when she'd been all alone in the world save for their little boy, was just shitty.

But he knew Devon well enough to know that even though he'd just chided him, reprimanded him for thinking badly of Joseph, it wouldn't stop there.

Devon could be obsessive. Not just where his work was concerned, and at that particular moment, Sawyer just wasn't capable of handling that.

For once, he was going to let Devon battle his demons by himself, because Sawyer had more than a dozen of his own beating him into the dust without any help from his best friend's.

# SIX

WAS it good to be home?

Sascha really wasn't sure.

Walking up the steps to the townhouse was a welcome respite from being tucked up in Cinta's home; the older woman had molly-coddled her until Sascha had wanted to scream.

But, equally, she'd wanted to hug Cinta too.

Sascha was feeling delicate, and that never put her in a good frame of mind.

She'd lost her baby and had spent a day in hospital recuperating from that ordeal. Another three at Cinta's had been what she'd needed to adjust, but moving on?

No, that wasn't happening anytime soon.

She wasn't sure she'd ever overcome giving birth to a baby with no heartbeat. There'd been more pain management, higher doses of the drugs because they didn't have to worry about the baby's health, no monitors beeping to keep the nurses updated with the child's stats. Worse than anything had been when she'd pushed the too-small form into the world and there'd been no cry.

Realistically, she'd expected that. She'd been foolish to expect a yell of rage at being pushed out of the warmth and into the cold, hard world. Had known to brace herself for the silence. But though it had been so different to Tin's birth, she'd still waited to hear it. Had hoped, beyond hope, that the doctors had been wrong.

But they hadn't been.

Even if they were, she'd have been too young to resuscitate. And at twenty-two weeks, she'd never have survived.

The last time Sascha had walked up these steps, she'd been about to become a mother of two. Now, all that had changed. She had Tin. And she was grateful for that. So fucking grateful. Even after what happened, she was so glad she'd been the one to fall, not him. He could have slipped and hit his head on the same steps that led to the store she'd been wanting to visit. He could have hurt himself, badly. And he was only two. So small. Too small to be dealing with any kind of trauma like that.

She regretted what had happened, deeply, but she'd never regret that Tin hadn't been the one who'd slipped.

Still, with his hand in hers, it was a different Sascha and a completely different Valentin who entered the Kensington house that had been Sascha's home for the last four years.

She didn't doubt that the men who traipsed in behind her felt different too.

There was no way they couldn't.

When she'd left for Scotland, with Sawyer and Devon at her side, the three of them were cheerful and happy at the prospect of being welcomed into the loving home that was Jacinta's and Hamish's place. Out of them all, Sawyer's was the only set of parents who accepted the six-some that they had going on.

Vasily, Andrei's grandfather, was aware of it, and didn't have a problem with it, but he didn't invite the six of them to his home in Moscow. Sascha didn't blame him. With his reputation, which he still had to manage, it would have garnered attention. And such attention in Andrei's family could trigger life or death situations.

Kurt's mother was a bitch, his father sounded like he had severe

PTSD and could barely function. Not without a cocktail of drugs and a bottle of Scotch, by the sounds of it.

Sean's... well, Deirdre and James were never mentioned that much. She knew they were snooty and that they looked down at the household the men had before Sascha had joined the fun and games. So, she didn't figure they'd get a kick out of knowing her son shared a woman with four of his best friends.

No, the only ones who truly welcomed them were Jacinta and Hamish, who were like Devon's parents too. Devon had been welcomed into the family after his mother escaped her abusive husband with a razor blade. Devon had found her and had run from his father to Sawyer's home. Ever since, he'd been with the Bennetts.

Between walking out of the Kensington villa and stepping into it now, there was such a sharp contrast that she was reeling. How different the world could be in no time at all.

Only six days had passed, but it felt like it should have been a lifetime. She already knew the sting of time passing, the world continuing as though unaffected, because she'd experienced tragedy far too often, but this? This was even worse than being the target of some assassin who'd been out to get her before she'd learned of her real heritage and inherited billions of pounds. It was worse than watching cancer suck the life out of her beloved mother. And it was a million times worse than knowing both her birth parents had been murdered thirty years ago.

Losing this child?

It was an ache that would never leave her.

They'd taken the train back. Sascha hadn't wanted the stress from a plane or car ride, and the train had seemed the kindest option even though it had taken such a long time to get back. It was dark already and way past Tin's bedtime.

"Up the wooden hill to Bedfordshire, young man," Sean said, the minute they'd closed the front door.

Though the little boy pouted, he squealed with joy as Sean swooped in, dragging him off his feet and flinging him into the air. As it always did, her heart caught in her chest until Tin was safely in his father's arms. But this time, her heart didn't just flutter back to life as was usually the case. It thudded with a bang, the terror almost knocking her off her feet as the fear he'd fall, that he'd hurt himself, flushed through her.

It took every ounce of composure she had to push the panic down and to toddle over to Sean so she could reach over to brush Tin's hair away from his forehead. "You sleep well, little monster."

Tin beamed at her. "I'm not a monster."

She forced a grin. "I am."

He narrowed his eyes. "Takes one to know one?"

"Exactly." She rounded her hand into a fist, amused when he did the same without prompt, and they gently bumped knuckles. "Night, baby."

"Night, mommy," he murmured, kissing her lips with a swift peck before Sean started to climb the stairs toward Tin's bedroom.

With the scent of Tin's baby shampoo in her nose, she watched them climb the period staircase. She'd stripped it a few years ago because the dark varnish made the hall gloomy. The men didn't give a shit what she did with the house, so long as she left their offices alone.

She wasn't sure if they'd appreciate her turning everything hot pink, but as that wasn't her color of choice, they'd never had to worry on that score.

Stripping off the dark varnish had been an arduous task, she remembered now, brushing her fingers over the honey-colored wood. They'd asked her several times why she hadn't just hired someone to do the job—and though she definitely could afford it—Sascha liked doing things by herself.

Such a hobby was why she was dreading going upstairs.

On the second floor, Devon's bedroom had been turned into a nursery before Tin's birth. Devon barely slept anyway, and when he did, he usually slinked into whichever bed Sascha was in that night. None of the men minded sharing her with him, because they all knew how tempestuous his sleep was. But, more than that, it was Devon.

Back in college, they'd created this household of five to keep Devon safe. There was no way they'd ever resent anything that Devon needed to stay fit and healthy.

She'd been the one who'd turned the room into a nursery for Tin, and though he was still in the bedroom, she'd used these really cool building blocks she'd found online, ones that were like giant Lego, to separate his room from where she'd put the crib and had decorated again.

She'd painted it herself. Had put the crib together, and had everything prepared in plenty of time for the birth.

Five months had passed in the blink of an eye, and she liked being prepared.

Now?

She wished she'd been lazy about it.

Now, she had a world that was in stasis. A reminder of something that should have represented the future but was firmly fixed in the past.

Kurt being Kurt, aka wonderful, reached for her elbow. "Let's have some tea."

She blinked, shaken from her thoughts. "Tea?"

He nodded. "It's too late for coffee."

"How about wine? Is it too late for that?" she asked, her tone rough and only half joking.

"No. It's not. Do you want some?" he countered, only he wasn't joking.

As she looked up the stairs again, she let out a heavy sigh. "No. A chamomile tea?"

"Of course." He pressed a kiss to her forehead and guided her to the steps that took them down into the basement kitchen.

She hated how unstable she felt on her feet. She guessed it was a mixture of the induced labor, which she'd still be recuperating from for several weeks, and the fall. She hadn't just hurt her back when she'd slipped. Her knees ached, and she'd twisted the left one slightly. Her lower back killed her and her stomach was one big bruise.

Grimacing with each step, she let out a shrill yelp when Kurt, huffing, swept her off her feet just as easily as Sean had Tin, and carried her down the rest of the stairs. "Why didn't you say you were hurting?" he grumbled.

"You could have warned me," she chided, even as she squirmed in his hold, the knots of pain in her back connecting, unfortunately, with his forearms.

"You would have refused," he said, haughtily. And Kurt knew how to be haughty.

It wasn't just in his German DNA, but it was ingrained. He came from an aristocratic German family, and his mother shouted that fact to the world.

Well, from what the others had told her, Margritte did.

She'd never met her, although, technically, Margritte should be happy Sascha was in Kurt's life. The woman was terrified her son was gay, and Sascha was proof that he was anything but.

Within seconds, she was down in the basement kitchen; her favorite place in the world.

She looked around at the new refurb that had been completed eight months ago, the new furniture and the new patio that opened up onto the yard so they could sit outside on the rare occasions it wasn't freezing cold.

It was home, and yet, it didn't warm up the bleakness in her spirit.

"Take a seat," Kurt directed, and she did as he bid, glad to let him do something.

Her men were like that.

They worked better when they had a task to do, a challenge to overcome. Just hanging around and hovering wasn't good for them.

More steps sounded, and she turned around, then regretted it. Slowing down as she twisted in her seat, the move triggering an ache that she ignored, she smiled, a tad wanly, at Sawyer and Andrei who had followed them to the kitchen.

The table was oak now, scrubbed down just like Cinta's. When she'd first moved here, it had been a white smorgasbord. A delight for any minimalist. Now? Nope. It was like a country kitchen with minimalist quirks to satisfy her men.

She had a station, not just a counter, and the station contained the oven and sink. The thick marble tops were a delicious amber/cream color and had gorgeous gold striations running throughout them. What she loved most though was the wide farmhouse kitchen sink. It was a nightmare to wash the dishes in—one drop and either her plates would crack or the sink itself, but it was worth it.

Unlike Cinta, she didn't have an Aga, but she had a wide eight-top stove and an oven that would make any professional chef weep.

The cupboards were a sleek cream that reminded her of the freshly churned buttermilk Jacinta bought from the local farm store, and everything was so warm and cozy that she spent most of her time down here even when she wasn't cooking anything.

And with five men and one small, growing boy, she cooked a lot.

As Andrei and Sawyer settled at either side of her at the table, she eyed them both. They looked drained, their skin pale.

Under their eyes, they each had bruises. The shadows were dark and told a tale of their own—they hadn't been sleeping.

That wasn't too unusual in their household, no one seemed to abide by any particular time zone, but still, this seemed a little more drastic than usual.

"Where's Devon?" she asked, even though she knew the answer.

"The office." Sawyer's tone was blank even though she saw his jaw tense.

He was angry with Devon, and she wasn't sure why.

Well, she *knew* why, but she didn't understand it.

Sascha had never stepped into a relationship with Devon expecting his reactions to be anything close to normal.

She knew he was a workaholic, and she knew he had control issues. He was always very likely to become obsessed with any puzzle he couldn't easily crack.

They were all well accustomed to him working eighteen-hour days, and carrying on for a full twenty-four if she didn't drag him out of his study. Either to eat, fuck, talk, or do something fun.

He didn't have enough of the latter, and Sascha had long since made it her duty to see that he had some downtime.

Being with Devon was quite overwhelming.

That didn't mean it wasn't worthwhile, because it was. His ability to love outshone most men's, but the difficulties stemmed from his brilliance.

Devon was a walking, talking, world-changer. And that was strange to be around.

He had the Midas touch, even if he wasn't interested in it. Whatever impossible problem he set his mind to, he solved and managed to alter the world with it. Be it a nation's economy or the way cryptologists handled their code.

Looking after him was more than that of a woman looking after her man. It was about protecting the potential in him too.

That was how this house had come about, after all. The five of them living together to make sure Devon was safe, to make sure that he was protected.

And when she'd fallen for him, fallen so deeply in love with him that she hadn't been able to see straight, she'd taken on that task too.

So, why Sawyer was angry, she wasn't sure.

Devon coped through work. He used it as a means of controlling his moods and his emotions, and she was used to that. She hadn't expected him to react any other way than how he had—by pouring himself into his work with a fervor that outclassed anything she'd seen of him in the past.

Not that it didn't sadden her. She didn't want him to emote that way. She'd have preferred for him to come to her, for them to talk things through, and for them to work things out as a team.

But that wasn't Devon, and there was no way Sawyer would ever change that.

She studied him, curiosity dragging at her heels as she murmured, "Aren't you working with him?"

Sawyer scowled. "No. I'm here with you."

She snorted, her amusement bleeding into the sadness that was weighing her down. "I can see that, honey. I just mean... you can be with him if you want."

Sawyer frowned, and she saw a flash of hurt bolt through his eyes like a streak of lightning. Before he could say anything, she tutted. "Now, don't be acting like that. I love your company. I always want more of it, but if you have things to do, things that will make you feel better, then you go do it."

He stared at her a second, then he shook his head. "We don't deserve you."

"You do, sugar." She winked at him even as she lifted her hand and moved it over to his. Cupping the balled-up fist, she murmured, "You do what you need to do to heal."

He licked his lips. "What about you?"

"I'll do the same." She reached out with her other hand and grabbed a tight hold of Andrei's. "The same goes for both of you," she said, looking over her shoulder at Kurt too, needing him to be included in this. Needing them all to know that they had to think of themselves, not just her.

They were grieving. The lot of them. Her pain wasn't any less than theirs.

She turned to Andrei, aiming for a bright smile and failing if his doubtful look was anything to go by. "What's the game plan tomorrow?"

He tilted his head to the side in that way Tin had come to mimic; his golden beauty was as strong as it had been since the beginning. Lines of strain were etched on his eyes, and there were the faintest strands of salt and pepper interweaving with the golden hair on his head, but he was still her Adonis. Still one of the most beautiful men she'd ever seen, with his gem-like eyes that could pierce her to the quick, and his strong, slender form that she loved to wrap herself around. And that accent? *Oy vey.*

"Why should there be a game plan?" he asked, his voice a rumble of Russian that, had she been capable of it, would have had her body stirring. Instead, there was the faint ache reminiscent of what she'd just gone through.

What that felt like, she'd never get over.

"Because you're you and it's Monday tomorrow," she mumbled, trying to sound positive and knowing she failed.

He narrowed his eyes. "It might be Monday, but I've had Jane cancel all my app—"

Before he could finish, she glowered at him. "You canceled all your appointments? What the hell for?"

"Because you need me. You need us."

"Yes. Of course I do," she snapped, her patience breaking. "And I've always had you. Look, you've never had to mollycoddle me before, and you don't have to now.

"You'll drive me crazy if the five of you hover around me, honey. You know that. You know how I work."

Andrei shook his head, and for a second, he seemed wordless. "This is different. You... we... *blyad*, the baby. You need us close."

She squeezed both their fists simultaneously then released them. Moving her hands to her lap, she pressed them between her thighs and asked, "What's going on?"

Sawyer's scowl was as big a giveaway as Nessie suddenly popping out of Loch Ness. "Nothing's going on. We want to be close to you. Not a crime, is it?"

"No, but it's out of character. Even when I got run over, you didn't hover. You came and went, and that's how I like it. How I've always liked it. You check in wi—" She stopped, her thoughts coming to a halt. "You feel guilty." Her tone was flat, mostly with irritation. She couldn't believe it had taken her so fucking long to work it out, but she'd hardly been on her best game this past week. And, even more so than she'd had with Tin, the baby fog had triggered some seriously dumb moments.

One time, she'd forgotten where she'd parked her car in the center of London. Only Sean, being the security conscious pain in the ass he was, had saved the day.

Without her knowing, he'd planted a GPS tracking device on the bottom of her Caddy. She hadn't had it in her to be pissed at him for being a stalker, not when she'd had to use the GPS tracker twice since that first time.

The whole 'baby turns you stupid' thing was a serious issue.

At least, it had been this time. Was that, she wondered, because she'd been having a girl?

A perfect little girl who should have graced the world with her presence? And would have, if her mother hadn't been stupid?

God, why would her men feel guilty when this was all her fault?

"No, don't be crazy," Andrei started, but she held up one of her hands to stall him. It was difficult with the tears burning her eyes like acid, but she needed to eradicate their guilt. Now. They had important work to do; she wouldn't fuck that up like she'd fucked everything else up.

"Don't say another word. I wasn't pissed before, but if you lie to me, I *will* get angry.

"We all lead our own lives, but we come together because we're a family. That's what we do, guys. We move in and out of each other's lives, coming together before heading off to take on our own particular sphere.

"You five are too busy to be hovering around me every second of the day, and I wouldn't ask it of you." She pursed her lips. "Nearly four years ago, in this very room, Kurt told me how it is. He said that the five of you were too busy to deal with a girlfriend of your own, but that together, as a unit, you could satisfy one.

"That's how we've been and how we'll always be. That's what I want. I don't want it to change. Do you hear me?"

"You're recuperating, dammit," Sawyer argued. "You need us."

"Yeah, but I'm not an invalid. I don't need the five of you around. If it bothers you so much, take it in turns." She waved her arm in the air dismissively. "I don't mind what you do. Make a damn rotation. Just..." She licked her lips, her anger coming to an abrupt halt. "Don't make me feel any worse than I already do. You being here makes things feel different. I already know things are, I don't need the reminder with the way you treat me."

Sawyer blinked and Andrei's brow creased into deep frown lines she'd swear hadn't been there before. At her back, Kurt approached. He squeezed her shoulder after he placed a mug of chamomile on the coaster in front of her.

He dipped down and kissed the crown of her head. "I understand."

She peered up at him. "You do?"

"I do," he confirmed. "You're overwhelmed and we're making it worse by acting out of character." He shot the others a look. "We'll figure it out among ourselves, but... Sascha, you're going to have to deal with the fact we want to be with you. Even if it breaks our usual MO. We *want* to be with you. Not out of guilt or whatever you might think, but because we *weren't* there for you when you needed us the most, and I know I'm not just speaking for myself here, sweetheart, but that kills me.

"It kills me that another man was there for you, caring for Tin, and holding things together for you, while we were just going on with our regular business. While we were completely unaware that our entire world had just crashed." He swallowed thickly. "I, for one, don't think I'll ever get over that."

She sighed. Maybe another woman would be angry, but how could she be?

It was circumstance.

That was all.

She swallowed, feeling the need to admit something to them both. "I could have gone and dragged Sawyer from the study. I knew he was working, but I also know that even if you are, and I want you,

you'll stop everything." She pursed her lips. "I wanted it just to be me and Tin that day."

Sawyer scowled. "What the hell for? It was a shitty day. Why would you want to go shopping in that kind of weather?"

"Because..." She winced. "I wanted to have another burger from McDonald's and I wanted to get your Christmas gift."

For a second, the three of them were quiet, then Kurt, his voice somber, murmured, "I'm not sure whether to laugh or cry."

She blew out a breath as she peered down at her lap. Tugging at a loose bit of thread on her sweater, she whispered, "You always get mad at me if I eat junk food. And I like to treat Tin with it too. I know it's stupid, but it's just..." She shrugged. "It's something my mom did with me. Every now and then, I'd have a Happy Meal. I wanted to continue that tradition without you guilt-tripping me about MSG and processed meat."

Sawyer shook his head. "Lass."

The phrase was enough to make her brow pucker. "What?"

He shook his head again, then he scraped back the chair and headed out of the kitchen. Eyes widening as he left, she whispered his name but he either didn't hear her or ignored her.

She let him go, and the others didn't stop him either.

Kurt's sigh was heartfelt. "I don't know if you intended to make him feel better, *Liebchen*, but you might have just made things worse."

"Huh?" she asked, staring at him blankly. "I-I just told you that I was the one who willfully went out without Sawyer. I went alone even though I knew it was really cold out. Why would he feel worse about that?"

"Because you were sneaking out for a craving, and you were sneaking out to avoid disturbing him. From work. Nothing important." Andrei sighed, even as he picked up one of her hands from her lap and began toying with her fingers. "The guilt we feel will take a while to disappear, Sascha. And even then, it might not go in its entirety.

"Nor should it. You are ours. We are yours. If the situation had been reversed, wouldn't you feel the same way? Wouldn't you hate yourself for having let us down? Because that's what I feel. What we feel. You love us. You trust us. And we broke that."

"No, of course you didn't!" she argued, horrified that was what they were thinking. "Look, life happens. It was just a stupid accident. Nobody is really to blame. We just need to move past this, don't we? And doing anything that is totally not our routine isn't the way to go about that!"

Kurt kissed her temple before he sat down where Sawyer had just departed. "We'll see."

And that was that, but to her mind, it certainly didn't bode well for the days ahead. They couldn't believe she thought they didn't love her?

It was so ludicrous she wanted to laugh, but laughter was something she was incapable of at that minute.

She'd have to prove that nothing had changed on that score, even if the rest of their lives would never be the same again.

# SEVEN

"WHAT?"

"Is that any way to be speaking to yer ma?"

Wincing the second he heard the waspish tones down the line, he murmured, "Sorry, Ma. Didn't realize it was you."

"What's the point of that fancy Caller ID if ye aren't going tae check the damn thing?"

Pinching the bridge of his nose as he sought patience, Sawyer murmured, "What is it? I dinnae have time..."

"I'll break yer off there, lad. You always have time fer me. Especially when I'm calling to check up on you all. How are ye doing?"

"How do ye think?" he demanded, barely managing to contain the snarl in his voice.

"I think yer all feeling like shite. Like you want to wreck the joint. Like yer could kill someone." She sniffed. "Quite natural, I promise."

He blew out a breath, well aware that only his mother could consider that to be quite natural.

"What about Sascha?"

"She's quiet."

"She'll come around."

There was such certainty in her voice that he found himself praying she was right. "Ma?"

"Aye, son."

"Why didn't you tell me you'd had a baby that died before me and Sheila?"

"When would have been the time to tell ye something like that?" Her caustic tone wasn't as spirited as it would usually be, which told him that, even all these years later, the hurt was still as fresh.

"That tone is exactly what scares me. The thought of that bairn still makes you sad. How is Sascha ever going to get over it?"

"It was different for me. I wasn't sure if I'd be able to have another bairn, but she already has Tin. That will make a huge difference. She has to move on. She doesnae have much of a choice."

"No one needs that kind of pressure," he argued.

"No," she said, agreeing with him for once in his life. "But she's a mother. She's used to it." When he released a shaky breath, she murmured, "It's okay, son. You just have to take all this one step at a time. Each day that passes, I promise, it gets better.

"Aye, I still hurt. I willnae lie to you. The memories are still raw, but in comparison to the day it happened? The days after? It's like the sun and the moon. I ache with what might have been, but I don't sob into my pillow at night anymore."

God. Was she trying to make him feel better or worse?

"I don't know what to do with myself, Ma. I don't know whether to hover around her or to keep my distance. And I can't take any cues from her. She keeps to herself. She's gone out a few times, but only for playgroup for Tin. I know she wants to keep his routine as normal as possible. But she's not even going food shopping, and you and I both know how much she loves that."

"She's not having stuff delivered in, is she?" Cinta demanded, sounding aghast at the very notion.

"Aye, she is," he admitted on a deep sigh. "If she's not doing something with Tin, she's sleeping."

"She went through a traumatic experience, child," his mother said softly. "She's grieving. She's grieving the past and she's grieving for the future she'll never have now. I have no magic words to make this better. You just ha' tae gi' her time. Time truly does heal the sting even if it doesn't take away the memory, but dinnae, for the life of ye, tell her that. She'll snap yer head off."

His lips twitched a little at that but not enough to form a smile. It seemed like a lifetime since he'd even wanted to grin, never mind laugh.

"All ye can do," she carried on, "is be there for her. Follow her lead. At the minute, she wants to sleep, but keep things normal for the bairn. That's good. That's what I mean by her moving on, even if she doesnae think she's capable of it now. She already is, because she wants things to be right for the wee laddie.

"When it happened to me, I just stayed in bed and cried for days. Yer poor pa was terrified for me. I wouldnae eat and I didnae want to drink either. Back then, things like post-natal depression didnae exist. Yer just had to move on and deal with it. But times are kinder now, and I'm glad. I wouldnae put another woman through that if she were my worst enemy.

"Just give her time, lad. Honest. Be there, aye, but let her come around on her own, and whatever ye do, make sure she isnae the one to close up the nursery. One of ye do it."

He cleared his throat. "Aye. Sean and I are doing it tomorrow. We've been putting it off tae, but Sascha will come around soon and we don't want her doing it."

"Good boys," she said approvingly, then on a sigh, murmured, "I love ye, lad. I wish you didnae have to go through this."

"Thanks, Ma," he said, his voice choked as he scrubbed a hand over his face. "I love ye tae." He let his hand run over his head to the back of his neck. As he did, he looked over the study that was his and Devon's domain. Not for the first time, Devon wasn't there and Sawyer didn't even have it in him to care.

His throat was thick as he worked up the courage to get out, "The casket arrived yesterday, Ma." The little coffin had traveled down to

London because Sascha wanted to be able to visit the graveyard near their house.

She blew out a shaky breath. "That will gi' her closure."

"It will?" He wasn't so sure. "The service is in two days' time. Are ye coming down?"

"O' course."

"You can always drive Sean's car down if dad isnae happy with flying."

"We'll see but I think we'll fly in. Hamish willnae like it, ye ken how he hates planes, but there's nothing about this situation to like, is there?"

He blinked, because she'd never spoken truer words, and he wished like hell she was wrong.

---

*"CHUNGA CHANGA, CHUNGA CHANGA."*

The tinny sounds coming from the bathroom never failed to make her smile, even today, when the last thing she felt like doing was laughing.

The Russian tune wasn't something she'd even try to understand, but the words *Chunga Changa* and *chudo barchik* were the only ones she could make out.

The song playing in the background was as corny as everything else she'd heard Andrei play at bath time, and she knew that sounded mean but it was just so different to anything she played for Tin that it amused her.

Tin had already been down to the kitchen to kiss her goodnight, but as she'd headed upstairs, she'd heard the song, had heard Tin and Andrei singing along together, and had to go and see what they were doing.

As always, when she headed upstairs, she turned her head away from the nursery, knowing she'd have to build up the courage to even look at the door, never mind walk through it, and made her way to the bathroom Tin had commandeered over the years.

With all his crap, it was easier just to give the room to him. Not that she was in there much. Bath time had always been a special moment between father and son. Not just because Andrei made time for it every day, carving the thirty minutes out of his packed schedule to laugh and tease the little boy, but also to sing with him in their mother tongue.

Today, his bright giggles were a welcome change from the bleakness that had been stalking her since they'd arrived home.

Tin was her light in the darkness; the reason she'd gotten out of bed ever since that day on Buchanan Street when she wanted nothing more than to curl up on the sofa and molder away there.

The stairs were getting easier, even though the ache in her body seemed to go soul deep. She'd forgotten how tough recuperating from labor was, and this time, there were none of the happy moments, just all of the sad and uncomfortable ones.

By the time she'd made it to the bathroom, she was a little winded, but when she popped her head around the doorway, she had to giggle. Andrei, in his expensive suit slacks and the silk shirt that clung to his strong body, was covered in bubbles. He had some on that shining mop of golden hair, a mop that matched the miniature version in the bath who, unsurprisingly, had fewer bubbles surrounding him than his father did.

"Now I know where those weird stains on your clothes come from," she teased, making Tin clap with glee and holler, "Mommy, mommy, mommy!"

Andrei grinned at her over his shoulder, totally unashamed at his current state. "*Pree-vyét*, Sascha!"

Tin, cackling, repeated the statement, "*Pree-vyét, mama!*"

Lips curving, she asked, "What does that mean?" She knew it was terrible that she'd never tried to learn Russian, but hell, there were only so many hours in the day, and having looked at a basic

Russian dictionary, all she'd given herself was a headache. That had been enough for a lifetime.

Andrei snorted. "What did we tell mama, Tin?"

"Hello!" Tin chortled.

Though she knew she'd mangle it, she repeated the word, and Tin, ever great for her ego, burst out into more giggles. He flopped back in the water, making a tiny tidal wave that had the liquid sloshing everywhere, all the while mocking her pronunciation.

"I'm starting to see why you're covered in bubbles," she said drily, as she stepped deeper into the room. Taking advantage of the toilet being next to the bath, she plunked herself down.

"*Kak dee-lá?*"

That had her blinking. "Huh?"

"*Tih krasahveetsa!*"

She tilted her head to the side.

"*Ty delayesh' menya schastlivym.*"

"What?" she demanded, grinning though as, with his heart in his eyes as he silently translated the words of love for her, he carried on:

"*Ty sogrevayesh' moyu dushu.*"

But her throat squeezed at the last one:

"*Ya lyublyu tebya.*"

Her smile was soggy as she repeated the one phrase she *did* know: "*Ya lyublyu tebya.*" 'I love you' – it was something she'd seen in her current obsession—Russian Bratva romance books. She loved them because they made her grin. She knew a real life Pakhan, after all.

Not every woman had that similar claim to fame.

At her atrociously pronounced declaration, Tin stopped giggling and turned to them. "*Ya lyublyu tebya, mama. Papa.*"

Now her heart *did* melt. She smiled at him then reached for his starfish pinkies and kissed them, even though they were soapy and dimpled from the water. "And we love you."

Reaching for the basket of toys that was suspended in a net over the side of the bath, she tugged the plastic suckers from the wall and let them fall into the water. When he hollered with glee and began throwing them, Andrei snorted.

"How are you doing?"

"What did you say to me?"

"Things you needed to hear," he said simply, his eyes gleaming like jewels as he stared at her from amid a sea of slowly disintegrating bubbles.

"Then shouldn't you have said them in English?"

He just smiled. "One day. When you're ready to hear them again."

Though she frowned, she didn't ask him what he meant because she couldn't—Tin hollered her name, his glee returning as Andrei picked up the sponge he'd soaked with water, and squeezed it over the little boy's head.

Even though it felt weird to laugh, it also felt good.

Tin's laughter made her heart both heavy and light, but her own? It made her want to cry, and maybe that was the release she needed.

Her eyes prickled with tears as she and Andrei took part in something that had only ever been 'male-bonding' before, and as Andrei taught Tin words, she made them both chuckle by saying them terribly.

It wasn't a good day, but it was a damn sight brighter than it had been twenty minutes before.

---

"WHERE HAVE YE BEEN?"

Devon, on the brink of stepping through the foyer, froze. He couldn't have looked more feckin' sheepish if he'd have tried, Sawyer thought, scowling down at his best friend from the top of the staircase.

"Nowhere."

That had Sawyer scoffing. "You only leave the feckin' house if there's something urgent going on. So, what gives? Where's the fire?"

Devon, now stepping out of his shoes, froze. "There's a fire?"

"Nae, ya fool. I just meant, where have you been?"

"You've been out again?" This time, it wasn't Sawyer doing the talking, but Sean.

Sean had noticed too? And what the hell did he mean by 'again?'

"Am I under house arrest or something?" Devon said on a low growl, unwinding his scarf from around his neck before he slung it onto the coat rack. "I didn't realize I had to account for my every action."

Taken aback, Sawyer tilted his head to the side as he studied the bags under Devon's eyes. The man never slept, but that seemed to be wearing on him more than usual—but then, who wasn't sleeping rougher now? The atmosphere in the house felt turbulent with all of their emotions. The grief threatened to suffocate the lot of them if they weren't careful.

Only Tin didn't seem affected, and Sawyer thanked Christ for that wee favor. He didn't feel like they had much to be thanking him for of late, but if the good Lord could make things easier on their boy, Sawyer would be grateful.

"Why are you so angry?" Sean sounded as puzzled as Sawyer was.

And the man wasn't wrong.

Devon *was* angry.

"I'm not angry," he immediately countered. "Why would I be angry?"

"That's what I'm asking," Sean murmured drily. His tone was cool, calm, and so damn clinical, Sawyer wanted to wince.

It was his 'shrink' voice, and even though Sawyer wasn't sure if Devon recognized it, he wondered how his friend would feel being psychoanalyzed at this given moment.

"Why aren't you?" Devon countered with a defiant tone. Hell, it bordered on belligerent.

"You think I should be angry?" Sean asked.

"Yes. I do. We should have been there with her. Because we weren't, the baby died."

"That's not your fault, Devon."

"Isn't it?" Devon sniffed. "Anyway, I like walking around the gardens. It's peaceful there."

Sawyer frowned. What the fuck? Had aliens abducted Devon? He never walked around the gated gardens that their neighbors, laughingly and snootily, called a 'park.'

Descending the staircase, he tilted his head to catch Sean's gaze. Wondering if Sean had spotted the obvious lie, he saw nothing hidden in the de facto head of the household's expression.

"It is? Well, next time, I'll come along. It would do us both good to be out in the fresh air."

Devon stiffened. "I'll tell you when I go out next."

Another feckin' lie.

Sawyer scrubbed at the back of his neck as he murmured, "I think we should have some whisky. That shite Dad bought for me."

"You mean the best bottle we have in the house?" Sean asked wryly.

"Aye, that one." Sawyer grinned as he took the final step to the foyer.

"Come on, Devon, you must be freezing. It's nice and warm in my study."

Shrugging, Devon stepped ahead, and took off for Sean's office. Before he could follow him, Sawyer grabbed Sean's arm. "When did he go out?"

Sean's gaze was calm as he murmured, "Every day since we've arrived home."

Gaping, Sawyer peered down the hall at the path Dev had just taken. "And you didn't think to mention it?"

"Why should I? Like he said, he's not under house arrest. I just thought he was walking. But that's twice today." Sean shrugged. "I thought that was odd."

"He's been off since Glasgow," Sawyer growled, running a hand over his head in agitation. He hadn't been watching out for his friend as much, and being in the dark about Devon's absences filled him with unease. That Dev had left the house at all without Sawyer knowing was damn unusual.

At the moment, unusual wasn't his friend.

"We've all been acting a little differently to normal. It's to be expected. We're grieving," Sean countered, his tone gentle. "And we both know Devon processes things in his own way."

"That anger though... that's new, Sean. What the fuck's going on with him?" Guilt filled him as he thought about how he'd been leaving Dev to fend for himself.

Dealing with his own grief, his own guilt had been more than enough for him to handle. Now, piling on the way he'd been neglecting Devon, who *did* process shite differently than any of them, just made him feel worse.

"He's grieving."

"He never gets angry."

"He's never lost a child before."

Sean's calmness irritated the hell out of Sawyer. "Why are you taking this so calmly?"

"How do you want me to react?"

Again, with the serenity. His shrink voice. It made him want to scream. "Like you're feeling something, mon."

"You think I don't?" Sean's eyes narrowed. "What makes you think that?"

"The fact you've been locking yourself up in your study with work and barely uttering a peep at the dining table. You barely say a word to Sascha."

"She wants to be left alone. I'm letting her deal with this her own way. What she went through is something we can never understand —I'm giving her time."

Sawyer wanted to argue with that but knew he couldn't. He gritted his teeth. "All right, but locking yourself up with work isn't going to do you any good."

"There's still a sick bastard out there stealing kids from their homes, Sawyer. You want me to just forget about that? I have other responsibilities," he snapped.

Considering Sean hadn't mentioned the child-killer case since that night before Sascha's miscarriage, Sawyer had to wince as yet more guilt cascaded over him. "I'm sorry," he said, his voice low.

Sean nodded. "It's okay."

"No, it's not. You're right. We all need time to deal with this."

"We do. But you're not wrong where Devon's concerned." Sean pursed his lips. "Something's definitely going on with him."

"I'll try to follow him the next time he goes out," Sawyer replied, but Sean shook his head.

"No. He's not doing anything wrong. Going outside is healthy for him. I thought he'd be holed up in his study like me, but he's getting out and getting some fresh air. He's moving himself out of his comfort zone. I like to see that. It's not unhealthy."

Sawyer frowned. "It's unlike anything he's ever done before. You and I both know he shuts down. He doesn't get angry. I don't like to see him that way."

"You think I do?" Sean shrugged. "Not much we can do save for riding it out."

Sean made to step away, but Sawyer grabbed his arm. "How are you doing, Sean? Really? Are you angry? At us? For not being there for Sascha?"

A scowl creased Sean's forehead. "Why would I be? I was there too. Sleeping off my damn drunk. No one's to blame. Not me for sleeping or you for working or Sascha for slipping. Life happens, Sawyer. We just have to roll with it. Even if it fucking stinks."

"What about this case?"

"It's giving me nightmares," Sean admitted. "But when don't they? I'll be all right."

"If you need to speak, I'm here, mon."

Sean blinked. "I know. I appreciate that, mate."

"You were pretty messed up that night," Sawyer said slowly as they started down the hall for Sean's study. "What happened?"

"Too much to talk about now," Sean replied, his tone darkening. "Plus, Sascha's in the lounge. I wouldn't want her to overhear."

That was the third time Sawyer had been lied to in the past ten minutes.

Did he have 'gullible' written across his forehead?

Striding into the study, Sawyer inwardly grumbled as he poured the three of them a whisky from the decanter Sean used for the gifts his dad sent every Christmas. He didn't usually let Devon drink it, but maybe the alcohol would calm him down, because even as he saw his friend was comfortable in his usual armchair, there was a storm brewing in his eyes.

The moment he saw it and processed it, he had to hide more of his unease. Devon panicked. He shut down. He didn't brood. The way he was looking reminded Sawyer of when they were stuck on a particularly difficult math problem.

Trouble was, that similarity didn't ease his concern.

Devon, with the bit between his teeth, was worse than a stag in rut. Combine it with grief that he didn't know how to process—Sheila's death all those years ago had proven that Dev had zero idea of what to do when someone died—and the anger and guilt that was twisting him up over Sascha's fall and the subsequent loss of their child...?

No, Sawyer had to amend his earlier thought. There wasn't a storm brewing in Devon's eyes, but a fucking tornado.

# EIGHT

"WHAT ARE YOU DOING?"

At Sawyer's words, Sascha jolted, and he tilted his head to the side, staring at her as *she* stared at the doorway to Tin's bedroom.

It hadn't escaped his notice that in the days since she'd been home, she hadn't put Tin to sleep once.

Their normal routine consisted of Andrei giving Tin a bath— mostly because he sang to their kid in Russian as he cleaned up the crap that Tin had managed to cover himself with over the length of the day.

It was the only time that they exposed Tin to another language, and they did so in as relaxed a way as possible.

When he was a little older, maybe five, they'd introduce him to German, but as that was far simpler than Russian, that would be easy for their smart kid.

So, Andrei managed bath time— no matter how busy his schedule was, no matter what kind of shit he had going down with the various power plays he was controlling at any given time, he made it back for that half-hour appointment he had with their son. Afterward, one of them tucked Tin in with Sascha at their side.

The last few days hadn't been like that. Well, not until last night.

Andrei had taken to bringing Tin to Sascha, where she'd kiss him good night and then they'd head off for bath time.

It didn't take a miracle worker to figure out why.

She didn't want to see the nursery.

But she hadn't said that. Hadn't even mentioned it. Hell, she hadn't even spoken that much since she'd come home.

Maybe that made sense, though. They were all quieter. The mood in the house somber and heavy with mourning.

"I-I need to clear the nursery. Tin needs his room back." The ache in her voice nearly broke him. God, what this woman could do to him.

He'd never thought a woman could bring him to his knees, but Sascha did. She had such power over him, but she never, *ever* took advantage of it.

She was his soulmate, and he'd made it so that she'd felt she had to hide her cravings from him. So much so, she'd been stupid, gone out in icy weather, and had fallen without him at her side.

Sawyer wasn't sure what that was, but he figured clusterfuck about summed it up.

Was he such a food Nazi that she hadn't felt like she could eat what she craved?

He knew how cravings worked. They usually represented some kind of lack in the mother's diet. But still, what diet required all the saturated fats in a Big Mac?

Hating himself for even asking the question, and knowing he needed to watch his words in the future when he talked to her about food, he murmured, "It's empty, babe."

She jolted again, and he frowned at her, wondering if she was truly as okay as she insisted she was. "It is?"

"We dismantled it a few days after we got home. When you took Tin to playgroup." There hadn't been that much to sort out. Just enough to break both his and Sean's fucking hearts as they packed away clothes they'd never use and gadgets that would never hold their baby.

It had been hard on him, so he was glad he and Sean had been the ones to handle that, not Sascha.

She seemed to sag, and he saw the relief on her face and he felt it in his heart.

Her pain reached out to him with tendrils that seemed to wrap around him. He could no more stop himself from moving closer than he could stop himself from taking his next breath.

He pulled her into his arms and murmured, "I'm sorry."

She tensed. "What for?"

"For making you feel like you had to hide your cravings from me."

She sighed, then let out a little chuckle that nearly broke his fucking heart. "Oh sweetheart, it was just a stupid thing. I'm the one who's sorry. I'm the one who put our baby in danger. I'm lucky you're still talking to me. That all of you can forgive me."

Horrified that she could even think that, he blurted out, "You weren't reckless, Sascha. You didn't know you were going to slip. And I know you. You don't see the world like the rest of us do, lass."

She leaned away from him at that. She didn't move out of his arms, though, just looked up at him. "What do you mean?"

His lips curved. "Haven't you realized it?"

She tilted her head to the side. "Realized what?"

"You're like a warrior."

"Huh?" Her brow puckered as she tried to figure out what he meant.

"Nothing gets in your way, Sascha. You take things full tilt. I love that about you, lass. You're strong and sure of yourself. You know what you want and aren't afraid to go after it; whether it's learning to dance, stripping this damn staircase, or deciding you need a burger. Just this time, we all flew a little close to the sun and we were burned for it."

She pressed back into his embrace and fell silent for a second. He didn't complain. It felt good to just hold her.

She'd been quiet— distant since they'd arrived home. She was recuperating and she needed the time and space to heal. He hadn't avoided her, made sure that he came and sat with her, ate whatever Kurt cooked for the family, and played with Tin while she watched on, but he'd stayed apart from her. Distant. Why?

Because he was second guessing himself.

Only once he'd put away the nursery furniture did he realize what he'd been doing. He'd recognized that his mother was right and he needed to rectify that.

He pressed a kiss to the crown of her head. "How are you doing, lass? Really doing?"

She was quiet, then in the smallest of voices, murmured, "Not good."

He squeezed her. "Are you going to contact the center?"

She shook her head. "No. I don't want to."

The hospital had given her information about support groups who could help her, *them*, deal with what had happened.

That she didn't want to go made him frown. "Is that wise?"

"I don't want to... I just want to be at home."

"And you can do that, you can be here twenty-three hours a day if you want. But that one hour might be wisely spent with people trained to help."

She huffed. "You think I want to go to one of those meetings by myself?"

"I never imagined ye'd be going by yourself, lass. Whisht. Have yer lost yer head?"

She blinked. "Wow. That was pure Jacinta."

He just rolled his eyes. "Well, have you? You didn't honestly think we'd let you attend a meeting like that without one of us there?"

She wriggled her shoulders. "I wasn't sure. You're not exactly the counseling type. Any of you. And Sean's a trained therapist!"

He snorted out a laugh at her umbrage, but he leaned down to buss her lips. "Well, get that out yer head. If you want to go, one of us will go with you." He shrugged. "Hell, all five of us can go, but it might raise eyebrows."

She sighed and started to say, "Frigging eyebrows..."

But the sound of the door slamming below had them both jerking in surprise. None of them were exactly the 'door slamming' types.

"Sawyer?"

It was Sean.

Scowling, Sawyer carefully untangled himself from Sascha's arms as he bent over the banister to holler, "What the hell's wrong with ye? Hollerin' like that, yer fool. It's a good bluidy job Tin's in playgroup or you'd have scared the shite out of him."

The angles of the staircases and the landings made it so that he had a clear view straight down to the ground floor. Sean, peering up at him, looked red-faced with... Sawyer's brow puckered. Anger? No, he knew Sean well enough to recognize sadness, and this was definitely anger.

"You need to come with me."

"Where?" he demanded, perplexed by the urgency in his tone.

"To the police station." Sean's nostrils flared as he firmed his jaw. For a second, Sawyer wasn't sure he was going to continue, then he did the equivalent of throwing freezing water over Sawyer's head by gritting out, "It's Devon. He's just been arrested for assault."

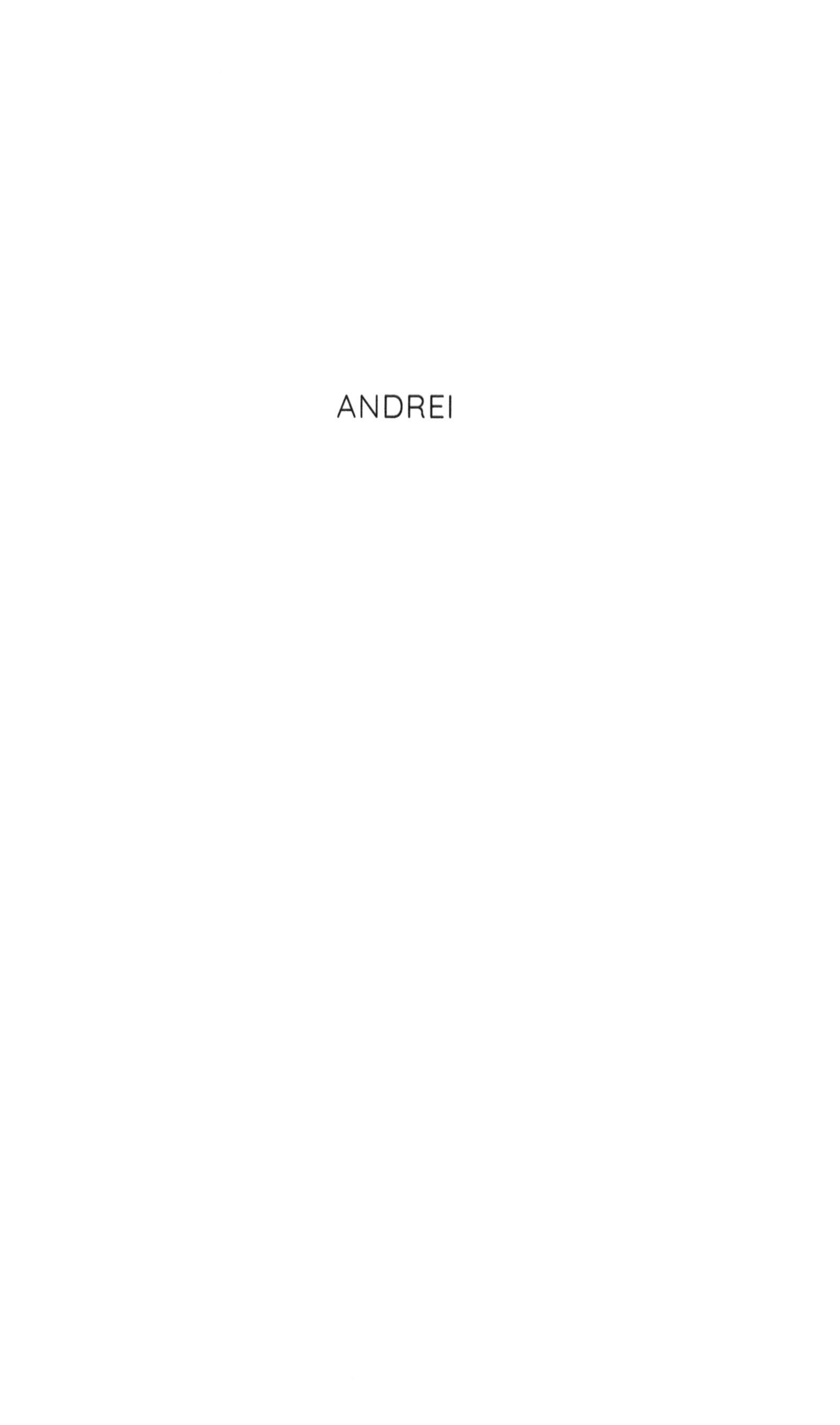

# ANDREI

# NINE

"YA DOLZHEN POPROSIT' *tebya ob usluge.*"

"What kind of favor?" Vasily, ex-Bratva Pakhan and Andrei Kirov's grandfather, asked, his tone suspicious and croaky, after a cough rattled from his throat.

"Are you smoking? I thought the doctor told you to stop." Andrei tried not to sound like a nag, but for God's sake, the man was ninety-three. He was intelligent. Had *all* of his faculties. The damn *starikashka*, old fool, should *not* need babying.

"He did. For that outrageous suggestion, I had him shot." Vasily's tone was imperious—but then, he was a Tsar in his world.

Andrei snorted. "I'll believe that when I see it. How *is* Dmitri?" Dmitri was a long-time friend to both his grandfather and the Bratva. The man could sew up a bullet wound faster than a Russian could down four fingers of vodka.

*Da*. He was *that* fast.

"He's well," Vasily groused, while mumbling under his breath about sawbones and incompetent physicians. In a louder voice, he stated, "He's better than me."

"Hardly. You're the one smoking against doctor's orders. Maybe you'd be healthier if you did as he asked?" *Please*, Andrei half-prayed.

"I have to die sometime, boy. I'm not going to stop doing something I enjoy just because that quack thinks I should." Vasily huffed. "Anyway, you're the one wanting some help. What did you want? Or was it just to nag me like an old woman? If you're trying to ingratiate yourself, then you're failing."

Sighing, Andrei pinched the bridge of his nose. "*Ya llublyu teblyu.*"

Vasily smiled—Andrei could hear it in his voice as he murmured, "I love you too, child. I'm well. I promise."

As well as a man in his nineties could be. "You make me glad that only the good die young."

That seemed to prick his grandfather's humor. "Be the first time anyone's been grateful I'm wicked."

Humming under his breath, Andrei decided to change that particular topic of conversation—phones could be tapped, after all. If the security services *weren't* interested in Vasily, they were idiots. Though technically retired, he was still a force to be reckoned with. "Devon's in trouble."

"What's he done now?" Vasily inquired, sounding more curious than anything else. "If he's solved another Millennium Problem without telling me first, I'll be pissed. Do you know how much money I lost by him, *and you*, keeping that to yourselves? Not only could I have wagered a fortune on it, I could have invested—"

Andrei rolled his eyes at the often moaned tirade. Vasily didn't seem to understand that it was the exact reason they'd kept him in the dark. "He was arrested."

There was silence on the phone. "Arrested?"

"*Da*." Andrei moodily stared over his desk and saw Sascha, the love of his life, staring at him from the doorjamb. She looked sad, but then, she'd been sad for weeks now. She'd taken the loss of their baby girl hard, and who could blame her?

He, himself, was still reeling, and he hadn't had to go through what she had. Not physically, at any rate.

Holding out his hand to beckon her close, relieved he was speaking in his mother tongue, he murmured, "I need you to make the charges disappear."

"Why?"

"Because I do." Andrei squeezed her thigh when she settled on his lap, a soft, warm bundle for his arms. As she nuzzled into him, his chair squeaked with the extra weight as he rocked back, finding the perfect spot that suited them both. When gravity cosseted them at that delicious angle, they stayed in a stasis, cuddling into each other like cooing turtledoves.

Only for Sascha Dubois would Andrei Kirov *coo.*

"That's no answer." There was the sound of a deep exhalation, telling Andrei the bastard was smoking while they were on the phone.

"I learned from the best."

"This is true." Vasily hummed, but there was a satisfied note to it. The old man always appreciated it when Andrei worked his wiles on him—he said it was the only way he could keep himself honed, as only Andrei could match him where intelligence was concerned. "How long ago was this?"

"Around a month and a half ago."

"Month and a half?" he spluttered. "How am I supposed to make anything disappear after such a length of time? Why did you not tell me sooner?"

"You can make anything disappear."

"In Moscow, *da*. But London?"

"You have people here. Don't make out like you don't."

"Tell me why."

"I have need of him for a project. He can't have a criminal record, though. If he does, he can't help me, and it's important to me that he's involved in this."

"The Veronian issue?"

Grimacing because he'd never been able to pull the wool over his grandfather's eyes, he rested his chin on Sascha's shoulder and hugged her close. She smelled good. Different. Her perfume was usually fruity, but this was cool. Refreshing. Unlike her, and yet, it suited her. A gift from Kurt, perhaps? Andrei pondered the likelihood of this as he inhaled the scent once more—only Kurt bought her perfume.

Sean had a tendency of buying her jewelry, Sawyer lingerie, Devon candy, and Andrei usually went for flowers. Even though it was trite and cliché—he tried to mix it up from time to time, but what did you buy a woman who had several billion pounds in her bank account and seemed to have no desire to spend it?

"It's with the Veronian government. You know they'd never allow someone with a record, a recent one, to work on their nation's finances."

"This is true. Prudes." He sniffed. "Some of the best brains in history were imprisoned at some point in their life. A man's not allowed any rebellion nowadays." Another sniff. "What's the offense?"

"Aggravated assault." He petted Sascha's thigh, trying to find comfort where there was none to be found.

This time, Vasily really did choke. It took thirty seconds for him to rasp, "Aggravated assault? *Devon?* I didn't think the boy had it in him."

Andrei closed his eyes as he rocked back. It was better than staring hopelessly out into his office. "*Da.*"

"Now Sawyer, I can imagine. Those claymores the Scots used to arm themselves with, well, stock him with that and a kilt, I could see him beating the shit out of anyone. But Devon? *Nyet.*"

"I'm pleased there's someone in this world who can surprise you."

"Only in that house of yours." He clucked his tongue. "I'll see what I can do. I have some strings I can pull." There was a low hum. "I want first dibs on when you put your legislation into practice. I'll be certain to invest in some Veronian debt before you do."

"That's insider trading," Andrei grumbled.

"So it is! I did teach you well, didn't I?" Vasily murmured, sounding delighted as he released a wicked cackle.

Andrei could just see him—cigar between his thin lips, a wide grin splitting his heavily creased jaw.

Sascha must have heard Vasily's laughter because she snorted at the infectious sound, making Andrei smile as he pressed his nose into her bright-red hair.

"What's the plan, anyway?" his grandfather asked.

Knowing better than to tell him he couldn't share such information, considering who he was, and knowing he was quite capable of having someone hack into Andrei's laptop to find out the details regardless, he murmured, "They're not cash poor, yet. They suffered a hit after those idiots went after the Royal Family. Investment in the nation dropped, and as they never envisaged such a sharp decline, their debt spiraled out of control. I've managed to put together some things that I think will encourage more investment, so they can at least bottom out."

"The UnReals, if I remember rightly."

"Yes. They've been eradicated now. The King's just had his first heir."

"I saw on the news. Girl child, correct?"

"Yes. First Crown Princess in the country's history."

Vasily grunted. "Women, women, everywhere, and nary a drop to drink."

Andrei winced. He knew for a fact that, ninety-three or not, the man could have any woman he wanted. Be it a street whore, a high-class prostitute, a politician's wife, or just a housewife from the capital.

Vasily was power personified.

That was why Andrei was asking him for a favor.

"It's good for the country's image. I'm actually going to suggest some plans where we invest in sectors to encourage equality in the government, as well as their businesses. It could foster a wave of immigration. A reverse brain drain, as it were."

Vasily hummed, and Andrei knew he'd bored his grandfather with talk of nonsense—equality didn't exactly exist in the Bratva. "How is she?"

"Heard her laugh, did you?"

"I'd recognize it anywhere."

"She's not doing too well."

"Can't blame her. One small fall and that's it. Life extinguished." Vasily exhaled noisily through his nose. "I'd have spared her that if I could."

"Me, too," Andrei whispered, his voice thick with emotion. Sascha stiffened a little as he pressed a kiss to her hair.

"I wish I could have gone to the funeral."

"I wish you could, too." Andrei's heart broke a little more. Not only at the ragged note in Vasily's voice, but at the memory of standing beside that tiny grave and watching a piece of his broken heart being lowered into the ground. "But we know what the doctor said. I'd prefer you safe and well, being there with us in spirit rather than the alternative. Being badass won't save you from the Grim Reaper."

"I hate being old," Vasily groused, otherwise ignoring his grandson's statement. "I don't feel old mentally."

"The mind is willing, but the body is weak," Andrei murmured, somewhat philosophically if his grandfather's harrumph was anything to go by.

"Give her my love?"

"Of course."

"Be patient with her, son. I say this knowing that, in my shoes, I wouldn't have been. I'd have..." He grunted. "I'd have tried to fix the world for her while raging at it myself. You must temper the side of your nature that's me."

"I'm just trying to be there for her."

"That's exactly what she needs. Are you going to take her to Veronia?"

"Of course. We're all going. Even if you can't sort out this shit with Devon, he'll be there, just not working if you can't help." Andrei had a few strings of his own he could pull. Though Devon technically wasn't supposed to leave the country until his sentencing and had lost access to his passport, Andrei had a few people in the government who'd help him if needs be.

"All of you?" Vasily sounded surprised.

"*Da*. We need a break. My liaison, the Duke of Ansian and Lorrena, has arranged for us to stay somewhere close to the palace."

"He knows about the household?"

Andrei hid a smile at the word 'household.' Vasily never outright mentioned the fact Andrei shared Sascha with the men that were like his brothers: Sawyer, Devon, Sean, and Kurt. "Not exactly. I just told him I wouldn't be visiting alone."

Vasily clucked his tongue. "Veronia would do her good. It's a beautiful place."

"Didn't know you'd been."

"It was a long time ago. You know how they feel about Russians," the old man grumbled. "Xenophobes."

Andrei's lips twitched. "Hardly. They're asking a Russian for help with their economy."

"They're asking for the Kirov Finance Tsar, my boy, not the Russians." Vasily sounded proud as punch at that.

Andrei didn't need his ego stroked, but it pleased him that Vasily was proud. He was a hard man to live up to. Even as the leader of an illegal mafia brotherhood, Vasily had made a fortune legitimately, as well as illegitimately. What the man didn't know about stocks and shares could be written on a matchbox. In turn, he'd passed that knowledge down to Andrei, who'd learned from his grandfather's hand.

"What of Tin?"

"You'll find out tonight. It's your weekly Skype call, isn't it?"

"*Da*. You should focus more on his Russian."

"I have been." He grunted. "He's only two, grandfather."

"He's Russian. He should know his mother tongue."

Knowing better not to argue, he murmured, "He's coming along. It's probably on par with his English now."

"This *is* good news. I shall practice with him tonight then." There was the sound of applause, and Andrei realized the old man was clapping with excitement—would wonders never cease?

Touched that Vasily was engaged with Tin, Andrei murmured, "He'll like that. You know you can call more?"

"Don't want to bore him with an old man," Vasily dismissed, then his tone turned curt. "What happened with the boy, anyway?"

Lips curling, because he was no longer talking about Tin, Andrei murmured, "Devon got into a fight."

"I managed to figure that out for myself, Andrei," Vasily clucked. "Who?"

"Nobody important."

There was a disbelieving hum, then, a grumble, "I'll see whose arm I can twist. I'll be in touch."

"Thanks, *Dzed*."

"You're welcome. Soon, Andrei. Soon." He cut the call, leaving the dial tone buzzing in Andrei's ear.

Placing his cell on the desk before him, he curved both arms around Sascha's waist and hugged her gently. "You need something, *katyonok*?"

"Just you," she said on a soft sigh.

Those two words about broke his goddamn heart. For the second time in as many minutes.

She meant them.

She didn't need anything but his presence, his embrace. And he knew she'd been doing this with them all. She came to each of them, at random times of the day, just wanting to sit with them. No words necessary.

If it wasn't so restful, it would have disturbed him, but it felt like a timeout. A moment in his day that was dedicated to her, and who was she if not the most important woman in his world?

Had they forgotten that?

In the almost-four years she'd been with them, had they started to take her for granted?

He didn't think they had, and yet . . . she'd suffered because they hadn't been with her. Tin was a rambunctious kid. He was strong for his age, too. If he'd been corralled by his dads, then Sascha would never have slipped, and—*blyad*!

What ifs were the worst.

"Did I hear you mention Devon's name?" she asked quietly.

He hummed. "Perhaps. Being taken in vain, I'm sure. I need Devon's help with this current project and Vasily was prying." He was lying, but it was to protect her. That meant it was more evasion than a falsehood, no?

"I love it when you speak Russian. It's the sexiest thing I've heard in my entire life," she murmured, half-sighing the words into his throat.

"I know you think that." If his grin was smug, then why the hell not? He had a woman fifteen years his junior on his lap who thought he was sexy. When wasn't that good for a man's ego?

'They' never told you about the crazy insecurities that came with being with a younger woman. The fear that you'd suddenly be too old for her. That you'd come across like a father figure. That she'd take up with a younger man because you weren't sexy to her anymore.

But Sascha never made him feel like that, so why he'd experienced the crippling doubt, he didn't know.

If anything, she made him feel virile. Stronger. More assured. And for a man who'd never particularly lacked in his confidence until he'd made her his woman, it was saying something.

"Why don't you speak it more?"

"Because you wouldn't understand a word I was saying," he commented on a laugh.

"This is true. In bed then. I want you to speak it more."

He cocked a brow at that, even as other things cocked to attention.

The past month and a half had been most unlike Sascha. After Tin, she'd been glad to be over the six weeks of healing the doctor insisted upon. This time? She hadn't been. But, naturally, the circumstances were different. Even if, physically, the labor had been easier on her than when she'd had to deliver Tin, who'd been very large at eight pounds three ounces, emotionally, the labor was another matter entirely.

"You do, huh?" he asked quietly. "I'm sure that can be arranged."

"I do."

"That your way of broaching this topic?" he teased, grinning when she nodded, her brow brushing against his throat.

"I'm scared." Her tone was bleak, but the words scored him.

"What of, *katyonok*?"

"Everything," she said on a whisper. "Isn't that stupid? How can you be scared of *everything*? I just am. I-I—"

"What, Sascha?" He kissed her temple. "Talk to me."

She blew out a gusty breath. "I just wish things could go back to how they were."

How could he argue with that? She should be close to eight months along now, and instead, they'd attended a funeral for the child who had never seen the light of day.

When he didn't say anything, she whispered, "I hate it here."

"Where?" He frowned. "The house?"

"Yeah. I hate going into Tin's bedroom. The nursery isn't there anymore, but I hate it."

Tension invaded his limbs. "We're going to Veronia soon."

"I know."

"A change might do you good."

"I hope so." She didn't sound convinced.

"Do you want to move, darling?" he blurted out the question because he was still reeling from this conversation.

He'd known she wasn't happy. *Blyad*, it didn't take a genius to figure that one out. But that she hated the house? That came as a surprise.

This was their home.

Had been for a long time. It had been their haven, but after Sascha, that haven had definitely morphed. This was just bricks and mortar to him. She made it a true home, and if she hated it here, then he was willing to do anything to take the pain away from her.

Even if Devon had to sulk about leaving his damn office behind if they moved.

"I don't know, and I hate being so goddamn wishy-washy." She made a grumbling sound under her breath, and he smiled a little, amused by her own irritation. This was what he loved about her. Even when she was drowning in unfamiliar emotions, she was self-aware.

Strong enough to recognize that she was floundering.

Rubbing his nose into her hair, so he could scent the pure essence that belonged to her and her alone, he murmured, "Whatever you want to do, we'll do." He winced at the idea, but had to ask, "Do you want to go back to the States?"

She snorted. "No."

Was he relieved? Maybe. They lived under the radar here, but Devon and Sawyer were big news in the States. If they lived there, there would be attention, and their unusual household would definitely cause titters of gossip.

"Why not?" he asked, wanting a reason rather than just a knee-jerk reaction.

"Because England is home. It has been for a long time, but it became that even more so when I met you guys. Your world is here. This is where we need to be."

"This isn't a matter of majority rules, Sascha. We want you to be happy," he remarked, his tone husky—arguing against something he genuinely didn't want, but was willing to cede to if it lifted her depression. "Wherever that is."

He felt her smile against his throat. "I know. I'm usually happy here. I'm just not at the moment."

He hesitated. They'd all, at some point, wanted to broach this topic with her but hadn't known if it was wise. "Do you want to speak with someone?"

She knew what he meant. "No."

The brusque retort pinched the skin around his eyes, but he took the hit and just nodded. "Okay. No worries."

The tension that had flooded her body at that moment hurt him. Physically pained him. At his easy acceptance though, she just blew out a breath. "Maybe someday. Just not yet."

She'd said that before, but every time they broached the topic of counseling, her rejections grew colder. "What about just speaking with Jacinta?"

"Maybe," she whispered.

"Have you spoken with her?"

"No. Not really." She hadn't been speaking to anyone. And she'd lost a shit-ton of weight, too.

Too much.

He rubbed his hand down her arm. "If you don't want sex, but think we do, you don't have to...I don't know... force yourself to do anything that makes you uncomfortable."

When she didn't reply, he thought it prudent to let the topic rest. He reached up and stroked his fingers over her head until he touched the curls that danced at her nape. Toying with those locks, he reached over with his free hand to knock his laptop out of sleep.

Studying the files, he started to read through the information he'd need to process before he called the Minister of Finance in Veronia tomorrow. Then, he felt them.

And a wave of uselessness filled him with resentment.

The tears wet his throat and rather than comment on them, he just brushed his lips over her temple and let her weep until, at last, she relaxed in his arms, tumbling into a stress-triggered light doze.

He clenched his eyes shut as the desire to do something,

*anything*, to make this better hit him. He knew they'd all been feeling useless recently. Had been wishing there was something they could do to make things right—hadn't that been why Devon had gone off and done what he'd done, dammit?—and yet, there was nothing anyone could do.

Andrei feared only time would heal this wound.

Nothing more, nothing less.

And that made him feel more out of control than ever, because in this matter, where he wanted to help, he couldn't. It was out of his hands, and that hurt like a bitch.

---

"TIN? What do you want for breakfast? Scrambled or poached eggs?"

He always went for scrambled, but she never stopped asking him; trying to make him eat more diversely was tough when the kid was insistent on copycatting Devon.

At first, she'd been rather pleased by how he always ate his vegetables without her having to tell him to. Because, hell, what mother wasn't happy about that? The kid actively, without even scrunching his nose, munched on broccoli.

Like it was a banana.

Or a candy bar, even.

Then, she'd realized why.

Devon ate broccoli. Loved the stuff. Especially with mint sauce, a weird concoction that was basically fresh mint macerated in vinegar and sweetened with sugar. Devon poured it on his vegetables like another person would drench their fries in ketchup.

That was how she'd put two and two together—she was definitely *Columbo* in the making.

Tin did the same.

Whatever Devon liked to eat, Tin did.

Spinach, check.

Avocados, check.

Chocolate pudding, nope—Devon hated the stuff, and guess who else did?

Tin had even started pouting about not being able to have wine with dinner, so she'd been giving him blackcurrant juice. The first time she'd made Devon drink it, so they could truly con Tin, who was far too intelligent for his own good. Devon hadn't appreciated the Ribena at first, but now he'd started having that instead of wine.

Regardless of her glum mood, her lips curved at the notion of the forty-one-year-old man-child drinking Ribena rather than good wine with his evening meal.

"Scrambled are just better," Devon told her, as he slouched into the kitchen, his feet padding against the stone flags before he slumped at the table, pressing his forehead to the wooden surface. "Aren't they, kid?"

She rolled her eyes at the muffled words, and rolled them again when Tin cheered, "Yes, papa," and, of course, dropped his head on the table, too.

*Of all the fathers he'd chosen to emulate, it had to be the weird one,* Sascha thought wryly, casting a look at the two heads that couldn't have been more different. Devon's so dark and saturnine. Tin's so light and golden. Two opposites and yet, Tin was intent on mimicking his father for all his worth.

"Why are they, though?" she questioned, eying the saucepan that was loaded with eggs and wrinkling her nose in distaste. To her, an egg was an egg, was an egg. Although, she'd fallen out of love with them last year when she'd tried and failed Keto. The fad diet hadn't lasted, but her loathing of all things bacon and egg had endured—it was enough to make her feel anti-American. What good-for-nothing American *didn't* like those staples?

It was akin to hating Reese's Cups, and yet, the prospect of eating eggs turned her stomach to the point she didn't care if Lady Liberty scorned her. Scorn be damned.

"You don't have to think about what you're eating. Eggs are

surprisingly complicated food, Sascha," Devon told her earnestly, and Tin, *of course*, looked up and started nodding in total agreement.

"Complicated?" She scowled harder. "How is an egg complicated?"

"Do I eat the yolk first or the white? And if I eat the white first, there's no flavor, but mixing it with the yolk just doesn't feel right." So said the man who covered his vegetables in mint sauce. "Should I dip with bread or sausage, and what about ketchup? And salt?"

She rolled her eyes. "I don't think the egg minds what your preference is."

"I mind," he countered.

"He wouldn't eat egg whites for about six years," Kurt commented as he stepped into the kitchen, his end destination her. He stopped at her side by the stove, pressed his hands to her hips, and pulled her back into his chest.

Of the five of them, he and Andrei were the ones who were least cautious with her. Even Devon, who really couldn't be careful without immense focus, was a little on edge around her, and she hated that.

She knew it stemmed from a positive place. They wanted to shelter her, cosset and cuddle her, so trod carefully around her. All the damn time. But God, that was starting to wear thin.

Devon made more of a mess of things when he tried to be careful, than he did at his most frank. Watching his words just made him panic, and when he panicked, he disappeared to his office for days at a time.

She liked that, though Andrei was a little more cautious than Kurt, neither had any issue in treating her as she'd once been and not like a china doll.

Kurt's fingers weren't soft on her hips as he held her in place. Not rough enough to leave bruises, but enough to make her feel the pressure of his touch. And the way he ground his cock into her ass? Another woman might have found it suggestive, but it actually relieved her.

It made her feel like the woman she'd been and not the lost soul she felt like now.

She wiggled her hips against him and smiled when he pressed a good morning kiss to the side of her throat—*after* nipping her shoulder. "*Guten Morgen, Liebchen.*"

"Morning, love," she told him, her voice husky as she tilted her head to let him kiss her on the mouth, too. He hummed under his breath then took a step back after patting her gently on the ass—he moved to the side to cover the motion from Tin who was susceptible to noticing shit like that.

Devon had done it once. Then he'd had to explain to Tin why *he* couldn't spank his mom.

That had been both awkward and hilarious. She'd made sure to watch, too, mostly just to see Devon squirm, because Tin was no ordinary kid. He was still young, but in many ways, he just wasn't. He was genius material, and Vasily had informed her that Andrei, as a child, had been a terror to guide because he'd been bored by everything.

Nothing had satisfied that wunderbrain of his.

She just hoped having five dads who'd experienced similar childhoods would save him.

She had a tendency of coddling Tin; he was her baby, after all. But the men didn't. They pushed him to learn, where she would leave him alone. Andrei was talking about piano lessons already, and Kurt wanted to start introducing German next year by the latest, when they'd already agreed that Tin wouldn't start on that until he was comfortable with Russian.

Trouble was, he *was* comfortable with Russian. In the last two months, it was like a switch had been flicked. Now, he and Andrei could natter merrily away in the bathroom for the nightly ritual that saw Tin coming out squeaky clean, and Andrei drenched all the way to his socks though he stayed on the dry side of the bath.

Hadn't she seen that last night?

Watching Vasily and Tin Skype was usually hilarious, but it had been boring because they'd done nothing but chatter in Russian.

What had she done to deserve having all these geniuses around her when she was just average?

Not even bothering to huff about that, because she had her own role to play here—Tin, for all he loved his daddies, couldn't sleep without a kiss from her, and he'd informed her that her lap was the best of them to sit in... a woman had to take her compliments where she could find them in this genius farm.

Serving the eggs in two bowls—two for Tin and a whopping eight for Devon who seemed to power through calories like nobody's business, the jerk—she seasoned with salt and pepper then brought the dishes over to her two guys. There was toast on the table, toast Devon was spreading with butter and cutting into small geometric shapes for Tin, and just watching him do that simple act made her smile.

It amazed her she didn't have to prompt them. They just did this stuff. Maybe she shouldn't have been amazed. Tin was theirs, too, wasn't he? And a father *should* take an active role in his child's life, but it never worked like that, did it?

At her dreadful mother and toddler group, she never saw a single dad. Yet all five of hers had made an appearance at one point or another—something that had definitely raised some eyebrows, but she'd just never mentioned the word 'dad' and had let them assume the guys were relatives. No, she'd never seen another guy there, and yet, her men always made a point of coming with her at least once every few weeks. Then, there was how interactive they were with Tin. How they helped him grow, how they helped shape him even though he was so young.

She'd really lucked out on the daddy scale.

"What do you want for breakfast, honey?" she asked Kurt, pressing a kiss to his crown where the dirty-blond locks smelled like his lime and mint shampoo. As she sniffed, she watched Devon pass Tin the shapes once he'd identified the geometric forms.

"I'm okay with toast today."

"You are?" She pulled back to cock a brow at him. "That's not like you."

"I'm nervous."

Sascha smiled, touched. "It will be okay." It always amazed her how such a talented writer, a true wordsmith, could have such little confidence in his work.

He winced. "What if I hat—," he eyed Tin, cleared his throat, and murmured, "dislike the cast?"

They'd made a point of never using the words 'love' or 'hate' because, *of course,* Tin being the precocious little monster he was, had fixated on them to the point that he'd told his doctor he hated her because she always stuck him with a needle. Then he'd told the dogwalker in the park he loved him when they'd met the guy once, and . . . yeah. It was just easier not to use those kinds of words around him.

The doctor had been offended even though Sascha felt sure most kids hated her, and she knew it—they'd just never told her. And the dogwalker had looked at them both like they were freaks.

Maybe they were, but she preferred her world to any fucker else's.

Even if her almost-three-year-old was starting to freak her out with how smart he was. Because, hell, *she* didn't always know some of the geometric shapes Devon cut out for him.

"There's bound to be someone you'll dislike. We can't like everyone, can we, Tin?" Devon's words were a wisdom that she really didn't feel like discussing after tossing and turning all night, and sleeping less than ninety minutes total. Sleep hadn't been her friend recently, and she was starting to feel the backlash.

"No, we can't like everyone, but we treat everyone with respect, don't we?" she countered, shooting her love a beady-eyed glance that warned him to watch his damn words.

"Unless they don't deserve it," Devon grumbled, ducking his head to avoid her eyes—well aware he was dancing with death.

*Goddammit.* They'd already had this conversation, and she'd warned him! Several times, too.

"Tin, we treat people with respect until they have proven they don't deserve it," Kurt tried to reason, but that didn't make it much better.

She foresaw a hell of a lot of trouble when it came time for school. Most of her teachers had been dicks, and hadn't earned or deserved her respect, but that didn't mean she hadn't had to give it to them!

"Seriously?" she groused, glowering at Kurt who smiled sheepishly. "I think I need my dad to visit."

"Why?" Devon asked, scowling. He and her father had a love-hate relationship. Well, not hate and not love just… Henry had a way of treating Devon like he was an alien.

An unwelcome alien.

An invading alien.

Devon, quite naturally, didn't appreciate the *ET, phone home* references.

"Because he's better at this stuff than you two, apparently," she complained, rolling her eyes when Kurt laughed, and Devon just looked even more perplexed. Blowing out a breath and promising to figure out a way to make Tin realize the importance of politeness, she mumbled, "Never mind." Then, she squeezed Kurt's shoulder. "What time is the meeting with the cast?"

"Twelve." He shot her a look. "Do you want to come with me?"

She shrugged. "If you want me there, I'd love to." And, actually, she wasn't lying. It would be nice to get out of the house for something that wasn't playgroup or grocery shopping. Not that she'd felt up to much else over the last few weeks, but it was time for baby steps.

And, in this house, baby steps involved meeting Hollywood stars.

Plus, she reasoned, she'd helped Kurt finalize his *Black Blood* trilogy. Together, they'd plotted the story and worked on the actual final file together, her helping him shape it to where he dreamed it could be.

As a result, the book had won yet more awards, and the trilogy had been picked up for a movie with a major production company in the States.

"Of course, I'd love to. It should be a good day. They're taking us to the *Holly*."

Sascha cocked a brow. "Expensive."

"And on their dime, too. Even better."

Snorting, because the six of them combined probably had more than the production company earned in a year, she murmured, "Who doesn't love a bargain?" When he winked at her, she had to laugh.

The sound had the kitchen freezing, though. And she saw Sean and Sawyer almost trip down the stairs as they hurried toward her. Their eyes were glued on her face, and the tableau seemed to be in a stasis as her laughter died off at how weird they were acting.

She frowned at them. "What is it? What's wrong?"

Kurt reached for her, and he encompassed her fingers in the warmth of his large paw-like hand. "Your laugh is beautiful, Sascha," he told her huskily, saying without uttering a word in front of Tin, that that was...

It couldn't have been the first time they'd heard her laugh since—

No.

She usually laughed when she joined Tin and Andrei in the bathroom, and she'd watched a funny movie last week, but... Did this laughter sound different? From the way they were looking at her, she guessed she had her answer.

Why were they reacting like this?

Sascha gnawed at her bottom lip, then turned away from them to round the station. "What do you guys want for breakfast?" she rasped.

"The usual," they both said.

But Sean was the one who murmured, "Do you need a hand in the kitchen?"

"No. I'm fine. Take a seat," she whispered and forced herself to focus on the dishes she needed to prepare for the morning meal.

It was better to think about that than contemplate the truth.

That her laughter could have been the first truly joyous sound she'd made in six weeks, disturbed her on a base level, mostly because she feared her depression had affected Tin. But, equally, that fear warred with the terror she felt at the notion of moving on. The baby was... Did her laughing mean she was forgetting—?

Swallowing, she switched off her brain and focused on Sawyer's porridge—she always made extra because he usually encouraged Tin to have some—and getting Sean's granola out of the oven.

Those mundane tasks were, quite frankly, all she was capable of.

# TEN

IT MADE her feel like a boor, but the restaurant wasn't her favorite. It was one of those places where money talked and only the number of Michelin stars counted. It didn't matter if a plate consisted of cauliflower jizz and sautéed, baked, sous-vided and cremated duck breast—it was in vogue, and little else mattered.

Mostly she was hangry. After that weirdness this morning at breakfast, she'd put off having anything to eat, thinking she'd be having something nice here, but she'd had a brain fart and forgotten that most eateries in the capital were serving shit like this.

There were four sections to the restaurant, and each one had their own hydroponic garden in play. One side grew basil, and from a distance, she recognized the other three sections grew rosemary, mint, and oregano. It made the room smell nice, she'd give it that, even if the clinical edge to the restaurant put her back up. Everything was white, gleaming white, which made the bright green herbs' color pop even more.

It was pretentious, as pretentious as the company they were keeping.

Making a mental note to have Kurt take her to her favorite café,

*Rossi's*, for some coffee and cake after this meeting—she intended on eating something nice today—she watched as Jennifer Houghton flirted with her man.

At first, it had been amusing.

Kurt had introduced Sascha as his partner.

They were always careful to introduce her as such. It could be interpreted in many ways, after all, and that was how they kept under the radar. By being circumspect.

In their position, the fact that they lived in a poly household with a child could, and would, feature in the gossip rags the instant it came to any dick with a camera's attention. Her men were too infamous and famous, and she hadn't exactly stayed out of the news with her past emerging in a big way and the small matter of her inheritance.

When her sister-in-law's case had gone to trial, and the details of the way Elizabeth Jacobie had murdered Sascha's birth parents had come to light, the press's interest was renewed with a vigor that had Sascha hiding and becoming reclusive for quite a while.

Coming to the media's attention again wasn't something she wanted.

None of them did.

And so, they introduced her as 'partner' and she just had to accept it if she wanted to maintain their under-the-radar relationship. In turn, this meant enduring women purposely misinterpreting the label and ignoring the obvious intimacy between Sascha and the man she was with.

Watching Jennifer fawn over Kurt swiftly grew tedious. She kept putting her hand on his knee and Kurt kept reaching for it, pressing it to the white linen tablecloth and patting it in a 'there, there' motion. It would have been hysterical if. ...

Well, okay, it wasn't.

Not at all.

She wasn't sure whether she wanted to bitch slap her, or just blow out a breath and wait for this meal to be over.

It didn't help that Matthew Dreyford, yup, *the* Dreyford, had taken a liking to her, too. Although, she wasn't sure if that was more his fascination with her money or the fact that she had a pretty face. She'd lost a ton of weight since her fall, had even dropped lower than her pre-Tin weight. She didn't particularly feel sexy. She felt, if anything, washed out, but it seemed like the men at the table were interested in her.

Which was, Sascha thought, one of the reasons why Jennifer was flirting with Kurt. She wasn't accustomed to sharing the limelight, even if Sascha didn't want anything to do with the limelight, period!

"You live in Kensington, don't you, Sascha?" Dreyford asked, as he speared up some kind of pumpkin mousse with crème fraiche that reminded her of Tin's baby puke.

"I do. Yes." She gave him a tight smile—how the hell did he know that?

"You'll have to show me the sights. Everyone knows how famous Harrods is."

"I doubt it's your first visit to London," she countered coolly, not in the mood for any of his bullshit. Kurt *had* to be nice. *She* didn't. She just had to be polite, even in the face of his leers and flirtatious comments—even though Kurt was right goddamn beside her.

And then, she felt like a shit. Because, hadn't she, just this morning, preached about being respectful? Devon was totally right. The bastard. Some people just didn't deserve respect.

God, she hated it when he was right, and she was trying to teach Tin an important lesson about not alienating the world. Tin was going to be the heir to a fortune that would make Bill Gates' kids weep. If they didn't make sure he wasn't an asshole now, then there was no hope.

They needed to start this shit young before it was too late!

Still, knowing she had to be polite even though the guy was a douche, she smiled at Dreyford in faint apology for her cool tone.

He grinned back, seeming to take the smile as something it most definitely wasn't: encouragement. "It isn't, but it's the first visit I'll have any time on my hands." His eyes lit up as they glanced over her, seeming to suggest he'd like to get his hands on other things.

Her mouth curled with distaste as his gaze went on a road trip, taking in her bright auburn hair that bobbed in large waves around her shoulders, the emerald blouse that pinched in at her waist, thanks to a high-waist pencil skirt, and managed to make her boobs look 'da bomb.' She had a pair of stacked heels on too, mostly to put her at the same height as Kurt—she was a shortass in comparison to him.

Still, this outfit wasn't for Kurt. It was for herself. She'd wanted to wear something pretty, so she'd dressed up. The skirt was black and fit her curves to perfection, but it was a rich velvet that felt lovely against her hands when she rested them on her lap. The gauzy blouse was more like gossamer, and she'd worn a bustier underneath it to dress it up—it wasn't too showy for a meeting of this nature, but it was a tad sexier than she'd grown used to of late. If it wasn't for Kurt, it sure as hell wasn't for this prick, either.

The last time she'd felt sexy was the night Devon and Sawyer had taken her to that tango club in Glasgow. The ache to be back then, to that time, created a physical response that made her stomach rebel the fancy duck confit she'd just forced on herself.

With a false smile, she murmured, "I'm sure you'll find someone who'd like to be your tour guide."

Of course, the dick didn't want to hear her rejection. "But I don't just want a 'someone.' It would be nice to see the capital from an American's perspective. I'm sure you know some haunts that most people don't."

Kurt's hand came to grab hers, probably because he was sensing the fact that she wanted to take her fork and stab Dreyford in the thigh with it.

Which part of her refusal was the man not understanding?

Even when she smiled out of politeness, it wasn't enough for anyone to think it was a come on. Hell, not even a prisoner who'd just been released would consider her smiles the 'green light.'

"Sascha has a young child," Kurt said gently. "Her days are busy."

She cocked a brow as he squeezed her fingers in silent warning. "Very busy." She shot Dreyford another smile and was pleased to notice he just grimaced, his eyes on Kurt's grip of her hand, as well as the way he'd slid his arm over the back of her chair.

He looked away, and she saw Jonathan Reynolds' smirk as he did. Cocking a brow at him in challenge, the executive producer just grinned at her and shrugged—he obviously didn't like Dreyford, either.

"So, Kurt, what do you think of the script I sent over last night?" that was David Masterson; the director and co-writer of the script based on Kurt's book. Kurt was helping to produce the movie also.

"I think it's almost perfect."

Jennifer pouted. "I noticed you cut four of my scenes."

Sascha, having read the updated script, harrumphed under her breath. Kurt heard her, and she saw his lips curve faintly. "Well, the story isn't really about Magdalena, Jennifer. It's about the Brandeberg family and the situation they're in."

Masterson rolled his eyes. "There are three sex scenes. That should keep the audience happy."

Jennifer narrowed her eyes. "We negotiated two."

"Originally. Bitch at your agent about that. He agreed with me, and you signed the damn contract."

"I wanted more lines," she countered, outright glowering at him now. Sascha sensed she hadn't read the contract and had taken her agent's word on faith.

Oops.

"I know you did, but this movie doesn't call for it. Maybe if we get the funding, the second one will allow us to develop your character more." But if the faint sneer on his lips was anything to go by, Masterson shared Sascha's disdain of Jennifer, even if he did like looking at her tits. This had her wondering if this particular casting had involved a couch and a blowjob.

Ouch.

*Catty.*

Still, if it fit, it fit.

Reaching for her wine glass, she took a deep sip and tried to pretend this hadn't been an awkward meal. But pretending didn't work, and it didn't get better when Dreyford and Jennifer began sniping at one another, and Reynolds seemed to find it amusing to rile them up even more.

Forty minutes later, her shoulders felt stiff as a board when Kurt wrapped her in her peacoat. It swirled around her ankles in a way that made her want to twist her hips from side to side to feel the faux fur lining tickle her calves.

"Did I tell you that you look gorgeous?"

She grinned at him, loving the taut, lustful expression on his face as he dipped his head and pressed a kiss to her lips. She opened her eyes at the last moment as she pulled back from him and saw Jennifer glowering at her over his shoulder.

Maybe it was stupid, but she smiled like a cat who'd gotten the cream as she turned away from the kiss. Then dismissing the bitch, she curled her arm through Kurt's as he hauled her into his side.

"I think, for your patience, you deserve some cake from *Rossi's*," he murmured under his breath as they walked down the silver-lined hallway—this restaurant felt like it was about to take off. Seriously. Could it be anymore sci-fi? The Starship Enterprise had more home comforts than *Holly*.

She peered up at him. "Stop reading my mind."

He laughed even as he reached down to peck a kiss to her temple. "The minute I saw you looking down at your cauliflower foam, I knew *Rossi's* was on the cards."

"Let's say it how it is, Kurt. It was jizz. Vegetable jizz."

A snort escaped him as he nodded at the maître d'. The man beamed at him, obviously recognizing the pair of them as they headed toward the door. The minute they did, the bright flash of cameras hit her retina, making her jolt.

Scanning the crowd in front of her, she wanted to groan with irritation. There were four paparazzi, something she should have expected considering Dreyford and Jennifer Houghton were having lunch with them.

She sighed and was grateful she'd tucked her face into the high collar of her peacoat as she headed out. It gave her some anonymity. Not much, granted, but enough to hide her features and expose only her eyes, as well as shield her from the bitter day outside—her original intent when she'd dipped her head under the collar's line.

Kurt just nodded at them, smiling at men armed with heavy-duty cameras even as his hand tightened about her hip as he guided her past them and out to the grim London day. The leers on their faces were almost sexual. But it wasn't really. It was a different kind of lust —for money. Greed coated their features until it dripped off their chin like drool.

Just being in their cameras' crosshairs made her feel dirty. God, she hated the spotlight.

*Holly* was in Mayfair. The exclusive address didn't impress her. She'd had better food just off Petticoat Lane where the famous market was held. In fact, she'd eaten better street food than she'd had in that damn restaurant, and eating here should have prompted her to realize this could have been a potential outcome. The paps hovered in Mayfair, waiting on celebrities and reality TV stars to fill their pockets and the pages of whatever rag they worked for.

The brick façades of the buildings were elegant here, rich. Their car was parked just around the corner—a minor miracle—and she was grateful to tuck herself into it because the paparazzi hadn't stopped herding them—with every clip of her heel against the neat stone sidewalk, she heard them scurrying behind her, clattering as they took shot after shot. At least two of them were trailing at their heels, which made no sense as they would make more money lying in wait for Jennifer and Dreyford. They were the stars, after all.

She did her best to ignore the press and murmured, "Don't worry about the car door. Let's just get out of here."

Kurt hummed his agreement, and as she peeked up at his face, she saw the ease on his features, the lack of strain, and realized how good his poker face was. The hand that gripped her own was tight, brimming with tension. But from the outside looking in, he was at ease.

The fact she was hiding her face would cause comment, but she'd prefer that. Better to be a mystery guest than have her name in the rags. The color of her hair might cause some chatter, but she doubted it. Red was hardly rare now, and speculation was one thing. Confirmed gossip, another.

Where she was concerned, the men were all gentlemen. No, she didn't need them to open the car door for her, and no, she didn't need them to open the door to a restaurant either, but she let them because she loved it. She loved that they thought about that shit, that they were preoccupied with her. But now Kurt knew not to waste time opening her car door, so she did it herself once he clicked the alarm on Sean's Maserati and slipped into the vehicle. The tight confines of her pencil skirt squeaked as she bundled herself into the passenger seat, keeping her face averted just in case the paparazzi tried to get another shot.

When he clicked the locks, he pressed the ignition button that fired up the engine. The throaty purr seemed to vibrate through the cab. It felt good, even if the chilly confines were anything *but*. It was cold and by the time they were swerving out of the parking space, the heat had permeated somewhat, the journalists had gone, and she could stop hiding her face.

"Still want to go to *Rossi's*?" Kurt asked, cutting her a look, his hands tightening on the wheel, and she looked at those spatulate hands, studying them a second before she nodded.

"I don't see why not. They leave us alone there."

"Good. I wanted to go, but wasn't sure if you would. …"

"Would what?"

"I don't know. I wasn't sure if you'd have the energy for it."

She frowned, thought about it. "If anything, that horrible meal made me want to go to *Rossi's* even more!"

"Why?" He shot her a quick look, so she could see how he'd cocked his brow.

"Because it was all bullshit, and that's not how we work."

"No," he confirmed, and repeated, "That isn't how we work."

"Plus, I deserve every damn calorie I'm about to gorge on."

She studied his strong hands as they gripped the wheel again, the fingers tightening with pressure while he drove them through the city. It wasn't as congested as rush hour, but there were still plenty of cars—enough to make her grateful she wasn't driving. She loved her Caddy, and took every opportunity to drive Baby, but, equally, it was great not having to have eyes in the back of her head.

It was also nice having someone chauffeur her from place to place. She was able to relax, while they focused on the nutcases on the road, avoiding anything from angry cabbies to sleek sportscars that were driven by lunatics who thought that because they drove a Lamborghini, they owned the road.

Still, there was a tension to Kurt that hadn't been there before, and it had nothing to do with the stress of driving through the city.

When they headed into Soho, she perked up as they drove down the side streets toward her favorite 'caff.' That was how they pronounced it here. She wasn't sure why, but even though *Rossi's* had left its greasy spoon days behind and was now a kind of coffee emporium, they were still proud to be a caff—on the walls behind the fancy coffee machine, as well as the line of drip coffee makers, there were pictures of the place through the ages. She'd often studied them as she paid her bill.

Eying the female clientele in their A-line skirts with petticoats, and the Teddy boys—a generation of young men who'd pretty much dressed like Elvis Presley with their velvet-trimmed drape jackets, drainpipe trousers, Brylcreemed quiffs, and who had been the rebels of their generation—she truly got a kick out of studying the people who'd frequented the place back in the Fifties.

She loved *Rossi's*. It was probably one of the only places she genuinely felt at ease anymore. The staff all knew her, and they knew

Tin, too. Most of them, after the fall, had come to her and hugged her, including Mamma Rossi, the family's ninety-year-old matriarch. Her gnarled fingers had patted Sascha's cheek as she'd promised, her voice throaty with too many cigarettes and the remnants of an Italian accent that had been away from the motherland for decades, "Things will get better."

The memory, to this day, still had the power to touch her. But, she forced herself to stay cheerful. Kurt didn't need her to be dour. After that bizarre meeting, he deserved some laughs.

Kurt pulled another miracle by managing to park about a two minutes' walk away from *Rossi's*, and as he took her hand, they were both more relaxed as they strode towards her favorite purveyor of cakes this side of the Thames.

"I swear, two nearby parking spaces in one day? I need to bring you along every time I go out."

He laughed, displaying white teeth, but even better—the glint in his eyes spoke of genuine amusement. "You can keep me on the dash, if you want."

"No, I'll just let you chauffeur me around. I swear, the traffic is getting worse." It was a common complaint among all Londoners because, shit, the traffic was never going to get any better.

The tinkle of the door opening heralded their arrival into the café that hadn't changed all that much in recent years. They'd started doing afternoon tea, which she was a fan of, and they'd changed some of the seating areas, adding more comfortable seats. The switch had made the place morph into a more chilled atmosphere rather than the working lunch vibe it had before.

She preferred the switch. Her favorite place to sit here had always been in the corner with a view of the busy street, but it had been popular with most of the locals so wasn't always empty. Now, there were more armchairs, more comfort, more of a likelihood she'd catch a seat, which made her love this place even more.

"Have you found that you cling to the places from before more?"

She blinked at that. "Huh?"

Kurt rubbed his nose as he took off his suit coat. It was smart, thick navy wool that highlighted his dirty-blond hair to perfection. Underneath, he wore a grey suit with a white button-down shirt and a navy tie. He looked like some kind of modern god, and she really, at that moment, could have given him a blowjob.

Yeah, that was how hot he was.

She could have slipped his cock out of his fly, dug her nails into his ass, and had him fuck her face.

And, oh boy, where that had come from, she wasn't sure.

Feeling her cheeks flush with the surprising force of the arousal that swirled inside her, she murmured, "Kurt?"

He grimaced as he draped the coat over the back of the seat and plunked himself opposite her. "I just noticed recently. You never like new places but love the old ones."

"Like?"

"Well, the *Holly*. It's new to you, so you weren't a fan. But if I'd taken you to *Roberto Corlino's* or *Devianz*, I know you'd have enjoyed it."

"That's because they don't serve crap like that," she grumbled, referencing restaurants they'd been eating at for a long time. "But maybe it *is* nostalgia. I don't know. I doubt it. If the food had been nice, and the company hadn't been dire, I'd have enjoyed the meal. But can you honestly say you did?"

He wrinkled his nose. "No. I can't honestly say I did."

That he repeated her words, pretty much verbatim, had her narrowing her eyes at him. The move made him smirk. "What?"

He shrugged.

"What?" she barked.

"It was . . .," he hesitated, "*different* seeing you jealous."

Sascha gaped at him. "'Different'? And I wasn't jealous." She'd totally been stalked by the green-eyed monster today.

"You were," he retorted, his tone amused. "You were jealous."

"Like you appreciated Dreyford gawking at my tits," she said with a sniff.

That had him waving a hand. "I'm used to men gaping at your tits, *Liebchen*. It's par for the course when you have a beauty at your side."

Despite herself, she preened. It was pathetic, but she did. She'd been feeling like a slob, so his words were a compliment that boosted her ego. Shameful, but true. "Doesn't mean you have to like it."

He conceded that with a nod. "I don't. But, like I said, I'm used to it."

"And you're not used to me being jealous?" She cocked a brow at him. "Which I wasn't. By the way."

"You were." He snickered. "Every time she put her hand on my thigh, I thought you were going to throw your wine at her."

Okay, so he'd seen *that*. She huffed. "Damn woman was all over you."

"And you know that you have no reason to be jealous," he commented softly. "Don't you?"

She shrugged. "I guess."

That made him scowl. "What do you mean?"

She hadn't exactly been putting out of late, had she? Men . . . well, they had needs.

"Sascha—"

Turning her head away from him, she smiled in relief when one of the servers, a woman called Rebecca, appeared at their side. "Hi, Becca. How's Tony?" Tony was her four-year-old.

"He's a nightmare," the younger woman groused. "Has decided he's forgotten his potty training altogether."

Sensing Kurt's confusion, because Tin was a year younger than Tony and had been potty trained for over a year already, she kicked him under the table. "God, kids, I swear they love just messing with our heads."

"Or our sheets," Becca grumbled, then she perked up. "No Tin today? You know I love giving those chubby cheeks a squeeze."

"No, he's with his dad." That was her go-to answer.

Becca cut Kurt a look—she knew him. She knew all of Sascha's men, the woman just didn't know they were exactly that. *Her* men. "Hi, Mr. Yeller. You want the usual?"

"Yes, please." He smiled at her, yet didn't seem to notice her blush when Becca looked at him. He then turned his attention back to Sascha who had to hide a smile of her own.

She'd lucked out.

Her men weren't just hot. They were turning into the sexiest silver foxes the world had ever seen. And to compound that, they weren't assholes about it, either. Even though a part of her wondered why Becca's heated cheeks didn't make her jealous but Jennifer Houghton's attention had, she refrained from maintaining that line of thought, and murmured, "I'll have some Victoria sponge cake please, Becca. And some loose-leaf Earl Grey."

Though she scrawled that on her notepad, she murmured, "We have some cupcakes with Earl Grey frosting. Want some?" There was a teasing smile on her lips because the woman knew her well.

Grinning, Sascha nodded. "Please. Pack up eight, will you? I'll take them home."

The server shook her head. "I swear, eight cupcakes. And you and Tin are tiny. I don't know where you put them." She wrinkled her nose as she carried on, "I'll be back shortly."

Kurt rubbed his lips before asking, "She thinks you eat everything you buy here yourself?"

Sascha laughed. "Yes. Well, that Tin and I share it, too."

Those royal-blue eyes of his darkened. "I wish it were simpler."

Because, after their little session with the paps she understood. She nodded and reached over to hold his wrist. The armchairs were tucked close enough together for her to hold his hand without feeling like her arm was going to drop off. As he laced their fingers, he asked, "Sascha, there is never any fear of—"

She shook her head. "Don't, Kurt. I don't want to talk about it." And she didn't. She had faith in her men, trusted them implicitly, but something about Jennifer had gotten under her skin.

"If you think we'd cheat on you because, what . . . you've been recuperating? I'm not happy about that, Sascha. That's a lack of faith that is very unfair. We've never done anything to encour—"

She held up a hand and peered over at him. "I know."

"Then?" he prompted.

"I don't think you'd cheat on me." She didn't. But she had, for that one moment's aberration. "I just didn't like Jennifer. That's all." And Jane, Andrei's PA, now that she thought about it.

She was used to her men being ogled. If he was used to it with her, then the same could be said with her quintet of hunks, but sometimes, some women just got under her skin.

Jennifer with the touching, and Jane . . . God, she was always laughing. That fake laugh, too. The one that womenfolk had created to stroke a guy's ego.

"When do children normally get potty trained?"

She reared back at that abrupt change of topic. Frowning, she replied, "Around two or three."

"Why did we potty train Tin at eighteen months then?"

With no choice other than to laugh, she murmured, "Since when did we decide what Tin does? He didn't like his nappies, so Devon told him he didn't have to wear them, don't you remember?"

Kurt frowned. "No."

"You do. You were writing *Schwarz*." That was the last book in his *Black Blood* trilogy.

"Oh, well, I don't remember much around then. My brain was a blur."

She chuckled, because he really was out of it when he wrote—that was no lie. "Well, Devon said he didn't have to, then Tin peed on the rug in the office."

"I'm sure Dev loved that," Kurt said, snickering. Then he squinted at her. "Wait a minute. He had that thrown away, didn't he? Was that why?"

"Yeah. He said that he'd forever associate it with a urinal."

Kurt snickered again. "He's such a prat sometimes."

She winked. "Our prat."

"True." He rolled his eyes.

"Then, because Tin is Tin and Devon is Devon, Dev showed him how to pee and crap, and ta-dah! We had a potty-trained kid." She cut Becca a look as she was on her way with a tray of drinks. "Don't say anything, though. I like to pretend that Tin is normal, and I'm having issues with potty training him, not problems deciding whether he should be learning German or the piano next."

When she wrinkled her nose, Kurt's guffaw made her grin at him. Of course, his laughter inspired some drooling from Becca who ducked her face to avoid eye contact with both him and Sascha.

With Kurt's strong coffee and her Earl Grey in hand, they settled back and looked out onto the road. It wasn't a restful sight. London could never be that, and maybe that was why she was tired of it. She'd always loved it. Up until recently.

"What are you thinking?"

She tilted her head to the side to take in both the street and him. "I'm thinking I've had enough of London."

Her blunt statement had him lifting his brows. "Really?"

"Yeah."

"Andrei mentioned you weren't happy here."

"He did?" She winced. "I should have guessed."

"We share the things that count, *Liebchen*," he murmured softly. "You know that."

"I do." She pursed her lips. "Did he tell all of you?"

"*Ja*, of course."

"Of course," she groused, then when Becca appeared once more with their goodies, she thanked her and forked up some of her cake, while Kurt tucked into his waffle with fresh cream and strawberries.

"Didn't you want him to share that with us?" he asked, cocking a brow at her.

"Not particularly. I was just thinking out loud." On a particularly shitty day. She'd gotten her period that morning, and the sight of it had just. ... Sascha blew out a breath.

This shit was hard.

She knew how to grieve. She did. But losing the baby? It was a gnawing ache that she didn't know how to ease; meanwhile, the world carried on, her men's busy lives continued, Tin didn't stop developing, and she was left feeling like the last month and a half hadn't actually happened. It might as well have been the day after the fall rather than a full seven weeks on.

He nodded, seeming to sense the turn in her mood. "Would you like to be in the country? Outside of the city? Or just a different house with no memories?"

She thought about the memories that house *did* contain, and the prospect of leaving it behind entirely filled her with dread. Then, she thought about what she needed, thought about what could be good for her as well as them, and murmured, "You know the family pile?"

Kurt snorted. "How could I forget?"

As one of the two legitimate heirs to the Jacobie family estate, she had every right to live in the palatial residence. It was deep in the heart of Surrey, close to London without being too far away, but was a link to her past, as well as a great place for a kid to grow up. All her guys could have as much space as they needed, but Tin could play in the grounds without her worrying, and he'd have more freedom than here.

Their Kensington villa had a yard, but it was small and enclosed. More like a courtyard than somewhere for him to play. When it rained, which it did a lot, it was totally unusable. She didn't doubt that it would rain in Surrey, too, but there were more options.

At her continued silence, Kurt frowned. "You'd like to live there?"

"It's an option. You know Edward's moved to be with the other Silicon Valley bigwigs." Her nephew, a tech billionaire and a guy fifteen years older than her—shit, it was weird being a young aunt—had left the UK behind after his mother and sister's trial—his name had been dragged through the gutter, even though he'd been innocent.

By association, he was vilified, so he'd made the move over the pond.

She couldn't blame him even as she felt for him. He'd lost his mother and sister the moment of their arrest. He'd learned his mother had killed her in-laws—Sascha's parents—and that his sister had helped their mother arrange Sascha's assassination.

It seemed incredible to associate such words with her. But, there were several billion reasons why, and those billions were now in her bank account while Elizabeth rotted away in prison on double murder charges, and Laura was serving time for conspiracy.

Edward hadn't done a damn thing wrong, but reading the press coverage on the trial, it would be easy to forget that. Even as she was sorry he'd been hounded by the media, she'd been relieved when he'd left for the States. Andrei had worked with him for a long time and seemed to like him, considered him a friend, but she couldn't be anything other than ill at ease with the man whose family had stolen hers.

Not that it was his fault, and her dislike of him didn't make much sense, but instincts were instincts. You couldn't avoid them or force them to conform.

"I'll talk to Sean about it," Kurt murmured after a moment's contemplation. He cut her a look as he forked up some more of his dessert. "I'm surprised you didn't."

"He's been busy."

"He's always busy. We all are Sascha, but that doesn't mean we won't make time for you. You need to remember that."

She sighed—this was becoming an often repeated and tedious topic of conversation among the men. "I know."

"No, I don't think you do, and look what happened because you didn't want to intrude on our work. You went out without Devon or Sawyer when you should have been tucked safely between them. It isn't your fault. It isn't ours. But we need to learn from that tragedy—you don't feel comfortable interrupting us, and you have to stop thinking that way."

She frowned at him, and though she tried to contain her irritation, her voice was waspish as she bit off, "I wanted to go shopping, Kurt. *Shopping*. And I wanted a goddamn burger. Do you think I don't listen? Do you think I don't know that Andrei is trying to save some country's economy and that he's hauled Sawyer and Devon in to help him? Do you think I don't know Sean is trying to stop some freak from getting his paws on another innocent child? And do you think I don't realize you're up to your neck in edits?"

"It doesn't matter. None of that does," he retorted, and his hand snapped out to grab her wrist. He held it firmly in his large, warm grip, then stroked the underside, where the many veins collected, with his thumb. That tender caress made her shiver. "You're all that matters. There will always be another crisis. Another problem. Another worldwide economic disaster to avert. That's how Andrei works. And Sawyer and Devon aren't much better. We both know the more complex and complicated it is for them, the more they love it. Sean will always be working on another case, and they just seem to get worse and worse, and I'll never not be writing a book. That is constant. That is our life. But it doesn't mean that you don't take precedence. You and Tin," he amended.

She bit her lip—but that was the only way she conceded to his words.

He reached forward to tug her lip free. "Whatever *you* want is best for us as a family."

"That's not fair to you guys." Her whisper made him frown, and deep in his eyes, she saw the welter of concern he felt for her but usually managed to hide.

"Life isn't fair, *Liebchen*."

Her throat felt tight as she managed to whisper, "Okay. I'll think about it some more. It's a big move."

"That's all I ask—that you think about it. Think if it will make you feel better." He studied her a second. "Don't forget, we're all heading to Veronia for at least four months, and then, if you want, we could go and stay in LA for a while. There'll be a shit ton of PR going on at some point in the future."

She cringed. "You know I can't be involved in that."

He shrugged. "Okay, but you can still be in LA."

"Devon won't fly that far."

"He would for you."

A wistful smile curved her lips. "Do you think? I thought he hated being near the ocean."

A snort escaped him. "If you're in the ocean, then I'm certain he'll be there, too. Let's just not take him scuba diving, okay?"

When he winked at her, she had to laugh, and as the laugh escaped her, a warm feeling took its place.

She could do this.

Not only because she had no alternative, but because she had these men at her back. Men who would brave planes and oceans for her, who'd move their lives from a metropolitan city to a country backwater, all for her.

With her five guys, the world was her oyster.

It was about time she started remembering that.

# ELEVEN

ANDREI EYED the bundle in Sascha's hand. "What is it?"

Sascha shrugged and placed the package on the coffee table. "I don't know. But it's addressed to Sean."

"Unusual time to have something delivered, isn't it?" Kurt questioned, his gaze moving to the carriage clock on the fireplace.

She slipped between them on the sofa. "I guess. It was hand delivered."

Andrei tensed. "It was?"

"Yes." She frowned at him even as she nestled into his side. "That's not unusual. You know messengers come for him at all times."

"I guess." Uneasily, he eyed the box. Sascha was right. Messengers came for Sean at all hours, just rarely at five-to-eleven at night. So, where this churning in his gut had come from, he wasn't sure, and knew he'd have to watch this new tendency he was battling. One that made him want to wrap Sascha up in cotton to keep her safe. That box held no danger. He was just being stupid. "Why didn't you take it into him?"

"Because he called out and said he'd be here in a minute." She reached forward, her hand hovering over her Kindle a second, before she grabbed a magazine she'd placed on the coffee table earlier. Tucking her knees under, she settled the blanket over her lap.

She'd been reading more, he'd definitely noticed that. Her wistful, watchful gaze darting from side to side as she devoured whatever she had on her e-reader at all times of the day and night. The magazines were new, too. She'd never read them before, but now, in the center of the L-seater sofa, on the lower shelf of the driftwood coffee table, there were piles of them.

Hell, piles was an understatement.

This month alone, she'd gone through around five a week. Everything and anything from travel guides to fashion journals. Things he'd never have imagined inspiring her.

She was changing. The stillbirth had done that, and he knew she was still trying to find level ground, but it was odd to learn that his woman continued to have the ability to surprise him.

The fire flickered, reflecting the golden tones in her auburn locks, and his gaze settled on the play of light for a few seconds while she settled deeper into the cushions, then he turned his attention back to the box.

"He's been working hard recently, hasn't he?" Kurt murmured quietly, and Andrei saw that he, too, was looking at the package.

"I figured he was using it as a coping mechanism." Sascha drew her finger over a picture of Mexican flautas. The recipe seemed to hold her attention for a second until she murmured, "We all have our ways of dealing with things."

"What's your way?" Kurt asked, cocking a brow at her.

Andrei could sense the question had surprised her. She stiffened, her finger suddenly pinning the page hard to the blanket beneath her. Because her tension filled him with sorrow, he leaned down and rubbed his chin against her hair. He needed to shave, so the silken strands tugged against his stubble, but she didn't seem to mind.

"I-I don't know."

Kurt reached for her hand, the one she was using to skewer the magazine to her knee. "You can talk to us."

She frowned. "I know I can."

"So, why don't you, *katyonok*?"

"What's to say?"

"I thought Americans loved talking about their feelings," Kurt teased gently, squeezing her fingers in an attempt to coax a smile out of her. It worked, but it was wan. Not like the usual beaming grin that made Andrei's cock hard.

"We do. But I'm not American. I'm British."

"Technicality," Andrei retorted, casting a look at Kurt. They both nodded at one another, having decided now was the time to discuss this matter. "You're American where it counts, and living two decades there counts the most. Plus, you switch back and forth to whatever suits your purpose." His tone turned amused. "Brat."

He felt her swallow, then she whispered, "Why are you doing this?"

"Because you're not making a decision, and you need to," he informed her quietly, pressing his nose into her hair. "We need you to."

"But why?"

He hated the tears in her voice, and by the strain on Kurt's face, he did too. "*Liebchen*, we wouldn't pressure you if it wasn't important. Yet, this house is obviously an issue for you. You wouldn't have raised the subject with Andrei if that were not so."

She lifted her chin and murmured, "Sean would never leave London."

"Why wouldn't I?" asked the man himself, and Andrei peered over at the doorway and saw him standing there, leaning against it.

Sascha gasped a little in surprise. "You love London."

"No, I don't." His smile was wry as he stared at her. "Don't put words in my mouth, darling," he chided.

"I'm not. You're the reason everyone moved here. You all lived in

Oxford originally," she retorted, her voice close to a squeak with indignation.

"I moved for the work. This was where I needed to be. But, more than that, it was the best place to be for transport. I can get anywhere in the country, and the world, by being here. That was my principal decision all those years ago, Sascha, but things have changed."

"You're as dedicated to your job as ever, and living in the countryside isn't exactly something I can see any of you doing. You're the least countrified people I know." She sniffed. "Kurt likes Starbucks too much even though he claims I make the best coffee in the country, Andrei loves Savile Row, Sawyer likes his twenty-four-hour gyms. ..."

Sean shrugged. "So? We can work out something there. Kurt mentioned the other day you were talking about the Jacobie family estate."

"Goddammit, you go crazy when I talk about any of you with the others. That was like the first thing you shared with me, that if I want answers, I have to ask the man himself."

"You're fair game," Kurt retorted, squeezing her fingers again. "You're all that matters to us. That means we need to discuss where your head's at, and honey, of late, I haven't had a damn clue where that is."

She gulped. "How can I tell you something when I don't have the answers myself?"

"Do you blame us for the baby's death?"

Sascha instantly ducked her head, and Andrei shot his friends looks. "No. Of course not."

"Then, what is it?" Sean stepped into the room and closed the door behind him. Moving over to the L-seater sofa, he sat down on the lounger sectional and pressed his elbows to his knees. Behind him, the fire roared, turning his hair darker, and putting half his face in shadow. "Why haven't you named her, Sascha?" he asked, his tone gentle, soft. Andrei recognized it as his 'psychologist' tone of voice. He'd have rolled his eyes if he didn't think Sascha needed to hear that from Sean.

"It's silly to name—" She cut off the words, tears clogging her throat before she could carry on.

"You cut yourself off there to refrain from lying to us," Andrei murmured, trying not to sound annoyed and failing if the way she stiffened at his side was any indication.

"I'm not lying," she whispered.

"Give her a name. Let's put her properly to rest. You know we still haven't picked out a tombstone."

Sascha reached up with her free hand and tugged at her lip. Then, after a minute, she stated, "I don't want to talk about this."

"Well, I do."

"Me, too."

"And I," Kurt finished, all of them in total agreement.

"What's the point? She's dead. I failed her."

Sean frowned. "How did you fail her? You made a decision that had no bearing on the baby. You wanted to go into the city. Whether you were pregnant or not, you could have fallen."

"I should have been more careful. It was my duty to take more care—every pregnant woman knows that. You're men," she hissed. "You don't understand what it's like. Every time I knocked my belly into the damn counter, I felt guilty. Every time you stretch a smidge too far, or do a little bit more work than you're supposed to do, you grimace and promise that you'll rest in the morning. It's what moms do."

"Of course, you do. That's normal. And you went shopping that day. Whether it was for a Christmas gift or to buy a burger. Either way, it doesn't matter. It was an *accident*, Sascha. There is no one to blame for that."

She sniffed. "I disagree." Then, even as Sean was narrowing his eyes at her, she tilted her head to the side and murmured, "I prayed that day, did you know that?"

Her hollow tone had Andrei frowning down at her. "I didn't even know you were religious."

"I'm not. But when I was in that ambulance, I prayed. I prayed so damn hard. And I carried on. When I hit the ER, when they told me there was no heartbeat. I carried on begging for God's help. I-I even begged him to take me instead. To let her live. I said that even though I knew I'd be leaving you all behind." Her fingers tightened on the magazine. "It didn't work."

Silence fell at her words.

Then, Kurt cleared his throat. "Well, I'm glad it didn't."

"Of course, you'd say that," she bit off, her words waspish.

"Nothing and no one is worth sacrificing you, Sascha. You're it for me," Kurt murmured, lifting their bridged hands to his mouth. "I loved our daughter, and I would give anything for you not to have gone through what you experienced, but I'd never swap her for you."

"That's because you're not a mother."

"No, that's because I'm. . . ." He gritted his teeth. "You weren't in your right mind then, Sascha. You weren't, because if you truly had been, you'd have been grateful *you* weren't injured, that *you* weren't being taken from us. What would Tin do without you? How would he feel? What life would he have without his mother there for him? And what about us? We need you, Sascha. You know our relationship is different than anyone else's. How could we move on without you?" His nostrils flared. "We couldn't. That's how. If you'd left us, if you'd made that sacrifice, we'd have been like ghosts."

"Don't be silly," she whispered, but she'd dipped her head again and was refusing to look any of them in the eye.

"I'm not being silly," Kurt immediately countered, then more stridently, he repeated, "I'm not. I mean it. We've waited a hell of a long time for you. Every child we have is a blessing, but you're the biggest blessing of all." Before she could make any kind of denial, Kurt released her hand, tucked his around her waist, then dragged her out of Andrei's arms and tugged her onto his lap. Before she could do more than squeal, his fingers were cupping her chin, and he was forcing her to look into his eyes. "You're my life, Sascha. You're our world. I don't care if that sounds intense. I don't care if it's extreme. We're men of extremes. We're men who live on the outside, on the fringe, and you're what makes us whole. These past three years have made me wish we'd known you sooner. You bring a light to our lives that no other possibly could.

"So, don't you dare tell me that you'd have swapped places with our daughter, because I won't have it. You'd have saved one life and sent the five of us and Tin to our personal hells."

She was trembling when he'd finished. Andrei saw the tremors quiver through her body like miniature earthquakes. But he also saw the tears and knew that somehow, Kurt's words had gotten through to her where other conversations on this topic hadn't.

Even as she was sobbing, Sean murmured, "Sascha, what should we name our daughter?"

A louder sob escaped her. Yet another, and another, until his heart felt like it was going to beat out of his chest. The agony in those sounds pricked his eyes with tears, and the need in him to soothe this pain was so immense, his body strained with tension at the inevitability of knowing there was nothing he could do.

When, eventually, she blurted out, "Camilla," he almost gasped with relief.

Hearing it, Andrei shot Sean a relieved look. The man who was like his brother nodded at him, his own relief evident. "Tomorrow, I will contact the stone mason, and have him create the tombstone."

She shuddered in Kurt's arms as he pressed her tighter into his embrace. He began to rock her from side to side, as though *she* were the baby, and as he did, he mumbled words to her in German. Though Andrei spoke the language, it was hard to hear the words Kurt uttered for he spoke so low. The words meant for Sascha alone.

He'd been right, though.

Kurt had been right on the money.

Another man, another family, might survive the loss of their matriarch, but not this one.

Each of them lived and functioned within their own particular sphere, but only Sascha brought joy to their days. And through her,

Tin. Camilla would have added to that joy, but with no Sascha, there was no joy. Period.

Maybe she was right. Perhaps it was something only a woman could understand. Something only a *mother* could comprehend, but he wasn't a mother. He was a father. And he was a man who adored his woman.

That, and a world with Sascha in it, were the only things that made sense to him.

When she started to calm down, he reached for the remote and switched on the television. Knowing they needed to take a step back after leaping ahead further in seven minutes than they had in seven weeks, he watched as the background noise lulled her into faint hiccoughs, and he turned on a news channel, preferring that nonsense to the other kind that was on at this hour—reruns of *Emmerdale*? He shuddered at the very prospect.

The sight of Sean on the news had him cocking a brow at the man in question who simply grimaced. Sean switched his gaze from the TV and reached for the box on the coffee table. As Sean pulled the two flaps apart, he frowned at the papers inside.

Andrei, not seeing anything unusual in the content—they looked like black and white photographs, something you'd find on CCTV stills—turned back to the news. He lowered the volume even as he strained to hear more.

"You never said another child had been taken." Sascha's voice was a rasp.

"I didn't see the point in upsetting you further."

"If I have to talk about things that hurt me, then you have to talk about things that hurt you." She turned to him, her lips wobbling as she whispered, "I'm not saying that out of tit for tat, I'm saying it because it's the truth. I never thought about it until Glasgow. Until you arrived there that night.

"You're so stoic, Sean, so rigid in some things that it's hard to believe you could be hurting about a case because you bottle things up. Well, that's as unhealthy for you as it is for me."

Sean cocked a brow at her strident tone, but he simply murmured, "There are some things, darling, that you don't want to know."

"Perhaps, but I want to know how you feel."

Sean's eyes trickled over to the news. There was another segment on now, but he replied as though they were still discussing the case of yet another child who'd been snatched. "Useless. That's how I feel."

Andrei narrowed his eyes at that. "Can we help?"

Sean shook his head as he got to his feet. Reaching for the box, he murmured, "This is work. I need to crack on."

Sascha studied him as he headed for the door. "Sean?"

He half-turned to look back at her. "Yes, love?"

"Camilla Angelique Dubois-Bennett."

Only Kurt didn't stiffen at the name; but then, why would he? He'd attended the body with Sascha. Had seen the baby.

"She was his?" Sean rasped.

"She had his hair," Sascha whispered, referring to Sawyer's bright red locks that were, crazily enough, redder than even Sascha's.

Both Andrei and Sean swallowed, but only Sean nodded as he closed the door behind him, shutting them into the lounge, and shutting himself out.

Andrei couldn't blame him. Feeling floored, he turned the volume up and tried to focus on that. Anything but Camilla Angelique Dubois-Bennett.

---

WITH UNEASE MAKING his brow furrow deeper than usual, Andrei began to pace the barrister's office.

Devon, as per goddamn usual, was calm when he should be stressed. He sat opposite their barrister, the attorney who'd be representing them in court, as cool and as collected as Andrei had ever seen him.

He had his legs crossed, one ankle pressed to his knee as he slouched back in the leather and chrome visitor's chair. Sean was at his side. He appeared more ruffled than usual but was engaged with their attorney because he was the only one who spoke 'lawyer bullshit.'

Andrei had a law degree, but economic and criminal law were so far apart on the scales that they might as well have been on opposite sides of the world. So, even though he understood the legalese, he wasn't calm.

Sawyer hadn't said a word, neither had Kurt. They were both by the door, standing like sentinels as they overlooked the interview.

"You can't say that you attacked him because he was stalking you, Devon."

Against his ergonomic monster of a desk chair, Charles Llewelyn rocked back. Not a hair out of place or a crease in sight of his four-thousand-pound suit. He fit in among the clean, minimalist lines of the office, but Devon didn't.

In his ragged jeans and old leather jacket and ratty tee, he looked like he couldn't afford to press the doorbell to this law firm, never mind hire the main partner to defend him.

"But he was," Devon countered, rocking back in the seat. "I warned him to leave me alone, when he didn't. . . ." He shrugged. "I was defending myself."

"There's no proof you were being stalked, mon," Sawyer grumbled, speaking for the first time since Llewelyn had started reeling off the potential sentencing issues that lay ahead for Devon if he lost the case.

With his grandfather not having contacted him with any news yet, good or bad, Andrei had felt it wise to attend this meeting.

Vasily was a Tsar in Russia but his spider-like reach only extended so far. There was always a chance he'd put too much faith in his grandfather's capabilities, even though he hoped he hadn't.

Devon might appear calm now, but Andrei couldn't see him dealing well with being separated from them, even for a short length of time. And *blyad*, Andrei wouldn't deal well with it, either.

Just the prospect of Devon being locked inside a cell made him want to pull his hair out.

His own anxiety and nerves were making him wish he'd brought some heartburn medicine from home. He should have known Devon would drive him to overdose on antacids this morning.

Running a hand over his head, he murmured, "Devon wouldn't say he was being stalked if he wasn't."

"There are several articles that discuss Devon's mental state and suggest he's paranoid."

Sawyer hissed out a breath. "Those articles were about a leak we were having. Corporate espionage, mon. He was bang on the money, too. We did have a bug in one of our company offices in New York."

"You couldn't report that, though, could you? So, all the prosecution knows is that Devon is renowned for being paranoid, so why not on this score, too? A mad genius, infamously famous for being kooky, has gotten it into his head that someone's following him, so he attacks?" Llewelyn shook his head. "No. That route leads to a prison sentence. We need to focus on the fact that where Devon beat his attacker was in a nasty part of the city."

"What were you even doing in Peckham? God, Devon," Sean half-growled, leaning forward and pressing his elbows to his knees as he glowered at him.

"I took the train there." He shrugged. "I wanted to clear my mind."

Andrei sighed. "Since when did you need to clear your mind outside of the house?"

"Is that rhetorical?" Devon demanded, twisting around in the seat to glare at him.

He winced. "I guess."

Devon settled back. "Look. I took the train, and Horowich was there at the station with me when I hopped on. He followed me to Peckham Rye and got off at the same stop I did."

"Maybe he was going home," Llewelyn inserted calmly, earning himself a narrow-eyed stare from Devon.

"Haven't seen him, have you?"

"Not without the bruises you bestowed upon him, no," this time, the attorney's voice was dry. "Even if I'd seen a before picture, he'd be unrecognizable now. You showed true rage when you attacked him."

"He was stalking me," Devon snarled. "I told him not to. He didn't listen. I warned him."

"He claims he was returning from work."

"Where does he work?"

Llewelyn leafed through his files. "Paddington."

"And where does he live?"

"Whitechapel."

Devon snorted. "You haven't looked at a map recently, have you? Or traveled on the underground?"

Sean frowned. "Charles, he isn't wrong. You wouldn't take the tube at a Kensington station if you worked in Paddington, and the trains wouldn't take you to Peckham if you lived in Whitechapel."

"He claims he was having lunch in Kensington."

"And decided to take the long way home?" Devon scoffed, then folded his arms across his chest. "Why haven't the police picked up on this? Did they just decide I was crazy and therefore in the wrong?"

Andrei dug out his cellphone from his pocket and plucked out Google Maps. As he studied the different subway stations in the area, he clucked his tongue. "Someone didn't do their homework."

Llewelyn simply blinked. "Whether or not Mr. Horowich *was* stalking Devon doesn't give him leave to beat the shit out of him." The attorney pursed his lips and rocked back in his seat. "Sean, you know that's not how this works. It isn't jungle justice."

Sean had known Llewelyn for a long time. Long enough for him to call in this favor. Llewelyn's caseload was enough to drown him, but he'd gathered enough time to represent Devon.

"If he was stalking him, then Devon would have a justifiable reason to feel threatened, though," Kurt countered.

"And that would give him a reason to go to the police with his concerns, not break the man's orbital socket, dislocate his shoulder, and puncture his lung via two broken ribs!"

Andrei winced. Since when had Devon been able to rain hell on a man like that?

Even as he was wincing, though, he had to face facts. Devon *had* done that to another person when, as far as he knew, Dev had never hurt anyone in his life. Not even his fucking father who'd practically handed his mother the razor blades she'd used to slash her wrists.

Though things had been unstable at home because of Camilla's passing, Devon hadn't shown any signs of deterioration–nothing to this extent. And though he felt like he was biased–because hell, this was Devon–Andrei knew that he wouldn't have done anything like this unless he truly had felt threatened.

But the law, as Llewelyn had stated, didn't work that way.

"You think a sentence is likely, Charles?" Sean fretted, clasping his hands together as he hung them between his legs. The way he was crouched forward stated that his asking the question was a formality. He already knew the answer.

"Yes."

Andrei felt them all, save Devon, deflate in the room. Why he was so calm, Andrei didn't know. Andrei wanted to shake him, demand to know what the fuck he'd been thinking of when he'd gone after Horowich the way he had.

Didn't the bastard care that this would wreck Sascha?

On the two previous occasions where they'd had meetings with Llewelyn, they'd encouraged her to stay at home with Tin and had fed her positive news. So much so that she thought Devon was close to being free and fucking clear because it was all a 'misunderstanding.'

How were they going to break the truth to her?

The answer was they couldn't. His grandfather would have to come through for them, even if Andrei had to bribe him with the promise of several month-long visits to Moscow this coming year.

Devon couldn't go to jail.

And that was that.

---

"WHAT ARE WE MAKING, MAMA?"

Tin stared at her expectantly, and she had to laugh. His eyes were like sparkly blue marbles glinting up at her. The intelligence within them was enough to boggle the mind, and it was for that reason, and that reason alone, that she asked, "What do you think we're making, Tin?" She waved her hand at the ingredients on the marble counter.

He tilted his head to the side, that mop of blond curls falling over his forehead as he scowled at the flour, eggs, butter, and coconut sugar. "I don't know. You make too many things with that stuff."

She grinned, then from under the counter, began shaking a bag at him.

"Chocolate chips?" he cried. "Cookies?"

She pressed her finger to her mouth. "Who don't we tell?"

"Papa Sawyer," Tin whispered.

"And why don't we tell him?"

"Because he's an alien."

She snorted at that. "I didn't teach you that one. Who did?"

His eyes twinkled. "Daddy Devon."

She was used to him mixing up his Papas and Daddies, but it always amused the hell out of her when he said their names afterward. She'd never thought she'd be in a relationship that required first names be tagged on after the title, but she wouldn't have changed a damn thing.

"You know that's mean of Daddy Devon, don't you?"

Tin, of course, shrugged—his hero could do no wrong. "I don't see why. I love him if he's an alien or not."

"Well, that's good to hear, baby," she teased, and then she moved around the counter to haul him onto the chilly marble. He wiggled his bum a second, prompting her to ask, "Need a cushion?" They were already breaking enough food hygiene laws to break Devon out in a rash, but hell, what was one more busted rule?

"Nope." This time, when he wiggled, she realized he was excited.

It *had* been quite a while since they'd done this together. Something last night's conversation over Camilla had urged her to remember.

The cookie recipe wasn't something she needed a recipe book for. It was glued to her retinas, but she prompted Tin, helping him do most of the lifting, even if he helped her with the weighing—he used a spoon to measure out the flour and sugar, and didn't even get much on the counter. She figured she had Devon to thank for that.

He wasn't exactly a neat freak in his office, but in other parts of his life, he was, and Tin, ever prudent when it came down to copying Devon, had noticed that. She wasn't even sure how that was possible, but when she'd watched Devon coloring with Tin, she'd learned a few things. Because Devon stuck his tongue out as he colored between the lines, so did their son. And Tin never went out of the lines, either.

This kid was spooky.

It was a seriously good thing she was used to being around weirdos.

*God love them.*

Mixing it with a spoon, she broke another rule and let him lick it clean as she dosed out the mix onto a baking tray. He sat there, watching as she placed them in the pre-heated oven, and clapped his hands as he glued his eyes to the clock on the back wall.

"They'll be ready in fifteen minutes, Tin. When's that?"

"When the big hand gets to number three."

"Good boy." She ruffled his hair and dipped down to press a kiss to his cheek. His little arms clambered around her neck to hold her close, and she picked him up, letting his legs hang loose as she whirled in a circle. His giddy laugh had her joining him, and that was how Sawyer and Devon found them.

"What's this I smell?" Sawyer asked in a grumbly voice, but he had a grin on his face.

"Cookies!" Tin squealed happily, immediately forgetting their vow not to say a word about the sweet treat.

"Chocolate chip?" Devon inquired, hurrying over to the oven to peer through the glass. "Score," he declared, pumping his fist—Tin quickly repeated both the word and the gesture.

Even if the gesture almost had him punching her nose.

"Easy there, champ," Sawyer remarked, chuckling as he hefted their son out of Sascha's arms and above his head. "Seat yer'sen down, wee laddie."

Giggling, Tin perched himself on Sawyer's shoulders and stayed there, even as his father took a seat at the dining table. She was used to the sight, even though it was still funny as hell. Tin, though, liked being tall, and he couldn't get much taller than this.

"How long?" Devon demanded, shoving his fists in his pockets as he stared longingly at the oven.

"When, Tin?"

"When the big hand gets to number three," he cried again, twisting to look at Devon. "I helped, Daddy. I counted everything out."

"Good boy, Tin," Devon immediately congratulated, but he didn't turn around, just kept his eyes on the oven.

"Do you guys want something to drink? Eat?"

Sawyer shook his head. "Whisht, lass. We just came to see you."

"Did the meeting go well?" They'd all headed out this morning.

Sawyer grimaced. "Not particularly."

"Need some sugar?" she teased, his tone pricking her with concern.

"Yes. Your sugar and cookies, too," Devon mumbled, honest to a fault.

Laughing, she murmured, "You're a little early to that party. You know they're better if you let them cool some." Hers got chewier, and Devon preferred them like that.

"No. I need one sooner than that. Andrei's changed the timeline on us," he complained.

"I'm sure he didn't do it on purpose," she replied, wondering why he sounded peeved. Devon usually thrived on that kind of pressure.

"Andrei doesn't care if he does something on purpose or not. Pompous. ..." Devon mumbled something that had Sawyer snorting but her tugging at her ear.

"Was I supposed to hear that or not?" she questioned drily.

"Not," Sawyer replied, then he shifted his gaze from her to her charm bracelet. "He's just miffed because we're going to have to go to Veronia sooner rather than later."

"Is that a bad thing?"

"Andrei knows I have to work myself up to flying," Devon countered, stacking his hands on his hips as he turned to glower at them. "He knows that when I have to go near the sea, I need even more time."

"He gave you three months, Devon," Sawyer groused. "Three. He's shifting it forward by a month."

"We're going next month?" Sascha inserted, her pitch soaring in surprise.

Sawyer nodded, but there was a plea on his face—one that begged her not to make a fuss about it. "Yes. Aren't you looking forward to seeing Madela?"

She rolled her eyes. "Yes, I can't wait."

Devon sniffed. "You don't *have* to wait. Not now Andrei's messed everything up."

"Is my name being taken in vain?" Andrei commented wryly as he stepped down the staircase, his feet making an appearance before his face did.

"In vain? Papa Sawyer, what's that mean?" Tin asked, tugging at Sawyer's hair.

"Nothing for you to worry yer head about, wee lad," Sawyer replied, and though Tin pouted, he settled down, his eyes big as he took in his father's face.

Andrei walked over to him and tugged Tin off Sawyer's shoulders and hauled him onto his own. Sascha swore the child had to feel more like a bag of flour than a little boy. The way they lugged him about—it was no wonder he enjoyed flying, the one difference between him and Devon.

When Andrei strolled over to the oven, he wrapped his arm around Devon's shoulder and said, "All will be well."

She frowned. "Why wouldn't it be?" Why did she feel like two conversations were going on here?

Andrei didn't answer, just cleared his throat and, to Devon, murmured, "Stop grumbling. You'll love it there. You know you will."

"Why?" Devon was definitely pouting—most unlike him, Sascha thought with a frown.

"Because it's warm. And that means Sascha can sunbathe."

Devon's eyes, like Tin's earlier, rounded as he turned to look at her. But she held up her hands. "Oh no. I'm not suffering with premature wrinkles just to make boy genius over there happy."

Devon pouted, but Andrei squinted at her. "What do I have to do to make the bikini happen?" he inquired.

She snorted. "Buy me one first."

He rolled his eyes. "Done."

"I'm not having you pawn that off onto your PA." The last thing she wanted was to tell Jane her damn size. "You want that to happen, you have to go into Harvey Nicks with me."

"I can deal with that particular torment if you try them on, and I get to watch."

"I'll come, too," Devon quickly inserted.

"Me, three," Sawyer said on a grin.

"Me, four," Tin commented, his voice squeaky with an excitement that told Sascha he had no idea what he was signing up for. The kid didn't mind shopping, but that was because it usually involved him getting new stuff. This would be about her, and therefore, it would bore him senseless. Not that it made him mean, it was just that the most normal thing about him was his attention span.

He *was* thirty months after all.

Sascha pursed her lips. "You can't buy me off that easily, Andrei Kirov."

His grin said he could do whatever he wanted, and that made her narrow her eyes at him. "Whatever my lady desires," he said magnanimously.

"I'll think of something," she retorted, and was saved by the bell when the oven timer went off. She didn't need to move, though, Devon had grabbed the oven mitts and was opening the door and grabbing the tray before she could do more than blink.

She was pretty proud when Devon, about to dump the tray on thc hcating pad, paused as Tin said, "No, Daddy, that's wrong. You have to put the cookies on that." He pointed to the cooling tray.

Sascha beamed at him. "Well remembered, Tin. We'll make a chef out of you yet."

"Give me a baker any day of the week," Devon retorted, and Tin, sensing the praise in the words, puffed out his chest.

She laughed at the sight, then asked, "Where are we staying in Madela?"

"In one of the Royal residences."

That had her eyes widening. "Seriously?"

Andrei grinned. "Thought you'd get a kick out of that."

"Just a tad," she whispered. "What kind of royal residence?"

"Xavier DeSauvier is my liaison. I told him I'd be bringing a party of six with me. He said he'd make arrangements that would put us close to the seat."

"What seat?"

"The government's seat," he explained. "Madela is the capital, but it's pretty big. The Royals' main residence isn't far from their Parliament."

"And that's where you'll be working?"

"To be honest, I'm not sure. I get the feeling King Edward does a lot of work at the Palace." Andrei shrugged. "It seems like he's the one we need to please. Not the politicians."

"Why?" Sascha asked, well used to the ways of the English monarchy where the Queen had little power over the government anymore.

"Because that's how it works over there." Andrei shrugged. "I think I'm a pet project of Xavier's. He's the Duke of Ansian and Lorrena."

"What makes you say that?"

"Because Xavier pretty much told me that whatever theories or agendas we come up with, we'll have to sell them."

That had Devon grumbling in the background as he poured himself some milk.

"They won't be cool enough yet," she murmured, cutting him a look as he eyed the molten treats.

"And you shouldn't be having any anyway. Not this close to dinner," Sawyer chided.

Devon just huffed. "Who died and made you king of the kitchen?"

Sascha lifted her brows. "Devon, was that a joke?"

Just as Tin had done moments before, his chest puffed out. "It was. It was good too, wasn't it?"

"Sounded like it belonged in a Christmas cracker," Sawyer groused.

"Speaking of, what will we be doing for Christmas? Will it be here or will we go early to have it in Madela?"

Andrei cut her a look. "I'd love it if we could have it in Moscow."

That had her jolting in surprise. "Really?"

"*Da*," he said with a grimace. "Because Devon was naughty that was Vasily's payment for him cleaning his slate."

Sascha's eyes widened again, even as she took a look at Devon who was hiding his face behind a big cookie—his cheeks were still bright red, though. Good. They should be, dammit.

When Devon had been arrested, and words like 'aggravated assault' had been bandied around at the police station, she'd been terrified at the prospect of him being locked away from her. And, the worst part was?

He probably would have been if some very expensive attorneys hadn't gotten involved.

She really hated that money talked, but equally, was glad it had.

And yeah, she knew that made her elitist scum.

"How did he clean that up?" she asked, her voice wary.

Andrei just shot her a look. "Best not to ask that particular question, Sascha."

She grimaced—knowing he spoke the truth. Jesus, Vasily's powers, and from such a distance, were unbelievable. It was frightening what he could do from Moscow.

"Guess that means you have two flights in your future, Devon," Sawyer said cheerily, and she just knew he was getting a kick out of Devon's suffering.

The man in question just reached for another cookie.

It was for the best.

That was the only place he'd find any comfort—Sascha wasn't peddling any on this particular topic.

Not when his arrest had scared the hell out of her.

She didn't even like to think back to that morning, and while it was the height of unfairness that Devon was free as a bird when he'd done what he had, she could only feel relief that it wouldn't affect their future.

Thank God for expensive lawyers.

The prospect of him being imprisoned had given her nightmares at a time when sleeping had been arduous anyway. So, nope, no comfort was coming his way Sascha-style. He'd just have to deal with the two flights and a rushed schedule without any interference from her.

# TWELVE

"THANK you for making this so painless."

Sascha snorted while she rifled through the rack of bikinis. As she bowed her head, the harsh overhead lighting in the store made her hair gleam, while darkening some tones to black. Even as he studied her, she was intent on finding something she liked.

"Hardly painless."

"Well, more so than Devon. The man's a big baby when it comes to flying." His grumble had her grinning.

"And you're not when it comes down to seagulls?"

He grunted. "That was one seagull. One time. *Blyad*, you'd think I started weeping whenever I saw them."

"Don't you?" she laughed, and danced out of the way when he growled and came for her. She hid behind a stack of bikinis that would have Devon's heart stiffening, never mind his cock. "You can guess again if you think I'm wearing *that*," Sascha immediately retorted, dancing out from behind that stack of bikinis and onto another one. "I need melon smugglers for these babies now."

He grunted. "You won't hear any of us complaining about the melons."

"No. Just me and my back."

"I'd like to offer my services as a bra."

That had laughter pealing from her. "Oh, for what purpose? General, everyday support or sports?"

"I'll gladly take on both challenges."

"You're too kind," she teased, and then picked up another low-cut blue bikini that matched Sean's eyes. Even as she did so, she eyed the pile and shook her head. "I can't believe you've talked me into a bikini."

"Technically, Devon did that."

She sighed. "I know. What that man can do with his eyes. Thank God, he doesn't realize it."

Andrei hid a smile—Devon *had* realized it a while back. He only used the technique for important matters like bikinis and larger portions for dessert.

"You look gorgeous in a bikini."

"I don't feel gorgeous," she groused, but it was mumbled more under her breath.

"Why would I lie?" he retorted easily, and the ease of his words had her peering at him, then shaking her head.

"I swear, you have some kind of filter where I'm concerned. It's like an ophthalmic Photoshop." She shrugged. "Who am I to complain?"

He smirked. "Exactly. Just enjoy the benefits," he murmured as he sneaked behind her, pressed his hand to her belly, and jerked his dick into the soft swell of her ass.

She snickered. "Perv."

"Hardly," he chided. "Fucking you in changing rooms is Sean's vice."

"True that," she said on a sigh that seemed reminiscent of the amount of fun she'd had in changing rooms over the years.

Shaking his head, Andrei murmured, "If you prefer a one-piece, go for that. You know Devon is just happy when the number of clothes you're wearing is less than two."

"He and Kurt should have been switched at birth. I swear, Devon is more German than Kurt."

"What makes you say that?" he asked on a hum, as he perused a particularly nice gold and brown one-piece that would make Sascha's hair pop.

"The fact that Devon is a born naturist. Only the fact that he knows Tin will start doing it, too, makes him control himself. I can't cope with Tin pulling that crap on me as well. Can you imagine if he tried to do it when we were out?" She pressed a hand to her chest. "I made Devon promise to always wear clothes when Tin's awake."

"That's why I haven't seen too much of his cock of late, then," he mused.

"Yes. That's why." Her prim tone made his lips twitch. "Tin already mimics Devon's every move, I'd like to try to avoid the worst of his habits until he can understand the repercussions of his actions."

Andrei decided it was prudent to change the topic. "You've got a busy couple of months ahead of you."

"I know." She winced. "It will be okay, though."

"Will it?" He cocked a brow at her. "You sure you're ready?"

"I was born ready," she teased, but her eyes were soft as she glanced back at him. "Thank you for asking, sweetheart, but no, I promise, I'll be fine."

"Moscow for Christmas, Madela for the next four months minimum, and then at some point, you're going to Germany with Kurt, aren't you?"

"Yes. Just for a week or two in late January, though. The production team wants to meet with him once their base is set up there."

"You don't sound too excited."

She shrugged. "What's to be excited about?"

"A Hollywood movie? Stars of the golden screen?"

That had her rolling her eyes. "Dreyford's a creep, Masterson, the director, probably picked Jennifer Houghton because of her tits, and that cat, I swear, drooled over Kurt more because he was taken."

"They certainly made an impression," he commented drily.

"Oh, that they did." She glowered at the one piece in her hand. "I mean, what's with that anyway? What kind of tramp goes after a guy she knows is taken?"

"Some women get their kicks like that, *katyonok*."

"Well, it's just wrong." She huffed.

"She probably thinks she'll be able to twist Kurt around her finger. Get perks, or something."

Sascha narrowed her eyes at him. "You could be right. She was bitching about not having enough lines."

"There you are then," he said. "She'd like to make him want her so that she can abuse his good nature."

"But I was there. Why would she think I'd allow that to happen?"

"Not all women are like you. Not all men are as faithful, either."

"Why am I different?"

"Because you are." His smile was gentle. "Kurt said it all the other night. You're our everything." Her brow puckered at his words, and he reached up to rub his thumb across her forehead. "There's no need to frown. You need feel no pressure."

She blew out a breath at his words. "How can I not? You make it sound like you can't live without me. That's a lot to handle when you have five men and a kid, Andrei." The last she muttered on a whisper as she peered over the stalls around them.

They were in a department store where different designers held different sectionals. At the moment, they were in the swimwear area, and their sectional was demure, with lots of browns, blues, and muted shades. Beside them, there were neon colors, and another held things like flowy kaftans and wraps. He'd never imagined himself standing amid such feminine fripperies, but for Sascha, he'd walk through the makeup stands, too.

That was the power she had over him.

"It need not be. Just be aware of how much we love you, and what we'll do to protect you."

She tilted her head to the side. "How do you know how to protect me when I don't?"

"That's a funny question."

She shrugged, but her eyes darted up to his and back down. "Maybe."

He reached over and tilted her chin up, so she was looking directly at him. "Explain, Sascha."

"I-I don't know what I'm saying," she grumbled, tugging her chin free from his gentle grasp.

Now why did he think that was a lie?

"I want to meet Margritte."

Andrei cocked a brow at her. "Have you asked Kurt?" He already knew the answer. Any mention of his mother's name had Kurt hiding his woes in Sauerkraut, and as far as he was aware, the house had been blessedly empty of the noxious stuff.

"No." She pursed her lips. "I think it's time. Don't you? In fact, I want to meet everyone's family. I'm here, and I'm not going anywhere." Sascha jerked her chin up. "I think it's time they recognized that."

He smirked. "This means war?"

Her eyes sparked fire. "So be it."

It probably would be, truth be told, if Margritte and Sascha were in the same room for long.

"I'll talk to Kurt about it."

She smiled at him, and he knew that was the answer she'd been hoping for. The little witch had just wrapped him around her finger.

Good thing that was the only place he wanted to be, he thought drily.

When his cellphone buzzed and he saw his grandfather's name on the Caller ID, trepidation flared to life. He reached down and bussed her temple. "I need to take this. You okay?"

She winked. "*Da*."

"I'll make a Russian out of you yet," he joked, laughing when she shooed him away. The minute he was at the other side of the sectional, he connected the call and greeted Vasily. "Everything okay, Grandfather?"

"When isn't it?"

Andrei sighed, relief powering through him with such intensity that he pressed his hand to the wall to prop himself upright. "You found something." It was a statement, not a question.

"Of course." Vasily sniffed. "My one impediment was the delay. It's harder to grease palms when the courts are in motion, but I have my ways."

"Thank you."

"I didn't do it for you."

That had him raising a brow. "You didn't?"

"No. I did it for Sascha. I have no doubt that Devon thinks he'd be okay in a jail cell so long as they gave him a scientific calculator, but Sascha?" he grunted. "She's been through enough."

That was probably about as much as Vasily would ever admit to knowing about their unusual arrangement.

"Regardless, thank you. You've taken a weight off my mind. We visited with his attorney the other day, and they said a custodial sentence was likely."

"Yes. It was," Vasily murmured. "Aren't you grateful I keep my fingers on the pulse?"

"The pulse of what?" he asked warily.

A cackle escaped his grandfather. "People in authority shouldn't sleep with hookers. No matter how high-class they are, there's always a pimp who can be bought."

Andrei wanted to groan, but how could he when his grandfather had yielded the result they needed?

"I don't need to know anymore," he grumbled.

"Prude," Vasily retorted, then he softened his tone, and stated, "Make the boy suffer. Don't tell him he's free and clear just yet, lest he takes it into his head that he's Rambo."

"I don't think that's a concern. He insists the man he attacked was stalking him."

Silence rang down the line. "Stalking him? As in following him around?"

"Yes."

"And you don't believe him?"

"I don't know what to believe. I'd prefer not to think he has a stalker, but the man, Horowich, had no justifiable reason for being in Peckham. At least, not according to the police reports."

Vasily hummed under his breath, and Andrei, recognizing what that meant, didn't bother to even wince when Vasily said, "Leave it to me."

Then, he cut the call.

Andrei didn't have it in him to be too peeved. Devon was free, Sascha wouldn't have to worry, and Andrei would be able to take his resident Brainiac to Veronia without any issues at Border Control. Throw in the fact that Vasily might discover something the police hadn't, and could shed light on the darkest corners of this unusual situation, in his eyes, it was a definite win-win situation.

---

AS SASCHA STARED straight up at the ceiling, she took advantage of the space in the bed.

Not that she appreciated the space, of course, but it was nice to spread out and starfish. She wiggled her feet, then wiggled her hands, and then she told each extremity to sleep.

She tried to make her calves and forearms do the same, but that was where she struggled with the meditation technique. Relaxing was hard.

Hard enough that she could empathize with Devon.

Since the accident, it had been tougher to catch some Zzzs.

When she stared at the ceiling for the next ten minutes, she rolled onto her side and picked up her kindle. She was in the middle of another Bratva romance, and this one had some scenes in it that made her edgy.

As she dove into the book, into the forbidden love story between the daughter of a police commissioner and a Brigadier in the Bratva brotherhood in Brooklyn Beach, she felt her pussy grow wet when the hero started spanking the heroine.

She knew what that felt like, after all.

Sascha had often felt the sting of Sean's palm against her ass. All her men were a bit kinky. All of them liked their pleasure with an edge. Sawyer had whooped her butt with a spoon once, and before she'd announced she was pregnant, Andrei had started to. ...

She swallowed at the memory and reached up to cup her throat. He'd cupped her there as he'd done today. When she'd been in the swimwear section of Harvey Nichols, he'd grabbed her chin, then lowered his palm to hold her throat.

His grasp had been firm. Strong. Unmovable.

And the memory had sent shockwaves through her pussy.

It wasn't the first time since the accident that she'd felt the stirrings of arousal. But it was the first time she acted upon it. The memory of what he'd done to her, combined with the sensual scene she was reading, had her sliding her hand over her belly and dipping under her pajamas to find some semblance of relief.

A part of her was content to move on, but another part felt guilty. The former held more power though as the need for release swirled deep in her belly. The ache was insistent. Too persistent to ignore. She'd loved the feel of his hand around her throat, and knew, from her books, that it wasn't too odd.

The notion of his being in control, of controlling even *that*–the oxygen she breathed–ignited fireworks in her bloodstream.

As she found her clit, she wasn't altogether surprised to realize how wet she was. She'd only read part of the scene, but thinking of the pressure of his fingers at her throat as he fucked into her, had done most of the work.

With the heel of her hand, she rotated her wrist to rub her clit while she explored her sex with her fingers. The liquid was slick and made it easy to slide two digits inside her pussy. As she pumped her hand, she closed her eyes and let the insidious feelings work against her.

With her other hand, she lifted her arm and covered her eyes with the back of her wrist. The move squished her head into the pillow, so when the door opened, she didn't hear the gentle click over the heavy sounds of her breathing.

What she *did* hear was the slight squeak of the bed as the mattress dipped under another's weight.

She wasn't sure whether to be mortified or turned on. It wasn't the first time she'd masturbated in front of her guys—Kurt, especially, loved watching her do that—but it was the first time they'd caught her in the act.

She turned her head and lowered her arm and found Sean there, his hand on her kindle as he perused the glowing screen. She watched him as he read, but didn't move her fingers away from her clit.

"Which part of this made you touch yourself?" he asked, and in the light from the screen, she saw the heavy lids that indicated he was turned on.

The simplicity of his reaction made her suck down a sharp breath as need slalomed inside her. Somehow, it was delicious for him to know what she'd been reading, and even more so that he knew what she was doing.

They were in the dark, and the faint light from the hallway wouldn't have illuminated much considering the bed was on the other side of the room from the doorway.

Her tongue felt thick in her mouth as she whispered, "The wand." The Brigadier hero had managed to magick up a vibrating wand. He'd tied it with duct tape to the heroine's thigh and kept it tucked tightly against her pussy. She didn't even care how much it would hurt later to have that duct tape removed, just the idea of it had her growing wetter.

He hummed under his breath. "Do you know what that's called?"

She stiffened. "Which part?"

His laughter washed over her, bringing her nerve endings to life again. "The scene."

The scene? Sascha frowned, but slowly rolled her head from side to side in response.

"A forced orgasm."

"I-I guess that makes sense." Especially because the guy had made the heroine come twice in barely any time at all.

Another hum. "I'm surprised you enjoy this kind of thing."

That had her hand stilling. "Why?"

About to lambast him for denigrating romance, he surprised her by murmuring, "I wasn't sure if you liked this kind of treatment."

"Just because I read it, doesn't mean I like it," she replied immediately. Then tempered that by adding, "But the kinky stuff? Why would you think I didn't like it?" Jesus, she grew wetter than a swimming pool whenever they did anything like that to her. And it didn't happen often enough for her liking.

Of late, with her sex drive in the dark after the accident, she'd been waiting for one of them to. ... She grimaced, unsure what she'd been waiting on.

One of them to take control?

To take control from her?

The notion made her grimace again.

"Sascha?"

Sean's voice wasn't hesitant, but there was a bite to it that made her freeze a little.

"Yes?"

"Do you need more from us than you're saying?"

Her eyes flared wide, but it didn't help. It wasn't like she could see much in the dark. "Umm."

"That's no answer." His voice was like silk now. It seemed to swirl around her, drawing her nerve endings to life in a way that made her want to shiver and wriggle against the sheets simultaneously.

"What do you want me to say?" It was a copout answer, but it was truthful. And even in the dark of night, she wasn't sure she could confess to wanting something she couldn't put into words yet.

Did she need more from them?

Maybe.

At this moment, she needed them to take this weight off her. A weight that Kurt had helped her with the other night, but it was more than that.

She needed to not be in charge, she guessed. She needed them to be.

A breath blew from her lips at the thought, but she struggled with how to formulate that into words without choking on them.

"Sascha?"

She stilled again and her voice was quiet as she whispered, "Yes, Sean?"

"Move your hand away from your pussy. And lay it on the sheet." There was something in his voice that she only ever heard Sean use when he was telling Tin off—and even then, it was for his own safety. Like when Tin had shoved two pencils up his nose and was dancing around the room—Sean had seen that before her, but he'd told their son off immediately for being silly, and, as they always did, had explained how he could hurt himself if he'd fallen over with the pencils there.

It was an odd tone to hear at that moment, but she recognized the authority in it.

Recognized it and wasn't perturbed by it.

She even obeyed.

Without conscious thought, she moved her hand away from her pussy and slid it out from her PJ bottoms. She lifted the sheet and pressed her hand to the top of it like he'd requested.

She felt his fingers trail over the back of her hand then up to her pointer finger. "My, my, how wet you are," he whispered, and he grabbed her wrist and lifted her hand in the air.

She knew what was about to happen, but even though she was prepared for it, she inhaled a sharp breath as he sucked both digits into his mouth and swirled his tongue around one, then the other.

A shiver rattled down her spine at the contact that immediately had her hips rocking and her thighs tensing. She knew what that tongue was capable of. Knew how he could make her scream, how he could make her moan and writhe with desperation.

He could give and he could withhold.

She knew that.

There'd always been that threat with Sean. It was the same with Devon, too.

Both would give when they wanted to. Unlike Devon, who could make her sob by withholding pleasure from her, Sean was generous and always left her satisfied. Even if it was by his will alone. She'd always known that about him, but it was funny how she only recognized how similar that was to the Brigadier in her book *now*.

He nipped the tip of her finger, then murmured, "Don't come unless I tell you to, okay?"

Sascha didn't have it in her to complain. "Okay, Sean."

Another hum. The vibration seemed to wriggle through her body, setting parts of her alight with a warmth like no other. "Get out of bed and strip for me."

She did as bade, seeing nothing wrong in the order as she slipped out and stripped.

"Now, roll onto your belly on top of the duvet."

While she cocked a brow at that, again, she obeyed. She heard rustling sounds and assumed he was stripping, too—a prospect that filled her with delight—and then she felt his hands on her ass.

The man's night vision had to be excellent for him to see her butt in the darkness of the room. There was little to no outside light that could illuminate the way for him, and yet, he seemed to be able to get his way around without turning a light on.

And, truth be told, she was glad for that.

Whatever experiment he was playing, she was glad it was in the shadows.

He squeezed her ass cheeks with both hands, rubbing them and drawing them apart. As the air kissed her ass, she bit her lip. She wasn't unused to being touched there—with five men, it was a go-to spot, and she was grateful she enjoyed it. But still, something about the way Sean was touching her made her supremely aware of the pucker.

When he released the mounds, her lips parted on a breath as she waited for what was about to happen. When it came, she closed her eyes and released the breath as his hand connected with her butt, making it jiggle.

She didn't even have it in her to wish her ass was tauter as he did it again. Three more times to make five.

"Do you know why I did that?" he asked, and she was satisfied to hear his voice was thick.

"Because you think I want it?"

That made him snicker. "No." His knees pinned her down by settling on either side of her lower thighs. His hands made fists, and he pressed them beside her arms as he leaned down and whispered in her ear, "That's for thinking you could leave us. I settled on five because I could give you a thousand and it would never be enough punishment for thinking you could abandon us."

She jerked back at that, but before she could utter a word, his teeth settled on her shoulder and he bit down. She yelped, jolting at the pain, then even as she winced, she let out a hiss as that pain settled deep in her belly.

*Why did that feel good?*

The question was wailed internally. She didn't verbalize it. Couldn't.

Just knew that ache felt right.

It made her blow out a breath again.

"That's going to leave a mark," he told her, and there was such satisfaction in his voice that it had the same effect as a blanket on a cold winter's day. She wanted to roll herself up in it like a goddamn human sausage—a thought that had her lips twitching. His nose ran down the side of her cheek, making her jump. "Do you like the idea of that?"

It came as a surprise to realize that yes, she did.

But she didn't say that, not until his hand slapped her ass again. "Do you like the idea of that? Of bearing my mark? Of people seeing it and knowing that your man gave it to you?"

"Yes, Sean," she whispered, and felt her pussy grow wetter at her timbre.

Jesus, was that her?

That sultry, submissive tone belonged to her?

She gnawed at her bottom lip as, after shifting his position, he murmured, "Spread your legs." She parted them, grunting as he pinched her butt. "Wider." She did, moving them apart to a degree that was borderline uncomfortable—she felt the strain in her inner thighs. Then, his hands made it all better as he stroked between her legs, coating his fingers in her cream.

Shivering, she murmured, "That feels so good, Sean."

He kissed her cheek. "Why does it?"

"I don't know."

"Would it feel different if I'd come in here and just rolled on top of you?"

She thought about that a second, then squealed when two fingers plunged their way inside her gate. God, she was wet, but they felt really big after months of inactivity. A shudder washed through her as she acclimated to the new thickness, and he let her. Let her breathe and relax in increments.

"Yes. It feels different."

As though to reward her for the answer, he carefully removed his fingers. But she clenched down on them, liking them there, wanting them there.

"Why?"

"Because. . . ." Why? Because he was acting on his own? Wasn't waiting for cues from her? Or, was he? Was he waiting for cues that she didn't know she was emitting?

His other hand pinched her butt again, making her firm the cheeks in response and let out a mewl. "Ow!" she cried, because shit, that stung like hell.

"Answer me then."

"I don't have a say in this."

"You always have a say in the things we do," he murmured, and his voice was so close to a purr, it sent shockwaves down her spine.

"I guess. But. . . ." She'd read enough BDSM romance to know how it worked. To know that she was in control because of how much she trusted Sean. When she didn't want to play, he'd have to stop if he was a good Dominant. But that didn't mean to say he *was* a good Dominant.

There was always that threat of having your wishes totally ignored.

A notion that stole her breath again.

Not in fear, but excitement.

"What made your breathing hitch there?" he asked, thrusting his fingers inside her again.

"I-I don't want to think, Sean. Let me stop thinking, please?"

He must have heard the plea in her voice because he didn't pinch her again, just fell silent as he stroked her butt. But even if he was contemplative, that wasn't enough for her. Not with his thick fingers filling her. She wriggled and writhed beneath him, and he surprised her by spreading his fingers apart, scissoring them wide.

He did that a few times, then he pulled out of her and half-leaped off the bed. About to grumble, she fell silent again when he ordered, "Don't move a goddamn inch."

That bite was back again, and fuck if it didn't make her cream harder.

She even stopped fidgeting, stopped rolling her hips and rocking into the bed. He'd only spanked her so far, but she knew what was in his bedroom. If he wanted to take this up a notch, the only thing he had close at hand was a belt. She sure as hell didn't want to be hit by a fucking belt.

The sound of his feet padding against the floor was the only indication she had of his proximity. Her eyes weren't covered by a blindfold, but they might as well have been for all she could see.

The blanket of darkness seemed to cosset her. Cushion her from the real world, and she loved that. She *needed* that cushion. Wanted him to wrap her in it for the moment, take her away from herself, and place her somewhere safe and warm, somewhere that was theirs alone.

She moaned when she felt the silk around her ankles. From the shape of the material, she knew it was a tie. "I'm going to grab your ankles," he told her, but it wasn't like he was asking for permission. He was advising her to prepare herself.

Sascha found she enjoyed that.

He could have just dragged her where he wanted her to go, but he hadn't. Even in this, Sean was a gentleman.

The Gentleman Dom?

Her lips twitched. Maybe.

Then, she squeaked anyway as he did as he'd warned. When he moved one foot wider than was comfortable, she didn't protest, curious as to where he'd take this. She knew if he hurt her, genuinely, he'd stop the minute she asked him to, but she didn't want to, and she knew that was where her faith in him came into play.

There was no need for a safe word with Sean.

She had no need to cry wolf. No need to beg him to stop, because the minute she did, that was the minute the fun would come to a halt, and this? Sure, she knew he was getting off on it. But for her? She really wanted this. No, a part of her *craved* it. Craved him.

He was always so in control. Always collected.

She'd never wanted to break that control, didn't even think she could. But now? The notion thrilled her.

Had he wanted more from her than she'd realized? Had he been holding back on *her*? The idea displeased her, but she didn't have long to be upset because she felt him grab the tie and heard the sound of fabric crossing as he knotted it to the foot of the bed. When he did the same with the other foot, she clenched her hands at the deeper ache in her thighs. She was spread wide open now, tied and fixed to the low footboard.

"How do you feel?" His hand slid over her calves. She'd pointed her toes in an arch, and she wasn't sure why, but he rubbed the taut muscles of her lower legs, which had her toes curling in delight.

"Like I can't move," she murmured drily.

"Well, you can't," he remarked, but she heard the smile in his voice. "How does that make you feel?"

She thought about it, then as the answer whispered in her mind, she pressed her face into the covers.

"Sascha," he warned on a grumble, and his fingers tensed on her calf. The prospect of being slapped there didn't fill her with glee, nor did it frighten her.

She wanted to be truthful, though, even if it made her uncomfortable. "Safe," she whispered.

He rubbed her leg again. "Really?"

"Yes."

"Why?"

God. What was this? *Trivial Pursuit*? She was tired of the questions, wanted nothing except to feel what he wanted her to experience, but the trouble with Sean was he liked to ask questions. He wanted to communicate.

There was no avoiding it, just as there was no avoiding him slapping her ass if she displeased him.

The very thought had her belly clenching. Surprise hit her as she murmured, "If you're in control, I don't have to think. If I don't have to think, I don't have to worry or be afraid."

This time, both hands moved over the curves of her calves, down to her ankles and over the soles of her feet.

"Count to thirty. If you don't move, I'll let you come."

Because she'd expected another question, she hesitated a second before she began her count. By number two, she'd realized his intent and clenched down hard as he began to trace his fingers over her soles.

Fuck!

He knew she was fucking sensitive there.

His tickling fingers had the numbers choking in her throat as she bit them out. Tension whipped through her frame as he carried on, making her legs want to tremble with the force she was putting on her muscles. A part of her wasn't sure if he'd class that as moving, but she genuinely wasn't. Normally, she'd be wriggling all over the damn bed, laughing her ass off and trying to avoid his hands. Now, she was as still as a statue even as all of her nerve endings were screaming at her to move, to avoid his touch.

By twenty-five, her eyes were wet. By thirty?

She wanted to scream.

Only the knowledge that she could wake Tin up prevented her from doing so.

When he stopped, she blew out several sharp breaths as her nerves carried on responding to the tickling treatment. "Oh, God! Oh, God! Oh, God," she rasped.

Who knew that could hurt more than the flat of his hand on her ass?

Jesus Christ!

"I didn't think you'd be able to stop yourself from moving," he murmured, and she heard the amusement in his voice. Though she wanted to growl at him, she didn't, because she felt the bed shift with his weight, and had to whimper as his hot breath washed over her pussy.

He stayed there for endless seconds, and she wiggled in place, trying to move her body down to meet him. She shifted her knees somewhat, but her legs were so wide apart that the movement was no real help.

Then, she felt him. His tongue, just the tip, against her clit. He fluttered it until she mewled, then he stopped, murmuring, "Ride my tongue." Her eyes widened in protest.

"How?" she shrieked. He was too far away to do more than tickle!

She whimpered as she rocked her hips, getting that feathery, fluttering sensation against the nub, but nothing that could satisfy her. Nothing that could do much more than ramp up her agitation.

A cry escaped her as she managed to pull one leg harder, releasing the strain on the other. That enabled her to move somewhat, but he just pulled back. Giving her only the tip of his tongue.

The sounds of her panting breaths seemed to echo around the bedroom, and before she knew it, she felt light-headed. She stopped rocking her hips, and pressed her forehead to the duvet. As she did, he moved closer, used the flat of his tongue to caress her clit and slide down her folds to thrust into her.

She released another cry, sharper this time, as delight filled her. The mental image of him with his nose pressed against her, getting as close as he could, filled her with lust.

He thrust into her a few times, then moved down to her clit. When he gave it an open-mouthed kiss, she wanted to die, and then, she stopped wanting that, preferring to live if he could just carry on making her feel this way.

"Come on, Sascha, sweetheart. You can come now." His gravelly voice, the words so husky and so close to her cunt, made a delicious vibration. As he sucked down on her clit once more, she felt the wonder come over her, wash through her very veins as it seemed to cleanse her of any and all negativity in her body.

The reasons she hadn't been able to sleep?

They disappeared.

The stress of having to pack up the house for the next few months?

Gone.

All she could think about was him. His mouth. His lips. Her clit. Her orgasm.

She fisted her hands into the sheet and moaned through the climax. It was powerful, enough to make her feet tug at the bonds holding her in place, but it was beautiful, too.

Colors seemed to flash before her eyes, and electric tingles bounced down her spine in a kind of merry jig that had her clenching her ass once more.

When he moved away, she blew out a tired breath, but though

she was exhausted, more than she would have been if he'd just fucked her, she protested when he began to unknot the ties from her ankles. "What are you doing?" she asked, aware that she sounded sleepy rather than sexy.

He hushed her, though, as he released her, tossing the ties on the floor, she assumed, by the sounds of the silk pieces whispering against each other as they tumbled to the carpet. Then, he climbed onto the bed beside her and carefully dragged the duvet out from under her. When he covered her with it, he shuffled close. For a second, she was unsure what he was doing, then she released a sigh and turned into him.

Pressing a hand to his belly, low down where she could feel the heaviness of his cock, she murmured, "What about you?"

"Not tonight." He kissed her forehead. "We have many nights ahead of us to play."

Her eyelids flickered at that.

*To play?*

Well, didn't that just fill her with glee?

Lips curving as she pressed her mouth to the side of his arm, she closed her eyes and, for what felt like the first time in months, actively welcomed sleep.

# THIRTEEN

THE MINUTE she stepped into the house, Sascha knew Jane was there.

She could smell the perfume, and after the crisp air of an early December morning, the vanilla overtones made Sascha wonder if she'd stepped into a cupcake factory or her foyer.

Okay, so that was catty, and she'd tried to like Jane. She really had. But Sascha had seen the way the other woman looked at Andrei, and was weary of it. She didn't mind a few ogles. Hell, she really liked Becca at *Rossi's* café in Soho, and she invariably gaped at whichever of her men Sascha brought along.

She wasn't jealous by nature. Not really. But when something became blatant? Yeah. It put her on edge, and that pissed her off, considering how floaty she'd been feeling these past couple of days.

It was ironic, perhaps, that today was the first day she hadn't felt the strain in her thighs after Sean had tied her up. She'd liked feeling that. Had liked seeing his bite mark in the mirror, and was grateful the remnants of that were still there, even if it was covered up by the sweaters winter weather necessitated.

A part of her knew she liked the physical mark because it was a claiming she couldn't otherwise have.

She'd never, all those years ago, realized how irritating it was not being able to lay claim to her men, and have them do the same to her.

She was in a kind of vacuum. No one, unless they'd seen Andrei, actually knew who Tin's father was. Sascha was aware that the small social circle she had—pathetically small, really, consisting of a few moms from the mother and toddler group she attended with Tin—simply believed that her men were actually *friends*.

Unable to marry them, unable to even state they were much more than her partner—which could mean anything in this day and age—created a lack of equilibrium that was heightened when it came down to other women who poached on her turf.

And in her own goddamn house, no less.

A shrill laugh echoed down the stairs, and she grunted as she slipped out of her jacket and hooked it in the hall cupboard. It was damp from a light shower outside, but she'd liked the brisk weather as she'd headed to the local corner shop for some extra milk. Tin loved the stuff, and she wasn't about to stop him from drinking it just because she'd run out.

Another laugh, followed by an, 'Oh, Andrei, you're so funny,' had her pulling a face at the hall mirror. When she did, she jolted in surprise as Devon asked, "Why are you making faces at yourself?"

Pressing her hand to her heart, she grumbled, "You startled me."

Devon tilted his head to the side. "I usually do."

His tone was rather dry. For Devon, anyway. Her lips curled at that, and she murmured, "I wasn't making faces at myself."

"You were. You were looking in the mirror."

She jerked her thumb at the upstairs landing. "I was making faces at that." Right on cue, Jane laughed.

God, Sascha loved Andrei, but he wasn't a fucking comedian. Especially not in work mode. Jeez, her sexy Slav could make paint drying look interesting when he went on about 'quantitative' this and 'statistical' that.

"At the landing?"

She hissed. "Do you have to be so goddamn literal all the time, Devon?" She glowered at him a second before she stomped forward, grabbed his hand, and dragged him down the last few stairs to the hall. Then, she carried on dragging him until they hit Sean's office. She barged in, nodding at Sean whose eyes flashed up to catch sight of them.

She ignored the fact he leapt to his feet and turned the whiteboards around. Because she knew what was on them, she didn't want the nasty details—Sean hadn't gotten that wrong. She knew, point blank, that was more than she could handle at the moment.

"Why would the landing piss me off?" she growled at Devon, even as she placed the milk bottle on the dresser beside the door. "*She* was pissing me off. Laughing like Andrei's Eddie goddamn Murphy or something." Sascha huffed. "It's sickening."

Sean snorted. "Sascha, there's no need to be jealous."

"I never said there was a need for it. I just said I was annoyed by how much she laughed."

Then, as she heard the words back, she grimaced at how irrational that sounded. A fact that was confirmed when Devon eyed her like he'd eye the Statue of Liberty if she'd wandered into Sean's office behind them.

"Should she laugh less?" he asked, apparently considering her question.

"Yes. It's false laughter," she explained. "Women do that shit all the time. It's to make a guy think that the woman believes they walk on fucking water."

He pursed his lips. "Is that a good thing?"

"What?" She scowled at him.

"To walk on water?"

For a second, she just had to gape at him, then she pressed her hand to her forehead and stepped closer to the fire. Tumbling into Devon's armchair, she stared at him, then cut Sean a look. "You deal with this one, Sean. Pretty please?"

From behind his desk, Sean rocked in his chair. He looked like some kind of oligarch who ruled a province from that very seat, but the twinkle in his eye that was for them alone always made her feel gooey inside.

How such a serious man could look like that, she wasn't certain, but she knew that though those looks were rare, they were precious nonetheless.

"It's time for a 'birds and the bees' conversation, Devon," he joked, making Sascha laugh even though she had to grit her teeth halfway through as yet another of Jane's cackles seemed to pound through the ceiling, ripe to attack her eardrums. Even Sean looked up, and he shot her a glance as he murmured, "She does laugh a lot, doesn't she?"

His tone was musing, enough so that she had to giggle. "I'm glad you noticed."

"Not until you mentioned it." He shrugged away the topic as though it was of no interest. "Devon, Jesus walked on water."

"How did he do that?" Devon frowned. "I can't walk on water."

"You're not the son of God."

"You're big-headed enough to think you're a god, though," Sascha grumbled, but her lips twitched.

"A math god," Devon agreed, and she did laugh this time because sometimes, and it felt as rare as digging up a diamond in their backyard, he *did* get jokes.

As she turned to look at Sean, curious where he was going with this conversation—his takes on these matters with Devon were always amusing to her—a picture on the back of his whiteboard caught her eye.

The last thing she'd wanted was for anything on that horrible thing to catch her attention. But the white-blond hair *did*. Despite herself, she got to her feet and slipped behind the whiteboards to look at that one image.

As she did, her heart dropped to her stomach, because this had to be the boy that had triggered Sean's drinking binge all those months ago. The reason why he'd driven to Glasgow, his need to see Tin a dull ache in his soul.

The boy had died because, according to Sean, the sooner the parents appealed to the killer, the quicker the bastard disposed of the child.

She gnawed at her lip as she took in the bright blue eyes that were like Tin's, the mop of white-gold hair. She could see the resemblance, could even see why, in a dark moment, Sean would suddenly feel the need to snatch Tin up, hold him tight in his arms, and never let him go.

"Sascha? I don't think—"

Hearing the wheels of Sean's desk chair scrape against the floor, she murmured, "It's okay, Sean. I can look away if I need to."

But she didn't.

There wasn't anything gruesome on the board, not like she'd half-feared. The prospect of murder scene photographs had always filled her with dread because that was always what the cops displayed in the procedural shows. But here, there was none of that.

In fact, she was surprised that she was surprised at all.

This was Sean, after all.

One of her men.

Incapable of doing anything the regular way.

The whiteboards were four feet by six feet, and there were three of them drilled together on hinges that meant they could curl up into a nest. As she stared at nearly twenty-feet of evidence Sean considered important, she got a glimpse into his working mind that stunned her.

She'd always known what he did for a living. Had, on the periphery, seen the strain it added to his features, and had always done her best to ease that for him. But as she looked at the workings of his brain?

Sascha found herself floored.

It was like some kind of mind map. But this was leagues beyond that.

He wrote in a type of code, too. Maybe only shorthand, but it meant she couldn't understand everything. She figured that was for both her and Tin's benefit. Although, knowing Tin and his burgeoning talents with numbers, he'd probably take such a code and consider it a challenge to best his old man.

Even though her lips twitched at the thought, she didn't allow a smile. That would have been barbaric considering what she was looking at.

There were pictures of four boys.

There was no visible link between them. They were all different races, had different hair and eye color.

"Should there be a pattern in why they're chosen?" she asked, her voice husky as she stared up at the whiteboard.

"Yes."

"But there isn't, is there?"

Sean's voice was heavy as he murmured, "No." It was also closer than it had been before. She wasn't altogether shocked to see him step around the board to look at her. "Come away, Sascha. I don't want you to see this."

"Does he abuse them?"

Something flickered in Sean's eyes. "No." He wasn't lying. She could read him well enough to know that.

"Why does he take them then?"

He shrugged. "I don't know."

*That* was a lie.

"I want to help." The burning ache had appeared from out of nowhere.

"You can't."

"Maybe I can." Suddenly, the need for a purpose consumed her. She *needed* to help. "How old are they?"

"About Tin's age. Not close enough to represent a pattern, though."

"Why?"

"I don't know."

"He's taken four now, hasn't he? Or are there more that aren't on here?"

Sean swallowed. "Yes. Four." He grabbed her hand and tugged her away from the board and into his arms. "Please, Sascha. *Please.* Let this drop. I-I don't want you connected with it."

The plea in his voice annihilated her. She let out a sigh and turned her face away from the smiling boys and into his throat. "Okay, Sean. Don't worry. I'll stay out of it."

"Thank you," he whispered on a shaky sigh, sounding more vulnerable than she'd heard him in years.

She reached up to run her fingers through the slight curls at the top of his neck. "It's okay. I think you were explaining something to Devon."

Feeling his cheek against her own hitch in a smile, she settled into him, trying to imbue him with a sense of calm that she wasn't really feeling. It was important to him that she didn't get involved, but the truth was, she wanted to help him.

Even if she knew this wasn't where her particular talents would come in handy.

Having a degree in Event Planning and Hotel Administration didn't exactly make her Agatha Christie, did it?

She reached up and turned her face to kiss his cheek. "It's okay," she repeated, then pulling away from him, she walked him to the desk, which he rounded while she perched her ass on the front of it.

Devon was eying them both with that usual way of his—like he'd just walked in on his parents' having sex. Goggle-eyed but not goggle-brained, he said, "You *are* right."

"About what?"

"Jane *does* laugh too much."

---

"WHAT ARE YOU DOING?"

Andrei looked over at Sawyer. "What does it look like I'm doing?"

He frowned at the large screen TV opposite Andrei's desk. "Making a schedule."

"Brownie points to you," Andrei retorted, rolling his eyes.

"Why, though? Thought that was what Jane was for."

"She has her uses. But this. ..." He shook his head. "Sascha wouldn't like it."

Sawyer snorted. "Pussy whipped."

"Like you aren't." Andrei cocked a brow at him. "You and I both know Sascha's intensely private about these matters. No way would she allow Jane to have a key for the house or know all of our travel plans."

Sawyer folded his arms across his chest. "Would be a damn sight easier if she didn't mind." He pursed his lips. "Think she's jealous?"

"Who? Jane?" Andrei asked, tone absentminded.

"No. Sascha." Sawyer grunted. "And she says I'm blind."

"Why would she be jealous?"

"Because Jane isn't exactly plain." Sawyer scowled at the thought, then shoved his hands into his pockets, so he could hunch his shoulders forward—the big, burly Scot couldn't have looked more uncomfortable if he'd tried. "And I've noticed the way she looks at you."

Andrei's mouth dropped open. "The way who looks at me? Jane?"

Sawyer snickered. "Your face. I swear. But yeah. *Jane.* She's got the hots for you."

"Where the hell is this conversation coming from?" Andrei demanded, sitting straighter in his chair.

"Because something got Sascha's knickers in a twist yesterday."

"'Sascha's knickers in a twist'?" Andrei repeated, feeling somewhat dumbfounded. "You can't be serious."

"I'm deadly serious." He grimaced. "I mean, I'm not blind. Jane's pretty. She's no Sascha, but she's attractive. I didn't think anything of it until Devon asked me why Jane kept staring at you. *And* laughing at you. He went on about Jesus and water, but I tuned out by that point."

Andrei shook his head. "Devon noticed that?"

"Yeah. That tells you how blatant she is. If Sascha noticed, you know she can be a cat."

That had Andrei laughing a little. "Amazing, isn't it? She has us wrapped into a more intricate knot than the Gordian variety, and she's worried about my PA."

"Does she have reason to worry?"

The question was phrased cautiously, as it damn well should have been. He sat up and glowered at Sawyer. "What the fuck are you insinuating?"

He raised his hands. "Nothing. I just. ..." Sawyer shrugged. "Wanted to make sure that it was one-sided."

"Why would you even question that?" he ground out.

"Because things have been difficult of late. Stuff happens in these kinds of situations."

"And, what? Because I'm from Bratva stock, I can't keep my cock in my pants?" He stormed to his feet and slammed his hands on his desk. "Until you mentioned it, Jane was a walking, talking laptop to me. I tell her shit, she spits out data. That's it. I'm about as interested in her as I am in that TV screen over there.

"Did I realize she had a crush on me? No. Because that would be like thinking the TV had taken a liking to me, and as far as I'm aware, we don't have to worry about AI for quite a while yet."

"I never meant to imply that it was because you're Bratva, mon," Sawyer retorted, but his tone was grumbly. Andrei knew he'd made the other man uncomfortable, and good. Sawyer damn well should be.

*Blyad*, Andrei's interest in Jane went no further than what she could do for him.

And he wasn't talking about sexually, dammit.

He'd only taken to having a PA because the situation with the Veronian government had added a bit of pressure to his schedule that he wasn't able to maintain on top of his other responsibilities.

"If I'd have even imagined Sascha would be jealous, I'd have hired a man. I don't care if they have a dick or a pussy so long as they can bring some semblance of order to my days."

Sawyer's lips curved. "It's strange."

"What is?" he growled.

"How like Devon you are in some things. I think I forget because of how you present yourself to the rest of the world. He got none of the charisma, and you got bucket loads, but you are like him, aren't you?"

"Like what?" he grumbled, taking a step back to sit heavily in his desk chair.

"You have tunnel vision, so Sascha is the only thing you see." Sawyer's smile deepened. "I shall report back to Devon that all is well."

He snorted. "Like Devon will even remember."

"He would. He was concerned about Sascha. Said she didn't need to be worrying about you cheating on her with the help, as well as dealing with what she's dealing with."

Andrei narrowed his eyes at Sawyer. "Are you intentionally trying to piss me off?"

"Not anymore," Sawyer said cheerfully, and just as Andrei started to hope the man would fuck off, he stepped deeper into his office. Resting his hands on the edge of the desk, he leaned over and whispered, "Did Sean tell you about the other night?"

"Which one?" he asked coolly, well aware the bite of his accent was audible in the two words. Tough. He *was* pissed off. Cheating on Sascha was incomprehensible to him.

She was *the* woman to him.

There was no other.

Didn't Devon realize that? Didn't Sawyer?

"Tuesday night." He jerked his chin up. "Said he'd tied her up, spanked her. She got off on it."

Andrei stiffened, all thoughts of irritation disappearing at this startling news. "She wanted that?"

"Seems so." Sawyer shrugged. "She's always been a bratty little thing. She takes whatever we give her, though."

"But to submit?" Andrei scowled. "I don't believe it."

"Talk to Sean. You know he doesn't exactly paint pretty pictures on purpose." He whistled. "And what a pretty picture, too." He straightened, so he could raise his hands and rub them together. "If she's into that kind of thing, then I'll gladly lead her astray."

Andrei chuckled. "You and me both." They shared a look. "Together?" Andrei asked.

Sawyer shrugged. "Don't see why not. You know Kurt and Devon don't get off on that shit."

"No. I'm surprised. Devon's such a control freak, after all."

"He is, and he torments her in his own particular way."

"You'd know," Andrei mocked, laughing when Sawyer grimaced.

"It will do me good to take her on with you. I'm sick of seeing the man's bollocks."

He had to chuckle at that. "Don't get used to the idea of seeing mine."

"I can hardly wait," Sawyer grumbled. "The man's an exhibitionist. I don't know why I'm surprised I see them more than my feckin' own." He folded his arms across his chest. "Sean won't share her."

Andrei shook his head. "*Nyet.*"

"Ever wondered why?"

"I *know* why." He pursed his lips. "He's a secretive man."

"Sean?" Sawyer frowned. "Hardly. The man's an open book where Sascha is concerned."

"*Da.* But where we're concerned? No. What happens between them will stay between them for the most part."

"He told me she got off on being tied up. That doesn't sound very bluidy secretive to me!"

"Well, it wouldn't. He was telling you, because he knows you get off on that stuff, too, and that will please Sascha. She's obviously going through some kind of. ..."

"Don't say meltdown," Sawyer said on a sigh.

"I wasn't going to. I was going to say renaissance. What happened has made her rethink everything, I suppose."

"Have you seen her kindle?"

Andrei frowned. "No. Why would I have?"

"I noticed it the other day. By chance. Sean mentioned it to me, too."

"What about it?" he growled, his impatience bleeding through.

"I saw a few words I've heard you and Vasily say over the years." He shot Andrei a knowing look. "When you're talking about your grandfather's work."

"Bratva phrases?" Andrei reared back, unsure if he was more surprised about that revelation or the fact that his PA apparently had a crush on him.

"Aye. Pakhan. Brigadier. Shite like that."

"On her kindle?"

He nodded. "She uses the family account to read. I looked it up."

"Why?"

"I was curious. She likes Bratva romances, mon."

"Bratva. Romances." Andrei shook his head—this time not in negation, but to shake the wool from between his ears. "That's a juxtaposition if ever I've heard one. By no way, shape, or form, is anything about the Bratva romantic."

"Apparently a lot of women disagree with you. And, from the way Jane looks at you, and Sascha, too, I'd imagine you're hot with the ladies. Tin's turning into a bonny wee lad because of you. I'd imagine you're prime spank bank material for a woman who likes that sort of thing."

"'Spank bank?'" Andrei blurted out. "You think she masturbates to that stuff?"

"Sean confirmed it."

"How many of the damn book does she have?"

Sawyer jerked a shoulder. "I don't know. Why would I? But . . . might be wise to—"

"Role play?" Andrei knew if his eyes grew any wider, he'd start looking like Tin when he thought the Devon-sized stack of pancakes was his.

"Don't see why not. Bring the lass out of herself." Sawyer grinned. "She might enjoy it."

"But would I?" Andrei countered. "That life is not romantic, Sawyer."

"It's a fantasy, Andrei. Give it to her. You're the one in the unique position of being able to do so."

"I suppose so," he murmured, his tone heavy. As he reached up to rub his chin, Sawyer moved away from his desk toward the open doorway.

"What are you going to do about Jane?"

"Do?" Andrei's scowl deepened. "Why do I have to do anything about her?"

"Because the way she looks at you. . . ." Sawyer shook his head. "She'll come onto you sure enough. You're not claimed, mon. She doesnae know that you're Sascha's. She'll think you're fair game and will make things awkward for you. Trust me. I know you've got that tunnel vision, but listen to a mon who doesnae, and who kens how women think."

Andrei scowled at that. "Bullshit. Since when do you know how women think?"

"Since I grew into my biceps, Andrei," Sawyer joked. "Just because I'm not interested, doesnae mean they're not interested in me."

Discomfited by the conversation, he grumbled, "See, my faith in you is absolute. You don't hear me asking whether you've acted on any of those offers."

"No. You're right." He dipped his head. "My apologies, brother."

Andrei sniffed. "I understand you're coming from a good place. I'll speak with Jane." He grimaced. "It doesn't seem fair to fire her. She hasn't done anything wrong."

"Not yet," Sawyer warned as he headed out of the office, not even giving him a backwards glance.

Was this a parallel universe?

He thought about Jane, tried to picture her in his mind's eye but realized that he couldn't, in all honesty, even do that. He thought she had brown hair, but it could easily have been blonde.

Then, he shrugged thoughts of his PA aside and turned his focus back to the schedule. Better that than the bizarre knowledge that Sascha thought the Bratva was sexy.

They were due in Moscow in just under eighteen days. In that time, they had to close the house up, have their things packed for not only Russia but their extended stay in Veronia, too. Knowing that Devon *did* hate to fly, he'd tried to narrow things down for him by flying straight to Moscow, then onto Madela in Veronia immediately afterward.

That presented a logistical problem considering there were six adults and a small boy to pack up. Truth was, he'd been enjoying making the arrangements. Sascha was predictably antsy about leaving these issues in the hands of others. And, as they led relatively sedate lives, their security wasn't as rigid as it could have been if they'd been in the public eye more.

Considering Kurt's sudden swell of fame, guards or extra security might become a necessity in the future. He'd made his name as the reclusive German author, however, so Andrei didn't think that was something Kurt was about to change, but he'd discuss the situation with his grandfather before he left for Veronia.

If anyone knew which company was the best to hire, it was Vasily.

As he checked into their flights, he stared at Sascha's name on the screen.

Was she really jealous?

Where had that even come from?

He wasn't sure, and taking into account this sudden need to be dominated, it heralded several questions in a conversation he'd prefer to have sooner rather than later.

# FOURTEEN

WHEN THE BEDROOM door closed behind him, Sascha cocked a brow at Andrei. "This isn't your room."

He cocked a brow right back at her. "I know it isn't."

She snorted. "Since when do you play musical bedrooms?"

"Since tonight." He grinned at her. "I thought we'd play tonight."

"Play what?" His grin deepened, and she jerked back in surprise. "He told you," she said on a whisper.

"Don't be mad," Andrei murmured, stepping deeper into Kurt's bedroom as he held up his hands in entreaty. "Not at him or us."

"I don't know if I'm mad or just disappointed."

He grimaced. "I'm not sure which is worse."

"Good." She blew out a breath as she folded her arms across her chest. "What did he tell you?"

He shrugged, aware that he needed to be careful here—Sean hadn't technically told him anything, after all. "I've learned that you like to play games."

She narrowed her gaze at him. "You're serious? That's what he said?" At his nod, she growled, "Yes, Andrei, I love playing *Jenga* in bed."

When he just laughed, she glowered back at him, and he murmured, "So angry, Sascha. Why? Is it based in embarrassment or fear?"

That had her stiffening, in more ways than one—he saw her nipples peak to attention through the silk chemise she'd worn to bed. A good portent, he thought, of things to come.

"How would you like it if I talked about what we did with Sean?"

Again, he shrugged, and sincerely, he told her, "If I thought whatever you shared would enhance my pleasure, I wouldn't mind."

"And that's why he told you?" she demanded, but her voice was squeaky. "To enhance my pleasure?"

He grimaced at the mocking bite to the words. "Yes."

"Why would he do that?"

"Because Sean isn't the only one who likes to play games."

"Stop calling it that," she snapped. "We didn't play *Monopoly*, Andrei. Nor did he lock me up in his dungeon." She huffed. "Unless, let me guess, you're all so into playing *games* that you have one locked up tight somewhere in the house."

"We thought about it for a while," he admitted, satisfied as her mouth dropped open and her eyes widened. "Not a dungeon, of course. More like a playroom."

"What?" she outright yelled this time. "When?"

"With the third woman we shared." He wafted a hand, not wanting to get into that. "Remember, most of our partners viewed us as an avenue for sexual exploration. Did you think we wouldn't use them back?"

"N-No," she stuttered, but she dropped her gaze to his mouth as she did. Why, he wasn't sure. "But, I mean, I didn't think. . . ."

"You didn't know. Why would you? We don't talk about it."

"B-But, who?"

"Sean, Sawyer, myself. Kurt isn't interested. He has his own quirks, of course. He did enjoy watching us at work. Devon, not so much."

Her mouth rounded into the most perfect, most beautiful O. "N-No," she agreed.

He pursed his lips. "If you only want that with Sean. ..." He let the words drift off and was satisfied when she scampered out from between the sheets. Her silk chemise pulled taut against her slimmer body, and he realized then that he missed her curves.

She hadn't been looking after herself, he noticed, and he knew that was about to become a problem.

"No!" she repeated, her hands darting forward, so she could tuck them between his own. "I-I, well, I guess it came as a surprise that Sean would share something like that, but I do want it." She swallowed. "I think I need it."

"Why? You didn't before." He cocked a brow at her. "You were content with our busy sex lives two months ago."

"Yeah." She wriggled, the muscles in her thighs suddenly straining. "But, I liked it when you—"

He let her pause for an indeterminate length of time, then prompted, "When I, what?" He reached up to cup her cheek a second, then he trailed the backs of his fingers down the side of her jaw. When he cupped her throat, she made a mewling noise that startled him into a quirking a brow at her. "When I, what?" he asked again, his thumb pressing down against the soft flesh in his grip.

"This," she rasped, arousal making her words husky. "I loved this. I loved when you got rough with me. I loved being spanked by Sawyer, or when Devon would pin me to the bed." She shuddered, and with her free hand, cupped his wrist. "I loved you tying me down and fucking me. It's been growing. This need. These urges. And now? Now, I don't want to think. I just want to feel. I want to feel like me again. Sexy and satisfied. I need you to guide me in that."

His eyes went to half-mast at that as he processed her words. "I said to Sawyer this morning that you'd gone through a renaissance. I don't want you to regret it, Sascha."

She blinked up at him with such trust on her face, he felt his very heart quiver in his chest. "I wouldn't, Andrei. Anything I don't like we don't have to do again. And you're right. This has been a learning curve for me. It's been. ..." She bit her lip. "We didn't have it easy at the start. What with the situation with the Jacobies. But, our life has been basically content. I feel like this is the first stumbling block. Almost like this has torn the blindfold from my eyes and has revealed that I am, actually, an adult."

"You were before, *katyonok*."

"I know, but this time I feel differently." She shrugged. "I just . . . I need something different. Maybe I'm opening the door to something that I'll regret, but we're always changing, aren't we? Growing. I'd prefer for us to grow together than to grow apart."

"Of course, but what if we do something you don't like? Something you don't expect?"

"I won't hold it against you," she reasoned. "Why would I? I want this. More than I realized." She reached up, and he saw there was a bruise on her shoulder. She lowered the strap and the silk gaped, revealing her tits, but that hadn't been her intent. "Sean bit me. You can't. ..." Sascha shook her head as her fingers trailed over the mark. "I didn't realize until recently how badly it was affecting me not being known as yours, and you not being known as mine. I like this. I feel claimed."

He frowned. "But you *are* ours."

"Jane doesn't know that," she whispered. "Jennifer Houghton, the female lead in Kurt's movie, she doesn't know that. Nobody does. Dreyford, the male lead, was coming onto me in front of Kurt because he doesn't realize I'm somebody's. This," she whispered, rubbing the bitemark. "Makes me feel claimed."

He'd never realized how the lack of a legal, open, and binding acknowledgment affected her. But, of course, he knew and understood the strain of having to be careful about discussing what they were to one another. It was irritating as fuck, especially as she was simply theirs in all their eyes.

Did she need a ring?

Would that make her feel better?

Or was her traditional upbringing making waves with this very non-traditional relationship she was in?

He reached over and touched the mark. "You like that?"

"Yes."

"Didn't it hurt?"

"It felt good. Right." She licked her lips. "And when I feel. . . ." Sascha broke off, "*weird*, then I touch it and I feel better."

He scowled at that. The bite mark wasn't a damn talisman.

His major concern was their leading her into something she couldn't handle. Something she was only broaching now because so many things were up in the air for her. She wasn't content with being in London, wanted to move to the country, maybe? And now this?

Was it too much?

Would exploring this new side of her be exploiting her?

Then, she reached up and tugged at the other strap of her chemise. When the silk pooled at her waist, he whispered, "You've lost weight."

"I know."

"This. . . ." He licked his lips. "I'm not like Sean."

"I never thought you were."

But he shook his head. "Sean leaves it in the bedroom. I can't."

She reached over and grabbed his hand. "Whatever you need."

"No. You don't understand." He forced himself to get the words out because, once he opened Pandora's box, he wasn't sure if he'd be able to close it. "You're playing at the moment. That's why I've been using that verb. But I don't want to play. If I open myself to this, I'll want it all the time."

"That means you've needed it since we've been together." Her tone was flat, then he saw the heat in her eyes. "Damn you, Andrei. Why the fuck didn't you tell me I wasn't pleasing you?"

He let out a growl. "Because you *were* pleasing me. I've never been so sexually satisfied in all my life, Sascha," he gritted out, then, he was amused because she preened at that, her chin soaring high with delight at his words.

"If you need this, then I need it, too," she murmured, scurrying closer to him. With her hair in a topknot and the silk settling around her hips after she'd moved, he realized how young she looked. Yes, there were shadows under her eyes, and yes, she did have some tiny frown lines, but she looked like an angel sitting there with curls tumbling around her throat.

"You don't know what you're asking for," he whispered, and his tongue felt thick in his mouth.

"I do. I've read enough to know that I like that. Just . . . break me in softly. Let me learn first what you want. What we need."

His cock had been at half-mast throughout this conversation, but now? It stiffened fully and to the point of pain.

"I'll punish you for disobeying," he whispered, reaching over again to trace the bitemark. "If I tell you to remember to eat. . ."–because she'd definitely been skipping meals to have lost so much so fast–"I'll expect you to obey."

That had her eyes flaring wide. "You'd punish me for that?"

"For anything I thought was for your own good that you saw fit to ignore."

He saw her pupils turn into pinpricks and knew he had her. A thought that had him blowing out a rough breath.

*Blyad,* was *he* ready for this?

It had been a long time since he'd explored this side of himself. And only today, after Sawyer's bull-in-a-china shop conversation, did he realize he'd enjoy opening himself up to Sascha if she was ready for that.

"Let's just take it slowly," he whispered, relieved when she nodded, seemingly aware that this was a first step for him, too, in many ways.

"Okay," she replied, then moaned as he dropped a hand to her breast.

"Do you like pain, *katyonok*?" He did as he'd never dreamed of doing, maneuvered her nipple between his fingers and pinched down hard. The sharp yelp she released had him withholding a groan, especially when her cheeks flushed and she quickly blew out a breath of air.

"I-I don't know."

"How did that make you feel?"

She swallowed, her eyes holding his for endless seconds, as he reached over and treated the other to the same treatment. He knew she liked rough sex. That he'd picked up on over the years. But to be dominated was a different matter entirely.

As he pinched her, she released a sharp breath and whispered, "Centered."

The answer wasn't one he'd expected.

It wasn't one he altogether liked hearing, either.

"Take off the night dress," he murmured.

"Kurt might be back soon."

"He's working, and if he caught the tail end of this, you know he'd enjoy the show."

Her lips curved in amusement, but she scampered off the bed and removed the chemise. As she did, his gaze swiftly took in the too prominent collarbones, the hip bones that had never been fully visible before. But the swells of her breasts were just as luscious as ever, and her waist was so small, he knew he could span it with his fingers.

She'd always been ripe, but now? Not so much.

If she'd wanted to lose weight, that was one thing. But depression had inspired this, making it another matter entirely.

"When I ask you to do something, you do it. Do you understand?" At her nod, he nodded back. "Kneel on the floor," he told her, watching with tender amusement as she did as bid. He was surprised though, because Sawyer was right. Sexually, she was a brat. A trait she was only just starting to reveal.

A part of him wondered if different aspects of her nature would reveal themselves with each of her partners, but at that moment, he didn't want to think about that. Was just content to think of the here and now.

"Spread your legs, let me see that pretty pussy."

Her mouth opened on a sigh as she complied.

"Are you eating breakfast?"

She blinked in bewilderment. "Sometimes."

"Every day?"

Shaking her head, she whispered, "No."

"Touch your clit," he directed next, watching as her delicate fingers traced the tender nubbin. She was sensitive there, like most women, he supposed, but she touched herself roughly, in a way that should have indicated the bite of discomfort wasn't something she was alien to.

He watched her fingers, studied the way the flush rose to her throat as she aroused herself, then he murmured, "I want you to eat breakfast. Every day."

"I'm not always hungry," she said on a moan.

"Stop touching yourself," he directed, and when she was slow to move her hand away, he bent down, grabbed her hand, curved it around her knee, and then slapped her inner thigh. She yelped, and he ignored it. "I told you to stop touching yourself."

"O-Okay," she whispered breathily.

"I also told you I want you to eat breakfast." He squatted in front of her and trailed his hand over the jutting hipbone then up to her collarbone. "You've lost too much weight."

"I thought you'd like that," she said on a pout, and he slapped her inner thigh again. Her hiss had him smirking.

"What made you think such crazy thoughts? When have we never loved your body?"

She blinked at that. "Men always like thin women."

"Well, the five men in this house don't follow that pattern, do they?" He cupped the swell of her tit. "We like you healthy."

"I am healthy."

"This isn't healthy," he retorted. "If I look at your back, will I see your ribs?"

"It's not a bad thing if you do," she argued.

"It is if you're starving yourself. Some bodies are naturally that way. Some aren't. You're not eating, Sascha. I've seen the small portions you have for dinner."

"Fuck," she growled. "I can't win. Sawyer says I eat too much, and you're saying I eat too little."

"Since when did he say that?" He knew for a fact those words would never have spilled from his brother's lips. Sawyer was as enamored with Sascha's curves as the rest of them.

She pursed her lips. "He never likes it when I bake."

"Yeah. Because he's a health nut. He's terrified you're going—" He bit off a curse.

"Terrified I'm going to what?" She reached over to grab his hand. A frown puckering her brow, she asked, "What, Andrei?"

"He wants you healthy," was all he said. "You should talk to him about matters such as this, but you should get it out of your head that Sawyer is unhappy with your form. All he cares about is your wellbeing. And cookies to him. ..." He winced, suddenly unable to stop himself from explaining, "Do you know how many people in his family have diabetes?"

Sascha reared back at that. "No."

"All of them." He pursed his lips.

"Hamish and Cinta don't. . . ."

"They do. As did Sheila, his sister. His cousins, his aunts, and his uncles." He shrugged. "Bad diets. They were poor, didn't have much money, so they made the wrong choices. You've seen the crap Cinta eats."

"She eats nothing but sugar," Sascha said, her mouth gaping.

"Exactly. Even though she's diabetic." He shrugged. "She's like my grandfather. Vasily says something will kill him eventually, so why deny himself his cigars? She feels the same with sweets."

"B-But. . . ."

"But nothing. Sascha, Sawyer worries about your health because he loves you. Never think he believes you're fat or anything like that.

He doesn't. He loved you before, and he, like all of us, celebrated each one of your curves.

"Limiting your food to be slimmer? Not necessary unless the doctor says so."

She blinked at him. "I can't believe I didn't know that. Why the hell didn't he tell me?"

"Because he's gruff and arrogant?" he grunted. "I shouldn't have told you, but I couldn't have you thinking you were anything other than perfect to us."

"Hardly that," she whispered, dipping her head, the coy move making his lips twitch.

"So, what are you going to do, Sascha?"

Her mouth twisted as she peered up at him through the fringe of her lashes. "Eat breakfast."

He nodded. "Good. Touch your clit."

Her eyes widened, and he could tell she wanted to argue. He cocked a brow at her until she reached between her legs and obeyed. "Do you know we love you, Sascha?" he asked, watching her rub her clit and only asking when she started rolling her hips in response to the caresses.

"Y-Yes, I know."

"So, why do you get jealous?"

A frown flashed over her brow, but she carried on touching herself.

"I just do."

That was no answer. "What do your books say about claiming?"

Her eyes flared wide. "My books?"

"The Bratva romances you apparently devour."

Her fingers stilled, and her cheeks burned. "What?"

"Did I tell you to stop touching yourself?" he inquired, eying her fingers until she started again.

"No."

"Well, don't stop until I do. And, what happens in the Bratva books, Sascha? Why do you like them?"

"They remind me of you," she whispered.

"Me?" He was about as unBratva-like as possible. "Why?"

"You're powerful. Just like Vasily. It's sexy," she gasped out the word, and he realized just thinking about that was getting her hot. "I know how clever you are, but when you . . . I mean, you're working with a Duke and a King to help a country's economy." A mewl escaped her. "Oh, God, I'm going to come."

He watched her, somewhat clinically, as she carried on, working herself higher, getting her to the spot . . . then he reached down, grabbed her wrist and pulled her hand away, as he asked, "In the Bratva books, what happens when their woman comes without their permission?"

Her eyes widened, and her tits began to wobble with each breath. "You never said I had to."

"No, I didn't. I wanted to see what you'd do. Wanted to know if you'd ask permission." He made a tsking sound. "Bratva men are brutal," he whispered, kneeling in front of her, resting one thigh between hers. "They beat their women." He grabbed her chin, held her firmly in place. "Not all, but a lot. Like my father did. He used his fists on my mother more than he touched her with love. Is that what you want from me?"

"N-No."

"Good, because that's not what I want."

He noticed relief didn't blossom in her eyes, which told him everything he needed to know—she trusted him.

Implicitly.

The next breath he took was so deep, he didn't realize how relieved *he* felt at that.

"I want to control your pleasure, Sascha," he whispered, reaching over to trail his tongue over the line of her jaw. Moving up to her ear, he sucked the lobe into his mouth and murmured, "Own it. Make it mine." The breath that soughed from her lips was shaky and lust-filled. "Do you want that?"

"Y-Yes," she whimpered.

"Why? Don't you want to control that yourself?" he asked, being devil's advocate.

"N-Not always. Not if you need to own my pleasure like I need you to."

Clever answer.

He smirked, nipped at her earlobe, as his hand cupped her throat once more. "You're a naughty little thing, *katyonok*." Then, he breathed, "Touch your pussy, get your fingers nice and wet, then put them in my mouth."

She released a whimper as he moved back, not edging far from her, just settling on his heels. She rimmed her pussy, gathered the juices, and then raised her fingers hesitantly. He opened his lips and sucked them into his mouth. She moaned as he tugged hard at them, curling his tongue around each digit, making sure he got every single drop of her cream.

"Wet your nipples, then pinch them," he directed as he moved to a standing position. When she obeyed, a rush of fire seemed to race through his veins, and he gritted his teeth as he reached for his fly and released his cock.

When he saw the purple head, he realized how turned on he was. Even grabbing a hold of his cock had him hissing with the pleasure of it. "You're going to suck my cock like I just sucked your fingers, Sascha."

Her eyes flared with need, and he watched as she nodded, eager to please him. She waited for him to move closer, then opened her mouth as he had. When he popped the tip in, he released a hiss. "Good girl," he whispered as she worked his shaft.

God, she *was* good.

She knew exactly what he wanted, needed. Just because his mindset had changed, didn't make his cock belong to a different person.

Fuck!

As she gathered enough saliva to suck him down properly, he began to carefully rock his hips.

"Keep your hands on your thighs," he ordered her, even as he grabbed the stalk of his shaft so as not to accidentally go too deep. He'd enjoy that another time, but not tonight. Not when things were so fresh.

He pumped his hips, loving that she complied, and loving that she let him thrust into her mouth as though he were thrusting into her pussy.

It took a hellishly short time for him to come, and when she swallowed every drop, he pulled his cock from her mouth and painted her lips with the mixture of cum and spit. She didn't even wince which surprised him.

"Show me your tongue," he commanded. "I want to make sure you haven't wasted a drop."

A panting breath escaped her that was half moan and half mewl, but she stuck her tongue out. He reached down and pressed his thumb to it, and murmured, "Tell me, Sascha, have you been good?"

She nodded, the eager motion made him laugh.

"But you're jealous of other women," he purred. "Don't you trust us?"

"Don't trust them," she mumbled around his thumb.

"Ah, but that's because you don't believe in your men." He tsked again. "That doesn't sound like you've been good to me. You've been avoiding meals, losing weight. I don't think you've been taking care of my woman for me."

Her eyes flared wide at that, but she didn't argue.

He hummed. "No, I think you've been bad." He leaned over, whispered, "What do you think happens to bad girls?" His eyes crinkled in a smirk. "In fact, what do you think *doesn't* happen to bad girls?"

Her chin trembled. "Andrei, no."

"No? No, you haven't been bad?"

She pouted. "That's not fair."

"I think it's very fair." He reached down and pressed a kiss to her cum-marked lips. "I think tonight is a good night to start as we intend to carry on. That means good girls get rewards for behaving, and bad girls get nothing."

"Andrei!" she said on a squeak. "Please!"

He shook his head, held out his hand for hers. The eagerness etched on her face as she slipped her fingers into his amused him. "Time for bed, *katyonok*."

She gaped at him. "No way."

Andrei just stared at her, hiding a smile as she huffed and reached down to grab her chemise. He reached for that first, though, and murmured, "I said time for bed, not time to dress."

She glowered at him and stomped over to the bed. As she continued glowering at him, he stripped. "Move over, please. I'd prefer your ass to be the one nudging Kurt's morning wood when we wake up."

Her lips twitched, but she scooted over. As he slipped between the sheets, he reached over to turn the bedside light off. When darkness shrouded the room, he murmured, "You won't always like it, Sascha. You should be aware of that."

She pshawed. "I'm seeing *that*."

Her snark made his lips twitch, but he'd expected nothing less. The truth was, it was a relief to hear the snark. That was Sascha. He wanted that *her* back.

And wasn't it damn amazing that this was the first time he'd heard that in eight weeks?

He turned onto his side, sighing with pleasure when she snuggled into him, apparently not too mad to do that. Placing his hand on her belly, he slipped his hand down between her thighs and cupped her there.

"Sweet dreams, *katyonok*."

Tension made her ramrod straight in his embrace, and he could sense her desire to scream at him. When she didn't, he was almost disappointed, then he was grateful because, surprising him again, she tumbled into sleep far faster than he'd known her to for several months.

He'd expected her to stay rigid with tension. Had expected her to ride his hand, to try to tease and entice him to force him to bend to her will. But the way she'd fallen asleep spoke of a bone deep weariness that, somehow, had been eased by what they'd done.

Did she really need this as much as she claimed?

He guessed they'd find out.

# FIFTEEN

THE MINUTE SASCHA took a seat at the table, Andrei hid a smile as she glanced at him from under her lashes. He'd never thought she could be more beautiful to him, but this coy, slightly shy aspect of her personality was beyond charming.

He loved the ball-busting, Devon-herding, Tin-wrangling side of her, but this one? It fired his blood in a way he realized he'd been missing.

She wasn't the most submissive woman he'd ever known, but they'd explore this path together, and he loved that she was comfortable enough with him to do that.

This kind of 'play' was about trust. Nothing more, nothing less, and he and Sascha had that in spades.

Having buttered a slice of bread for Tin without having cut it into many-sided shapes as Devon did, he reached for two more slices and buttered those as well. "Strawberry or raspberry jam?" he asked quietly, when she fussed over the mess Tin had made between him putting the bread down and his son picking it up.

*Blyad*, the boy was a disaster with food.

He fully expected to return to the kitchen one day to find the walls painted with spaghetti hoops—both Tin and Devon being the culprits, naturally.

"I'm not hungry," she murmured, the words close to automatic as she wiped Tin's brow.

Her words had him narrowing his eyes. "You're not, hmm?"

There was a silken threat to the words, and they ensnared her attention like nothing else could. She jolted, then her gaze crash-landed on his. She licked her lips then whispered, "I'm really not."

"You need breakfast," he countered. "Doesn't she, Tin?"

"Mama, you do!" Tin chirped, and Andrei wasn't ashamed at using their almost three-year-old to coerce her into eating. "Breakfast is the most important meal of the day."

The way he parroted the words was pure Sawyer. The kid even rolled the 'r's in 'breakfast' and 'important.'

Sascha grumbled, "No fair."

"I can't show you how naughty it is not to eat breakfast with little eyes and ears watching and listening. But remember what I said last night? It comes with rules, Sascha."

There was a low warning to the words that, surprisingly enough, had her inhaling a rough gasp of air. "O-Okay?"

He cocked a brow at her. "Okay?" That was it? No more arguments?

Jesus, she'd enjoyed last night more than he'd credited.

She nodded. "Strawberry, please."

He smiled at her, satisfaction roaring through him as he spread the preserve over the bread. It wasn't even a victory on his part. He'd manipulated her via Tin, but someday soon she'd come to understand what he meant when he said he'd be taking care of her.

She didn't know how he could be when he was in this zone. Submissives weren't alone in having a mindset. Doms had them, too. And Andrei took his responsibilities seriously. Always had, and that was before the love of his life had kneeled before him yesterday evening.

Sascha truly didn't realize what she'd brought into the open, he feared.

Andrei swallowed as he leveled the jam neatly and evenly, covering the slice up to each corner. When it was perfect, he cut it into squares, then began working on the next slice.

After it was just so, he lifted the plate and handed it to her. As he did, he saw she'd been watching him, her eyes wide.

"What?" he enquired.

"I didn't know you were so exacting."

Because he tried not to be. He didn't want to be a control freak. And yet, what Sascha wanted from him would stir those feelings into being once more.

He liked everything just so, but living with four men, a woman, and a small boy didn't always allow for that. Now? Sascha had invited this side of his nature to the party and Andrei was certain he was pleased about that.

There was no reply worth giving her, so he just studied her, ensuring she took a bite of her breakfast. It wasn't as healthy as he'd have liked, but it was something.

"What are you doing today?" he asked her, trying to take his mind off things he couldn't control. Yet.

"I'm going to take Tin for a walk. He wants to see the fish in the park."

"It's freezing outside," he stated, peering out of the French doors onto their small back yard. "And I'm Russian. I know what freezing is."

Her lips curved in that Mona Lisa smile that could bring *him* to his knees. "Some fresh air will do us good. Tin's been cooped up like a hen, haven't you, baby?"

When Tin began to cluck, Andrei chuckled as he reached for his coffee. "Tell me when you go out, and I'll come with you."

"Nope," she told him, her tone cheerful. "I already know you have appointments today. Last night doesn't change things to that extent, Andrei. You still have things to do, and I still have a life to lead. You don't need to watch over me at all times."

Didn't he?

Because he knew he was being ridiculous, he nodded in agreement. "Okay." He wasn't the only one feeling as wobbly as a newborn foal taking their first steps.

"I thought there'd be more of an argument," she retorted, surprise lacing her tone.

"Disappointed?" he asked drily.

"No. Just shocked."

"I want to take care of you, not smother you. You're right. You can handle a walk."

"I'm glad I have your vote of confidence," she jibed, but her grin, when it appeared, was like the sun shining through the clouds on a grim day.

"Always, *katyonok*," he purred, reaching over the table for her hand. When she slipped her fingers through his, they both squeezed, and Andrei breathed a sigh of relief.

Today was the first day of a change of direction in their relationship. Whichever path it took them down, as long as they were together, he knew they'd be okay.

She was his *vtoraya polovinka*.

His soulmate.

There was no alternative for them than to find the path they needed. That was how it worked with soulmates.

---

"STARING at the pond will do you no good."

Jumping a little, Sascha looked at Devon who'd taken a seat at her side. "What are you doing here?"

"I like it here."

"Since when?" she asked, her tone somewhat suspicious. Not

because she didn't believe him, but because Devon's answers sometimes felt about as relevant as a mouse at the dining table.

"Since Glasgow."

She stiffened but relaxed immediately. "Ah."

"Yes. Ah."

"Do you like the water?" she asked, curious as to why he'd been coming into the gardens when he'd never been interested before.

The communal park wasn't overly large, but it was enough. The land belonged to the neighborhood and was locked, with each resident having a set of keys to permit them entry and to keep 'hooligans' out. Well, that was what Mrs. Berringer had declared at the last Neighborhood Watch meeting anyway.

Sascha hated locking herself inside. It just felt a bit too much like the *Secret Garden*, and while that was cool in the movie, in real life, it felt weird to lock oneself into an outdoor space.

Probably the size of two tennis courts stacked side by side, most of the vicinity was taken up by a large pond that contained koi fish. That was where Tin was. He was less than five feet away from her, near enough for her to grab if he happened to fall in, but it wasn't likely. There was a low stone wall around the pond, but a larger glass barrier kept children from falling into the murky liquid—or, she thought drily, to stop little hands from trying to catch the fish.

She had no fear of Tin hurting himself in its depths. He'd been in deeper baths!

Still, the darting of gold seemed to ensnare him, and when she wanted some quiet time, this was always the place to go as the fish kept him occupied while her brain could float away.

There were several benches dotted here and there, and the garden itself was shrouded with trees and bushes that made the park feel quite intimate, she supposed. Almost like an external sitting room.

It surprised her that Devon liked it here, though, considering his preferences seemed to be his office, whichever bed she was sleeping in, and the kitchen, those were pretty much his go-to destinations.

"I didn't know you'd been popping out to sit here." Something else that shocked her. She wondered if Sawyer knew, and if he did, why hadn't he told her?

"I like it. Helps me think."

"Me too," she murmured quietly, and releasing a breath, she moved closer to him and rested her head on his shoulder. When his head tilted to the side and rested on hers, her lips curved as she watched Tin stare into the pond. "I'm surprised it hasn't frozen over."

"It's not cold enough for that."

"It frigging feels like it," she grumbled—wrapped up in the quilted peacoat he'd bought her as well as thick gloves, hat, jeans, and a sweater, she wasn't exactly *warm and toasty*.

"Well, that's because you run the house hotter than a furnace."

She snorted. "I don't."

"You do. It's about five degrees hotter than we used to have it."

"No way."

"Way."

Puffing out her cheeks, she just shrugged. "I get cold."

"I imagine you do." He hummed under his breath, and the tune pricked her attention.

"What's that?"

"A Nocturne by Chopin. I was listening to it earlier."

Curiouser and curiouser. "You don't listen to classical music often, Devon. Are you okay?"

"Of course. I was bored with the silence. Tin wasn't in my office. I'm used to his chatter now."

That about melted her damn heart. Could such an admission be any cuter? "You like him being there? I wasn't sure if he was a nuisance or not."

"Oh, he is, but I love him for it anyway," he replied, his tone cheerful, and goddammit if that didn't make her love him a little bit more. Which should have been impossible, because she loved the difficult, stubborn jerk like crazy.

"Is that why you came out here? Because you saw us head for the garden?"

"Yes. But I like it here," he said again. "It helps clear my mind."

Because she could only imagine the shit that went through said mind, she didn't comment on that. "Devon?"

"Yes."

"You know Andrei's managed to clear it, so you don't have a record?"

He tensed a little. "Yes."

"Do you feel guilty about that?"

They'd never talked about what had happened, *why* Devon had assaulted a stranger when it was so out of character, and it seemed strange to her now. Why hadn't they discussed it?

She'd guarantee he'd discussed it with the other guys, just not her. But she was his partner. Shouldn't he share crap like that with her? And, mad as it might be, this was the first time she'd really been able to talk to him without Tin listening in, or one of the guys around.

She wanted to discuss this with him alone, and here, in the quiet gardens, it felt like a good time.

"Do you want the truth?" he asked, his tone cautious enough to make her withhold a smile.

"Of course. Why would I want a lie?"

"Some people prefer lies."

"When have I ever?"

He shrugged. "Then, no. I don't feel guilty. He deserved it."

"Why?" His strident tone surprised the hell out of her. "Why did he deserve it? You didn't know him, did you?"

"No. But he knew me."

There was a woodenness to the words that garnered her attention. "What do you mean?"

Silence. "Nothing."

"Devon. Don't be silly. Tell me what you meant," she insisted, pulling away from their cuddled position, so she could stare at him.

His eyes, those rich, azure pools, stared back at her. They were almost guileless, but Devon was no ingenue. Even if he was a little more naïve than most would credit a man of his age for.

"You won't believe me."

He sounded so matter of fact about it that she tensed. "Why wouldn't I?"

"Because *they* didn't." He jerked his chin up, which nudged his head back—towards the house.

"None of them?"

"No. They didn't." He leaned forward, and pressed his elbows to his knees as he murmured, "I explained why, but the attorney just told me to be quiet."

What on Earth? She reached for his hand, and even though she couldn't feel his palm through their gloves, she squeezed his fingers. He looked darkly handsome against the graying sky, and the grim wintergreens and brackish browns of trees that were hibernating for winter. His black felt coat highlighted his golden coloring, and made his black hair pop all the more.

"I'll believe you."

"You'll say I'm being paranoid, too."

She cut him a look, unsure of how to respond to that. Once upon a time, one of her men, either Sean or Sawyer—she couldn't quite remember which—had told her Devon was quite capable of being paranoid, of having paranoid delusions.

She'd watched *A Beautiful Mind*, so she got *it*. She did. Devon wasn't crazy, even if she teasingly said he was. Not really. He just saw the world differently than most. But paranoia? That felt like a whole different ball game.

Releasing a breath, she murmured, "Hit me with it."

He pursed his lips, then, his nostrils flaring, murmured, "The bastard was stalking me. When I told him to stop, he pretended he wasn't, and..." he shrugged. "I saw red."

"I SWEAR Tin has more luggage than all of us put together," Andrei grumbled as he stared at the cases in the hallway.

"He needs a lot of stuff that your grandfather is unlikely to have hanging around at his house," she retorted drily. "Stop whining."

"I'm not whining," he countered. "It's just. . .," he grimaced, "a lot."

"Good thing we're flying first class then, isn't it? And that we can afford the excess luggage?" She laughed when he rolled his eyes, but he just folded his arms as he watched her rifle through another bag as she checked to make sure she'd packed something she considered vital.

"We can buy things there, you know?" he asked, unsure if she realized that.

"You mean, they accept money in Veronia, too?"

Her gasp and the way she clutched her chest had him growling, "When did you become so sarcastic, *katyonok*?"

"It's being around you lot," she countered. "You've made me the woman I am today." Her wink was sassy as hell, but it was so nice to see her being herself again that he just shook his head at her. His girl was coming back to life, and it was a delight, and a relief, to behold.

"I thought it would be our fault."

"Of course." She beamed at him, then she tilted her head to the side. He turned around to see why and saw the shadow at the door. Before he could reach it, the key sounded in the lock and Sean appeared.

His friend appeared harried, his shoulders hunched, not only against the cold but against whatever stress was plaguing him.

He jerked in surprise at the sight of them both hovering in the foyer and demanded, in a tone most unlike his usual calm voice, "What the hell are you doing here?"

Sascha gasped at the biting note, but Andrei murmured, "We're just packing."

Sean glowered down at the luggage then shook his head at the sight of the eight different bags. Before either of them could say another word, he tucked his briefcase into his chest and maneuvered around the cases and Sascha, his destination evident: his office.

"What the hell was that about?" Sascha demanded, turning to frown at Sean's retreating back.

"You know how he gets with his cases," was all he said, but he stepped forward, pressed a hand to her shoulder and murmured, "Carry on packing. I'll come and bring the bags downstairs, okay? Don't carry them yourself." There were another four suitcases waiting for him.

For once, she didn't argue, her attention still on Sean, even though he'd slammed the door to his office closed behind him. She nodded as he headed down the hall after his friend.

Sean was not one to lose his temper. He was the most sedate of the lot of them. A true Brit, calm and collected, to his bones.

He didn't knock. That was a house rule. Just closed the door behind him, and pressing his back to it, Andrei stared over at Sean who was seemingly glowering at nothing.

Maybe it was the time of day, or maybe it was simply the first time he really looked, but Sean wasn't sleeping. The dark shadows under his eyes, the strain around his mouth, it all spoke of a deeper symptom, and Andrei had the feeling that symptom had less to do with their stillborn daughter than the rest believed.

"I think it's time you told me what's going on, don't you?" The man was entitled to be grumpy, but snapping at Sascha? That was beyond uncharacteristic.

Sean jerked at that, and Andrei gathered he hadn't even realized he'd entered the room. "Andrei? Is it time for dinner?"

He scowled. "No, it damn well isn't time for dinner."

"Then what's wrong?"

"I don't know. That's what I'm asking you."

"There's nothing wrong." Sean tilted his head to the side. "What made you think there was?"

"The fact you're walking around like a ghost."

"Don't be ridiculous—"

"I'm not," Andrei cut off. "I want to know what's going on. What aren't you telling us?"

Sean narrowed his eyes. His hair was shaggy and in need of a cut as he ran a hand over it. If he was trying to smooth it into some semblance of order, he failed. That alone spoke loudly. Sean was the neatest of them all, and Andrei considered himself pretty OCD when it came down to it.

It was unlike Sean to keep things to himself. Where Sascha was concerned, not so much. But with him and the others? Yes. Sean shared his caseload with them, often seeking advice or asking to simply run a theory by them.

He hadn't done that since Sascha had. ... Well, since she'd—

He sliced that train of thought in half. That was a path he didn't need to go down today. "Sean?" he prompted instead.

His best friend closed his eyes as he slouched back in his desk chair. "Andrei, you really don't want to know."

"Why don't I?"

"Because you're busy."

"I am, yes," he murmured easily, when wasn't he busy? "But never too busy for any of my family."

Adam's apple bobbing, Sean whispered, "You'll think I'm crazy."

"Why would I?"

"Because I sound it. Fuck. I sound like Devon."

That had Andrei scowling harder. "Like Devon? What are you talking about?"

Nostrils flaring before he opened his eyes, he murmured, "You know the day Devon was arrested?"

"How could I forget?" he asked drily.

Sean firmed his mouth. "He used his call on me."

"I know. And you arranged for the solicitor. ..."

"Yes. I did. But he told me something."

"What?"

"When we got to the hospital after Sascha had given birth, there was a man there."

"A man?" Andrei's eyes rounded. "Who the hell was he?"

Sean grimaced. "Your reaction matched ours. When she fell, he was there to help her. He stayed with her through the journey in the ambulance and all that day, he was with Tin."

"Why am I only just finding out about this?" he growled.

"Because I didn't realize it was important, dammit. Not until recently."

"What's changed?"

Sean swallowed. "I forgot about him. Didn't think anything of it. I was just grateful he'd been there for Sascha when we hadn't been." He sucked down a breath. "But when Devon called, it brought certain matters to light, and I've been investigating them."

"Investigating what?" Andrei demanded.

"Devon said he. ... Well, the guy was called Joseph Santorini." He quickly swept his hand over his hair again. "Devon said he attacked the guy that day because he thought it was him."

Andrei blinked. "Devon said he attacked a stranger because he thought it was the man who'd helped Sascha in Glasgow?"

"Yes."

"But it wasn't?"

"No. The man Devon assaulted was a guy called Christopher Horowich."

Andrei processed that but failed to put two and two together. "Where are you going with this, Sean?"

"Devon was due in court, and I also knew you asked Vasily to look into a way of ensuring Devon didn't walk out with a criminal record."

He felt no shame for asking for something illegal from his grandfather. Sometimes things had to slide for the greater good, and Veronia's economy would falter without Devon at Andrei's back as he spearheaded the investment drive. "Yes. I did," he retorted, somewhat bullishly. "I'd get grandfather involved again, too."

It wasn't the first time Andrei had used his grandfather's many resources, earning Sean's disapproval with each occasion. Although, in this instance, it sounded like Sean had wanted to make sure Devon wasn't punished. A fact that had him frowning.

Yet more uncharacteristic behavior.

"I wasn't sure if Vasily would be able to do anything, so I did some looking myself. Then Vasily contacted me," Sean carried on, his voice hoarser now. "He sent me a picture of Christopher Horowich."

"What about it?"

"He looked just like Joseph Santorini."

Andrei blinked. "Similarities or twins?"

Sean shook his head. "No. No way. Not even close to identical twins. It was him. Santorini."

"So, he was using a false name?" Andrei asked.

"Apparently, so. Devon really did beat the shit out of him, but Vasily sent me a shot before the beating. It was definitely the guy in Sascha's hospital ward."

Andrei thought about the ramifications of that. "Which implies, what? The man's been stalking us?"

Sean's jaw firmed, showing the steely pressure he exerted upon his lips. "The man's been stalking me."

"*You?*"

"Yes," Sean whispered. He pushed some papers forward, and as he did, his voice was thick as he carried on, "After she fell, I don't know, I had a bad feeling. I called in some favors. Got the footage from the store's security camera. Then, when I realized what I was seeing, I called in some more."

Andrei peered down at what appeared to be a storefront. There was a man in an expensive suit crouched down against the front steps that led to the doorway of a store which sold tartan products. He looked like he was tying his shoes. In another shot, you could just see his face, even though he was half-burrowing into his scarf. "Where is this?"

"Buchanan Street," Sean said hoarsely. Then he pushed another picture toward him.

It was a picture of the same man, still crouched down, but behind him, Andrei saw Sascha and Tin. His eyes widened at the sight, and he straightened when he saw something in the stranger's hand. "What's that in his hand?" He tilted his head to the side as he brought the photo near his face.

"A bottle of sunflower oil," Sean whispered bleakly.

Andrei swallowed, but it was hard. His throat couldn't seem to do it, couldn't seem to make the natural motion. "No. Sean, no."

"Yes, Andrei," he breathed, his face crumpling. "Santorini made sure Sascha fell."

Cupping his hand to his mouth, Andrei shook his head as he gathered the photos together. "No," he gritted out. "No."

Sean's eyes were wet as he stared at him. Then, he closed them, the guilt shredding him from the inside out, and Andrei realized he knew the true meaning of agony.

# KURT

# SIXTEEN

WITH HIS COCK in his fist, Kurt wondered if he'd died and gone to Heaven.

Or maybe not, because surely Heaven wasn't this beautiful?

Wasn't so goddamn ripe and curvy and wet...

He grunted as his thoughts worked in tandem with the sight in front of him.

Sean never shared.

Never.

Except with Kurt.

And fuck, Kurt was excruciatingly grateful for that as he watched Sascha moaning on the bed, writhing and wriggling under Sean's domination. She looked even more beautiful on the grand four-poster bed that took center stage in this bedroom.

They were in Vasily's home, deep in the heart of Moscow. Amid the classical furnishings, the Titian paintings, and the luxurious *objets d'art*, Sascha fit in well. Her luxurious form belonged to another time, another age, where women had been rounded and curvaceous—without shame.

Still, the sight of her bound to the bed was both a delight to behold and a stark surprise.

The men Kurt considered his brothers had always been kinky bastards. It was ingrained in them down to the bone, but they were also considerate lovers. This side of Sean, Sawyer, and Andrei's natures would never have revealed itself to Sascha if she hadn't wanted it.

Of late, that was all she wanted, and they were all happier men for it.

Well, except Devon. He was, as always, in his own world. Happy if Sascha smiled and down if she didn't. Things were far simpler for Devon than the rest of them, but even as the thought crossed Kurt's mind, he felt foolish. Nothing was ever simple where Devon was concerned.

Nothing.

Running his thumb over the tip of his dick, he smoothed the bead of pre-cum around the glans. He wanted Sascha's mouth on him, wanted it like he'd wanted nothing else, but the sight of her was too delicious to ignore.

Splayed on the grand mattress in one of the bedrooms in Andrei's grandfather's Moscow mansion, Sascha's arms and legs were tied to each post of the bed. Her wrists and ankles were bound with hemp rope before the strands were plaited and knotted to the columns. She was facedown, her eyes blindfolded, a silk tie folded and wrapped in on itself and shoved in her mouth. Sean had instructed her to insert earplugs too, ensuring he controlled her sense of taste, sight, and sound.

With each whack of his palm against Sascha's rounded buttocks, she released a garbled number.

The gag wasn't ideal.

Kurt knew from experience that Sean liked to hear her cry out, liked to have her respond, verbally, to his dictates. But in Vasily's home, it was awkward, and neither of them wanted Andrei's grandfather questioning why unusual cries escaped their bedchambers.

The old bastard would know what was going on, but he'd ask just to make Sascha blush.

The *Arschloch*.

Reaching under to cup his balls, he gently squeezed them in his palm and rubbed them together, sometimes twisting when he felt his arousal overcome him, needing to edge slightly because the sight of Sascha was enough to make him want to come again and again.

As he jacked off—slowly—he heard Sascha cry out from behind her gag, "Seven."

He tilted his head to the side as Sean gave her three more rapid spanks. She counted swiftly then sobbed as the sting had her hips twisting against the sheets.

She couldn't seem to get used to the spanks. Her butt, with that creamy skin of hers, was so sensitive, and a part of him wanted Sean to bite her there, just to see how she'd respond. He wasn't into this scene like his brothers were, but he sure as hell enjoyed watching it.

Fuck, he'd get off on anything that involved Sascha.

Although, gimp suits were most definitely off the cards.

"She only earned ten," Kurt commented when he saw Sean retrieve a hairbrush from the dresser beside the sofa where he was sitting. Noticing the vein pulsing in his brother's forehead, as well as the tensed abs Sean had revealed when he'd come into the bedroom wearing nothing but a pair of jeans, Kurt was curious as to what his brother was about.

"I never said how many sets of ten," Sean retorted, his mouth tight with an anger that was unlike him.

Kurt knew not to be concerned for Sascha's butt. When it counted, Sean would be the height of controlled, but still, Kurt knew the rules the three men were starting to demand of Sascha were important to them; to Sascha, even. But for some reason, she was continuing to rebel.

She wanted this.

Kurt saw it in her eyes when Andrei would bite her bottom lip when he kissed her, leaving behind a bruise that would last for days, and had her swallowing whenever she laved it with her tongue.

He saw it in the flush that overtook her creamy skin as Sawyer spanked her.

And it was more than evident in the way she could and would climax under Sean's dominance.

There was no coercion here.

Kurt knew the three men had only started introducing this kink into the bedroom because Sascha had told them she wanted it.

But her rebellion was evident, and the result of her punishments seemed to be of endless fascination to her.

Was it a concern?

Perhaps. This desire to be dominated had been born of grief, after all. A grief he could easily understand considering the loss of their beloved baby girl.

Was this the healthiest way of dealing with the emotions her grief had triggered? Who was he to say, was all the answer Kurt could come up with.

Different strokes for different folks, and there was no doubting the fact that Sascha needed a stern hand at the moment. She wasn't looking after herself. Plain and simple.

Eat breakfast. That was rule number one, for example.

Hardly complicated, no?

She made breakfast for them every day, and four times out of seven, she wouldn't eat it.

That resulted in a punishment.

Another rule was that she wasn't to leave the house without telling someone where she was going.

That might have seemed a tad over-the-top but Sean, with Vasily's help, had learned she might be in danger by association. They hadn't told her that, but they had conveyed that Sean had managed to collect a stalker, something that put the entire household at risk.

For whatever fucking reason, she would pop out to the store

without telling them, or head to the newsagents around the corner for a paper.

Another punishment.

There weren't many 'rules.' But what they were was a kind of guidance—measures the men had implemented to ensure her health, welfare, and safety.

Sean was angry today because she'd broken another rule—Devon had walked in to find her crying in one of the many lounges in Vasily's house, and when he'd asked why, she'd lied.

Devon, being Devon, naturally hadn't realized she'd lied. Sean had discerned the mistruth when Devon had asked him if they ought to take her to the hospital—she'd excused her tears by saying she'd stubbed her toe.

But according to Devon, she'd been sobbing like her heart was broken, and that was why he'd thought she was in extreme and intense pain.

That little interlude was why Sean was here today.

The bouts of emotion weren't something he was punishing. It was the fact she was hiding it. That she'd lied to Devon about it.

Because, rule number two was no lies. And if she lied to Devon or Kurt, by proxy, Andrei, Sawyer, or Sean would punish her for it.

The 'no lying' rule seemed more appropriate for their two-year-old, Tin. But Sascha, for some stupid reason, kept hiding her grief. Worse still, would lie about it and try to put a brave face on the situation.

That was why Sean was mad. Because they'd told her she was to express her feelings. He was a shrink, after all, he'd know what to do. And considering she was refusing to speak with anyone about their daughter's stillbirth, well, Sean wasn't pleased with her avoidance.

That was why he strode back to Sascha's side, practically vibrating with his anger at her. It didn't bleed through when he hit her left butt cheek with the hairbrush, though. He was, as Kurt had known, controlled to the max as the wooden paddle connected with her ass. The flesh turned instantly pinker than mere seconds before, and she released a wail as she twisted in her bindings, her head tilting so that she could shoot an accusative look at Sean that was totally wasted on him—mostly because he'd expected her reaction, but also because most of her glare was hidden behind the blindfold she wore.

Sean didn't even command she count this time—if he pulled out one of the earplugs, she could have heard his dictate.

He just gave her four more sharp hits to the left cheek and five more to the right.

By the time he was through, she was sobbing, and Kurt's cock deflated somewhat. Her little wriggles on the bed spoke of her need to try to burn off the pain, but it didn't work. How could it? Then, she released a sharp scream as Sean rubbed the sore skin, palming the thick mounds and massaging the tender flesh.

Her forehead pressed into the mattress, and by the time he was done, she was panting so hard, Kurt was concerned she'd hyperventilate behind the gag.

Sean must have been equally as troubled because he strode to her side, carefully pinched one of the earplugs, and pulled it free. "Sascha," he commanded, his voice strident as he unknotted the gag and released the tension in the fabric. "Calm down."

Her sobs increased in volume, enough so that Sean caught Kurt's eye, his concern evident.

"Is she having a panic attack?" Kurt asked, his words a rasp as he voiced his worry.

"No, but she's working her way up to one." Sean moved onto the bed, and though he wasn't fully nude, he pressed himself half on top of her. She stiffened as he settled himself, covering most of her as he tucked her into his hold. When he relaxed, she also did, but her breaths were still snuffled squeaks from her nose.

Though he usually watched, Kurt couldn't stop himself from getting to his feet and striding over to the other side of the bed. When the mattress dipped at his weight, she turned her head slightly, and Sean took advantage of that move to pull the tab of the tie from between her lips.

"Kurt?" she asked huskily, and he had to smile. Sean hadn't announced his entry to the room, after all. Kurt was invited in after Sascha had been trussed up like a turkey on the bed before Sean had gone off and changed out of his more formal clothes into the old pair of jeans he wore currently.

"How did you know?" Kurt pressed a kiss to her head.

"You smell like a forest."

His brows rose. "I do?" His lips twitched as, mirroring Sean, he covered her other side, so she was blanketed by them both.

"Yes. You do," she whispered.

"Can you breathe okay?" Sean questioned. "We're not too heavy for you?"

"No, you're perfect." Her voice was low, but she relaxed into the mattress, seemingly content to lay there in silence.

Hell, Kurt wasn't too displeased by their proximity either, and as her breathing calmed, she started to relax further, and he found himself closing his eyes, appreciating the warmth of the embrace, the peace of this haven they made together.

"Why did you hit me so hard?" she asked after a few seconds.

"I didn't," Sean countered.

"My ass disagrees."

"You'd have told me to stop if you'd wanted me to."

She fell silent at that, seeming to process what he was saying. Kurt saw her gulp, then she whispered, "Yes, I would have done, wouldn't I?"

Sean's top lip quirked up in a slight smile. "You would." He wriggled on the bed slightly, getting more comfortable in his position. "Your punishment isn't over," he warned when she released a sigh as he covered her once more.

"You said ten," she sulked.

"And like I told Kurt when he said the exact same thing, I never said how many sets of ten." A low growl escaped Sean's throat. "You lied to Devon, Sascha. We both know that isn't as easy as it sounds.

The man's like a human lie detector at times. You can pull the wool over his eyes, but lying to him? That took intent."

"I didn't want to talk about it. I get sick of talking about it!" she screamed, the sudden shrill sound had Kurt jolting in surprise.

Sean immediately shifted and spanked her bright-pink ass. She released a howl, and her body bowed as she tried to alleviate the ache. For a second, Kurt and Sean just focused on her, then when she began to sob, Kurt's throat felt thick with tears, too.

"You have to talk about it. If you did, then maybe you wouldn't keep on having these outbursts," Sean told her, his tone like gravel, and that alone was telling. He was having trouble containing his emotions as well.

"I don't want to," she whispered. "I just want it to stop hurting." When her bottom lip quivered, Kurt's heart melted.

"Then we have to give you something to take your mind off that particular hurt."

Kurt knew the words should have come from Sean, but instead, they came from him. Where they'd found their source, he wasn't sure, but seeing the conflicting needs inside her was something he couldn't bear.

She needed them, and he couldn't help but fear the fact that they were failing her in some intrinsic way.

Her breath quivered from her lips as she processed his words, and she twitched slightly, turning toward his voice. "What kind of thing?"

Kurt fell silent, unsure how to answer now he'd made that declaration—fuck, he should have thought about the consequences of his words!

Before he could speak, however, Sean murmured, "More rules."

She tensed, and a swift pant escaped her lips. Her body rippled underneath their heavy blanketing weight, and Kurt could swear he could scent her arousal. It seemed to blossom out of nowhere.

"I don't want more rules," she countered breathily.

"I think your body disagrees with you," Sean retorted, his tone dry. "And what did I just say about you lying to us?" He gave a sharp tap to her butt, one that had her moaning this time as he slipped his fingers down over the curve of her ass and slid them into her pussy.

She was wet.

The sounds were clue enough, but the way she moaned as he finger-fucked her, the way she writhed? Jesus, Kurt wasn't sure if he'd be able to stop himself from blowing his load.

The sounds of her slick heat being fucked by Sean's fingers were masked by the moans she released and then when Sean stopped, the groan that escaped her lips resonated deep in Kurt's fucking soul.

"No!" she whined, bucking her hips.

"Yes," Sean ground out. He jerked his chin at Kurt who rolled back to let him crowd her from above. When he topped her, he bowed his head and placed his teeth about the fleshy part of her shoulder. Just the way he gripped her had her calming, though small whimpers still escaped her.

It was so primitive that Kurt wasn't sure what the hell he was seeing, but her response to Sean was undeniable.

He released her and, with one hand, reached between them. Kurt heard the sound of his zipper being lowered, and Sascha did, too—if the way her head tilted was anything to go by. When his cock was in his fist, he pressed it to the plump ass cheeks and rested the heavy weight between them.

She moaned and murmured, "Please, sir? Please?"

The flash of delight in Sean's eyes was enough to make Kurt shudder. "Why should I do what you want, when you don't do what I want?"

His retort seemed to have her stymied until she whispered, "I'm trying."

"Trying's not good enough, is it?" Sean growled. "Trying is the difference between working to make you come and not ignoring your needs entirely."

She froze at his words, her limbs tensing as she seemed to still all over. A shudder whispered through her body, and she suddenly went slack.

"I'll try harder."

"Not good enough," Sean whispered as he nipped the upper curve of her ear. "I want your one hundred percent, not just ninety-five. What use is ninety-five to me?"

Sascha licked her lips. "But I—"

"No," Kurt immediately countered. "No buts. You don't even take your punishments like a good girl, do you?"

That had her biting her bottom lip. "I-If I let you punish me, will you—?"

"There's no letting me do anything," Sean ground out. "Is there?"

This time, her chin trembled. "P-Please, sir? I'm sorry I was bad. I'm s-sorry."

The sounds of her pleas were a double-edged sword. It went straight to Kurt's cock, but equally, he didn't like his strong, sassy Sascha sounding so defeated. Still, this was a defeat of a different variety.

In her own way, Sascha was totally in charge here.

That was the beauty of the Submissive's relationship with her Dominant. Unless she wanted it, the Dominant could do sweet FA—fuck all.

Grunting, Sean murmured, "Sorries mean nothing. Everyone can say sorry. I want action, Sascha, action. Now, you're going to prove to me that you want this, want me in this way by being a good girl for your punishment, aren't you?"

Her lips parted as she whispered, "Y-Yes, sir."

Sean shot Kurt a triumphant smile, and he pointed to the rope he'd tied above her head. "Unravel the bindings, I want her on her back."

Though she released a whimper, she remained silent as Kurt picked at the knots. They weren't as tight as he'd thought they were, but to someone unaccustomed to being bound, he had no doubt they felt restrictive to Sascha.

She was their Queen.

Had been for years now, and she wasn't familiar with being tied down. If anything, she was used to soaring.

Though it concerned him that she wanted to be bound, equally, he was just relieved that she was willing to express her needs in some small way.

When she was free, she didn't move, even though Kurt could see the relaxing in her biceps and thighs as the pull of the ropes ceased straining her muscles. When Sean tumbled her over, so she was on her back, Kurt released a hissed breath at the sight of her.

God, she was lovely.

With her ripe tits, curvy waist, and strong and sleek thighs, she looked like sex personified to him. There were stretch marks on her belly from carrying two babies, and her breasts weren't as pert as maybe they'd once been, but he only knew that because she'd complained to him about that after giving birth to Tin. He didn't see the difference. He couldn't, truth be told. He just saw her. This sexy minx who belonged to him, who was ripe and sassy and vibrant with life that pulsated through her veins. It transmitted itself to him, and energized him in ways he couldn't begin to describe.

When he saw Sascha naked, he just saw his woman.

Nothing more, nothing less.

He couldn't stop himself from reaching over and touching her breasts. Andrei had definitely been there recently. There were teeth marks on the curvy swells, and the sight of them wasn't as unusual as it might have been. Even before they'd begun embracing this side of their natures, a side that had been put to pasture for years, they'd all marked her. It might have seemed adolescent, but there was nothing hotter than their marks, their love bites, on her throat and tits.

Sean slapped his hand. "She's being punished."

He grimaced at the chastisement but understood when he saw Sascha had arched her back and was actively seeking his touch.

"Tie her hands to the posts," Sean ordered again.

His lips twitched at being bossed around, but he complied, loving how the new position spread her legs to the point of discomfort. He looked at where Sean had tied her ankles and saw that he'd knotted the fastenings at a different point on the bedposts. She was wider than before, and he could see the tension in her calves and thighs because of it. The strain made them looks as sleek and as powerful as a model's, and fuck, did he want those bad boys wrapped around his hips as he slammed his way inside her.

Grunting at the thought, he grabbed hold of his cock as he maneuvered on the bed. The mattress dipped as he crawled to the footboard and watched as Sean did the same—his hand on his dick as he stroked himself to the sight of Sascha's gleaming pussy.

She was bare—another rule. She'd always had a landing strip, but for whatever reason, Andrei had insisted on this new amendment to her routine. Kurt wasn't about to complain. Going down on her was like slurping up hot, wet silk now.

The juices seemed to flood freely from her sex, slipping out until his mouth watered with the need to taste. She was aroused—if he hadn't seen it in the flush on her cheeks and tits, or the way her body shuddered at the slightest caress, here was his proof.

"Now then," Sean started, but he stopped to clear his throat, and Kurt couldn't blame him. Sascha on a bad day was enough to make a man pause, but at this moment? She was like a wet dream come to life. "I'm going to spank you, Sascha, and you're going to count, and you're going to ask me for the next one."

Her chin quivered. "Yes, sir."

For a second, Sean froze, then he grinned slightly. "Don't you want to know how many spanks?"

She licked her lips. "May I ask?"

Kurt shot Sean a look, and this time, they shared the grin. "Well done, Sascha. Yes. You may ask, and I'll answer: ten spanks. To your pussy."

Her nostrils flared. "Thank you, sir."

The way she said that, breathily and excited and tense, all at the same time, made his cock feel like it would burst. Sean didn't reply, just climbed off the bed. This time, he didn't retrieve a hairbrush, but from one of the drawers, he gathered a long, thin stick.

The cane was reed-thin, and he winced at how hard the sting was going to be against such tender tissues.

He'd have argued, but fuck, he wanted to see her back bow, those delicious tits of hers jiggling as she tried to overcome the strain.

When Sean returned, she released a breath, and he raised the reed high and with minimal force, slapped it down against her thigh. She yelped, more out of surprise than pain, Kurt thought, and her shaky panting breaths were evident that she was taken aback rather than suffering.

The sound of the whoosh had been epic, though, and Kurt understood why Sean had done that.

"Hold open her pussy lips, Kurt," Sean whispered, his voice so low he could barely hear it.

Kurt, swallowing, reached forward and did as bid. The minute he touched her cunt, she moaned and wriggled on the bed, her hips arching as she sought the kind of caress she'd need to get off.

Sean caned her thigh once more. "None of that. You'll get your pleasure if you're a good girl."

Sean, Andrei, and Sawyer all had their ways about them.

Sean appreciated behavior modification—punishing Sascha was something he enjoyed. Andrei liked to control pleasure—orgasm denial was his chastisement of choice. And Sawyer was a blend of the two, but he liked bondage more than the others. He'd have Sascha hogtied if she'd be amenable to the idea.

The very notion was enough to make Kurt's cock seep pre-cum. Even as aroused as he was, he had to wonder if, in all their years together, they'd have been able to contain their kinks or was this inevitable? Like night following day?

Vanilla relationships were easier, but when had any of them ever been vanilla?

In truth?

Five men shared Sascha, and she was fine with that. Why hadn't they always realized she was fine with things being a tad unusual in the bedroom?

Sean maneuvered himself between Sascha's thighs, and though he didn't rest much weight on her, he straddled one of her legs as he carefully positioned the reed against her cunt.

He didn't move.

Not for endless seconds.

Sascha's breathing grew heavier and heavier, until she was outright panting until sweat sheened on her skin, and she was gleaming with it. Her tits jiggled and her nipples turned into hard, ferocious beads he wanted to bite more than he wanted his next meal.

Then, when she looked on the brink of another panic attack, Sean tapped her.

Right on the clit.

For a second, she was silent. Almost as though she wasn't sure whether the kiss of the reed to her pussy was anti-climactic or not. Then, the mewl that escaped her was long and low, and her belly muscles tensed in a way that told Kurt, she'd have rolled up into a ball if she'd been able.

That mewl went on for a lifetime, and it was hardwired into his system until, eventually, she panted out the pain and whispered, "Thank you, sir. Number one. May I have another one, sir?"

Such compliance was alien to him where Sascha was concerned, Kurt realized. She wasn't exactly argumentative, but she had fire. Spirit.

Kurt didn't want to kill that, even if he wanted to find a way to help her cope with the grief she was experiencing at the moment.

The Sascha of before was another person from the Sascha of now, and it could well be that this would be what brought their woman home to them.

"Good girl," Sean purred. "Kiss her clit, Kurt, in congratulations."

Kurt's lips twitched as he leaned over and curled his tongue about the nub. He slurped down on the tiny pearl, sucked hard until he felt

Sean's hand in his hair as he tugged Kurt away from the delicious pussy they'd all made theirs years before.

"Hold her wide open again," Sean directed, and Kurt did as bid, content to leave this in Sean's hands for the moment.

He tapped her in quick succession, barely giving her leave to whisper the words he wanted to hear before he'd hit five.

Her little nub was bright pink, and the skin around it was flushed with a hectic red. Kurt's mouth watered with the need to taste it, and Sean nodded at him. "Give her what she needs, Kurt."

She released a long moan until Sean angled himself better on the bed. "I want you to come, Sascha," he commanded. "You don't even have to ask before you do."

A happy squeak escaped her as Kurt began sucking her clit once more, and then the caning started as Sean changed his original punishment. The yelps merged with moans as Sean caned her tits, leaving faint pink lines on the tender flesh.

They weren't bright pink, weren't hard stripes that would bruise, but they'd leave faded marks in the morning that would declare to all the men what had happened the night before.

As Sean caned her, she jerked and juddered while Kurt ate her out.

It took a surprisingly short time for her to come considering the discomfort she had to be under, and Kurt, despite himself, was proud of her for being able to focus on doing as Sean demanded.

He felt Sean's fingers in his hair once more as he tugged Kurt away from her juicy cunt. She was bright pink again, but this time from pleasure, not pain, and was so wet, it would be better than Heaven sliding between those drenched folds.

Before his eyes, Sean reached forward and produced a silver butt plug.

When he saw the fur behind it, Kurt had to grin.

So, Sean had picked up on that, too?

"Get it nice and wet, Kurt," he ordered and, carefully, held up the fur tail, so it wouldn't brush her skin as Kurt grabbed the metallic plug and, with no ado, slid it inside her.

The cold silver burned as it went in—that much was obvious as she grunted at the contrast of her molten heat and the chill of the plug inside her.

He fucked her with the plug a few times then, on Sean's nod, slipped it out and slid it between her spread cheeks—that was how wide her thighs were, it had opened all of her nether regions to their delighted gaze.

When her ass accepted the plug, she finally felt the fur against her skin and mumbled, "Oh, what's that?" Then, she realized she'd forgotten herself. "Sir. I meant, what's that, sir?"

Sean beamed at her, not that she could see it, and murmured, "My little pet needed a tail, so I bought her one."

For a second, she froze, then she whispered, "Pet?"

"Yes. *Pet*," Sean half-purred.

"W-What does that mean, sir?"

"It's the kind of submissive you are. A naughty little pet that needs to be trained."

When her breasts jiggled as she released a deep sigh, Kurt wasn't sure what was going through her mind. But she didn't say anything, she kept silent if anything.

Sean didn't seem disappointed by her lack of response, just slipped between her legs, grabbed a firm hold of his cock, and slid home.

Before she could do little else than jolt in surprise, he began to fuck her.

Hard.

The bed shook with his thrusts, and the wail that escaped Sascha had Kurt reaching over to press his hand to her mouth.

Her tongue popped out to tickle his palm, and the little rebellion had him grinning. But Sean, upon seeing that grin, seemed to take it as a challenge.

The look of intent on his face changed. Morphed into something else.

He reached between her legs and pinched her clit. When she squealed, he seemed to let up some, but he carried on fucking her so hard the bed shook with each thrust.

A low, keening sound escaped her, and Kurt watched as her hands turned into fists as she held herself still for Sean's fucking. Then, she began to arch her hips and rock her pelvis, taking everything he had to give and asking for more.

Sean's grin turned pained as he ceased pinching her clit and began to rub. Hard and fast. Quick little caresses that had her struggling against her bonds. When he was close to coming, Sascha was so high, so strung out, that Sean winced when he pulled out.

Her expletives could be heard from beneath the gag of his hand, and though Sean grinned, it didn't stop him from grabbing a firm hold of his cock and jerking off onto her belly.

As his seed pooled there, sinking into her creamy skin as though it belonged there, he began to smear the liquid on her. Then, he reached over, pressed one hand to the side of her head and motioned with the other to Kurt. He removed his palm, and she immediately hissed, "You bastard."

Though they both carried on grinning, Sean barked, "Open your mouth!"

When she complied, instantly, it seemed to soothe the beast inside him. He thrust three fingers into her mouth, plunged them in and out roughly until she was moaning again.

When she'd come to love such rough treatment, Kurt wasn't sure, but she was glowing brighter than the sun under Sean's care, that was for damn sure.

Even as he shook his head at the sight, he jerked to attention when Sean murmured, "Suck Kurt's cock."

Not one to be left out, he moved so he straddled her chest and carefully tapped the tip of his cock to her lips.

They parted immediately, taking him into the warm, wet cavern that could be beaten by one thing only—her cunt.

He thrust into her with care at first, then when she made encouraging noises, began to move a little faster, a little harder.

She wasn't gasping for air even though the position had to be uncomfortable, and she didn't gag, either. Then, when she did, he jerked in surprise as her teeth grazed his shaft. Tilting his head back, he saw Sean was eating her out, and deciding to forgive her, Kurt did something he thought Sascha would appreciate.

He didn't want to hurt her.

That wasn't his bag.

But this went beyond him.

Somehow, it went beyond Sean, too.

Sascha felt she needed punishing, and though she was so beyond wrong, Kurt felt like he had to give her this catharsis.

It was wrong on so many levels that he also knew, but it didn't stop him from grabbing a firm hold of her hair and tugging her head back as he began to thrust into her mouth.

The lazy moan that was garbled around his shaft said it all, and as she milked his dick of all he had to offer, he felt her tense, close to orgasm.

Then, she tensed in a different way when Sean obviously stopped his machinations.

Kurt, leaning over Sascha, panted as he made sure every drop of cum slipped between her lips. Then, when he was done, he climbed off of her and sank back, unable to stop himself from turning into mush as the orgasm and what he'd just seen went to work on blowing his brains out.

Sean didn't suffer a similar fate.

If anything, he seemed recharged, energized by what was happening.

"Please?" It was one word. One. Single. Word. And yet Sascha drew it out so it was like a litany, and when Sean began to undo her fastenings, unknotting the bindings while Kurt watched on drowsily, she started to sob out the words, "Please, sir?"

Sean ignored her as he moved about the bed, releasing her from her bondage. When her arms and legs were free, he reached for some oil that he'd left on the bedside table, poured it onto her thighs, and handed it to Kurt.

Though it was hard when he felt like he was made out of limp spaghetti, he gathered himself together and poured the oil onto her torso and arms.

The sheets would be a mess tomorrow, but it wasn't like Vasily's staff were going to complain, was it?

He hummed under his breath as he stroked and massaged Sascha's taut arms. Her body seemed like it was vibrating. Whether that was from suppressed rage or need, he wasn't actually sure.

As Sean dug his thumbs into the insteps of her feet, she released a grunt, and her hips arched in response.

When Kurt was done smoothing the oil into her skin, rubbing her biceps, which had been taut for well over twenty minutes, he sank back on his heels and began to maneuver the blindfold out of place.

Sean hummed when he saw the tears pooling in the tiny crevices of her sockets, and he reached over and began to lap at the liquid as it spilled free.

"W-Why, sir?"

"Good girls get treats for good behavior," he told her simply. "Are you going to eat breakfast tomorrow?"

She released a shuddery breath. "Y-Yes."

Kurt, because he felt like it was important she know this was true, murmured, "You don't have to eat a lot, Sascha, just enough to keep your energy levels high."

Sean hummed again. "Sascha knows I'm not asking her to stuff her face. I want her healthy. That's all. And not eating breakfast when she has a lot to do throughout the day is silly, isn't it?"

Her lips quivered as she peered at him through glass-green eyes that were liquid with tears. "Y-Yes, sir."

"Why is it?" he asked, obviously trying to press the situation home.

"Because I have to chase Tin around half the day." Her lower lip popped out.

"What's another reason?"

"Because I don't need to diet."

It still astonished him that she thought she was fat. Every time this came up, Kurt had to shake his head at the notion that the woman who epitomized perfection didn't notice it.

"Exactly," Sean growled, then he reached for her tits and squeezed them. "I love these as they are." He dipped his head and began to kiss her stomach, trailing his tongue over the dips and swells of her belly before pressing a kiss just above her navel. "I love you as you are," he told her, whispering the words as he peered up at her.

She began to tremble, and though she nodded, Kurt wasn't sure if she believed Sean.

Laying on his side, he reached over and with his pointer finger, tilted her head, so she was looking at him. "You want this, don't you, Sascha?"

Her eyes widened. "Of course."

A frown puckered his brow. "You don't have to do anything you don't want."

"I know." This time, there was a faint growl to her words.

"I think Kurt is inexpertly trying to ask why you need this now when you never did before." Sean's voice was wry as he leaned back on his heels and zipped up his fly.

Her gaze cut to his swiftly disappearing cock, then to his eyes. "Because I've never felt this out of control before." The simplicity of her statement floored Kurt.

"Why do you feel out of control?" he asked quietly, needing to know, needing to understand.

She shrugged. "I wish I knew." There was a sorrow to her words that had anger nipping at his heels, but as he didn't really know where it was aimed, he released it on a long, slow sigh.

"You'll tell us if you don't want this?" he insisted.

She blinked. "Of course." Her lips formed another pout. "I'm not too happy about being left hanging."

At her grumble, Sean spanked her thigh. "You just said you want this, so you can't grumble because you didn't follow the rules you agreed to uphold."

When she winced, the point hitting home, Kurt just sighed.

Whatever the hell was going on with her, Sean didn't seem too distressed about it. He'd be the one to know. With his many degrees and doctorates in psychology, he had to know a thing or two about grief, didn't he?

Shooting him a look, Sean just smiled.

Somehow, that smile said it all.

Yes, this was unorthodox.

Yes, this might not have been the best way to handle grief, but this was what their woman needed.

And whatever Sascha needed, she got.

# SEVENTEEN

A SHRIEK ESCAPED Sascha when she surged from the depths of the water and saw Devon perched on the side of the bath.

"Devon, how many times have I told you not to do that?" she complained, as she always did.

He grunted. "It's not my fault you're always underwater when I come in."

She narrowed her eyes at him. "Did you knock on the door like I told you?"

"Yes." He huffed.

"And why didn't you wait if I didn't answer?"

He blinked at her. "Does it matter?"

Because evasion wasn't something she was used to from Devon, she frowned. "Of course, it matters when you scare the shit out of me whenever you sneak into the bathroom while I'm underwater."

"What do you do under there, anyway?" he groused, his hand trailing through the liquid silk that was just this side of scalding. "It can't be good for your brain. The water's too hot."

She snorted. "It's not too hot. I'm not burned."

"That's because you're used to it." He shook his head. "See, that's why you need me here. To make sure you don't cook yourself in some kind of bath bomb stock."

Sascha wrinkled her nose as he peered over at the small tray of bath bombs she'd brought with her. Yeah, there was no way she was wasting this bath—whenever she came to Moscow and Vasily's house, she used it.

Half-pool, half-bath, it was like a really wide dipping pool. Submerging herself under the surface was never difficult. It was too deep. She didn't have to cling to the side to hold herself down in the depths, could even mushroom float, bobbing around as she chilled out.

Problem was Devon seemed to have an issue with the bath. For whatever reason, he had some sort of radar system set up for whenever she used the damn thing. He'd sit on the side while she floated or wriggled around in the bath and stun the shit out of her when he sneaked in to watch.

Hell, Sascha was down with watching. What had happened last night was proof of that.

She felt like another woman when one of her men took her while another looked on, but there was. . . .

A breath gusted from her lungs as she sighed. Sascha was reading too deeply into the situation.

"Just knock and wait next time," she tried to get him to agree.

He pursed his mouth, looking remarkably stubborn as his upper lip firmed while the bottom flattened out.

The expression was far too much like the one Tin made when she tried to get him to eat something Devon didn't like.

With a grunt, she tipped her feet, deciding to lay flat out on the water level. Sure, it put her naked body in Devon's line of sight, but her pussy was off limits today.

Aunt Flo had visited, and knowing Devon, he was aware of that. It wouldn't have surprised her if he'd set one of his alarms to run in sync with her ovulation cycle.

The thought had her rolling her eyes, then he surprised her by asking, "Why do you like it?"

"Like what?" she replied, turning her head to the side to look at him. "The water . . .? I like how big the bath is more than anything. I don't have that many at home. You know that."

But he was shaking his head. "No. I didn't mean the water. I meant, why do you like when Sean, Andrei, and Sawyer boss you around?"

Her lips curved. "I wouldn't call it 'bossing me around,' Devon."

"No? I would." He frowned down at his hand, which was still trailing in the liquid. "I don't get it."

"What's not to get?" she replied gently. If anyone else had asked, she might have huffed, told them it was her damn body, and if she wanted it bossed around, that was her prerogative.

But Devon was confused, and while she loved the man, he wasn't at his best when he was confused.

What was an ordinary state for most men and women, not understanding a situation could have Devon derailing, spiraling into a level of panic she'd witnessed more times than she liked. Sure, over the years, it was less than a handful of times because her men knew just what to do to calm him down, plus her presence in his world had helped level him out, too. Throw in Tin? The baby hadn't inspired panic even if his reactions and responses weren't exactly logical. If anything, that had brought another level of serenity to Devon's world.

Her lips curved as she remembered him asking why Tin drank so much if he was only going to pee it out seconds later.

Of course, that had precluded him going through every book on newborns Amazon had to offer.

Okay, maybe not *every* book, but it had damn well felt like it. Especially when he'd been quoting facts for about six months after his binge-reading session.

Still, those times when he did spiral never grew less concerning. She was used to him being slightly vague. Like he was in another world. His brain ticking away even as he kept up most conversations —about twenty seconds behind.

What she wasn't used to was him being unresponsive.

She hated that. Hated it with a passion and always did her best to backtrack, to help him through whatever was confusing him.

"It makes me feel safe."

The admission might have been torn from her with the way she panted afterward. It was dredged from the very foundations of her soul, and she knew that she would not have shared that particular insight with anyone else, not even Kurt.

He was the most 'emotional' of her men, the one she found it easiest to share that kind of stuff with. But even with him, she had been pretty reticent about this new side of her sex life.

"Why though? Do you like them hitting you?"

Her throat closed at his words, at his choice of verbs. "They're not hitting me, Devon," she whispered, her voice low and thready. Not just with surprise but with concern.

If the ocean represented the world, Sean, Kurt, Andrei, and Sawyer were Devon's lifeboat. They kept him safe from the unknown perils of the open sea. In that analogy, she was a life jacket. Always there, always making sure he was safe, too, but more protective than proactive.

The last thing they needed was for Devon to question the role the four men had in his life. Hell, they weren't just 'men.' They were his brothers.

She'd never seen closer siblings before, and the bond each guy had was something everyone should aim for.

They knew each other's secrets.

Knew each other's sins.

And loved each other regardless of them.

"My father used to hit my mother, Sascha," he stated quite calmly, even if there was a tornado brewing in his eyes as he looked at her steadily. "I recognize the sounds."

Her throat clutched.

Dear God, how had she forgotten that his father had abused his mother?

Mouth trembling as she waded to the side of the bath where he was seated, she pressed one of her hands to his and then slid the other up his exposed forearm. In a T-shirt and ratty jeans, he shouldn't have looked as handsome as he did.

Somehow, Devon had the ability of making a Chewbacca shirt look hot.

Yeah, made no sense to her, either.

"Devon, they're not hurting me."

"You cry out. In pain," he gritted out.

"I know I do." She bit her bottom lip. "It hurts."

"So, why . . .?" The question trailed off as his confusion seemed to soar.

"I like that it hurts," she whispered.

He reared back at that. "You like it?"

Closing her eyes, she leaned her forehead against his arm and whispered, "It feels good."

"I don't understand." If the words weren't enough to tell her that, his flat tone was.

"I know. I can tell." It was on the tip of her tongue to say she didn't understand, either, but that was a surefire way to have him dipping his toe into the vortex of panic.

Everything was so cut and dry with Devon sometimes. It made maneuvering around him impossible on some days, yet a joy on others.

Of all her men, there was something about him that brought a deep and intrinsic joy to her world.

Before Tin, he'd always been able to make her smile. He kept her grounded in a way. There was no BS allowed around him, not without him calling her out on it, at any rate.

But after Tin? That had just settled even more. Watching her baby boy with her lover was not only more entertaining than TV, but also, it was inspiring and heart-warming.

Devon was unique enough never to be irritated at just how constant Tin's mimicking was. Anyone else? Yeah, they'd have snapped by now. With all the love in the world, it was irritating. Tin was relentless. He followed Devon—when he couldn't move independently, it had been with his eyes. Then, after he'd learned to crawl, he might as well have grabbed hold of Devon's leg and let the man walk him everywhere because Tin was stuck to him like glue.

Parents weren't perfect. They weren't always patient. They got tired and stressed, had their own shit to deal with, too. Being followed around, having your every move copied while you were in the vicinity? Every day. For years?

That shit?

Yeah, she wasn't sure if she'd have been patient enough to deal with that.

But Devon?

He took to it like a bird did to flight.

It never fazed him. Never irritated him. It just was, and God, she loved him for that.

Fuck, she adored him for how great he was with Tin. For how much he loved their son when, she knew, the guys had all feared he'd never really know what to do with a kid being in the house.

Devon had proven them wrong in spades.

His earnestness triggered something in her, though, something that forced her to open up to him when, of late, she'd been hunkering down.

"I like the pain."

His hand gripped hers. Tightly. So tightly her fingers ached, and that was proof enough that he wasn't himself. Devon was usually controlled when he touched her. Even when he was in the throes of orgasm, he'd never have held her as tightly as this. "Why?" he rasped.

"It's a release. It lets me feel." She licked her lips. "I feel so out of control, Devon. So . . . unlike myself. I don't know what I'm doing. Where I'm going. Each day is so strange to me now.

"It made sense before. My days weren't like a routine, and they were never that boring." Boring wasn't a part of your life when you had five very different men under the same roof with a little boy who looked set to take after his fathers on the genius front. "But I had a purpose. That purpose was to make a baby. I guess that sounds dumb, but it was like I had a checklist in my head. Nine months. Give or take a few days. That was my to-do list. Make a baby.

"Now? Now I failed?" Her throat thickened once more, making her wish she had some water to drink, not just laze around in. "It's like nothing makes sense."

He fell silent at her words, but his grip on her hand relaxed slightly. She felt the soothing stroke of his thumb against the back of her hand, and it made her shudder as she pressed herself tighter against him.

"There are moments where nothing makes sense," he told her, his voice almost grating. "Where I feel like I'm going to go crazy, go insane if I can't get a handle on things. I want to blow up, want to implode. Want to scream, and yet, even uttering a word is beyond me." He sucked down a shaky breath. "Nothing makes sense," he repeated, and she knew how terrifying a prospect that was for him.

Her lips curved slightly though as she realized what he was trying to do. . . .

Rationalize this state of mind she was in, compare it to what he went through.

And the craziest thing? He wasn't half wrong, she recognized.

That was how she felt.

Out of control.

Like she was spinning and spinning and spinning with no chance of it ever stopping. Of never being able to just stand flat on two feet, to gaze at the world around her without feeling dizzy.

"Yes," she confirmed. "That's how I feel. Everything did make sense before, but now. . . ."

"You're lost," he inserted, his other hand coming up to stroke her hair back from her temple. "But you're not, Sascha. You're never lost. I'd never allow it."

The statement was arrogant, but it amused her enough to make her smile. "I know. I'm never lost when I'm with you." And she didn't just mean Devon. She meant all of her men. "But it's a different kind of lost. Like a purpose that's gone fallow. I can't seem to get over that."

"And them hitting you helps?" he asked, sounding pained.

She released a breath. "They don't hit me, Devon. They spank me."

He pulled away slightly, and she peered up at him, seeing his lack of understanding. "That's just a synonym."

Sascha had to snort. "Maybe? I don't know. I just know I like it."

"My mother hated it," he whispered.

"I'm not your mother," she whispered back. "And they're not your father. Andrei, Sean, and Sawyer love me. They only have control over me because I give them that control. The power is with me, Devon. With your mom, it wasn't like that. Your father was in control, and he abused her."

Devon flinched, and while she regretted hurting him, it was important he understood she was nothing like his mom, and her men were nothing like his father. "I didn't think you were her," he told her gruffly. "I didn't sneak into the bathroom to see my mother naked." His nose wrinkled with disgust at the thought.

"I'm very relieved to hear that," she teased, finding it hard not to laugh at his expression. But, his words were more telling than their face value. "You used to sneak into the bathroom with her, too?"

"I don't do it all the time with you," he murmured, then like he was confessing, whispered, "Not all the time, anyway. Sometimes, I just check on you then go before you know."

Her eyes flared wide at that, and for the first time, she felt irritated. "Dammit, Devon!"

He didn't seem to hear her, though, he was lost in his thoughts as he whispered, "One time, I came home from school. We had a chauffeur, and he used to bring me back." Her tirade was on permanent hiatus at his words.

Devon never spoke about his childhood.

Never.

She wasn't sure if the sound of her breathing was enough to disturb him from this tale, and that was the last thing she wanted.

"About two years before she killed herself, she'd started drinking. My dad hated it, but he never stopped her. I didn't know why. I wished he had. But I used to see him . . . he was the one who would top up the decanters, and he was always the one who'd serve her when he got back from post." He shuddered. "She'd do the stupidest things. Her lies became a reality at some point."

"What do you mean?" she asked, murmuring the question so as not to break his train of thought.

"She'd lie about falling down the stairs or walking into doors." He scowled at that. "Do you know, I've never walked into a door? I tried. I tried to because I couldn't understand why she did it so often. . . ."

"It was an excuse, sweetheart. A justification for her bruises," she explained, unsure if he understood that. Her voice was thready with sorrow for what he'd witnessed.

"Oh, I know," he refuted easily. "I just wasn't sure why it was her go-to excuse." His shrug said it all, she guessed. "When she started drinking, I saw her, though. She *would* trip up and fall into the door. She did fall down the stairs. She fell asleep at the breakfast table, even. One time, I thought she was going to drown in her soup!" He shook his head.

"Did you think she was going to drown in the bath?" she inquired, understanding where he was heading with his tale now.

He shot her a look, stared deep into her eyes, and slowly, nodded. "She insisted on a bath every afternoon. I-I think it was to avoid me for a little while longer after school."

Her heart twinged with agony at his words.

"I'd come back to that house—" Not a home. Never a home, she knew. That was wherever she and the guys were. "—and the first thing I'd do was head upstairs to her bathroom. They had a connecting bath, and she used to leave the door open. I'd sneak into the bedroom, although she was so drunk I didn't have to sneak much, and I'd peer through the door to make sure her head was on the pillow she had on the rim.

"I'd check about ten times until I heard her pull the plug." He shuddered. "I hated that bathroom. And then, when she slit her wrists in there, it just. . . ."

"Consolidated that hatred," she ended, wishing she could take that memory from him, while knowing it helped forge the complicated man she loved into the creature standing here today.

"Yes," he said quietly.

She fell silent a second. "Okay. You can sneak in. But I'm never going to hurt myself, Devon."

"No. You have Sean, Andrei, and Sawyer to do that for you."

His blandness had her flinching. "It isn't like that," she argued.

"No? Then what's it like?"

For the first time, she saw the flash of fire in his gaze. Huffing, she pushed off from the wall and headed to the opposite side of the bath. Staring at him, she let her anger soar, let it hold free rein as she thought about what he was saying.

"I like it," she bit off. "The pain is freeing, that's for sure. They temper it. They're always careful with me. I know that. I can feel their love and concern surrounding me at all times. But more than that? I like their rules."

He shook his head. "How can you, Sascha? That's not like you."

She cocked a brow at him. "I like breaking them, Devon. I like breaking those rules."

For a second, he was silent, then he tilted his head to the side and smirked. "That makes sense."

Despite herself, she had to laugh. "It does?"

"Yeah. It does. You're not subservient, Sascha. Not submissive or. . . ." A breath gusted from his lips. "You're not the kind of woman to allow men to control her, I guess is what I'm saying."

"And that's the biggest compliment you've ever given me," she retorted, amused when he shrugged. "Some of the rules are for my own good. I know that. But I like the consequences."

"You know they really do love you?"

The question, after all the revelations, jolted her. "Of course!"

He sank back, and she saw his features relax.

He'd doubted that?

"Devon, I know they adore me," she told him roughly.

"You don't need to do this for their love, is all I'm saying."

"I know, sweetheart. I know. It's not—" She winced. "Sometimes, I wonder why I didn't realize before they liked this stuff. It makes me feel bad. Were they missing out when I wasn't interested in this? Wasn't I enough for them?" She bit her lip, dipped her chin, then, after a moment, admitted, "And if I don't like it forever, if I change my mind and stop wanting this from them, will they always miss it? Will I be wrecking something perfect with this fucked up headspace I'm in?"

"You're grieving, Sascha. We're all grieving. And they'll always love you. You complete us, love," he told her, his tone soft like saltwater taffy mid-chew. "Life is a cycle. That's one thing I've learned. We'll go through phases. Maybe this is just one of those phases."

She could sense how badly he wanted to believe that.

Nodding though as she contemplated his words, she finally said, "But deep down, and as selfish as it sounds, I'm not doing this for them, Devon. I'm doing it for me."

He stared at her, seemed to scan her for the truth, and then, whatever he'd found seemed to settle him because he murmured, "Good. That's all I needed to hear."

And then, he got to his feet, stripped, and joined her in the hot, silken depths of the tub.

# EIGHTEEN

SASCHA FROWNED as she took a seat at the breakfast table.

"This goddamn plug," she growled under her breath as she tried to get comfortable and knew it was impossible with five inches of metal shoved up her ass thanks to Sawyer.

Just because she had her period didn't mean she didn't need the reminder to eat breakfast, he'd informed her.

God, it was a wonder she hadn't smacked him.

A tampon *and* a butt plug?

That was just mean, and why the hell she hadn't told him to fuck off, she wasn't sure.

*Chalk up another* what the fuck is wrong with me *moment,* she thought on a huff.

Releasing a slow breath, trying not to blow her top, she grabbed the armrest and tilted down so that she wasn't sitting on the curve of her ass but the upper slopes of it.

If she looked like she was slouching, so be it.

When she looked up and saw Andrei and Sawyer smirking at her, she reached up, scratched her nose with her middle finger, and flipped them off. Though Andrei cocked a brow at her, an expression that said her ass would pay for that bit of insolence later, Sawyer just snickered.

She couldn't stop herself from grinning at him and the amusement he found in this situation.

Andrei and Sean were so breathtakingly intense. She loved it. Without a doubt. But Sawyer? With his ability to laugh as she bitched at him in bed, as she bucked him off, forcing him to control her, to take her harder, faster. . . . Cue sigh. She loved that just as much.

He was the light to his brothers' dark, and she needed that. Needed them all so goddamn much that just thinking of a life without them was enough to break her fucking heart.

When tears welled in her throat, she dipped her head and gritted her teeth.

Those thoughts were stupid. Stupid, stupid, stupid.

Why was she constantly thinking such fucking things?

The only time she didn't, when her brain was free and clear from all the crap swarming her synapses, was when she was in bed with one or two of her five men.

When she was focusing on them, on what they were doing to her, only then did she feel like she could take a deep breath.

"Why are you sitting like that?"

The question, unsurprisingly, came from Devon. His head was tilted to the side as he took in her slumped position.

"It's more comfortable," she informed him, her tone a little stern to get him to shut his mouth.

"How is that possible?" he countered then, just her luck, mimicked her.

When Tin, their toddler, spotted his father's behavior, he too slouched in his seat, which almost had him slipping out of the damn thing as it was more of a booster than a proper highchair.

Sean, accustomed to the chaos of life with Devon, and life with

Devon *and* Tin, grabbed Tin by the back of his shirt and hauled him up. Which, of course, had Tin giggling like it was the funniest thing he'd ever done in his life.

Despite herself, Sascha found her lips twitching. When Sean grinned at her, outright declaring war, she huffed out a breath and grumbled, "I'm being punished, Devon."

Her voice was too low for Tin to hear, and considering Devon was next to her, it wasn't hard to be discreet, especially when the table was so damn huge.

Vasily lived in the Russian equivalent of a family estate. It was like Downton Abbey by an architect who'd been drunk on vodka.

Each room was far too big and would be damn cold if there weren't huge fires roaring in every hearth. It was an environmentalist's nightmare, but a lot of people lived under this roof.

She wasn't sure she wanted to know their each and every role because Vasily was a supposedly retired Pakhan in the Bratva, but they'd all been polite and kind to her, so who was she to judge?

With the fire, the clink of the knives and forks as the others ate, and Tin's chuckling, Devon shouldn't have had to clarify, "Punish?"

Sawyer sighed. "For God's sake, Devon, I've already told you what's going on."

Because he was annoyed, his Scottish brogue came out thicker than usual. At the sound of that, rather than his words, Sascha thought, Devon turned to stare at her, a piece of toast in his hand.

She spied it, then looked into his face. Realizing he was giving it to her, she had to smile at him.

"Saving me from myself?" she asked.

He stared at the toast. "They can't get mad if you have just one slice."

"That is the height of logic," Sean informed her, and she looked over at him and saw his focus was on her.

As was every other man at the breakfast table.

Except for Vasily who was on the line with someone, barking

orders by the sounds of it as he doodled on the newspaper in front of him.

Thankful he wasn't privy to this conversation, she reached for the toast. When Devon shook his head, she frowned then licked her lips when he raised it to her mouth. Swallowing thickly as he angled it for her to bite, she did as bid and chewed.

It was dry in her mouth, and as had been the way of late, she wasn't sure whether she wanted to spit it out or swallow. She *was* hungry, but it was like a corporeal hunger. Her stomach was, but her head wasn't.

It was damn confusing, that was for sure.

Huffing out a breath when she reached for her orange juice and swallowed down the butter-drenched piece of toast, she turned back and saw Devon was waiting.

This was new.

"What's going on?"

His lips twitched. "Nothing, Kitten."

Her eyes flared at that as she turned to Sean who wasn't looking at her anymore, if anything, his attention was on his phone as he stared at the screen. There was a pucker she recognized that came from work, and though she had to sigh at his inability to have a break even at breakfast, she accepted another bite of toast.

Combining Sean's labeling her as 'pet' the other night, and then this 'kitten' by Devon of all people, Sascha was left wondering what the fuck was going on.

There was also a reason he was hand feeding her.

She didn't want to think about why his attention twisted her up inside.

It was like. . . .

A breath escaped her.

Almost like the sun was finally touching her skin after a long, cold winter. Which was hilarious considering she was in the Russian capital in December! Cold? Cold? She hadn't known the meaning of the word until she'd found her way to Moscow.

When she heard a bitten off, "*Da*," Devon handed her the piece of toast and let her eat the rest herself, his gaze flickering from her to Vasily once.

That look alone told her he'd started because the older man's attention was elsewhere, and he was stopping because Vasily had the focus of a bird of prey.

Even though she wasn't hungry, she carried on eating. It was the first time in her life she'd been like this. If anything, food had always been a comfort to her. There was nothing she loved more than drowning herself in carbs and saturated fats when she was down. At the moment, though, that just wasn't doing anything for her.

God, she wished she could get out of this funk. But it seemed to follow her like a shadow, hovering over her shoulder, waiting to pounce.

The sound of a throat clearing jerked her attention from how hard it was to bite, chew, and swallow a piece of goddamn toast, to the man at the head of the table.

Said table was over twenty feet long and would have seated over a hundred in its day. They were at the bottom end near one of the fires. The carver chair Vasily used was too close to a throne for comfort, and yet it suited the old bastard.

And yeah, he was a bastard.

With that wily twinkle in his eye, the loose tongue that made Devon look closed-mouthed, and a brain that was more like an AI databank than a human organ, Vasily was unusual to say the least.

He was also dangerous.

The only thing that kept her safe, she felt certain, was Andrei's love for her, and Vasily's adoration of his grandson.

Okay, it also helped that ever since she'd gotten with the guys, they'd been visiting the old man a lot more. From barely any kind of visits in the twenty years since Andrei had moved to Britain, to five or six times a year now.

Vasily would kiss her feet if he could have knelt on the ground, Sascha felt sure.

"Andrei . . ." The rest occurred in Russian, but she recognized her lover's name in his native tongue.

It was unlike Vasily to speak in the other language when they were around, and the rudeness had her narrowing her eyes at Andrei who didn't look anything other than confused.

"*Da*," he murmured softly, then switching to English, asked, "When?"

"Today."

Andrei hummed under his breath as he reached for the cafetière and poured himself a coffee. When he turned to Sawyer and asked, "Are you ready to roll out that software?" Sascha narrowed her eyes because, without a doubt, that was weird.

Whenever Vasily did fall into Russian, Andrei usually explained whatever it was the old man had said.

Before she could ask, Sawyer murmured, "Yeah. We can roll out the draft rehearsal."

"What kind of draft rehearsal?" Vasily inquired, his ears pricking up in a way that had Sascha hiding a smile behind her tumbler of orange juice.

Vasily, as was the way with crime lords, appreciated tidbits of information he could use to make a shit-ton of money.

After their visit here, they were heading to Veronia for a few months. Or however long it took for Andrei to help revitalize their economy, which had been suffering ever since there'd been an anti-royal rebellion against the former king and queen—something that had resulted in a tragic end for the queen.

She wasn't entirely sure what the fuck they were doing to kick-start the economy—when did she understand the jargon they tossed around like two kids playing ball? What she did know, as per damn usual, got her hot.

It was strange.

Since she was a little girl, she'd never experienced grief like this, and yet, her emotions were all over the place to the extent that she'd never been more ready to be dragged out of the pit of depression that grief sunk her into.

It was almost like she was willing for any and all distractions, and if that distraction ended with a cock sliding into her mouth or fucking her so hard and fast she had rug burns on her ass, she was fine with that.

Gnawing at her bottom lip as she thought about the other night when Kurt, for the first time in their relationship, had been *rough* with her, she turned to find the man himself and saw he was staring at her.

There was a brooding look on his face, but there was a fire to rival the one in the hearth as their gazes clashed and held.

He didn't like that she was exploring this side of herself, and she wasn't sure why.

It wasn't the first time he'd expressed his doubts about her sudden cravings for something she'd never wanted before, but there was no soothing those doubts of his.

She didn't want to be made love to.

That was what it boiled down to.

She didn't want tenderness. She didn't deserve it.

The thought had a breath shuddering from between her lips, but she jerked back to awareness when Devon, still slouched at her side, groaned, "This is so bad for your back, Sascha."

She had to laugh. "Trust me. I know." Did she ever. It wasn't the first time one of her more dominant lovers had insisted she wear a butt plug to breakfast—it was supposed to encourage her to remember to follow the rules. She'd grown so accustomed to having to wear one of the damn things that it actually wasn't a hardship. Until she had to sit upright at a table.

Then, it sucked ass.

With the toast finished off and her glass of juice empty, she knew she'd followed rule number one.

She'd never met a bunch of breakfast Nazis before, but that was exactly what this lot was. Still, having complied took the edge off her nerves. When Sean had denied her that second orgasm which had looked set to blow the other one out of the park, something inside her had melted.

Fuck, she'd never craved something so badly in her life.

The knowledge that he'd denied her would stick with her for a long time. And it wouldn't make her angry.

Hell, no.

It made her hot.

So fucking hot, it was a wonder she didn't set fire to the table.

Where this craving for his domination came from, she wasn't sure. Where the need for Sawyer's and Andrei's found its source was just as much of a mystery. She just knew she needed it like she needed her next breath.

These men owned her, body, heart, and soul. It was only right they provide the solace she needed to get through this phase in her life, where getting out of bed in the morning was fucking harder than learning Japanese with a constant hangover.

Devon seated himself straighter, groaning again as his body adjusted to the new position. When she caught Kurt's eye again, she smiled at him and blew him a kiss.

He was a tad surprised at the gesture, but he caught it and pressed it to his lips in a move that should have seemed practiced but somehow wasn't, and was the cutest shit she'd ever seen in her damn life.

The knowledge that these men would give her the Earth, as well as the fact that Tin needed her, were the only things that made getting out of bed possible.

Vasily grumbled, "No hanky panky at the table."

She snorted. "How was that hanky panky?"

He narrowed his gaze at her. "You know the rules."

She blew him a raspberry which had him hiding a grin. He liked when she didn't follow his every word like it was the letter of the law, and didn't listen to him like he was some kind of cult leader with a Jesus complex.

Sure, in this house, to his people, he was the leader. But to her, he was her boyfriend's grandfather. He loved Reese's cups when she brought them for him, and could dive into any cryptic crossword known to man and solve it in under a quarter of an hour—even the Times' one, which she cut out for him every morning and saved in a folder to bring him when they visited.

The first time she'd come to Russia, it had been with Andrei. Of course, her men had followed, too, but Vasily hadn't known that.

The next few times, they'd stayed at a hotel, and then gradually, Vasily had invited them all to come after he'd informed Andrei that nothing should happen in front of him if the invitation was to remain extended to them.

Why he thought she'd be willing to partake in a damn orgy in front of her partner's grandpa, she didn't know, but had been relieved to be invited into his home. With Tin, and the amount of shit they had to traipse around, it was just easier to leave the crap here and use again. It wasn't like the old man didn't have space to store it all.

"What are your plans for today?" Vasily asked Sascha, and the question was so strange, she frowned at him.

"Why?"

He huffed. "Can't a grandfather-in-law take an interest in his granddaughter-in-law?"

"A regular one, maybe." She squinted at him. "What's going on? Why are you acting weird?"

Vasily threw up his arms. "I am being polite."

"Exactly," she told him sweetly. "It's weird."

Andrei snickered. "She has you there, *Dzed*."

Sawyer laughed. "Aye, she does have a point, Vasily. You're not exactly known for your manners."

"I'll have you know I'm very polite when the company requires it."

"And I haven't required it up until now?" Sascha retorted, quirking a brow at him.

He huffed again. "Look, what are you doing today? I'm curious. I want to know." He gestured with his hands in the way all Russians seemed to do. It was like he was beseeching her while also commanding her to speak. Pinching the air with his thumbs as he wafted them about.

Every Russian she'd ever met did it.

Andrei included, and because he did it when he spoke Russian, Tin, who was learning the language, had started to do it, too, which was cute as fuck.

"Nothing. I intend to read." She had some research to do.

"Read? What do you intend to read?"

Okay, so this was just getting weirder. Vasily wasn't an average relative. He was interested and curious and genuinely cared, but he wasn't the sort of man who remembered birthdays or who gave a shit about how you spent your day while you were under his roof.

In the many visits to this mansion, he'd never once asked her what her plans were, and why he'd begun now made her all the more suspicious.

"Books."

He growled. "You're about as informative as the KGB."

"I try," she mocked, then conceded, "I want to relax while Sawyer and Kurt teach Tin how to swim."

Because there was nothing relaxing about watching Tin in the water, she knew she had to go to the opposite side of the house.

The trouble was, Sascha had this burning need to wrap Tin up in cotton. Miles and miles of it. So many fucking miles, he'd probably suffocate under its mass, which wasn't exactly the point.

She released a shuddery breath at the prospect of her baby learning to swim, and maybe he saw the genuine terror etched on her face because Vasily didn't mock her. Instead, he murmured, "He will love the water. Andrei did. He was good swimmer as boy. Strong swimmer."

Sometimes, Vasily had a habit of dropping articles like 'a' and 'the,' and it was usually always to do with Andrei. The man was so proud of his grandson, and it was almost as cute as Tin making gestures in the bath when he spoke in Russian.

"He'll be okay," Kurt assured Sascha, and she shot him a weak smile.

"I know he will be." She'd brought enough flotation devices to keep Venice from sinking.

She began to toy with the crumbs on the tablecloth beside Devon's plate. As she swirled through them, she made little shapes here and there as she thought about what she'd be researching today.

Ordinarily, she'd be binging on romance novels, devouring them like she couldn't devour a piece of toast.

But, as it was, she wanted to know what it meant to be someone's pet.

She wasn't sure she liked the idea.

She wasn't a fucking dog.

The thought had her pouting. Dog, her ass. A cat, though? A kitten like Devon had murmured earlier?

Hmm. Yeah. That fit. She loved napping, didn't she? Could be snarky at the drop of a hat, and though she wasn't a bitch, she had grown accustomed to being the Queen Bee of her little world.

Grinning at the thought, she hid her smile behind the tumbler lest Sawyer see it and think she was altogether enjoying her 'punishment' too much.

---

GETTING Tin in a flotation device was like asking an octopus to stay still while a sushi chef decided to chop him into bits.

The kid had developed more arms and legs in the last few minutes than Kurt's patience could handle. Sawyer's, too, if the sweat on his brow and the throbbing of his cheek was any indication.

The swimming pool and the area itself were heated. And when Kurt said heated, he meant heated. He and Sawyer were perspiring like they were under the midday sun on a Hawaiian beach. Fuck, he felt sure vacationing on Venus would be cooler than the temperature Vasily kept the indoor pool at.

Hell, if it were frigid, maybe Tin wouldn't be so goddamn energetic.

Sometimes, Kurt was relieved he had four other men to rely on where his son was concerned. How one-parent families coped was beyond him. Seriously, each and every single parent the world over deserved a goddamn gold medal and a five-star vacation to Maui.

"Why does it have to be so bluidy hot in here?" Sawyer groused, reaching up to swipe at his brow.

"I don't know," Kurt rejoined. "Maybe because we'd freeze to death after we got out of the water?"

"I'd have thought they'd like that. Have you seen those videos of those nutcases jumping into frozen ponds, getting out, then heading into the sauna?" He shuddered. "Madness. Sheer madness."

Kurt's lips twitched then, while Tin still insisted on wriggling around like some kind of cat on LSD, he grumbled, "Tin, if you stay still and let me put this vest on you, I'll. . . ."

The kid froze, well aware a deal was about to go down.

Jesus. Kurt was certain at Tin's age that he hadn't been that smart.

With a huff, he carried on, "A cookie?"

Tin immediately started struggling.

Sawyer snorted. "You have to start higher than that, mon."

"Isn't the best way to start low and then bid higher?"

"Who's the economics expert here?"

Kurt snickered. "Andrei."

A grunt escaped the Scotsman. "After him."

"You," Kurt conceded. "Still, aiming high with kids never seems that wise a move to me."

Sawyer shrugged then murmured, "And what would you like, Master Tin?"

Their little shit peered up at Sawyer, all baby blues and white-blond hair. The kid would double as a cherub if said cherub had the brains of someone triple his age. "A book of Sudoku."

Kurt winced. "Not more Sudoku."

Sawyer folded his arms across his chest. "Now, you know your ma told you no more Sudoku."

Tin's bottom lip popped out. "I like it."

"I know you dae," Sawyer said softly, "but you can't do it all day, every day."

That the kid was obsessive in a house full of obsessive geniuses didn't exactly come as a surprise.

Of them all, Kurt was the most normal one, and he didn't sleep when the creative bug bit him, forgot to shower when he was in the middle of a manuscript, and barely remembered what day of the week it was when he wasn't writing, never mind when he was in the middle of the process.

Normal in their house was pretty much Sascha.

She didn't read economics journals for fun. Didn't eat, drink, and breathe math. Didn't watch TV to learn something, and didn't have to line up every mug in the kitchen cupboard by size, color, and function.

Sascha, as weird and as wonderful as she was, was regular in their peculiar household. Something that was hitting home all the more now that Tin was showing signs of his father's genius—though he was *their* son, and *they* were his fathers, biologically, he was Andrei's.

Andrei. The economics whiz kid who made a Pakhan proud, and had royal clients begging him for help.

Normal. Nope.

"How about I introduce you to crosswords?"

Vasily's voice was a croak, but in the glass walls of the pool house, it carried. He didn't appear overheated in his velvet smoking jacket, just looked like he belonged in a classic Sherlock Holmes movie. He took a seat on one of the loungers, groaning as his old bones settled into the comfortable chairs. When Tin ran over to him, squealing with delight at his grandfather's presence, he hugged him the minute Vasily opened his arms.

Kurt had to admit it was a touching sight. Especially knowing what Vasily was capable of.

Sometimes it was easy to forget the man's power. When he complained of aching joints and an inability to piss in less than five-minute stretches, the Pakhan seemed far away, leaving behind an irascible man who'd fought Kurt's ancestors during the Second World War.

"Now then, what do you say to some crosswords?" Vasily chucked Tin under the chin. When Tin replied, his childish voice loaded with glee, Kurt had to grin as pride swelled inside him.

Their boy was two. *Two.* And already he could speak three of his parents' native languages.

Vasily cut Kurt and Sawyer a look. "Let me dress Tin for the water."

Sawyer, eager to pass the chore onto another, strode over and handed Vasily the vest. With little to no fuss, Tin allowed himself to be dressed in the safety device, before Sawyer, a hand on his son's shoulder, guided him over to the water.

"Now, when are you allowed to run and jump into the pool?"

Tin peered up at him. "When I'm wearing this."

"Good boy." Sawyer scrubbed his hand over Tin's head. "Why do you have to wear this?"

"So Mommy won't castrate you."

Kurt snickered. Even though Tin butchered the word, it was audible enough for Vasily to laugh, too.

"That's right. And why don't we want Mommy to castrate me?"

"Because you like your bits where they are."

Sawyer beamed at him. "You learn fast, son. All men like their bits exactly where God intended."

Tin, peering up at his redheaded da, parroted, "Where God intended."

"You ready to jump?"

Tin giggled. Before Sawyer could even finish his question, their little hellion had taken off and dive-bombed into the water.

Vasily chuckled as the spray went everywhere, even dampening his jacket. Leaving Sawyer to dive into the pool with Tin, Kurt crossed to the lounger at his side.

"All is well?" he asked quietly.

Vasily tilted his head to the side. "Why do you ask?"

"You grimace when you sit down."

"I've been doing that since I was forty-eight. That bullet to my spine. . . ." He grunted. "It might have nicked it, but God, I feel it every day."

Kurt narrowed his eyes at the old man. "You know what I mean."

"I swear you're all like hens clucking around the yard. I'm old. I'm ill. I'm dying." He thrust his hands into the air. "It is, as Sascha would say, time for you to get with the program."

Kurt laughed a little. "Is it so terrible that we care?"

Vasily shrugged. "I suppose not. It is more than an evil old man deserves."

Leaning back against the lounger, Kurt crossed his feet at the ankle. "You can't be wholly evil."

"Why can't I?" Vasily asked, sounding put out at the question, enough to make Kurt laugh.

"Because Andrei wouldn't love you as much as he does, and Tin wouldn't, either. Kids are good at reading people."

Vasily hummed at that. "I suppose you are right. The child does love me."

"Indeed he does." Kurt's smile was small, but it was there nonetheless. He rubbed his chin as he asked, "Any news?"

"Best you speak with Andrei on that. He told me he wished to be the go-between."

That had Kurt frowning. "Why?"

Vasily shrugged. "Why does that child do anything?"

His lips twitched at the notion of Andrei being a child, but then, to Vasily, what else would Andrei be?

Kurt shot him a look. "Where is he?"

"On the phone with Madela as far as I know."

When Tin squealed, Kurt's mouth curved into a wide grin as he watched Sawyer getting drenched by a toddler.

Laughter brayed from the old man at his side as Sawyer's hair flopped into a tangle around his face. "Come here, ya wee monkey," he grumbled, grabbing Tin, lifting him out of the water and dangling him overhead. "Surrender!"

Tin's giggles had his tiny body vibrating as he shrieked, "Higher, Daddy, higher."

"This bairn has no sense of danger," Sawyer groused as he raised on his tiptoes and stretched to accommodate the 'bairn's' request.

In less than a flash, Tin threw himself out of Sawyer's arms and giggled as he bounced in the shallow end. From the sounds of it, Tin was a water baby.

"You are good fathers," Vasily murmured softly.

"We try."

"With so many of you, it must be easier." He stroked his chin where a thick beard grew. Looking at Vasily was like looking at a white-haired Andrei. The same strong brow, obstinate chin, and clear ice-blue eyes that even age hadn't blurred. Andrei's hair was white-gold, whereas Vasily's was now like silver. Still, he had a full head of hair and a thick beard, giving Kurt the impression of a lion's mane.

Fitting, considering Vasily was the King of his very own jungle.

"It is a wonder we have not adapted this way earlier," Vasily mused. "Our children would be better cared for, *da*?"

Kurt shrugged. "Not necessarily. But having more than two parents does make things easier if one of us has to work. And it rounds out his education, that's for damn sure."

Vasily sniffed. "Education? What, his skills at mimicking?"

A grin flashed over Kurt's lips—Vasily had noticed Tin's penchant for mimicking Devon. "It does no harm."

"Why the strangest of you all, though?" Vasily questioned, sounding perplexed.

"I think you answered your own question," Kurt joked. "Devon, in his way, is very melodramatic and spontaneous. We're less so. He's far more interesting to copy."

"This is true."

"What pisses you off more? That's he's mimicking at all, or not copying Andrei?"

When Vasily huffed, Kurt snickered, and the two of them fell into a surprisingly comfortable silence.

They'd known each other for a long time. Or, at least, *of* each other. Vasily, unlike most of their parents, was always in the background. There was rarely a week when Andrei didn't call the old grouch, even back at college. If he didn't, it was because he was busy, and even geniuses couldn't remember everything without prompt. Sascha prompted now, so Andrei was more in contact with his grandfather than ever before.

Kurt liked that.

He wanted Tin to have as many experiences with Vasily as he could. Though the old man seemed intent on outliving them all, he wasn't in the best shape and was nearer a hundred than anyone liked to count. He couldn't live forever, so whatever time he had, Kurt wanted Tin to know him. To love and to remember him.

Sawyer had a great relationship with his parents, Andrei had Vasily, and though his and Sean's family still lived, they weren't in contact that much.

Kurt's father suffered from a severe form of PTSD, and his mother, Margritte, was a socialite who claimed Kurt's divorcing his ex-wife had ruined the family name and their standing in polite society. She'd never approved of his brothers, had always believed them to be living together in gay harmony deep in the heart of Kensington.

Kurt's mother, if it wasn't already evident, was a homophobic bitch. Not having her in his life wasn't something that disappointed him, but he knew it bothered Sascha. She was intent on visiting his folks in the New Year, if he couldn't dissuade her, that is.

The last thing he wanted was to start the year with his mother's pinched expression spoiling everything, and considering how up in the air things were with security, it made sense that they stuck together as they headed to Veronia.

At least, he hoped Sascha would see the sense in that. Wondering what his chances were, he reckoned he had a higher likelihood of getting out of this pool room without getting wet than he did of convincing Sascha a visit home was the last thing any of them needed.

# NINETEEN

SASCHA WASN'T ENTIRELY sure where the noise was coming from, but she'd been hearing it all afternoon.

It was a dull thwacking sound and considering she'd been hearing that a lot of late, it hit home.

Literally.

Was someone being spanked in Vasily's house?

Considering the grandson's proclivities, it would come as no real surprise that the grandfather would be a kinky bastard, too. With his advanced years, she wasn't sure whether to applaud him or to crinkle her nose at the prospect of him doing his *thing*.

The house was huge.

Three stories tall, about two hundred feet wide. It was baroque in style, and in the sunlight—which came infrequently this time of year—certain parts of the edifice glinted and glittered because the cornices were decorated with honest-to-god gold.

Yeah. It was that kind of place.

The sort of home you saw in documentaries on PBS, not the sort you imagined people actually living in.

It was mind-blowing, really.

Here she was, investigating the weird sounds coming from somewhere in the building, as she walked around a place steeped in history.

Vasily had proudly informed her that he wasn't the only prince to have lived within these walls.

The man's ego knew no bounds, and even recognizing that he was royalty in his particular *criminal* sphere didn't make up for his arrogance.

Only the fact that he adored Tin, Andrei, and even her because of the joy she'd brought to his grandson's life made him bearable sometimes.

As she stepped down a long corridor, which was lined with suits of armor, her flats slipping against a parquet floor she was grateful she didn't have to polish, she heard it again.

Tipping her head to the side, she followed the faint sound. The only reason she was seeking it out was because it was such a weird noise. From a distance, it had been difficult to discern it wasn't sexual. Only instinct had been the reason for her getting off her ass and leaving her computer behind to investigate.

As the sounds grew louder, more frequent, too, she heard the grunts next. These definitely weren't sexual, but they were coming from behind a door.

It was an innocuous aperture.

Just like any of the hundreds of doors in this damn palace.

But this one?

It seemed to glow.

Around the frame, she could see light shining from behind it, and while that wasn't unusual—many rooms in the property were used, after all—something about the noise had her stepping closer rather than backing off.

A scream sounded.

It seemed to ricochet in her head, making her heart pound faster, and her lungs strain for air.

It had been so sudden, coming out of nowhere, that she felt the atavistic flight or fight response deep in her system kick in.

Only her curiosity kept her in place which, considering this palace belonged to a Bratva man, was probably the height of idiocy.

Reaching for the doorknob, she curved her hand around the handle and carefully, in half-inch increments, turned it.

She sucked in a breath as the faintest squeak made itself known, but when more thwacks came, shuddering from somewhere inside the room, she felt more confident in opening it without the occupants realizing it was her.

As the door opened, she peered inside.

There were a set of steps that led down to what she could only assume was a basement. A bare light bulb glowed overhead, the old-fashioned filaments burning into her retinas before she looked down at the steps.

There was a weird smell coming from whatever room was down below. She didn't recognize it, but it reminded her of hospitals. Disinfectant and some bleach, maybe?

Biting her bottom lip as her imagination ran away with her, it didn't take her too far because if her common sense had been firmly in place, then she'd have backed the fuck off and scurried back to her room as though the hounds of hell were nipping at her heels.

And even though she was alone, she felt the moistness of each panting breath that escaped her lungs as though they were physical entities.

Another thwack sounded, and realizing she was in over her head and had no right to be nosing in on shit that was none of her business, had her backing off.

Finally.

Then she heard it.

A faint whisper.

Her head tilted to the side as she recognized Sean's voice.

*Sean?*

What the fuck?

A flurry of Russian sounded and even though she wasn't accustomed to hearing Andrei speak Russian, not outside of Tin's bath times, she'd know his voice anywhere.

His words were as guttural as when he sank inside her and fucked her sore.

She licked her lips at that. Had she misunderstood? Was something going on down there? Something that involved Sean and Andrei with another woman?

Her heart plummeted.

For all the years they'd been together, they'd had to hide their needs from her. The ones that had sprung to life from the darkness in her soul appeared out of nowhere, like a flashlight turning on thanks to a sudden drop into a Stygian gloom. But it hadn't been the same for them.

These needs of theirs? Their kinks?

They'd been years in the making, and over three of them with her had been spent in vanilla sex.

She'd read enough BDSM romances to know that a Dominant's needs always outed themselves. She didn't give a damn what Christian Grey swore to Ana. Kinks always revealed themselves. Just as they had with her men.

But before she'd decided she needed that in her life, where had they gone to have those kinks of theirs seen to?

As sickness welled inside her gut, nausea churning away with a power that made her feel certain she was about to vomit here and now on the staircase, there was another scream.

The sound was so piercing it made her jerk back in response. It came as a surprise, but also, a relief.

That thought alone made her feel like a sick bitch, but whatever her men were, they were *not* gay. Hell, most of them weren't even bi-curious, even if Devon did tease Sawyer about appreciating the view of his balls as his brother fucked Sascha. And that scream, without even an inkling of doubt, came from a man.

Because whatever the hell was going on down there had something to do with her men, she felt more confident in descending the damn stairs and investigating exactly what the fuck was going on.

Stupid? Definitely.

But curiosity got the better of her.

As she padded down the stairs, grateful for the soft soles of her slippers that made each step soundless, she tried not to grimace as she felt the bare brickwork under her feet.

The temperature hit next.

Followed by that strange smell and another one . . . she wasn't sure why it stank of ammonia down here, not until she reached the end of the tunnel-like staircase and could peer around it to the room beyond.

What she'd imagined she'd see, well, as vivid as her imagination could be, she didn't come up with this.

She wasn't even sure if she'd have preferred to see her men with another woman, because, yeah, that was how fucked up *this* was.

Swallowing, she took a step closer to the gathering of men in the center of the large basement.

The room ran as large as the house, and it was cold. Fucking cold. It seemed to sink into her bones and made her irritated that she was wearing only a thin cardigan because even though it was frigid here, Vasily kept the house as warm as she remembered her childhood in New Mexico being.

In some rooms it was so damn hot, they could have used air conditioning!

Wrapping her arms around her waist, she slipped into the ten-strong gathering and watched as a man larger than a linebacker, with biceps as large as an American football player, and fists meatier than a ham, slammed into a face she recognized.

Her tongue felt too thick in her mouth, and when she released a sharp breath, the air whooshed from her lungs as they expelled air in time to the spluttered cough that escaped Joseph Santorini's mouth.

Beside her, the stranger stilled. She felt his focus but ignored it.

She was in no danger here.

The only people in danger were her men and Joseph Santorini if she didn't figure out what the hell was going on and put a stop to it.

A bark of Russian came from the man who'd noticed her, and she felt the attention of everyone in the room focus itself on her. Well, the Russian speakers. Sean was slow to the party, but when he saw her his eyes widened, then he grimaced.

"What the fuck is going on?" she bit off, her voice a rasp as she tried to process the surreal situation.

When she'd fallen, and the accident had kick-started her early labor, Joseph Santorini had been the man to help her. He'd waited with Tin. He'd stayed by her side as her baby brain had finally righted itself, allowing her to remember the Kensington house's phone number. When her men had arrived, he'd disappeared.

She knew her guys hated that they hadn't been there for her, but whatever the fuck was happening in this basement had no logical explanation as far as she was concerned.

As Sascha studied the man who had helped her after her fall in Glasgow, she felt pity strum through her veins. Pity and guilt. Especially when she saw the reason for the ammonia-like stench in the air.

He'd peed himself. Not just once. She didn't know how many times. Parts of his pants were wet, other parts dry. There was a puddle under his dangling feet. He was shirtless, and his body bore the signs of a very bad beating. He was torn up in places, bruised in others. Blood had pooled here and there until he looked more like something you'd find swinging from a butcher's hook than a regular human being—especially when she looked at his face.

His once-handsome features were almost unrecognizable. His eyes so swollen that she had to wince as she realized he couldn't even see her they were so badly damaged.

Her hands curled in on themselves as she spat, "Someone had better explain what's happening here before I lose my shit."

"Lioness."

She narrowed her eyes at the one word. She recognized the

Russian voice and turned her head to find Vasily amid the crowd. He wasn't, in point of fact, all that difficult to find.

On a comfortable seat with blankets covering his legs to ward off the chill, he looked like a King watching over a tourney between knights. Except there was no honor in this particular fight.

Not when Joseph's arms were strung above his head, knotted at the wrist then hung over a hook. His shoulders were splayed, the blades visible on either side of his chest from the position. She couldn't begin to imagine how much pain he was in, but she could try to bring an end to this sorry scene.

"What have you done?" she demanded, glowering at her grandfather-in-law.

"What needed to be done," he stated simply, and she flared her eyes at him in surprise.

When she cast a look at Sean, who was cozied up in a coat as was Andrei, she realized the only people who weren't dressed for winter —because that was how damn cold it was down here—were herself, Joseph, and the man beating the crap out of him. In point of fact, the human bulldozer gleamed with perspiration.

Beating the shit out of people, apparently, worked up a sweat.

"Explain," she insisted, taking a step out of the crowd. When the stranger to her side grabbed her arm and tried to stop her, she slammed her knee into his groin and spat, "Don't touch me."

The man swore then groaned as he cupped himself, leaning over at the waist as he tried to absorb the sting of her attack.

She ignored him and moved through to the small circle where Joseph was strung up.

He was gross. There was no other way of describing it. Covered in blood and drool and piss, he was so far from the man she'd seen on that Glaswegian shopping street that it was obscene.

What she couldn't understand was why.

To Sean, she demanded, "Tell me."

His jaw worked, and he stepped out of the crowd toward her.

Joseph was not only trussed up like a cow's carcass in an abattoir, but he was also under a blinding light. One that seemed to illuminate each and every wound on his body. It was only as Sean moved toward her that she realized the crowd was more or less in shadow, and her eyes took a second to adjust. If they hadn't, she'd have seen the file in his hands sooner.

Without asking, she held out her hand. Whatever the justification was for this travesty was evidently within the folder.

Her heart stuttered in her chest as she tried to process exactly what was going on here as she stared deeply into his eyes.

What stunned her the most was the utter absence of regret.

He didn't look ashamed, either.

More . . .

*Sheepish?*

The notion had her frowning.

Tin was sheepish after he drank too much juice when she told him not to and peed his pants.

Sheepish was like the facial expression equivalent of eating humble pie.

You knew you'd done wrong, didn't exactly regret what got you into trouble in the first place, but knew the person who'd warned you could hold it against you forever if you didn't totally accept the fact that you weren't in the right.

It staggered her to think two of her men could be involved in this disgusting scene, and then, her thoughts shuddered to a halt as she pulled her gaze from Sean's, even though she felt sure it would be harder to separate two ten-ton electromagnets, and finally dropped to the file she'd opened while staring at him.

When she saw the case file that, after a quick scan, appeared to show Devon's assault on the man he insisted was stalking him, she frowned.

When she saw the picture of the man he'd beaten, her eyes widened in response because she hadn't thought he'd be capable of that, too.

But, when she saw the picture beside that, the man who he'd beaten, she flinched.

It was Joseph Santorini.

He wasn't called that in the case file, though. His name was Christopher Horowich. She recognized that name. The men discussed it when they talked about the repercussions of Devon's actions. She knew they tried to avoid speaking about it when she was in the room but, dammit, she wasn't five, and she insisted on listening to *some* of it.

Devon had told her that Horowich was stalking him, and that was why he'd attacked him.

But this?

This was a whole other kind of fucked up.

"What's your real name?" Sascha muttered as she turned back to the man hooked up to the ceiling.

Andrei stepped from out of the crowd this time, and his polished shoes tapped against the bare concrete floor as he approached her. He and Sean looked so polished, so pristine, and it seemed wrong when she glanced at how broken the beaten man was.

When Andrei put his hand on her shoulder, she stilled, not wanting his touch at that moment, but he ignored her. Squeezing her gently, he murmured, "His real name is Horowich. Turn the page, Sascha. But brace yourself."

She stiffened further at his side but did as she was told. She couldn't have stopped herself from turning that sheet of paper over if her life depended on it, but when she saw the grainy CCTV footage, at first, she wasn't sure what she was seeing.

Then, as Sascha peered at the images, she saw the little sweater that was Tin's favorite. She recognized the bobble hat she made him wear when it was cold out, and, at his side, she recognized herself.

For a second, she was so bewildered at the sight of her on closed-circuit footage that she didn't know what to make of it.

Then, when she realized she and her son were in the background, not the forefront of the picture, she peered closer at the photo.

When she saw the man crouched on the ground, maybe ten feet in front of her, she thought he was tying his shoelace. Then, as she flipped to the next shot, she saw he wasn't. Saw he had a bottle of oil in his hand and that he was carefully trickling it on the ground.

It didn't take a rocket scientist to figure out what the fuck he was doing.

The close-up shots were zoomed in so much that she could even read the brand of oil the bastard had used.

When the next shot revealed Horowich's face as he looked left and right to make sure he hadn't been caught, she felt sick to her stomach.

This man had. . . .

*He'd wanted her to fall.*

Then, when she had, he'd stayed by her side, had traveled with her to the hospital, had ingratiated himself to be close to her and Tin. He'd watched over Tin while she was in labor.

"Tin," she moaned, unable to think of anything other than the fact that this monster had been alone with her baby for those hours while she'd been incapacitated. "What did he do to him?"

"We asked," Sean lamented, his tone low and soothing. But there was no soothing the ravaging beasts that were eating at Sascha's soul. "Tin said the nice man played games with him."

Her lips quivered at his snarled 'nice man.' "What kind of games?"

"Innocent ones," Andrei assured her, hauling her into his side. "He was safe. Horowich's intent was not to harm Tin."

"No. Just me."

"I don't think he intended on you losing the baby. He was after a story."

A story?

Her heart about broke then and there. "You mean to tell me he's a journalist?" The breath soughed from her lungs as she stared up at him, knowing her heart was in her eyes and it was breaking.

His head dipped. "I'm sorry, *katyonok*."

Her mouth quivered. "It's not your fault." For a second, she stood there, processing this news in a den of thieves while the man who'd perpetrated her early labor stood there like a living, breathing punching bag.

It was hard to process.

Hard to come to terms with the reality of what they were saying. But the images weren't saying anything. They were *showing* irrefutable evidence of what had happened.

For months, she'd suffered.

Guilt at going into a snowy, icy shopping area without her men. Shame at losing her baby. At not being good enough, *strong* enough to keep her child.

And none of it was her fault.

She should never have fallen.

Her baby should still be in her belly. She should still be safe and warm inside her, waiting to come out and see the world. But instead, she was buried in the ground, would never have the chance to live, to bring joy to her family because of this man.

She was in shock.

Sascha knew that.

It didn't take a genius to figure it out.

Shivering, her skin was clammy with a bizarre kind of sticky warmth that was part and parcel of what her body endured as she tried to deal with the ramifications of what she'd just learned.

Quietly, she sucked in a breath, her gaze still on the file as she asked, "How long have you known?"

Sean cleared his throat. "A few weeks."

"Since before we came here?" Rage blossomed inside her. "And you didn't think to tell me?"

She felt like her skin crawled as she stared up at him, her anger making her temperature skyrocket.

"No," he admitted.

Her mouth firmed. Their dynamic had changed. There was no

denying that. No denying the fact that she got off on the way these men controlled her, but only because she *allowed* it. Craved it, even.

But she'd never asked to be treated like she was Tin's age.

Had never asked to have her opinions and wishes shoved aside as though she wasn't past the legal age for consent.

"You seem to forget that I have a brain between my ears," Sascha told him, her voice strangely silky. "Which part did you think I couldn't process? Which part of my pain did you think you could ignore?"

She didn't mean to.

Really, she didn't.

But that last word, it boomed out. Reverberating around the walls like a stray bullet that ping-ponged until it died out in an eerie echo.

"I was trying to spare you more pain," he countered, but he narrowed his eyes, and she knew he was getting too big for his boots with this domination shit because that look? It was his 'you're pushing your luck' look.

Well, fuck *that* and the horse he rode in on.

She closed the file and slammed it against his chest. "What's happening here?" she repeated the question she'd already asked two or three times since she'd realized exactly *who* was having the shit kicked out of him.

"An eye for an eye," Vasily murmured from his throne, but he'd tipped back in his seat, his eyes at half-mast as he stared at her.

There was a dare in his gaze, but more than that, she saw a bewildering admiration relax his features.

Why that was, she couldn't say.

Gulping in a breath, she whispered, "You mean to kill him?"

Vasily cleared his throat. "Kill is such a harsh word."

For a second, she gaped at him, then she gaped at her men. "And you think that's okay, do you?" She kept her focus on Sean, mostly because she expected more from him.

Sean worked on the *right* side of the law. Not the left, for fuck's sake. He wasn't dirty. This wasn't in his nature—

But what *did* she know about him?

Sometimes, she wondered.

She truly did.

For years, he'd hidden the fact that he got off on binding her to a bed and fucking her hard and fast. He'd been a gentleman. Surprising her with his kinky ways, she supposed, but those kinky ways were nothing compared to what he put her through now.

He was softly spoken, highly intelligent. His brain ran through puzzles like a computer, and he put himself under so much strain because the cases he dealt with as a criminologist put human lives at risk. He had the smarts to save someone who'd been abducted by a killer . . . he wasn't a killer himself, was he?

She licked her lips, trying to figure out what to do. Where to go from this.

But what she couldn't ignore was the body strung up at her side.

What she couldn't ignore was the burning fire in her soul that demanded justice.

For a second, she wasn't sure if she could breathe. She felt torn, twisted in two separate ways. One path was the path of sense, of justice. The other insisted on vengeance for her daughter. . . . Put a knife in her hand? She wasn't certain if she wouldn't send the bastard back to his maker.

Horowich was a journalist.

He'd wanted a story, so what? He'd decided to fabricate one for himself?

But there'd been nothing in the news about her miscarriage. Had been nothing *anywhere* that detailed what she'd endured.

It didn't compute.

Why hadn't he published that? Revealed all the salacious details to a public who wasn't interested in some random heiress, the minute he had a computer in front of him?

She reached up and rubbed her temples where an ache was gathering. Hell, it was more than gathering. It was blooming, spreading from one side of her head and diving off into the other.

God, how she wanted this to be a dream, but, unfortunately, it wasn't. This was reality.

And reality sucked.

# TWENTY

"WHAT WERE YOU WAITING FOR?"

The question escaped her lips before she could contain it. She didn't want to ask the man who'd been tortured. Didn't want to acknowledge him, but that fire in her gut wouldn't allow her to hold her tongue.

She wanted answers.

Andrei's hand tightened on her shoulder, and though his aftershave was a sweet and sultry scent that usually had her thoughts heading for the bedroom, this time, it didn't.

She pulled free from him, rejected his touch.

They'd lied to her.

They'd all fucking lied to her, because she knew, without a shadow of a doubt that was the truth.

Okay, so maybe not Devon.

If he'd known, he'd have blurted it out before now. The man was incapable of keeping secrets. Even official ones. One that required him to sign a document declaring it was an act of goddamn treason if he spilled the beans on any of his work. . . .

Yeah, even that didn't count.

Before she'd started working for the guys, they'd hired Polish and other Eastern European housekeepers to clean the house in the vain hope they wouldn't understand Devon when he spilled state secrets.

That was how bad he was at keeping them.

So, no, Devon hadn't lied to her, but the others had because Andrei and Sean wouldn't have kept this shit to themselves, would they?

"Well?" Sascha demanded, stepping closer to the beaten man, and approaching with care considering the puddle around him wasn't something she wanted to stand in.

"He is in no state to talk," Vasily countered, and she released a hiss.

"Whose fault is that? What was this about if you weren't going to ask him questions?"

"Fun?" Vasily retorted, cocking a brow at her in a way which felt like a flame to a pool of gas.

She wanted to scream. No, better, she wanted to hit him with something. *Anything.*

What the fuck was he doing? Sitting there like some feudal lord of old, beating up men who did his grandson harm, corrupting that grandson who, until now, until her, had been a law-abiding citizen.

The sheer logistics of bringing Horowich here blew her mind.

They'd kidnapped him.

Transported him across Europe, brought him here, then imprisoned him.

They'd beaten him.

And now what?

After all that, they weren't going to let him live, were they?

For the first time, she felt the shadow of the Bratva crawl over her spine. Except this time, it wasn't a shadow. It felt like it loomed overhead, and she understood how fucking petrified Damocles must have been having that damn sword dangling above him.

Worse still, a part of her wished. . . .

Her mouth grew dry as she tried to stop herself from processing that thought.

But she couldn't.

Couldn't lie to herself, couldn't hide from the truth.

She wished she'd never heard those thwacks. Wished she hadn't followed her nose and sneaked down here.

If she hadn't, she wouldn't know what was happening and. . . .

God, how big a coward was she?

"Can you make him speak?" she bit off, her aggression aimed at Vasily, no longer her lovers.

She felt the sharp sting of their betrayal but, more than that, fury writhed inside her at Vasily's role here.

He'd helped do this.

His empire had brought this bastard here.

"Not much," Vasily retorted coolly, and when he glanced at Horowich, the banked flames of his own anger were evident for all to see.

Vasily was the epitome of controlled. But today? That control was on hiatus.

He was enjoying this, she realized.

Enjoyed the punishment, and though she wished she didn't understand, she did.

She really fucking did.

Behind her, someone called out something in Russian. Vasily tossed back a reply, and then there were heavy retreating footsteps, boots that clomped against the ground as whoever it was, walked away.

Within thirty seconds, though, they returned and she felt, rather than saw, the shuffling. When a man broke through the crowd, a vial in his hand, she half wondered if they were about to add 'poisoning' to the list of charges. Then, the guy opened the small jar, and the sickly-sweet stench poured free from it.

He wafted it under Horowich's nose, so close it almost rubbed his skin. Maybe it did, because Horowich flung his head back to avoid the vial as he coughed and retched.

*Smelling salts*, Sascha realized, as Horowich gasped down air like he'd been unable to take a few solid breaths in hours.

When she looked at the state of him, she had to wonder if there was more truth to her unfortunate thought than she liked.

The bastard's head twitched from side to side as he sought an escape route, but there were none.

Not unless he thought he could get through seven high-level enforcers—after all, they wouldn't be here if Vasily didn't trust them, would they?

Sascha swallowed when she felt his attention come to her.

She'd mistaken the slits of his eyes earlier. Had thought they were too swollen, too puffy for him to see out of. Instead, he'd just been unconscious.

Now, though, she saw the second he processed who she was and felt his flinch down to her very bones.

"Why?"

The question had his jaw tensing which, in turn, seemed to trigger a deluge of pain.

"Why?" she demanded again, refusing to back off, rcfusing to let go of this subject.

Sascha felt like a bulldog who'd been given a bone and was refusing to let loose.

She wanted answers, and fuck if she wasn't about to get them.

"Story," Christopher Horowich gasped out.

"Story? What kind of story? I'd already miscarried," Sascha remarked. "Why didn't you publish anything then?"

She could see the headlines, and they were enough to make her shudder with revulsion at having her personal life spilled out in black and white again.

Having already endured her past being spread out like a picnic and devoured by the vultures, she couldn't even imagine having her very recent tragedy picked to pieces, too.

"You six. You . . ." His breath rasped from his lungs, and it was evident there was fluid or blood or something in them. It shadowed his speech and the air that whistled in and out of his mouth. "Poly."

Biting her bottom lip, she tried to control herself. She really did. But. . . . "You mean you engineered my fall so that you could get close to me? Maybe find out more about my relationship status?"

He huffed. "Status? Slut."

Her eyes widened. Did her ears fucking deceive her? "You can not be slut-shaming me when you're strung up like a piece of back bacon about to be cured. Are you fucking kidding me?"

Before he could say another word, his head tilted back, and he released a long, loud moan. Her nose wrinkled as he pissed himself once more then seemed to pass out.

Stepping back from the mess that was the piece of shit who'd wronged her family in so many ways she wasn't sure she could even begin to count them, Sascha turned on her heel and walked through the circle of men.

She didn't head out of the basement. Just away from the spotlight.

Out of that bright beam, the shadows seemed to overtake everything, even herself.

He'd wanted a big story.

Had wanted to reveal, to the world, that Sascha Dubois was engaged in a six-in-a-bed sex romp with five geniuses.

One infamous economist, two Nobel-Prize winning mathematicians, a renowned criminologist, and a Pulitzer-prize winning author.

She could see it now.

Could see the ruins of her life as they tried to maneuver that kind of gossip.

They'd never have any privacy again. . . .

She ran her hands through her hair as she tried to focus on that. Because *that* was better than the knowledge of what else he'd done.

Jolting when someone stepped straight into her path, and she walked into them, she tensed when she realized it was Sean.

"Calm down."

"Don't you tell me to calm down," she snarled, hurling herself out of his arms.

Not that it did her much good.

Finding herself in Andrei's, she tried to struggle, tried to free herself, but couldn't. They wouldn't let her.

Instead of wasting time and energy on something that wasn't going to happen, she pressed her forehead to Andrei's shirt and allowed herself to weep.

"Why didn't you tell me?"

When Sean approached from behind, she felt his heat sink into her very bones as he sandwiched her between them. "Because we didn't want you to have this burden."

"Burden? The truth shouldn't be a burden."

Andrei snorted. "Don't be naive, Sascha."

Her throat thickened at his rebuke. "Don't talk to me like that," she snapped. "We're not upstairs now." Sascha spat the latter out on a hiss, and though he stiffened, he dipped his head in understanding—his chin brushed her temple, and she shivered at the bristles of his stubble against the tender skin.

"No, we're not, but you're not thinking clearly."

"That's where you're wrong," she countered. "I haven't been thinking this clearly in weeks. Do you know what it did to me? Do you? Thinking that I wasn't fucking woman enough to look after my baby? That I was too goddamn stupid to realize I couldn't do it all, that I shouldn't have gone out to the store without my big strong men at my side? I felt like a pussy. Like a big fucking wimp who couldn't do shit right."

"And we've told you," Sean ground out, practically in her ear. "You weren't to blame. You're not a pussy, and you don't need two men to watch over you, you don't need to be looked after like you're infirm, Sascha. The reason you should have one of us with you at all times is because we want to be with you."

She stilled at that. "You can't always be—"

"I'm well aware of that, but one of us should be. You're in an unusual situation. A situation that the bastard back there wished to exploit. There has to be some advantage to being with all of us."

That had her frowning. "I'm not a chore you need to schedule."

"I never said you were," he bit off, and she knew she was angering him.

Well, *good.*

He'd damn well understand what she was going through, wouldn't he?

"What Sean is trying to explain is that you're our world, Sascha," Andrei told her softly, leaning back, so he could cup her chin and tilt her head up so that she could look him in the eye. "When a man, or men, in this case, loves his woman as much as we do, we change our lives to suit her."

"But I never asked for that."

"Doesn't mean we're not going to give you that. What happened in Glasgow was an aberration. You think you feel guilty? That's nothing to how Sawyer feels. He told me that the area is renowned for being slippery. Anyone could have fallen, never mind someone whose center of gravity was out of sync," Sean told her softly.

She frowned at his words, then whispered, "Now isn't the time for this."

"Isn't it? You seem to be questioning the basic tenets of our relationship—"

"No, I'm not," she growled out. Where the fuck had he gotten that from? "I'm questioning the fact that you kidnapped a man, dammit."

"We didn't," Sean dismissed, and his tone was enough to have her narrowing her eyes.

"By proxy, you did."

"Actually, they didn't," Vasily murmured, and she jerked as she realized he wasn't over in his throne as he had been earlier. Instead, he was leaning on a stick a few feet from her.

Vasily's men had gathered in a tighter circle around Horowich, to give them privacy, maybe? Either way, she almost felt sorry for them because it stunk over there.

"Why am I not surprised you took this on yourself?" she snapped, not even feeling any amount of trepidation at challenging the man.

"Because it was my place," he murmured quietly, calmly almost. "Your hands were tied. All of you. But mine weren't."

"Why did you involve him?" she spat, slamming her hand into Andrei's chest, glaring at him with every ounce of accusation she possessed.

"I had to, *katyonok*. Devon could have gone to jail if I hadn't. I needed him to help sort things out for us. Wipe the slate clean."

She shuddered at the thought of Devon in jail.

Knowing him, he'd probably think he'd have a good time, and maybe he would. But being controlled? Told what to do and where to go. How to sit and what to eat?

No.

He'd go mad.

Well, madder than he already was, and maybe she was being a bit mean there because he wasn't crazy or anything, but the way he led his life was certainly unusual.

As far as she was aware, in the seven days since they'd arrived in Moscow, Devon hadn't slept.

No.

Not a single night through.

"Exactly," Andrei mumbled. "Throwing him inside would be like throwing a puppy into a lion's den."

Her mouth worked, but she couldn't argue with his reasoning.

Releasing a shaky breath, she whispered, "Why did you do this, Vasily? Why not just leave him to the law?"

"Because they would have done very little," he countered, "and, also, because even if it had come about that he'd gone out of his way to engineer your fall, he might have had to deal with a manslaughter charge, but, Devon would still have had to go to court."

The lack of justice in that statement hit her like a ton of bricks. "M-Manslaughter? Not murder?"

Vasily shrugged. "Who knows with that pathetic justice system they have over there? I wasn't about to leave it to chance."

"You can't just dole out punishments, Vasily! You're not a judge."

"No, but I know of several in the area." He grinned at her, showing teeth far too perfect for a man of his age.

"You can't kill him," she whispered. Even though deep down, she truly did want an eye for an eye, but that wasn't her.

It wasn't them.

*It couldn't be.*

Horwich had stolen so much from them but not their honor. Their sense of right and wrong.

"Andrei has already made me promise I wouldn't," Vasily harrumphed.

She turned back to the man she loved. "You did?"

"*Da*," he told her gently, reaching up to cup his chin. "I didn't want him on our conscience when he's the one who should be rotting from the inside out."

Licking her lips, she asked, "Why are you letting them beat him?"

"Because I only have so much control, *katyonok*," he ground out. "Just because I asked grandfather not to remove this pest from this earth does not mean I do not want vengeance of my own."

Her eyes widened a second, but then, she settled down, pressing herself into his chest. "I should have known."

"Yes, you should, naughty girl," he whispered.

She bit her bottom lip and rolled her forehead over his pec. "What are you going to do with him?"

"Treat him like the scum he is," Vasily told her brightly, his tone far too chipper for this dark, dank room.

Christ, she'd never be able to see this house in the same light ever again.

Shuddering so hard that Andrei ran a hand down her back, she whispered, "And what does that entail?"

"Our prisons are not little holiday homes. He will go to one and rot inside for a very long time. And, if we're lucky, one of his inmates will do the job I wish to complete this day." He said the latter on a huff as he turned around, his cane thumping heavily against the exposed brick floor as he retreated to his chair.

"How's that possible? He hasn't committed a crime here."

Andrei snorted. "If you think my grandfather isn't capable of manufacturing one, then you've definitely underestimated him."

As she processed that, processed the man's power, the circle seemed to open up and a sliver of space broke through. She saw Horowich hanging from the hook, and even though it undoubtedly made her a bad person, she felt no guilt.

If that did make her a horrible person, then Horowich had helped forge that in her.

She was who she was today because of his actions.

Losing her baby had changed her.

She was no longer as light and as carefree as she once was, and even though Sascha had freaked out at what was happening down here, she hadn't gone ape shit. Wasn't threatening to call the cops or involve the authorities as the daughter of a cop should.

No.

The darkness he'd helped forge inside her meant she was fine with his punishment. His death on their hands was too much, but his punishment?

No, she could live with that.

If Vasily was right–and he had to be, otherwise she knew Sean and Andrei would never be complicit with it–Horowich would receive little to no punishment for her fall.

How a solicitor could reason away him pouring oil on the ground was beyond her, but he wouldn't be here if her men had believed there was a solid case that would put him behind bars.

And, though it was evil of her to think it, from inside a Russian prison, Horowich wouldn't be selling any tales about Sascha's love life.

Protecting their unit was something they all had in common. After this bastard had forced his way into their world, had destroyed the life of their unborn daughter. . . . Call her a bitch or a woman scorned, or just call her a momma bear who felt as though her vengeance was satisfied.

# TWENTY-ONE

"ARE YOU OKAY?"

She stiffened at Andrei's question. Turning her back to him, she mumbled, "Go away."

Of course, he ignored her. The bastard. She heard his bare feet padding against the wooden slats, knew he was close.

"Which part of 'go away' didn't you understand?" Sascha snarled as she shot him a death glare over her shoulder.

Andrei, sighing, murmured, "Sascha, we need to talk about this."

His white-blond hair was mussed. Hell, mussed wasn't the word. It was like he hadn't brushed it in days, but she knew that wasn't the case. He'd obviously been running his fingers through it since the last time she'd seen him at the dinner table when he'd been as refined and polished as Vasily insisted.

They didn't have to dress up, exactly. But they weren't 'allowed' to wear the same clothes from breakfast at the evening meal. Vasily sulked if they broke his house rule.

"I'm not happy, Andrei," she whispered, seeing the fatigue in his eyes and, despite herself, hating it was there.

When he flinched at her words—a not too unexpected reaction—

she murmured, "I want him to be punished but that. . . . What happened downstairs? It was all kinds of wrong. I'm ashamed I was a party to it."

"Vasily . . ." He blew out a breath as he took a seat on the edge of the bed. It relieved her that he sat on the opposite side than her, and she hated that.

Any distance between her and her men was the last thing she needed or wanted, and yet, from Sean and Andrei? Yeah, that was how she felt at the moment.

She'd thought she'd known them. But hell, she'd thought she'd known herself.

"It's no excuse, but this was always going to happen, Sascha. As long as my grandfather still lives, he will see to it that we are shielded."

His words had her staring at her feet.

What had seemed so right down in that dank cellar, now felt so shady.

"I-I can't believe that I haven't called the police," she whispered, almost to herself. "What happened to Horowich was. . . . I mean, he deserved it." She winced. "Didn't he? After what he did? But . . . it was wrong, Andrei. That isn't how the world works."

He turned to look at her over his shoulder. "It isn't how it *should* work, *katyonok*," he corrected. "But it is. Especially in this part of the world. Vasily has half the police force in the city on his side. They'd never see any charges through."

"And isn't that as unfair as a court not finding Horowich guilty for what he did to me?"

His words were thick in response to the truth in her question, "Of course. But life is unfair. If it wasn't, you'd still be pregnant, Sascha." He ignored her flinch. "We'd still be waiting for her to be born, and she wouldn't be at the bottom of a grave in Kensal Green cemetery. Our love wouldn't be the fodder of some journalist's lust for fame and greed for the profit it would bring him—"

"I get the picture, Andrei," she bit off, holding up her hand to ward off any more of his justifications. "Life isn't fair. But that doesn't mean we have to make it worse."

She sat up. Having always drowned in the overly large bed, it felt even bigger now. On the sea that was the mattress, she was a tiny buoy who was barely keeping herself afloat amid the devastation a tidal wave had just wrought on her world.

"We don't make things better by doing what we did, Andrei."

He shrugged. "There was no alternative."

"How can you say that?" she snarled.

"Because Horowich's lawyer had already approached Llewelyn, our attorney."

She frowned. "He had?"

"Yeah," he agreed roughly. His hands pulled on the faded jeans, which covered his bottom half. Truth was, she'd never seen him so nervous.

"What did he want?"

"He was holding us to ransom."

Those words settled in her soul. "Oh."

"Yeah." He cut her a look. "'Oh.' He was holding our unusual family to rights, and we weren't about to have that."

"What he did, that was illegal—"

"And throwing a fucking cup of oil on the ground for you to slip wasn't? It was aggravated manslaughter at the very least," he ground out. "And the bastard thought he could exchange Devon's freedom and his own with justifications over how weird it is for you to be shared by five men?"

She sniffed, and somehow, in that entire sentence, what pissed her off more was, "*You* share *me*, buddy."

His head whipped around to look at her, and though he was gaping at her, she kept her eyes narrowed on him. "That's all you have to say?"

"No. I have plenty to say. But remember that." It wasn't a threat, but it was a command.

She wasn't sure why she wanted to ram that home, just knew it was imperative.

They weren't in control.

He cleared his throat. "I told Vasily about what was happening."

"You did that on purpose," she stated, knowing that to be the truth. "You knew he'd react."

Andrei, no shame on his face, nodded. "I come from a violent world, Sascha—"

That had rage exploding through her. "Fuck you, Andrei. Fuck. You. You don't get to use your past as a bullshit reason for justifying what we did yesterday. You don't get to say it's okay to beat the shit out of someone, torture him, then put him in some Russian gulag because he hurt me!"

"Don't I?" he bit off. "I was protecting us. Protecting you and Tin. Vasily did what had to be done."

"And that's what scares me," she whispered, raising her hands to cover her face. "We committed a crime yesterday."

"You don't make a pregnant woman fall without knowing there's a risk you'll damage the baby." His voice was as frigid as the temperature outside Vasily's overheated walls. "Horowich knew what he was doing. As he poured that oil, as he insinuated himself into your ambulance, as he stayed with Tin—God only knows what he asked our son. How he peppered him for information. Thank Christ Tin is too young to understand what happens in our house.

"But, don't forget, Sascha. Killing Camilla wasn't enough for him. He *was* stalking Devon, and only the fuck knows if he was following the rest of us. Even knowing what he'd done, he didn't let up. He wanted the big score. Greed is one of the seven deadly sins for a reason."

"And wrath isn't?" she snarled back. "I'm not saying what he did is right. It's so beyond wrong we might as well be on the other side of the universe to him. What I'm saying is that what *we* did is wrong too."

Andrei got to his feet and stacked his hands on his hips as he did so. "Maybe it is but justice had to be served." For a second, he stared at her, not a word passing from his lips until he murmured, "Sean and I, Devon, Sawyer, and Kurt, we have a lot to lose if news of our relationship goes live." Before that particular strike could hit home, before it could score into her like a dagger slicing through sinew and muscle, he carried on, "But none of that matters. What terrified Sean and I is what happened the last time you were in the press." He shook his head. "You didn't cope well, Sascha. You hid away from the world, hid away from us. You burrowed away in the living room, and . . ." He blew out a breath as he pushed his hands into his pockets, splaying his arms as he murmured, "I think I could cope with many things before I had to see you go through that again."

Her brow crumpled at his earnestness. They'd already been through so much as a unit.

Attacks, miscarriages, revelations, and now *this*.

She swallowed thickly. "Andrei?"

He seemed to brace himself, his features settling like stone as he stared at her. "Yes?"

"I love you."

Air hissed from his lungs at her words. The relief on his face, had she been standing, would have brought her to her knees.

"And I love you, *katyonok*," he told her, his voice husky. "But that doesn't change what happened yesterday."

"No, it doesn't," she conceded, turning her attention from him and placing it on her knees—they were the safer option. "But, as always, it's the best place to start."

"This is true."

She gnawed at her bottom lip. "You won't do anything like this again, will you?"

"I make no promises," he rasped. "Whoever hurts you, threatens you—" His voice broke off. "You have to understand, my darling, we're not rational where you're concerned. None of us are."

She blinked at that. "Did you involve the others with Horowich?"

"No." His head sliced to the left in outright rebuttal. "It is the burden Sean and I chose to bear alone. You were never supposed to know, Sascha . . ." He winced. "They simply know Horowich has been dealt with."

She stared at him, for the first time, her features betrayed her scorn. "You mean to tell me that my household of geniuses didn't figure out your story was shady as fuck?"

"Devon and Sawyer are knees deep in the Veronian project." He shrugged. "You know what they're like. When I told them there was no repercussion to Devon's attack, not even Sawyer did more than breathe a sigh of relief before getting back to work.

"Don't forget," he informed her, "we'll be headed there after the New Year."

She frowned. "And Kurt?" He and Sean were close. Always had been, always would be. It hurt her to think Kurt had kept something like this from her.

"No. He didn't know, either. It was our burden to bear," he repeated grimly.

"And you'd bear it again and again, wouldn't you?"

His eyes flashed. "I'd kill for you, Sascha."

For half a beat, her heart stopped, then it whooshed to life once more. She closed her eyes, unsure whether that was the greatest compliment of them all or the worst.

"I don't want you to kill for me," she choked out.

"If we'd lost you *and* Camilla, Horowich wouldn't be alive to complain about being locked away in a Siberian jail cell," he told her, his tone grim.

Her bottom lip trembled. "That's too much—"

"Too much what? Love? Sascha," he ground out as he rounded the bed and grabbed the hands she'd pressed to her knees. "Whatever you say, I come from a violent past. Before I went to Oxford, you have no idea the sights I'd seen. Things that had transgressed in this very house. Violence is in my blood," he told her, his tone stark. "I don't expect you to understand that, but understand that Vasily works to a different code, and by proxy, for as long as he's alive, so do I.

"I am a good man," he rasped. "I am a decent man. I will help those who need help, protect those who need protecting. But where you're concerned, I'm never going to be rational."

She stared at their bridged hands, her eyes watering at his admission.

Did she deserve such devotion?

Did she even want it?

The truth was, she'd never thought she'd be put in this spot.

Men didn't. . . .

Christ, she'd been lucky if her exes had remembered their anniversary and bought her some chocolates. They sure as hell would never have gone to these lengths to protect her, to avenge her.

They wouldn't have run into a burning building to save her.

They wouldn't have come after anyone who hurt her.

But these men, *this* man, wasn't an ex.

He was one of the loves of her life.

And he was different.

She knew that.

He hid it better than Devon. But over the years, she'd seen how similar they were. How close they were to the brink of madness.

Their dedication was such that it bordered on the ridiculous sometimes. Both would deny themselves food and sleep for their work. Both would run themselves ragged in the line of 'duty.'

And there was no hiding the fact they did have a duty, either.

No, it wasn't like her father. They weren't cops or firemen or soldiers who put their lives on the line. Instead, there were economies that depended on them.

Millions, maybe even *billions* of people who relied on their work, on their mental capacity.

They had more responsibilities than a king, she knew, and Devon wasn't the only one who benefited from the hive that was their home.

Andrei needed their little household as much as Devon did, but he was suave, had more charm, and could literally talk her out of her panties if he so chose. Devon would simply pull her panties down to get to his prize—her.

She released a shuddery breath. "I'd better make sure nothing else happens to me then, shouldn't I?"

It was a huge responsibility to bear, but that was love, wasn't it?

There was no choice. No comeback or take backs. Accepting the good and the bad was part of the sacrifice of giving someone your heart and holding theirs in return.

He squeezed her fingers. "You needn't wrap yourself up in bubble wrap. I'm not deranged, *katyonok*."

Her lips twitched. "Mad. Bad. And dangerous to know, though, hmm?"

For the first time, the tension in his body seemed to seep away as he winked at her, and though this situation was still all kinds of wrong, she had no alternative but to smile.

# TWENTY-TWO

"WELL, THIS IS AWKWARD."

Devon tilted his head to the side as he looked at Kurt. "What is?"

"Can't you sense the atmosphere?"

He blinked. "No. What kind of atmosphere? It feels warm enough to me."

Kurt grumbled under his breath. "Do you always have to be so literal?"

"In all the years you've known me, when have you known me *not* to be literal?" He frowned. "In fact, you should take comfort from it."

Kurt narrowed his eyes at that. "What? Why should I?"

"If I'm ever abducted by aliens who want to harvest my brain, you'll be able to tell the difference, won't you?"

Rolling his eyes, he reached for the bowl of potatoes Andrei passed his way. "That's supposed to be a comfort? Anyway, what's to say they won't take my brain instead of yours?"

Devon seemed to think about that as he dished out some cabbage—Russians almost beat Germans in their love of the vegetable. Which was fine and dandy if he'd been an average German, but instead, he hated the stuff. "I don't think they'd want your brain."

"Why the hell not?" Kurt demanded with a scowl.

"Because you're a creative type. They don't need that."

So, they'd gone from a hypothetical alien species who wanted to harvest human brains, to an otherworld society deeply into eugenics.

Grunting, he commented, "How do you know what 'they' need? Maybe they have enough walking, talking calculators out there already?"

Devon's lips pursed. "That's true. But I doubt it. The probability is–"

"What are you two arguing about?" Sascha asked, her hands motioning for the bowl of potatoes.

"A hypothetical race of extraterrestrials who only want the brains of mathematicians and not writers," Devon replied immediately, not seeing the idiocy of their conversation.

God, the man needed to learn to prevaricate.

Sascha blinked, but otherwise didn't mutter a peep. Why would she? She'd lived with them all long enough to know that Devon was capable of talking about the most random shit.

As she served herself some mashed potatoes, Vasily inquired, "Why would they want more scientists or logical thinkers? They've already mastered the art of space travel. Surely they'd be fine with their own technology."

Kurt grinned at him when Devon pondered that. "They'd want other alternatives."

"Why would they?" Sean countered. "They've mastered what we haven't been able to–the ability to cross a galaxy with a manned spacecraft on the hunt for new species."

Devon huffed. "I think this is getting a bit technical for Christmas dinner."

"Only because yer losing," Sawyer retorted, making everyone around the table–save Devon and Tin–chuckle.

Tin frowned. "Why everyone mean to Papa?"

Devon beamed at him. "That's right, bud. You tell them."

Sean snorted as he dished out some pureed carrots onto Tin's plastic dish. "Tin, we're not being mean. Papa is being silly."

Tin's head wobbled from side to side. "No. Papa's brilliant."

"Let me guess who taught him that word," Sascha remarked drily, shooting Devon a soft look.

Kurt snorted. "Egotistical *Arschloch*."

Devon sniffed. "How is it egotistical? I'm rather clever, aren't I? Tin is, too. We recognize each other's brilliance."

"And what am I? Dog food?" Sascha cocked a brow at him, and though Devon was surprisingly useless at catching nuance in a conversation, with Sascha, he was like a detective.

"Of course not, love."

She smirked. "But I don't have any awards."

He puffed out his cheeks.

"And my money wasn't earned, but inherited."

Sawyer laughed and clapped Sascha gently on the back. "It's Christmas, lass, give the lad a break."

She grinned at Sawyer. "Isn't that all the more reason not to?"

"What kind of logic is that?" Kurt retorted, amused despite himself.

"The womanly kind." She winked at him, and Vasily coughed.

"None of that at the table."

"None of what?" Devon asked, frowning.

"Flirting, boy. Flirting." Vasily grunted. "I swear, for someone so smart, you're damn stupid sometimes."

Before Devon could reply, Kurt handed him the turkey platter. Vasily, though he wasn't best pleased about it, had conceded to a traditional Western Christmas dinner on the family's behalf. Though the man wanted to turn himself purple with beets, he'd conceded to having borscht for his starter while the rest of them began their meal with smoked salmon.

As they served themselves their dinner, the chatter was light and non-confrontational after their initial discussion about aliens and brain harvesting—*all in the workings of a regular twenty-four hours in their household,* Kurt thought drily.

But, as had been the way for the past few days, Sascha was brooding.

He could see it. Sense it.

Kurt even thought Devon could.

It wasn't like before. Before, the grief on her face had been evident for one and all to see.

Now?

It was almost as though she was angry, and the anger, well, he wasn't certain where its aim was pointed. He knew she had her period, but he wasn't Neanderthal enough to blame her hormones. . . .

Even if she was acting decidedly odd.

As he forked up the delicious turkey Vasily's chef had prepared on their behalf, he eyed his fellow diners.

Sean and Andrei weren't exactly free from strain, either, and that was something Sawyer had noticed, too. They hadn't discussed it, but Kurt had seen the sideways glances his brother was giving the rest of them, and if Devon knew the difference between left and right, Kurt felt sure he'd have sensed the tension also.

As it progressed, the meal was surprisingly enjoyable.

Each diner seemed to be making a conscious effort to relax, and even Tin was happy after opening what had felt like a thousand Christmas presents. Kurt had kissed Sascha in thanks for wrapping all the damn things.

Of course, Tin being Tin hadn't been gifted the regular things like toys. He had books. Dozens of them, and each one, he'd squealed over.

His biggest squeal had come from the Sudoku game that was a little too old for him, but Devon—though aptly enough, not always on planet Earth, was hyper-vigilant where Tin was concerned—had promised to play with him, so they didn't have to worry about him swallowing the pieces.

Although, worry was an odd word.

Worrying about Tin wasn't like worrying about a normal child. *Not that any kid was particularly normal*, Kurt thought, especially not after he'd had his eyes opened at his monthly visit to the playgroup Sascha insisted Tin attend to 'socialize.' If those hellions were considered normal, then he was relieved Tin was weird!

But Tin never did anything that was worrisome. He was just too smart for his own good.

Kurt feared, if he had any worries, that he'd turn out like Devon. On paper, that wasn't too bad a thing. The man was a millionaire, after all. Had success dripping from each and every breath, and he might as well shit gold because the financial markets worldwide stood up and listened if he had anything to say on certain matters—especially if he and Sawyer issued a joint statement.

But . . .

The only reason Devon was the man sitting here today was because he'd been cared for all his life.

Not by caregivers, but by his friends. They loved him. Loved him enough to stay together after university, to live in the same house even though each of them could afford bigger and better ones on their own. He'd had their support, their comfort, their love since his late teens, but there was no guarantee that Tin would find that.

If Tin was as clever as Andrei, whose IQ was close to Devon's, and with his propensity for mimicking Devon, that was Kurt's singular concern.

Devon had thrived in their household. And when Sascha had come along? He'd soared.

But they were unusual. Their household wasn't exactly common, was it? Sascha's tastes were considered outré in most circles, weren't they? And there was no guarantee Tin would find someone who'd...

He brought those thoughts to an abrupt halt.

If there was one thing Kurt was learning about being a father, nothing was certain. Everything changed. And going along for the ride was the only option available to any of them.

As he took a deep sip of the Pinot Noir Sean had selected for the meal, he tried not to feel uneasy. Tin was only a toddler, and they had childhood, puberty, then the terrible teens to get through before they even knew what he was capable of.

Somehow, that didn't exactly calm him.

---

"YOU'RE QUIET," Sascha murmured, hours later as she climbed into bed beside him.

Kurt blinked up at the ceiling of the four-poster bed that was his whenever he stayed in the house.

He'd counted the cracks in the wood, the slight slivers that let in light in the morning if he didn't cover the bed with the curtains that were supposed to keep the hot air in and the cold air out.

Well, that was supposed to be the case.

In Vasily's home, everywhere was warm.

If the FBI happened to look over Vasily's place with a heat map, Kurt felt certain they'd think he was trying to grow weed here.

Tropical temperatures had nothing on this house.

Case in point, Sascha climbed into bed with nothing more than a skimpy T-shirt on and he wore only his briefs.

It might be minus twenty outside, but inside, it was as warm as the Seychelles.

"I'm just thinking."

"You've been thinking all night."

He grimaced. "Lost myself in a thought."

As she lay down beside him, she propped her head on her hand as she tilted onto her side. "What kind of thought?"

His laugh was self-deprecating. "It's foolish."

"Most thoughts are," she told him softly, resting a hand on his belly, "when we lose ourselves in them."

Starting to gnaw his bottom lip as he gathered himself, he blurted out, "What happens if Tin doesn't find someone like you?"

She stilled at that. "Like me?"

"Yes. Someone who'll put up with our craziness."

A breath soughed from her lungs. "I don't put up with all your craziness," she countered, and when he rolled his head on his pillow, so he could look into her eyes, he saw something that confused him.

Frowning, he reached for her, tilting her chin up with his fingers when she dipped her head to avoid his gaze. "What is it? What's going on? You've been tense for days." He winced. "Tenser than usual, I mean."

She huffed. "Thanks, Kurt. You make me sound really uptight."

He shrugged. "You have been of late."

"You're good for my ego, aren't you? Is that what you mean by putting up with you?" Though she sounded like she'd taken offense, when she rolled her eyes, he knew she hadn't.

"What is it? You asked me to explain my thoughts, well, I ask the same of you."

"You wouldn't believe me if I even—"

"Try me," he interrupted.

She cleared her throat. "Why were you thinking about Tin at dinner?"

"Because Devon is so fucking weird, and Tin wants to replicate everything he does." When she stilled again, he snorted. "See? Now you're worried, too. Don't lie."

She winced. "Well, not worried. Devon came from a completely different background, that was never going to help him. Environment plays a major part in–"

"What?" he prompted. "Devon had it hard. Don't get me wrong. His father was a bastard, and though I feel bad for his mother, it doesn't mean I forgive her for leaving Devon with him. But even if they'd been perfect, it wouldn't have changed the way his brain works."

"Maybe not, but at least we're understanding and forgiving. He'll be with people who *get* him and don't try to ostracize him." She patted his belly. "You're fretting for no reason."

"Am I?" he asked, gloomily. "Anyway, it's your turn to spill the beans."

She winced at his statement, then curled into him. Burrowing her face in his arm, she hid from him and the rest of the world, he thought, as she fell silent, and he let her.

He wasn't the kind of man who pressured a woman to speak when she didn't want to, yet he *was* the kind of man who was persistent and relentless, but simply not aggressive with it.

Eventually, after minutes, maybe even twenty of them later, she whispered, "I didn't fall in Glasgow. That day. It wasn't an accident."

Though he stiffened at her words, he released his tension on an exhalation as he pressed his mouth to the top of her head. "Why would you say that?"

"Sean showed me proof the other day."

"Of what?"

"Of . . ." She swallowed thickly. "The man who helped me when I fell, who stayed with Tin . . . h-he did it."

"Why?"

"Because he was a journalist looking to make a story."

Fury roared through him. Not only at the prospect of someone trying to find a story by making a pregnant woman fall, but also, from the fact that Sean hadn't told him dick about this.

"Why the fuck is this the first we've heard about it?"

"I-I don't think they were going to tell anyone." Her voice was breathy, and he could hear the tears in her words.

Only knowing she was on the brink of crying stopped him from leaping off the bed, heading for Sean's room, and demanding what the fuck he was thinking by not keeping him in the loop.

Then, her phrasing hit him.

"They? Who are they?" he asked.

"Him and Andrei."

Kurt narrowed his eyes as he released a hissed breath. They knew, the bastards, and hadn't thought to tell the rest of them?

"I think he involved Andrei because of Vasily." She shrugged. "It doesn't matter."

"It does. It really fucking matters." He ran a hand through his hair. "I can't believe they didn't tell us about this."

She shrugged. "I only found out by accident, Kurt. They were keeping it to themselves."

"Why the hell would they do something stupid like that?"

Her lips curved, and he almost gaped at the fact she had the wherewithal to smile at him while revealing this news. "You sound so German."

He grunted. "I *am* German."

"I know, but I only hear it when you're angry." She released a deep breath. "I didn't mean to get you mad."

"I'm not mad at you, *Liebchen*. I'm mad at them. They had no right to keep this information from us."

"You won't like the reason," she half-mumbled, pleating her fingers and stretching them slightly.

"I don't like what they've done, either, but at least understanding their behavior might make me feel better."

"I doubt it." She sighed. "A few days ago, I just . . . I heard a noise. It reminded me of when they're spanking me. I guess I was scared."

"Scared? Of what?"

"That they were spanking someone else."

He gaped at her again, not sure his eyes could bug out much more than what they were doing now, but the prospect of her even thinking one of them was cheating on her was ludicrous. "You thought they were sleeping with someone else?"

"Hardly sleeping." She shrugged. "I hoped it was Vasily, the old pervert, thinking the apple doesn't fall far from the tree, you know? But it wasn't.

"The sounds came from behind a door that I've never even noticed before. It's like any door in the outer corridor on the left wing."

He frowned when she stalled. "Go on."

"I went downstairs, and Horowich was there."

Kurt reared back. "Horowich? The man who Devon assaulted?"

She swallowed, and the gesture while automatic, seemed so difficult to accomplish. Blowing out a breath, she whispered, "He was the journalist. H-He's the one who staged my fall."

With his head spinning, Kurt sank back into the pillows and stared up at nothing. That was all he could do.

Because he knew what she was about to say, he didn't ask what Horowich was doing in the cellar. She needed no prompting to continue, "He was tied to a hook, beaten and bloody while Vasily's men, Vasily himself, and Sean and Andrei looked on."

Neither of them spoke for a handful of moments. It was so quiet the chiming of the grandfather clock in the corner of his room sounded so overly loud that they both flinched.

Reaching up to rub the back of his neck, he asked, "Where is he now?"

"Some Russian prison." She gnawed on her lip before she bit out, "I condoned it."

"You didn't have much choice," he instantly countered. "They made a move without consulting any of us. Our hands were tied from the start."

As rage bubbled inside him, he knew it stemmed more from the fact he'd been kept in the dark than the act they'd perpetrated.

Unable to help himself, he lifted an arm and tugged her close. She nearly launched herself at him, cuddling up to him as though she had ten arms and ten legs. He thought she couldn't get closer to him if he tried, and he *was* trying.

He wanted the comfort as much as she did.

There was a dark pool inside everyone's soul. Some could preach they were good and pure, but when it boiled down to it, when a loved one was hurt, everyone wanted justice. There was a reason Sean and Andrei had acted the way they had—introducing Vasily told him everything. If they could have acted within the law, they would have done. Though their keeping this a secret came as a surprise, he knew them too well to think they were acting so rashly out of a desire for 'an eye for an eye.' They were far too rational to seek that alone.

No, there would be justification, but that wouldn't be something Sascha could or would understand.

She was a cop's daughter. Trained, from birth, to respect the letter of the law.

Kurt . . . well, he'd been taught by the Stasi *not* to always approve of the law. Law and politics ran hand in hand sometimes, and he'd learned that by losing his grandfather and father to the torments of a prison where they'd been tortured as political enemies of the state.

"I feel so guilty, Kurt," she whispered, breaking into his thoughts.

"Why?"

She stiffened, but he hummed under his breath as he pressed a kiss to her head. "You understand why they did it, don't you? Without even knowing the facts."

"Yes. I do," he answered, tightening his arm around her when she tried to pull away. "Horowich hurt you, didn't he?" he asked, the question rhetorical.

He felt rather than saw her gnawing against her inner cheek—her chin was tilted against his shoulder, after all. "Y-yes."

"We lost Camilla because of him, didn't we?"

"Yes," she whispered.

"And, no matter how pissed I am at their keeping me in the dark about this, I know for a fact they wouldn't have acted this way without reason." He gritted his teeth in irritation. "What reason I'm not sure, but—"

Sascha broke in with a voice so quiet he strained to hear her as she whispered, "Andrei said Horowich was trying to bargain with them. Dropping the assault charges, if we didn't pursue his involvement in my fall."

"And why the hell would we have agreed to that?" His tone, in contrast to hers, was a loud boom which made her jolt.

She turned her face into him, and he wanted to scream when he felt the wetness of her tears against his skin. "Because he had evidence of our relationship. He said he'd agree to keep quiet. . . ."

And like that, everything clicked.

"Ah," he murmured softly.

"Ah," she replied.

For an age, they lay there in silence. Not saying anything, not doing anything, just 'being' in each other's embrace.

The darkness outside grew heavier as midnight approached and went, then, only God knew how long later, the bedroom door opened.

In all that time, neither of them had slept, neither of them had uttered a word.

Kurt wasn't sure what to say, wasn't sure what to think.

He wanted to comfort her but knew there was little point. She couldn't understand, not truly, why Sean and Andrei had acted on their intel the way they had. Neither could she justify her own reasons for not putting a stop to what she'd seen.

As the light in the hall broke into both their pensive moods, they saw a familiar shadow. They were far too accustomed to Devon popping up in their bedrooms like a jack-in-the-box—he slept where Sascha slept. *If* he slept at all.

Stepping into the room, he silently closed the door. When there was barely any illumination in the room, Sascha croaked out, "We're awake, Devon. You can switch on a light."

"Why aren't you asleep?" Devon inquired and, Kurt wasn't sure why, but he sounded exhausted. "You're always asleep at this time." He clicked on a light, and for a few seconds, Kurt just blinked as his eyes adjusted to the new brightness.

When he saw him, he saw the fatigue lining Devon's face, the shadows under his eyes.

"Come here, baby," Sascha told him, lifting an arm.

Devon padded forward, his steps still silent as he approached the bed. He turned off the main light via the switch above the nightstand and clicked on the low lamp.

He didn't strip, just climbed atop the mattress and huddled up beside her, sandwiching Sascha between him and Kurt.

The bitch of it was, had they been awake without such thoughts in their head, he knew they could have started something. But as much as Kurt loved losing himself in Sascha's body, there was no relief to be found tonight.

She'd told him something that would forever change their world, and dealing with the repercussions was all he could handle.

"Why aren't you asleep?" Devon asked.

"What time is it?"

"Just after four."

Sascha clucked her tongue. "And you're only just coming to bed. You didn't sleep at all last night."

He released a heavy sigh. "I know. There's too much to do before we head to Veronia next week."

"There's no point in running yourself into the ground, sweetheart," she crooned, turning away from Kurt for the first time that evening to allow Devon to snuggle into her more.

Kurt didn't mind, if anything he was touched, as always, by how she was with Devon. Having her accept his brother's quirks, and watching her act on that, just made him love her all the more.

She lifted her arm, and Devon curled into her, pressing his head to her chest. She started running her fingers through his hair, gently at first until his breathing leveled out and Kurt knew Devon was asleep.

"You should get some rest too, *Liebchen*," he told her gently.

A hum escaped her. "I know. I will."

His lips twitched. "If you say so." Kurt bent over and pressed his mouth to her head again. "Thank you for loving him."

She stiffened. "Don't say that. He, as well as the rest of you, are my gift."

He turned so that he could stare down at her. "You really think that?"

"Yes, even if two of you have gone off half-cocked like something in a Tarantino movie." She blew out a breath. "I'm going to try to sleep," she told him, obviously keen to avoid returning to that subject.

He couldn't blame her.

Nodding, he dipped his chin and pressed a gentle kiss to her mouth, then rolled over to switch off the light Devon had turned on before he'd climbed into bed. As he moved beside her once more, he felt her breathing change as she succumbed to sleep, too.

Slumber wasn't so quick to come for him, though.

He spent the rest of the night listening to his brother and the love of his life's breaths, finding comfort from that when everything had just changed.

And not, he believed, for the better.

# TWENTY-THREE

"WHY DIDN'T YOU TELL US?"

Andrei blinked at Kurt's abrupt intrusion, then stiffened when he must have read the anger on his face. He held up a hand, which irritated the hell out of him, before Andrei turned his attention back to the computer and murmured, "Jane, do you think you can deal with that before tomorrow?"

"Yes. Of course. Is everything all right?" Andrei's PA inquired.

"Yes," he replied brusquely. "I'll call again tomorrow at four." Though he nodded at her, that was as much of a farewell as he gave his PA.

Though it could be considered rude, they were all aware that Jane had a crush on Andrei, and until recently, Andrei hadn't realized it. Until Sawyer had pointed it out, then had spent the four weeks since joking about Andrei's blindness—when Sascha wasn't in the room, of course.

He'd never exactly been the height of friendliness. Kurt had seen him interact with Jane far too often to fear she had a snowball's chance in hell of taking his attention from where it belonged—on Sascha—to her. She could wear the tightest pencil skirts in the world and drop as many pens as she wanted, Andrei had tunnel vision, Kurt knew, and that tunnel was fixed firmly on Sascha.

"She told you," Andrei said on a grimace.

Kurt's mouth curled into a sneer. "That's all you can say? Yes. She told me when you should have. You and Sean. I can't believe you kept this from me. From us."

Rocking back in his chair, Andrei sighed tiredly. "It just happened."

"Kidnapping a man doesn't *just* happen. Holding him captive and beating the shit out of a man doesn't *just* happen, Andrei. Spout your bullshit at Sascha, but I won't believe you."

The room was paneled with stained wood, which made it darker than the meager outside light had a hope in hell of combatting. With two desk lamps on and a blazing fire in the hearth, Kurt could still see the play of shadows on his brother's face as his expression revealed more than Andrei would appreciate.

He read anger in his tightly furrowed brows. Sorrow in the curve of his mouth. His pinched eyes spoke of guilt, and when he rubbed at them with his forefinger and thumb, he also conveyed his fatigue.

"Sean and I asked grandfather for help with Devon's case. I needed him to come to Veronia, and the case was getting in the way of my timeline. I just wanted to erase things."

"The hand of justice comes with five-pointed stars now, does it?"

Andrei had the grace to wince at the reference to the symbolic stars Bratva men had tattooed on their chests. "Look, you know Devon would do far more good in Veronia than him doing his penance in a jail cell would ever achieve."

Because he didn't disagree, he didn't reply, but that wasn't to say he approved.

Andrei's temper sparked at his lack of an answer, and he bit off, "Sean contacted grandfather, too. I think he realized after our talks with Llewelyn that we didn't have much chance of getting Devon free and clear. When Sean asked him to look into it, Grandfather sent him the CID case file. From the before and after shots, Sean recognized Horowich as being one and the same man who was with Sascha when she was brought into the hospital after her fall."

Kurt strode away from the door and headed toward the large mahogany desk Andrei was using. The books lining the walls in their antique shelves dampened the sound from outside in the hall, making it so all he could hear was the crackling and hissing from the fireplace.

Resting his hands on the desk, he asked, "Then what happened? And don't bullshit me, Andrei. I should have known from the start."

He was glad to see his brother wince; it meant his rejoinder had hit home.

"Sean explained the situation to Vasily, who had someone hack into the cameras on the street where Sascha had her accident. He found pictures of her and of Horowich spilling oil onto the sidewalk where she was about to fall." Andrei closed his eyes, then tilting his head back, he carried on without opening them, "We approached Horowich's barrister with this information, and he came back with a counter-offer–let this drop or have all our dirty linen aired in public."

"So, what? You decided to have him strung up and beaten half to death?"

Andrei scowled at him. "You tell me you wouldn't have watched, too," he bit off. "Sascha's so beyond traumatized by losing Camilla that she's a different woman half the time! Our family will recover from losing Camilla, but it will take years. All because that bastard wanted an in."

"Do you hear me arguing?"

"Well, it sounded like a criticism."

"It was. Of *you* deciding this. Without me, Sawyer, or Devon."

"Devon would have told Sascha," Andrei instantly dismissed.

"I wouldn't. Nor would Sawyer," Kurt pointed out.

"Why put the burden on you?" he countered. "Do you think I like that I enjoyed seeing that bastard having the shit kicked out of him?"

"No. Don't you think I'm angry that I did miss out on it?"

Andrei jolted back. "No. No way," he retorted. "I don't believe it."

"Why? I'm a man, Andrei, aren't I? Someone hurt my woman." He tilted his head to the side. "Did you punch him?"

"Vasily wouldn't allow it."

"And you listened?" Kurt replied, stunned by that answer.

"He said it was for the best."

"Because you wouldn't have stopped?"

Andrei dipped his chin. "Perhaps. Are you going to tell Sawyer?"

"I don't know. It will just piss him off. Some things are best left forgotten, but the trouble is, Sascha isn't dealing well with any of this."

"No. I know." He released a heavy sigh. "I wish she hadn't realized what was going on."

"She thought one of us was cheating on her."

That comment had Andrei scowling. "Why the hell would she think that?"

"Why do women think anything?" he retorted.

He mumbled, "See what I mean? Sascha would never think like that before. What with Jane and now this? It's not like her. I hate that someone has broken something inside her."

"What you did to Horowich . . . that isn't going to repair anything," Kurt warned him.

Andrei ran a tired hand through his hair. "I know," he admitted. "I know."

---

"HAS SASCHA FINISHED HER PERIOD?"

Kurt snickered. "Feeling frisky, Sawyer?"

Though he released a snarl, that wasn't the only sign that Sawyer was horny. He ran a hand through his hair, something he did infrequently because his red hair was thicker than fucking wool and snagged easily.

"She's been weird this week, hasn't she?"

His comment had Kurt stiffening and shooting Sean a look. When his brother merely carried on reading one of the documents in front of him, Kurt heaved a sigh, sensing that Sean wasn't going to answer. "She's a homebody," was all he said, figuring that would be the best explanation. As well as the easiest.

"So? She's used to traveling now. At first, I thought it was because it was shark week, but now . . ." His voice petered out.

"Shark week?" Devon crossed his feet at the ankles as he pondered that. "Because of all the blood?" He snickered. "Very clever, Sawyer."

The man in question rolled his eyes. "I'm a comedian, Devon. Didnae ye ken that?"

Devon sat up. "When did this happen?"

"When did what happen?" Kurt asked, confused. "Shark week? This last week, Dev."

"No. When did Sawyer become a comedian? Why didn't you tell me until now?"

Sawyer waved a dismissive hand and, utterly ignoring Devon, mumbled, "She's distant."

"She's grieving," Sean rasped, his voice deeper than usual.

"When hasn't she been since Camilla?" Sawyer replied, his brow puckered. "I'm nae taking anything away from her with that, but I just don't understand what's different between this past week and the last."

Kurt, feeling slightly hot under the collar, cleared his throat. "Is it her first period since . . .?"

Sawyer blanched. "Christ, is it? I havenae asked. I didnae really want to know."

His lips curved. "Me, neither." Rubbing his chin, and well aware he was bullshitting to protect Sawyer and Devon from the heavy weight that was the truth of Sascha's grim mood, he carried on, "It has to be painful. That first time after. . . ."

Sawyer's grimace said it all. "I thought she was getting better. Did you see what she'd been researching?"

"No. What?" Sean asked, his brows high.

"Pet play." Sawyer grinned. "She must have liked that tail we got her."

Kurt snorted, but Devon grumbled, "It's gross."

"Hardly, mon," Sawyer countered. "It's natural."

"How is it natural?" Devon retorted. "She's a woman, not a dog."

"I think she's a kitten, actually, Dev," Sean murmured, his tone close to absent-minded, meaning he was only half-focused on their conversation.

"A kitten?" Devon squinted at that. "It makes no sense."

Sawyer raised a hand and began ticking down with his finger. "She's either a brat or a pet, Dev. She's insubordinate but likes a firm hand. The rules make her feel safe, but she likes to break them and reap the reward. She's too naughty to be an out and out submissive."

Devon rolled his eyes. "God forbid she'd just be a woman."

Sean grunted. "We're well aware you don't approve, but Sascha wants this."

"I know she does," he replied, surprising all of them.

"You do?" Kurt inquired, tilting his head to the side as he took in his brother who was seated at the side of the fire, a sulky pout on his lips. "How?"

"I asked her."

Sawyer groaned. "You didn't go putting any funny ideas into her head, did you?"

"What kind of funny ideas?" was all Devon said. "Like the fact she didn't have to do this stuff if she didn't want?"

A growl escaped Sean—that alone was enough to have everyone jolting in surprise. Sean was, after all, the most controlled of them all. "We do this for her."

"Bullshit. You're telling me you don't get a hard-on over this shit? Watching her demean herself in front of y—" Devon's mouth tightened. "My mother would have barked if my father had asked her to.

Remember that when you're getting her to do shit that would make any average person blush."

It was Sawyer who growled this time. "Are you trying to tell me you think we three are like your da?"

Devon shrugged, but the look in his eyes spoke of his concern. "I think there's a fine line between consent and force."

"I don't appreciate the implication, Devon," Sean rasped.

"You don't have to like it. You just have to listen to it and abide by it. Sascha isn't one of the women you'd take to those clubs back in the day. She's our woman. Our wife. Whatever she wants, do, but be aware she might not want it forever. Do you hear me?"

"Aye, we hear you. Loud and clear." Sawyer wasn't affronted, though, and that was enough to surprise Kurt. More than anything, he appeared stunned at Devon's concern. Considering Devon walked around with his head in the clouds for most of the day, Kurt could understand.

He himself wasn't altogether easy with Sascha's sudden need to submit. Like Devon, he felt more comfortable believing it was a phase. Even though he knew that wasn't how these soul-deep desires went.

His love of watching wasn't something he could avoid. He'd had to embrace it or go mad. Perhaps this was the calm before Sascha's storm?

They wouldn't know until the hurricane hit them, but he hoped the clear up wouldn't be too traumatic.

For all parties involved.

---

WHAT WAS IT ABOUT GOOGLE?

You made one questionable search and until the end of time, the rest of the search results were loaded down with porn.

After yet another failed attempt which resulted in porn that had her eyes flaring at just the sight of the thumbnail, she huffed out a sigh and signed out of her computer.

She was grouchy.

There. She'd admitted it. Grouchy with a goddamn capital G.

Rubbing her temple, she tilted back against the window seat and stared out at the grounds beyond, where acres of trees and bushes looked like bumps on the horizon thanks to how loaded down with snow they were. It was bleak. As bleak as her goddamn mood, and for the first time in too long, she was bored of feeling that way.

Bored with a capital B.

"Mama."

Turning to stare at her son who was supposed to be sleeping in his cot, she murmured, "Hey, baby." Climbing to her feet, she grimaced at the sight of his flattened mouth. "I know. The next time we're here, we'll get you a bed."

"Beds are for big boys," he retorted, his tone as grouchy as she felt.

"I know."

"I'm a big boy, Mommy." She knew he wasn't just making a statement there; he was making a demand. One that insisted she agree with him.

Despite herself, she had to laugh. "Yes. You are. A very big boy."

At her back, she heard someone chuckle, and seeing Vasily, she narrowed her eyes at him. Remaining silent though because Tin had heard the laughter and seen his grandfather, he released a squeal of excitement that she certainly didn't feel.

Tin was all arms and legs as she heaved him out of the cot, and Vasily tutted. "You really do need a bed, don't you?"

Tin, sensing a kindred spirit, nodded. "Yes, *Dzed*, I do, I do."

She let him down and watched as Tin scrambled over to Vasily's side. The kid always had a shit-ton of energy. Didn't matter if he'd woken up from his nap or not.

With her eye on the pair of them, she retreated to the window seat as they switched to Russian. She didn't mind. It amazed her that

Tin had picked up the language so swiftly. She'd heard him babble away with Andrei, but with Vasily? The two of them seemed to be able to talk far more than she'd have imagined.

Resting her head back against the paneling behind her, she looked out onto the yard once more. She was aware of what they were doing in her peripheral vision, and even if she didn't trust Vasily, she trusted him with Tin.

That made no sense, she knew.

Tin was her everything. Her baby boy. He was more precious than a two hundred-carat diamond, yet she knew Vasily would protect Tin with his life.

The diamond? Not so much. That would be smuggled out of the country before she could do so much as sneeze.

The two of them played for a while, building shit and getting more joy out of knocking the towers down. She took advantage of Tin's attention being held by someone else and closed her eyes.

She wasn't asleep, though, so when Vasily approached, she could level a look his way.

"Sulking doesn't suit you."

Narrowing her eyes at him, she murmured, "Who says I'm sulking?"

He sniffed. "Me."

"Well, contrary to popular opinion, Vasily, you don't know everything."

"No? I know you're making my boy's life miserable."

She cocked a brow at him. "I am? Well, I didn't realize I was. I just thought I was trying to come to terms with crimes so heinous we could all be locked up for twenty years," she spat.

He pursed his lips. "You know there is no comeback."

"That doesn't reassure me."

"How can that not reassure you?" he retorted, waving his hands in the air.

"Because the very fact we can do this and get away with it is so beyond wrong that I can't stand it." She sucked down a sharp breath. "Anyway, I'm not making Andrei suffer. Not intentionally, anyway."

"You need to do something with yourself."

Her eyes flared at that. "Excuse me?" The old bastard wasn't about to lecture her, was he?

God help him if he called her lazy.

"I mean you're too smart for this."

"For what?" she demanded, her tone close to dangerous.

He grunted. "Stop spitting fire at me," Vasily retorted. "As much as I love Tin, and as much as he's one of the smartest children I've ever known, you're more than that, Sascha. You're more than just a mother."

She winced. "Don't say that."

"It's not offensive what I say," he retorted. "I just mean . . . being a mother is a full-time job. I saw this with my wife. God rest her soul. With my son and then with Andrei." Considering Vasily never mentioned his failure of a son, especially not around Andrei, those words came as a surprise. "But when you are grieving, stewing in that grief is never wise. You must move on. You must do something to take your mind from these things."

Sascha blinked up at him. "Moving on isn't as easy as you'd think. Not when I shouldn't have had to move on in the first place."

His lined face creased more with his shared grief, and as he reached for her hand, she didn't pull back, not even when he pressed it to his chest, just above his heart. "I feel your pain, Sascha. I am not a mother. This, I know. I wasn't a good father, but I was a good grandfather. I will continue to be until God takes the breath from my lungs. I will do things that most people wouldn't dream about doing as they rest, safe in their beds, for him and by extension of his love, you. But I feel your grief. I understand it.

"One thing you learn in this life of mine is pain. You don't grow attached. You learn not to. But now and then, someone slips through the cracks, and you learn to guard them. To guard them so well that you will kill for them. Commit the worst sins in their name."

"That doesn't justify—"

But he didn't let her finish. "I make no justification," he told her. "I see no reason to."

God, she wanted to smack the arrogant ass.

His lips twitched at her mutinous expression. "I merely explain that people always slip through the cracks, and they will always cause you pain. There is no shoring yourself against that kind of ache, but I know what it is to feel how you do." He rubbed her hand with a tenderness she didn't associate with him and let her fingers slip from his grasp. "You are a good woman, Sascha. And you are rightfully unhappy about what happened, but more than that, you're a smart woman. Your grief is yours to own, to possess, but don't let it own you."

He reached forward to pat her cheek. His hand scented faintly of his expensive cologne and the cigars he smoked that Andrei cussed him out over every time he saw the old man lighting one up.

"I'll take Tin with me to the pool. Andrei said he wanted to get in another lesson before you leave."

"Swim, Mommy. Swim!"

She nodded, her throat too thick to reply, and watched as the youngest and oldest members of her family left the room together.

Vasily had touched a nerve, that was for sure, but was he right?

# TWENTY-FOUR

"TIN," Sascha warned. "Don't."

The little man pouted at her. "I like it."

That seemed to be his justification for most things at the moment.

Painting his toenails?

He liked it.

Liberally coating himself in Devon's aftershave?

He liked it.

The nail varnish had, quite naturally, spilled over Vasily's eighteenth-century Aubusson rug as well as most of Tin's pants.

And the aftershave?

Even Ivan, one of Vasily's right-hand men, who had sinus issues and couldn't smell dog shit if it was right under his nose—that was a fact, and Sascha didn't want to know how everyone *knew* that—had been able to scent Tin a mile away.

Christ, the astronauts in the International Space Station could smell her toddler.

She rolled her eyes because, the bitch of it was, the little monkey couldn't open either product without outside help.

Because everyone had far too much sense, everyone save for

Devon, he was the reason Tin was currently covered in her very expensive face cream. Head to toe.

He looked like something from a David Bowie video because—wouldn't you credit it?—the moisturizer had a shimmer to it.

Even in the miserable Russian noon day sun, he was shining brighter than a diamond.

His current mission?

To lick the cream off his arms.

It was times like these, when Tin did regular shit, that she wondered why she worried about him. Sure, he was a genius in the making. Sure, he loved Sudoku when most kids couldn't even read yet. And sure, he was going to be speaking three languages fluently before his fifth birthday, but he still had the same curiosity as a child.

Unfortunately, he also had a father who was an enabler.

Sighing, she turned to Devon and ground out, "Really? Did you *really* not see an issue here?"

He peered up from his laptop with a hum. His eyes were blank. Well, they weren't. They were focused on what he'd just been reading. She could have talked to him in Romulan, and he'd have understood as much as she'd just said.

Running a hand through her hair, she peered down the private jet and saw most of her men were working, meaning she had full guardianship over Tin.

Did that make it her fault he was glittering like a disco ball?

Or was it Devon's for opening the jar?

Pondering that a second, she decided it was Devon's fault. She elbowed him in the side and mumbled, "Stop opening things for him."

"What things?"

"Jars. Bottles. *Anything*. He wants you to open anything more dangerous than a pen, tell him to come to me."

"Pens aren't dangerous."

"That's my point." Although . . . "Wait, don't open pens for him, either." She had visions of him drawing all over the jet's upholstery, or Sharpie-ing the Duke's walls—that was where they were staying, after all. A Duke's ancestral home.

Vasily had just laughed at the electric-blue stain on his priceless rug.

A Duke?

Yeah, she couldn't see that going down so well.

With a huff, she elbowed him in the side again. "Don't open anything for him."

"Not even a water bottle?" Devon frowned at her. "He needs to drink, Sascha."

"I'm not saying he can't. I'm saying get him to come to me to open things." She was resolute in this. Water wasn't dangerous, but Devon wouldn't take notice if it was a bottle of water or a bottle of juice.

Bright-blue nail varnish was as hard as blackcurrant juice to get out of ancient and antique soft furnishings.

"Jesus," she whispered. "Why didn't I make us stay at a hotel?"

At least at a hotel, everything had a price tag. In an ancestral manor, furniture wasn't just furniture. It was *objets d'art*. Priceless.

Well, until Tin got his mitts on it.

"Hotels aren't as comfortable, nor are they as close. There's nowhere appropriate near the palace," Devon informed her, his nose back on the document on his laptop.

Grimacing, she conceded with a huff and sank back against the plush leather sofa.

The jet was Vasily's idea of a going away present.

It wasn't like they couldn't afford to travel via private jet, but she preferred to have a small carbon footprint. To the Pakhan—retired, her ass—carbon footprints were meant to be ignored. And, when she'd climbed aboard, it would have been churlish not to use the damn thing.

God, it was gorgeous.

Comfortable seats everywhere, actual desks, individual seating without all the bulky electronics that came with first-class perks. This was like a flying living room. Considering Tin was noisy and sometimes pulled tantrums when they flew—he had bad earaches occasionally—this was a solution she didn't want to get used to.

"Are you nervous?"

Devon tilted his head to the side at her question. "Nervous?"

"Yes. Nervous. You know, are you anxious about what we're about to do?"

He frowned. "Why would I be? It's a puzzle."

Her lips quirked. "Like father, like son, I guess."

"Uh huh. Tin likes puzzles, too," he confirmed like she didn't already know.

Sascha folded her arms against her chest and cast another look around the cabin. Kurt was using red pen on a copy of the film script he'd received last night. Sawyer had his legs crossed at the ankle as he read from a sheaf of files. Sean was engrossed on his computer, and Andrei was on his phone, scowling at something he was reading.

They always had something to do.

It half amazed her, half made her feel like she was lazy.

Even now, when they could be relaxing, they weren't. She knew most of them had put in a few hours on Christmas Day itself, and yesterday, for New Year's, they'd all been in the offices Vasily allotted to them, because yep, his house was large enough to have *several.*

Whereas she?

What was her purpose?

Vasily was, she hated to admit, right.

She bit her bottom lip as she watched them. There was a peace to be found in just viewing them as though they were a movie. Christ, they were a dream come true to drool over, truth be told, but she felt a bit like she was wandering and getting lost.

When her role had morphed from that of housekeeper to that of 'their woman,' her duties had changed, too. Sean had hired more maids, had insisted she stop doing the laundry, too. She managed the household accounts and cooked. That was it.

Of course, there was Tin to look after, and he was a handful, but it just. . . .

She sighed.

Why was she feeling so restless?

Because she'd expected to be preparing for the chaos of a new baby?

Since that option was no more, did she feel like a ship without a rudder? Aimless? With no direction in mind?

Goddamn Vasily for getting into her fucking head.

"Why are you huffing?"

She blinked, surprised Devon had noticed. He'd seemed engrossed in whatever he was doing.

"Sorry. I didn't mean to disturb you."

"I'd have told you to move if you were disturbing me," he replied, frustrated, and she had to laugh. "I didn't, did I?"

"Nope, you didn't."

"So?"

"So?" she countered, lips curving at his impatience.

"Why are you huffing?"

"I'm bored, I guess."

"Bored?" He turned back to her so that he could look her square in the eye. "Do you want sex?"

She snorted. "No. Do you?" She'd seen a bedroom, though, and if they ever flew private again, she could join the mile high club.

Several times.

"Later. We'll be there soon. I don't like being interrupted."

Despite herself, heat unfurled in her lower belly at the rasp in his voice. She elbowed him, again, in the side. "I wasn't talking about sex."

"Why are you bored then?"

"Sex isn't entertainment," she retorted.

"No? It entertains me," he countered.

"That's because your brain is weird and thinks of sex as a hobby. Some men take photos, others go hiking, you like to suck my clit."

He licked his lips. "I do. Very much."

A laugh escaped her again. "I know. My clit appreciates the attention," she confided, making him grin.

"Good to know." He rubbed his chin. "Do you want a book to read?"

"No. I have my kindle." She blew out a breath. "Sorry. I'm just on edge."

"Why?"

"Not sure." That wasn't a lie either.

"Are you excited about staying in Veronia for a while?"

"I don't know. Not really. I mean it won't change things, will it? It will be like being home, just somewhere else."

"And you say my brain is weird. There's a huge difference between Veronia and England."

"There is?"

"Yes. It's warmer."

She giggled. "This is true."

"Plus, there are plenty of things to do. We're stuck in the city for the most part. Tin doesn't know the countryside all that well. We can do things."

"What things?"

He pursed his lips. "Things."

"Can't think of anything off the top of your head?" she teased, knowing this idea of his hadn't been building for a long time.

If it had, he'd have researched it, and if there was one thing Devon was great at, it was research.

That was why she had the best vibrator this side of Christendom.

That thing had enough power to make her eyes roll back after one buzz.

"I'll look into it," he informed her, his tone grouchy because she'd caught him off guard.

"Good. Well, that's something to look forward to."

"I know why you're antsy," Kurt murmured, and she tilted her head to encompass him in her look.

"Why?"

"I haven't had anything for you to edit for a while."

She wrinkled her nose. "I don't edit. I just suggest things."

"You do a better job than the editors at my publisher," he countered, tapping his pen against the desk. "Hell, you'd be better at checking this script than I am."

"Huh?" She held up her hands. "No way. That's the final script, isn't it?"

"Yes. You can handle the responsibility, Sascha," he chided. "You know the story as well as I do."

"Hardly," she countered.

"We discussed it often enough," was all he said as he got to his feet, red pen and script in his hand. When he tried to pass it over to her, she shook her head, and he grunted, then plunked it on her lap. "You'll do fine."

"It's *your* script!" she retorted.

"Think of it as *our* script."

As she shuffled in her seat, the papers jostled with her. When they almost slipped between her knees, Devon caught them for her. As he secured them, he said, "You have something to do now, don't you?"

Kurt grinned at her. "It's a weight off me, Sascha."

She frowned. "The director wants your eyes on it, Kurt. Not mine."

"That's because he doesn't know you helped me perfect the trilogy. Directors don't read dedications it would seem," he joked.

Her cheeks grew pink as she remembered the dedication he'd shown her on the hardback edition of the final book in his Black Blood series. He'd signed it for her, and it was on her bedroom shelf back home.

Silly or not, it was one of her prized possessions.

She bit her lip. "Are you sure?"

"Absolutely," he encouraged. "If you have a question, just ask."

Blinking at him as she gulped, she turned her attention to the script before her.

It wasn't like what she was used to seeing. The font was horrible, like a typewriter's, and the spacing was weird. She saw where Kurt had made notes, underlining words, highlighting whole sentences. As she moved through his edits, she got a feel for what he was looking for.

She'd never been privy to his conversations with the production company. Not because he'd excluded her, simply because a lot of it went down on the phone, and Kurt had a Bluetooth earpiece.

If she'd wanted, she had no doubt he'd have included her in a conference call, but she'd never have thought to ask about it.

As she started to read the thick script, something inside her settled. Felt less restless.

It wasn't a permanent solution, but it helped.

For now.

---

THE HOUSE WAS ENORMOUS.

About a twenty-minute drive from the main airport of the capital city, the seat of the Duke of Ansian and Lorrena made stately homes she'd visited in the past, when she'd toured the south of England as a newly arrived émigrée, look small.

This place was epic.

It had a huge lake in front of it too, and to the side, a gigantic glasshouse. The drive alone was longer than some roads back in London.

As they meandered down the white gravel-paved drive in the car the Duke had waiting for them at the airport, she felt excitement stir for the first time.

They were actually going to be staying in this place!

When they pulled to a halt, the large doors opened. They were about twenty feet in length, minimum, and out walked someone dressed like a penguin.

She wasn't sure why she was surprised there was a butler on staff here, but Sascha was.

Epic.

As the butler organized with the chauffeur for the luggage to be removed, he immediately guided them into the hall.

While the men gathered around a large central table that was loaded down with a vase of flowers so large it had to empty a florist's shop, she peered around the comfortable foyer.

Overhead, there was a glass dome ceiling which let in some wonderful light, especially as the glass was stained with yellows and blues that made the dust motes in the air seem like they were dancing.

There was a mezzanine floor with wooden supports that were carved into gleaming ropes which twirled around one another, and the tapestries alone had her gawking at the majesty of the place.

When Tin pulled at her hand, she bent down to speak with him even though she kept her eyes glued to a beautiful Lalique vase that decorated a wide side table.

"Mommy, I need the potty."

She nodded and turned to the butler who appeared to have overheard.

"If you'd step this way?" he intoned, but she waved a dismissive hand at him.

"Please, just tell me where it is. We'll be fine on our own."

He smiled at her, his brown eyes twinkling as he looked down at Tin, making her wonder how long it had been since the ducal seat had children living in it. From what she'd read, the Duke was a renowned and unashamed and unapologetic bachelor.

Considering he had to be drowning in pussy from his title alone, never mind his wealth, she couldn't exactly blame him. And having seen his picture, as well as the King and his brother's, this family seemed to create only handsome men. There was no way she'd have settled down if she were in his shoes.

"There's a more comfortable bathroom up those stairs, ma'am," the butler informed her. "Take the corridor to the left, and it's the fourth doorway down."

She smiled back, happy that he wasn't anti-kids because Tin was the kind of boy who needed people on his side. His white-blond hair, bright baby blues, and pouty mouth made him look like a cherub.

Until you realized he was the opposite.

She wasn't sure if the devil had cherubim but considering his curiosity, Tin was no angel.

Hauling him up into her arms, she dumped her bag in Devon's hands and headed toward the stairs.

As they approached the corridor, Tin decided that playing with her new dangly earrings and somehow getting them caught in *his* hair was imperative.

"I swear, kid, you're half cat," she grumbled as she tried to untangle them.

Making it to what she'd figured was the fourth door, she opened it, expecting a bathroom worthy of an architectural magazine.

What she got wasn't a bathroom, but a bedroom.

An occupied bedroom.

At first, she didn't think anything of it. Then, when she realized who was standing by the window, in the Duke's arms—okay, understatement, because the Duke was definitely engaged in tonsil hockey here—she nearly dropped Tin.

Perry DeSauvier had hit the press as the girl-next-door who was soon to be the Queen-next-door. There'd been no avoiding her picture in the media, and there'd been no evading the deluge of gossip about the Veronian royal family after the previous Queen had been assassinated a few years ago.

So, though she'd have liked to think she was wrong, the Duke was definitely feeling the Queen up.

"Xavier, would you pass me—?"

Her eyes cut to the person behind the voice, and when she saw who it was, she really did drop Tin.

The Queen and the Duke.

With the King in attendance?

What the fuck was happening here?

# SEAN

# TWENTY-FIVE

LIFE HAD a funny habit of throwing shit someone's way when they weren't equipped to deal with it.

But sometimes?

Sometimes life just had a real fucking laugh at your expense.

That was life for Sascha Dubois at that moment because, seriously, somebody somewhere was fucking with her.

She wasn't gaping at a King, a Queen, and a Duke after they had some post-sex cuddles, was she?

No.

That just couldn't be.

It could. Not. Be.

Cheeks bright pink, she could do little other than stare at the trio who were gaping right back at her.

It was one of *the* most awkward moments of her life and she'd given birth. She had a lover on the spectrum who came out with the most random, and most mortifying shit when the mood struck, and then she had his mini-me in the form of their son.

She was used to awkward.

Awkward was her bitch, and the way to make it that way was to laugh. To laugh so hard that everyone just realized you'd taken it as a joke.

But this?

Here?

Nope.

That wasn't going to cut it.

Then, just as shit got really awkward, and Sascha was talking *super* weird with no one having a clue what to say *or* do, Tin begged, "Mommy, pee pee. 999."

999 was their emergency code—the Brits' version of 911. What better way to teach him that number than to equate it with toilet situations—at least, that had been Kurt's idea. Oddly enough, it had stuck fast.

Eyes widening, Sascha blurted out, "Shit. I forgot."

"Bad word, Mommy. Bad. Bad. Bad."

Fuck.

Trust him to remember that now. But, thank God for kids. Without a word, or maybe another squeak, she retreated from the bedroom without a backward glance and turned to the left to where she figured the bathroom she'd initially been searching for was located.

With barely enough time to get Tin on the damn toilet, she made it.

After she'd lifted him high enough to wash his hands, she turned him around, grateful that he was still young enough to enjoy being hugged by her.

There'd come a day when he'd be anti-hugs and anti-kisses from Mommy, and while that would suck, it would suck harder when she opened the door and stopped procrastinating, because she didn't doubt she'd be facing the firing squad.

She wasn't frightened, per se. She was here with Andrei, after all, and the King and Queen needed him to kickstart their economy again. They also needed Devon and Sawyer... They wouldn't kill the mother of Andrei's son, would they?

"Mommy, you're hot."

Sascha winced as she pulled back. "Sorry, kiddo." The hug, in their winter coats that were fit for a Russian winter, as well as the warm temperature of the bathroom, had made both their cheeks flush.

A tap sounded at the door. "Ma'am?"

She closed her eyes as she tried to process what the hell she was about to say, before another tap sounded and Tin started wriggling to get down.

"Mommy, door. Door!" he repeated, and with both feet firmly on the floor, he hit the ground running so he could yank open the hugely ornate aperture—this was one grand bathroom.

Her hope that the door would be too heavy for him was immediately wrecked when three concerned faces peered through the opening. Spying them, she blurted out, "It's okay. I get it. More than you can imagine."

Perry DeSauvier's shoulders straightened, and with a cool tone, she murmured, "There's nothing to get. Xavier was comforting me. I've had a bad day."

Sascha's lips curved in a smile, and though she'd probably regret being blunt later, she wasn't born yesterday and wasn't about to be treated like a fool. "Honey, I like to be comforted that way too."

Perry's cheeks flushed. "You don't understand."

"I understand perfectly. I get it. Don't worry." Sascha bit her bottom lip. "I mean, I *seriously* get it."

Was the way to avoid being hit by an assassin trying to keep royal secrets classified as easy as just admitting the truth? She really fucking hoped so.

"There's nothing to get," the King, Edward DeSauvier retorted coolly. "My wife had some bad news. She and Xavier are very close."

Tonsil-hockey close. Yup. Sascha had seen that. She'd seen that loud and clear. But obviously they weren't about to admit it, and though she was on the brink of letting things go just to get the hell away from this conversation—she'd have agreed that blue was black by this point—Tin destroyed her plans. Yet again.

Why had she wanted kids again?

"Kiss," Tin yelled. "You kissed. Mommy kisses lots too. Daddy Andrei and Daddy Devon lots. Daddy Kurt—" He made smacking sounds with his mouth. "Papa Sean and Sawyer too." More smacking sounds. "Lots and lots of kisses," he said with a giggle that had Sascha's cheeks burning.

Amusement lit the Duke's eyes where before there'd been cool disdain. "Lots of kisses, hmm?"

Sascha felt her core temperature soar even more—had Tin told anyone else about the 'lots and lots of kisses?'

God help them if he'd told someone at playgroup!

"I, um, I meant it when I said I get it." She shrugged. What else could she say?

Queen Perry's eyes were bugging out, and Sascha couldn't blame her. Whatever she had going on with a Duke and King, well, that was nothing to the *five*—count 'em, *five*—men Sascha had to juggle on a daily basis.

She cleared her throat. "M-My..." Shit. Her what? "They'll be waiting on me." She'd never stayed as a guest somewhere before. Aside from Vasily who totally knew the score.

The King—the *freakin'* King—tilted his head to the side. "You're with the economists."

It wasn't a question. But neither was it a statement. Hadn't they run a security check on her or something? Shouldn't they know who was wandering about their corridors just waiting to barge in on highly secret situations?

Clearing her throat, then realizing she couldn't speak, Sascha just bobbed her head.

"All the economists, apparently," Duke Xavier mused, and Sascha was grateful when Perry elbowed him in the side.

Then, a thought occurred to her. "Oh my God, I was supposed to curtsey!"

A snort escaped Perry. "I think we're way past that stage now..."

The way her words trailed off let Sascha know she was supposed to introduce herself. "I'm Sascha Dubois," she whispered, her tone close to shy, and Sascha didn't particularly consider herself *shy* but shit, this *was* the first time she'd ever met royalty, for God's sake. She was entitled to blush, especially when she'd just caught the Queen kissing the Duke and not the King. But God, she couldn't blame her. Xavier was *fine*. Before her thoughts could derail even more, she mumbled, "This is Valentin. My son."

"Tin," he grouched. "Not Valentin."

When he said his name, she had to smile because it sounded so incredibly Russian that there was no evading exactly who is father was.

She said it like Americans did. Close to Valentine, like the holiday. But Tin? Nope. She couldn't even reproduce how he said it. There were all kinds of dips and dives in the few short syllables that made up his name.

"Well, it's a pleasure to meet you, Tin," Perry graciously told him. She pressed one hand to her knees as she bent over and, with the other, reached out to proffer the other to him in a greeting.

He took it, his small, undoubtedly sweaty palm sliding against the Queen's, and he murmured, "You're like Mommy."

Her lips curved. "I am?"

"'Merican."

Sascha barely refrained from rolling her eyes. Seriously? The kid could say Valentin and speak Russian and say all kinds of shit in German, but her country? Her fucking country? Nope. He slurred that.

Jesus.

"Yep, I'm from Tennessee," she informed him. "I haven't been back in a while though. Your ear's good too. I've been having lessons to sound more queenly."

Xavier snorted. "You can tell how well they've been going."

She reared up at that and pouted. "No fair."

The minute Sascha saw that pout, she realized she hadn't misunderstood, *at all*, what she'd witnessed between them. Of course, she knew she hadn't. There was no misunderstanding that kind of tongue-fucking the Duke had bestowed upon his cousin's wife, but that pout? Yup. That sealed the deal.

Sascha pulled that kind of move when Sean or Andrei were teasing her. It usually ended with her slapping one of them on the belly, then sliding her hand over said belly and sometimes, if she was in the mood—and she was usually in the mood—slipping it down to their cocks for a quick fondle.

Not that she expected Perry to do that in front of an audience. Although it would have been amusing to behold, that was for damn sure.

Edward, apparently sensing that Sascha had discerned the level of intimacy between his wife and cousin, leveled her with a look. She tilted her head to the side and shot him a flustered smile.

"Look. I'm—" She winced. "I'm really rich. I don't need to sell your story or anything."

"Story! Yes, Mommy! Tell me a story. I'm tired. I want to go to beddy."

Sascha's lips curved, and even the men and woman smiled at his chortle of glee at the prospect of a story. She pressed a hand to his shoulder. "I just—I won't say anything."

A muscle ticked in Edward's jaw, but he dipped his chin, making Sascha wonder how that move could be so regal. How did they teach that? Were there classes on how to make the everyday folk feel like scum? "You'll all be signing an NDA so—"

Sascha wafted a hand. "Oh, don't worry. I'm used to signing those. I had to sign one when I moved in with—" She cleared her throat. "Well, yeah. I'm good with NDAs."

Perry snickered. "Good to know." This time, the hand she held out was for Sascha. "Perry." Apparently, the surname or the title wasn't required—and fuck, yep, it wasn't. Sascha figured it was like money—royals never carried it, did they? Nor did they need to 'carry' a surname.

"Sascha Dubois," she whispered, trying not to feel awed by the fact she was shaking hands with a Queen. Even if that Queen probably had a similar upbringing to her.

"Yes, you already said," Perry teased, "but it's nice to put a name to the blush." When the other woman shot her a wink, somehow, Sascha knew she and this Queen were going to get on great. Before Perry's men—and yeah, they were her men—could say another word, she stepped forward, grabbed Tin's other hand, and as a unit of three, she motioned toward the hall. "I can show you to the bedroom you'll be using."

"You can?" Her brow puckered in surprise.

Perry shot her a look. "Yep. I run things around here."

This wasn't even a palace and even Sascha knew that the Veronian Royal Family lived at Masonbrook Palace. Did that mean Perry managed both households? With that in mind, Sascha mused, "That's a lot of running."

"Damn straight. It keeps me out of mischief," Perry joked. "Anyway, as far as I recall… there are five economists downstairs, correct?"

Sascha shook her head. "There's technically just one. Two are mathematicians, but I think Sawyer does something with statistics and Devon tends to make patterns. At least, I think. What they talk about usually goes over my head, and to be honest, I don't really care.

"That sounds so bad," she added, "but seriously, it's so boring and so hot at the same time."

Perry laughed. "Yeah, I know how that works."

"Then there's Sean. He's a criminologist, and Kurt…" She smiled. "He, well, I don't know if you know the series, but he wrote *Black Blood*?"

"Kurt Yeller?" Perry cocked a brow at her. "As if I *couldn't* know that name. Jeez. That series was hardcore. They're making it into a movie, right? I can't wait."

"Yeah." She winced, realizing how dour her tone was, then tried not to be such a killjoy and pumped some enthusiasm she wasn't really feeling into her voice: "I've met the stars. They're good." *Good.* That was about as much as she had to say on the flirts that were the stars of Kurt's movie adaptation. Jennifer Houghton, the main female star, had flirted up a storm with Kurt, and Matthew Dreyford had definitely been trying to get into Sascha's panties.

"I wonder if they'll try to have a premiere here in Madela. I know Xavier and George are working hard to make the city more..." She sighed. "Well, more of everything. The little snafu we had with the revolutionaries set us back a step or two."

"Understandable," Sascha agreed. "But it's safe now, right? Has been for years?"

"Yep. But the UnReals are sticky boogers."

Sascha snorted at that. "Sticky boogers?"

Perry's eyes twinkled. "I have a three-year-old." She patted her stomach. "And another two on the way, apparently."

"Wow. That's going to be a handful."

"You know how it works. It's a damn sight easier with a lot of fathers around."

"That's true." Sascha tilted her head to the side. "Are you secretly walking us to our doom? Is there a room for firing squads at the end of the hall?"

"There's a room for everything else," Perry answered cheerfully. "But nope. Not that. Edward's right. You'll be signing an NDA, and I do actually remember you from the press. You went through that trouble with your parents, right?"

"Understatement," Sascha replied with a shudder. "The press are not my friends, that's for sure."

"Well, that means *we* can be friends, right? I'd like that. It's hard not talking about my relationships with people. Do you seriously have five guys?"

She snickered. "Yep."

"Wow, brave woman," Perry whispered. "Three is tough to keep up with, and they're always all over the place too. Like, if I'm, you know, sore, one of them usually has to fly to Berlin or something, then the other is buried in his lab. It gives me a break."

Sascha shrugged. "They don't attack me en masse."

A laugh escaped Perry. "Shame."

"We heard that."

The growled words came from behind them, and Perry, eyes still twinkling, shot the men a smile and blew them a kiss.

With a grin, Sascha looked straight ahead, and then stopped walking when Perry did too. "This is your room. I didn't know about Tin though. Does he need a special bed?"

Sascha shook her head. "No. He's okay in a single."

"Phew. Well, his room is just off yours." She reached up and tapped her chin. "Your... partners' suites are all on this floor also. Is that a problem?"

Sascha blinked, finding it surreal to be having this conversation, period. Never mind with a Queen. "Why would that be a problem?"

"I like to be close to mine."

Well, that was intriguing. "How do you wrangle that in a palace?" Sascha blurted out.

"Secret doors," Xavier said drily, making her jolt in surprise because she hadn't really anticipated an answer.

Damn, those NDAs must be ironclad, either that, or she had a trustworthy face.

Perry chuckled but tapped her nose. "Ways and means."

"Sounds like it," Sascha teased, and suddenly, the next few months ahead of her in Madela really didn't seem too shitty. In fact, it sounded like it would be awesome if it meant she could hang around with someone who understood her life—how it worked, how complicated it was in some facets, and how simple it was in others.

She beamed at the Queen, and though it was totally inappropriate, she grabbed her and hugged her. It felt strange to hug another woman, and she realized that she hadn't hugged someone who wasn't her guys or Tin in a very long time.

Perry started at her abrupt move, but she squeezed Sascha back.

"I'm looking forward to getting to know you," Sascha stated, well aware it was forward, but unable to help herself.

Perry's grin appeared slowly. "Same here."

---

"SASCHA'S BEEN GONE A WHILE."

Devon's statement had Sean lifting his brandy and taking a sip. His gaze didn't move from the hearth where a roaring fire seared his retinas.

The burn as the brandy went down felt good, as did the heat in the room, and the comfortable leather under his butt as he sank into the Chesterfield. The distance from the UK felt even better.

"She'll be putting Tin to bed. You know how long that takes when he's overtired," Kurt stated, his eyes glued to a newspaper. Ever since he'd passed over the responsibility of reviewing the script for his new film a few hours earlier, he'd taken on a lighter air.

Sean, knowing Kurt far too well for any of their own good, understood. Kurt hated rereading his work. And though the man considered it an honor that his grand oeuvre was being made into a major motion picture, his ego wasn't so damn enormous that he enjoyed seeing how the screenwriters had changed it.

"It's only six," Devon countered, sounding put out at the prospect of Tin going to bed, something he confirmed with his next words. "We were going to mess around together after dinner."

"So? After all that traveling? He'll be out until tomorrow," Sawyer said with a grunt as he read through a file he had on his lap.

They were all doing something save for Sean who, technically, *was* doing something too—drinking.

He intended to get drunk.

Rip-roaring drunk on very fine Armagnac.

There had to be some advantage to staying at the private home of a Duke, for Christ's sake.

"I wanted to play with him," Devon repeated, pouting at having his playmate snatched away by the Sandman. Sean's lips curved at the truculent tone—even in his deepest, darkest moods, Devon could usually shine a light onto the quagmire.

"You don't want to play with him. Not when he's tired. You know how whiny he gets," Andrei pointed out.

Sawyer snorted. "Devon definitely knows, because that's a trait Tin gets from him."

Devon scowled. "That makes no sense. I don't sleep and I'm not whiny."

"You are with Sascha."

"Since when?"

"Sascha." Sawyer mocked Devon's English voice, and did a good job of it, too, considering he was a Scot, "I didn't sleep last night. Can you suck my cock? That will put me out better than Valium. Sascha, I need to leave the house, will you hold my hand when we go out? You can ride my face in the car on the way back if you want to."

Though Sean wasn't in the mood for laughing, he had to join in at that—Sawyer's jibes were too fucking true not to.

Devon sulked for a second, his brow furrowing as he stated, "I don't ask her to suck my cock. She just does it."

"Lucky bastard," Sawyer grumbled.

"Like she doesn't suck yours," Devon retorted. "I saw her the other day at Vasily's. You didn't look like you weren't being coddled."

Sawyer shrugged. "I was being coddled."

"Then what's the problem?"

"No problem," Sawyer retorted with a grin. "Just saying how it is."

Kurt cleared his throat. "He's only teasing you, Devon."

Sean's heart skipped a beat. Kurt—always the pacifist.

"Why, though?"

Kurt sighed. "Because he's a shit?"

That had Devon nodding in complete understanding. "Oh. Right. That makes sense." He rubbed his chin. "I still wanted to mess around with Tin."

"You can tomorrow."

Sascha's voice had Sean looking over at the doorway where the love of his fucking life stood watching over them. He wasn't sure how long she'd been standing there, but from the amused quirk to her lips, it was quite a while.

She moved into the room, ignoring the other seats, and focused on the sofa where he was seated. As he'd known she would.

Sascha had some kind of inbuilt radar where they were concerned. It was something they'd all remarked upon over the years. She knew when one of them was down, knew when one of them was pissed. She'd appear, either with cake, a smile, or a sexy skirt, and she'd make them feel better.

Sascha was...

Well, she was a tonic, and they'd let her down.

That's all they kept on doing. Letting her fucking down. If he didn't love her so bloody much, he'd let her go. That was how hard this latest development was hitting him. He'd brought danger into their world, and he'd never forgiven himself for that.

Lifting an arm when she pressed into him, he curved it around her shoulders, loving how she nuzzled into him.

"Where were you?" he asked softly.

"I met the Queen," she replied, a slight laugh in her tone.

"You did?" Andrei butted in, sounding surprised.

"Yep."

"I didn't realize they were here." He tilted his head to the side. "We've been in here since we finished the tour earlier."

"Getting drunk by the looks of it," she stated, eying the tumbler in Sean's hand. "It's not like you to drink, sugar."

No. It wasn't. He hadn't gotten drunk since Camilla's death, but it was that kind of day.

He pressed a kiss to the crown of her head. "Bad day."

"Really? You've been with us—I didn't see anything wrong."

He shrugged. "The trouble with being online all the time." That was the problem with flying private, there was easily accessible internet. Where he could have remained in ignorance for an extra few hours, instead he'd learned the unpalatable truth while stuck fifty thousand feet above the ground.

"What happened?"

Releasing a breath, he murmured, "Nothing. I'm just processing some emails I received earlier."

Sascha studied him, and reading between the lines, hazarded a guess, "Processing what happened with Vasily?" Though they shared a look, the memory went unspoken.

Horowich, the journalist who'd been stalking their family, hanging from a hook. Beaten to shit. Black and bloody for his crimes against Sascha and the daughter she'd been carrying. The child who'd died because Horowich had tried to insinuate his way into their lives. For a story. Nothing more, nothing less, than a desire for front page news.

"Yeah," he admitted, and it was only half a lie. He'd sanctioned the kidnapping of a murderer... that was something to process, but it wasn't the topic at the forefront of his mind. He just didn't want to share that with her yet. Hell, he *couldn't*.

After the situation with Horowich, how could he reveal this to her?

"Well, I'm glad it's hitting you hard. So it should."

His lips twitched, and he was doubly glad he'd kept quiet now. "I'm glad I can rely on you to keep me grounded."

She shrugged. "You wouldn't be normal if it didn't affect you."

"*I'm* okay," Andrei protested.

"And you're not normal," she countered, but there was a faintly amused note to her voice. "How can you be, growing up with Vasily as an influence?"

That had him scowling at her. "I'm not a sociopath."

"I concur, he isn't," Sean stated drily. "He's just desensitized to violence."

"Didn't need a degree in psychology to figure that one out, bud," Sascha retorted.

"What are you guys talking about?" Devon piped up, and Sawyer looked over at them, curiosity in his eyes.

Sean cleared his throat, well aware that Devon and Sawyer were in the dark where this topic was concerned. Wanting to keep it that way, he said simply, "I happened upon one of Vasily's business transactions."

Sawyer's eyes widened. "Shit. I missed it?"

"Be grateful you did," Sascha said with a huff, and Sean had to admit he loved how uncomfortable she sounded. She didn't like hiding things from them. Didn't like it one bit, and it was evident in the tension in her frame. "It was like something from *Fight Club*."

"Shit, now I'm really pissed I missed it."

"And I'm the bloodthirsty one?" Andrei responded with a grumble, the papers in his hand rustling with his irritation.

Sawyer flipped him the bird.

"What happened?" Devon inquired, his head tilted to the side and his eyes narrowed in such a way that told Sean this topic wasn't about to die a death.

Dread filled him as well as shame, but before he could blurt out his sins, Sascha murmured, "They took out the trash."

Sawyer grimaced. "You're shite with the details, lass."

"Let's be grateful for small mercies, *ja*?" Kurt threw in, cutting Sean a look that had him tensing. Had Sascha told Kurt what had been going on?

Unease filled him. "Best to let sleeping dogs lie, Devon."

"That would make far more sense if it was children."

It was a testament to how out of sorts Sean was that he didn't understand what Devon was talking about. Scowling at his best friend and brother, he asked, "Children?"

"Why would it be an issue if you woke a dog up. Now a baby? One that's teething and just fell asleep?" Devon shook his head. "Tin made me wish we could give babies Valium."

Sascha snickered. "Your ma tried to convince me to dope him with whiskey, Sawyer."

That had him rolling his eyes. "Get them hooked while they're young. A fine Scottish tradition. She'll do the same with haggis. Just you watch."

Sascha's nose crinkled. "No way is my son eating bits of bits of bits of animals."

"Bits of bits of bits? You do realize you consume those every time you eat those crappy hotdog sausages?"

"I'm feeling judged for my choice of hotdog," Sascha retorted, pinning Andrei with a glare. "Do I say anything about all the vodka you drink when you're in Russia? Nope. I don't say jack so don't judge my hotdogs."

Andrei smirked. "You're judging Sawyer's haggis."

The Scot raised his hands. "Don't get me involved in this fight—especially not over haggis. Now, blood sausage? I'll fight yer to the death, Yankee."

"How many times," Sascha grumbled. "I'm not a Yankee. I'm from the West Coast. I'm from Arizona, for fuck's sake."

Sean lifted his glass to his lips and took a deep sip of the liquor he'd been consuming since the butler had shown them into this room an hour or so ago. Covering his smile, he watched as Braveheart went to the wall with Merida from *Brave*—Sean knew *all* the Disney flicks now thanks to Tin.

As the two squinted at each other, Devon butted in, "You like Yankee Candles, Sascha."

"So? What does one have to do with the other?" Kurt inquired, peering over his specs in confusion. "It's just a name."

Devon shrugged. "They're candles. From America."

Sascha snickered. "You're so literal sometimes."

He sighed. "You're only just realizing that *now*?"

"Was that a joke?" She released a false gasp and clapped a hand to her chest. "Be still my heart."

"No, don't be still," Devon blurted out, eyes flaring wide with sudden distress. "Keep it beating!"

Sascha softened and slipped out of her seat, headed over to

Devon, and as smooth as silk, lowered herself onto Devon's lap. She reached up to kiss him, then said, "It will beat as long as yours does, Devon."

He frowned at that. "I'm older than you, Sascha."

"So?"

"So? We have a son. You need to live for him."

"Well, this got existential pretty fucking quickly," Andrei commented on a low laugh. "Can we talk about something far less deep? Like how Sascha accidentally met the Queen of Veronia and we didn't know about it?"

Sascha turned to look at Andrei and shrugged. "We bumped into each other in the hallway."

"You bumped into her in the hallway and were with her for ninety minutes?" Andrei cocked a brow. "Pull the other one."

"The other what?" Devon questioned.

Sawyer hissed out a breath. "Shut up. You and your damn phrases. I swear. How can you remember all those codes and forget metaphors and sayings?"

Devon grinned. "It's an art form."

"It's a pain in the ass is what it is," Sascha told him, but she softened the words by pressing a kiss to the end of Devon's nose.

She wasn't the only one softening.

Sean felt everything inside of him relax at the way she handled Devon. She was always so at ease with him. She never made him feel bad for being a little unusual, she accepted him—flaws and all. Even if, as she'd said, some of those flaws were a supreme pain in the arse.

"Let's get back on track," Kurt retorted, sitting up in his seat. "The Queen? Even I want to hear this one."

"We got to talking about men."

"Men?" Sean wasn't the only one to tense up at that. "Why would you be talking about men?" he rasped.

Sascha peered down at her lap. "We both have them?"

Devon reached up to cup her chin, then he used that soft hold to tip her head back so she had to look him in the eye. "Explain," he ordered, his tone unusually insistent.

She soughed out a little huff. "Do I have to?"

"Yeah. You told someone about us?" Andrei inquired, his brow furrowed. "I think we deserve a little clarification here. Especially considering we're in Veronia on business."

Sascha reached up and began tugging on her bottom lip, something she only did when she was running on nervous energy. "Perry's like me. She's got something similar going on, I mean."

"Going on?" Kurt sighed. "Explain, Sascha."

"I swear, you never stop yakking on, lass, but now when we need you to talk you go silent?"

She scowled at Sawyer. "I'll remember that."

"Please do," he responded smugly. "And I'll make sure you do in bed."

Devon grunted. "Can we not turn this into a weird conversation about how you like to tie her up?"

There were many things wrong about this discussion, but Sean wasn't sure what to focus on. Devon's persistency in correlating the way Sawyer, Andrei, and he got off on 'tying' Sascha up, as he phrased it, with the way his father had beaten and terrorized his mother was a gross concern. But the fact Sascha might have revealed their secret to another person was equally as worrying.

"Are you trying to tell me that the Queen has more than one man?" Sawyer pressed, bringing their conversation back to the original concern.

Sawyer's disbelief had Sascha scowling at him, then with a huff, she got to her feet and headed over to the fire. For a second, she stared down into it. The quiet in the room was broken only by the crackling flames, but all eyes were on her. On Sascha. *The* woman.

"You can't think we're the only people in the world like this," she said after a few moments more of silence.

"Nay, lass, I dinnae think that, but I dinnae think the King of a feckin' country would be—" He looked like a goldfish with his mouth opening and closing the way it was. "I mean, are you trying to say that—"

She shot him a dirty look, then, she winced and, slouching back over to Sean and curving herself into him, admitted, "I walked into the wrong room. Saw something I shouldn't have." She cleared her throat. "Tin did too. It was... awkward."

What Sascha had just revealed held great importance.

They kept their secret under wraps for a reason, and Sean was certain the royal family did the same.

This could affect them all. Their lives, their careers... Not that he wanted to think about his career at the moment.

Fuck.

Maybe this was the exact distraction he needed.

# TWENTY-SIX

SEAN'S NOSTRILS flared but her words had his eyes twinkling with amusement. Amusement was better than the Inquisition she'd just been dealing with, and it was a relief, truth be told. Not only because she didn't appreciate feeling like she was under arrest, but also because something was going on with him.

Sean wasn't a heavy drinker. Not at all. Yet here he was again, drowning his sorrows in alcohol. That wasn't like him, and at least her barging in on a very royal kissing session had interrupted his train of thought.

Right from the beginning of their relationship, Sascha had been able to discern who needed her the most.

They were men, after all. Shit at sharing their feelings, impossible to make open up unless they were ready to talk, which was never. She could read them, though. And yeah, that sounded like BS spouted in romance books, but she could.

Sean? He got this tick in his left eye. It flickered and fluttered. Sawyer? He'd crack his knuckles. Andrei's accent deepened, which was the most noticeable because he spoke with a sharp English accent, so even the hint of Russian had her on red alert. Kurt's accent would deepen too, but he'd start jogging more and he hated jogging, so that was a big clue. Kurt would also hang around in the kitchen if he was ill at ease or uncomfortable with something, wanting to be around her rather than his problem—be it with an editor, his publisher, or a character in one of his books.

Devon?

Well, Devon was rarely stressed in a regular way. Thank God. His meltdowns were few and far between, but when they happened, the entire house quaked. He looked at her as though she could solve the mysterious labyrinth that was his brain, could rip apart his demons, and bring peace to his world like she'd soothe an itchy rash with calamine lotion.

She wasn't an angel, far from it, but Devon? He looked at her as though she was.

"What *did* you see?" Sean asked, reminding her that, until now, his left eye had been ticking so damn much, he'd looked like he'd been fluttering his lashes at her.

Well, the lashes on the left side.

Yeah, it looked damn odd, and Sean? Nothing about him was odd. He was hot. With a capital H.

"Perry making out with the Duke," she whispered, her cheeks turning pink at the memory, "and then the King, Edward, walked in so I knew she wasn't cheating but that it was a thing, you know?"

"Why are your cheeks pink?" Devon inquired. "You've seen far worse than that, Sascha."

"Yes, you've well and truly ruptured any and all of my innocence, Devon, fear not. I'm just remembering how goddamn embarrassed I was.

"Me and Tin were standing in the doorway, I saw them kissing, then the King walked in, then just when I think my heart was about to explode, Tin went and reminded me that he needed to go potty." Sascha slapped her hand against her head as the room erupted into laughter. "Trust me, we're never being anyone's guests ever again."

Sean, amid his laughter, hugged her tightly into his side. "Tin really said that?"

"You bet he did. After making several comments about kissing." She rubbed her temple. "Anyway, when you have an introduction like that, things progress quite quickly. She's pregnant and wants Tin to meet her daughter, Alice. They're the same age."

"After all that, you wrangled a play date for Tin?" Andrei gaped at her, then he slapped his knee. "That's it, you're helping me when I have to deal with those boring trade delegations."

Sascha snickered. "You'd be better off asking Tin to help. He was the one who broke the ice. With a sledgehammer."

Sean chuckled. "I wish I'd seen it."

"I wish *you'd* been the one to take him to the bathroom. Total FML moment." She blew out a breath. "Anyway, didn't take much to figure out what was going on, and with Tin spilling the beans about how many kisses I give to his daddies—" They all groaned, and she nodded at them self-righteously. "—the cat leaped out of the bag pretty damn quickly."

"So ye shared war stories?"

"Hardly war stories, Sawyer," Sascha teased, finding a little humor in the situation now that it was well and truly over. "I didn't think I'd ever be able to look her in the face again but Perry is... well, she's like me. Just regular in an irregular situation."

Sean frowned. "That's a funny way of phrasing it."

"I'm a *funny* kind of girl," she joked, leaning over to kiss him. It was prim, not at all meant to entice, but intended to soothe whatever had him so tense. "I just meant... I don't think either of us planned to have *several* men in our lives, and yet, it couldn't have worked out more perfectly. For me, at any rate."

If anything, the words that were meant to ease his tension further, had him stiffening up. He reached for her hand, squeezed it, and gruffly said, "I'm calling it an early night."

The room, as a whole, gawked at him.

Sawyer declared, "It's barely seven o'clock, man. We haven't even had dinner yet."

"Headache."

And with that, he strode off, leaving Sascha staring at his back. She didn't try to follow, thinking she would confront him later in private.

"Do we even know where we're sleeping?" Andrei asked, making Sascha laugh.

"You didn't think to ask?"

Sheepishly, he admitted, "No."

Narrowing her eyes at him, she retorted, "You were going to leave it down to me, weren't you?"

"Maybe."

"What am I? Your PA?" She snorted at the thought. "How is Jane anyway?" Christ, it had been good to get away from the London house just to avoid his manic assistant.

Sascha swore if she heard Jane cascade into laughter one more time, she'd want to smash the woman's laptop in with a rolling pin.

Andrei frowned then shrugged. "Her usual self. She's been quiet today though. Must be because we were traveling."

Sascha hummed under her breath. "She's weird."

He shot her a look. "She's just an employee, Sascha."

"So, she's a *weird* employee. You're funny, love, but you're not that funny."

Devon piped up, "Jane does laugh a lot at your jokes, Andrei."

Shooting him an approving look, Sascha got to her feet once more and went to perch on his lap. Okay, okay, favoritism, but fuck, he was too cute not to use as a seat.

"Sascha isn't the only funny person in the room," Andrei responded, but his lips twitched as he shot her a knowing look before averting his attention to whatever he was reading.

He looked comfortable, tucked in an armchair beside the spitting fire. The room suited him. It was paneled in wood, filled with books and comfortable leather furniture. From armchairs, sofas, lounges, and little futons. It was a man's room. Sascha could even smell the lingering scent of cigars, but it wasn't brash, just spoke of a time when this had been someone's smoking room. She could well imagine men in velvet smoking jackets sitting in here, bitching about their wives, and playing a game of cards as they swilled down whiskey after their meal while said wives drank tea and talked about polite, *boring* things in another parlor.

This place?

It was history made real.

A Duke lived here, and a King and Queen roamed its halls.

Sascha wasn't sure whether to be impressed or just astonished.

"I don't like her." She wasn't sure where the words came from, wasn't sure why she was pushing this when she hadn't before, but now just felt right.

"I know you don't. Sawyer told me, but I can't simply fire her because my wife doesn't like her, Sascha. She's good at what she does, and she's dedicated."

If they *were* married, then this wouldn't even be an issue. "Because she wants in your pants," she retorted coolly.

He sighed. "And what if the only person I want in my pants is you?"

"They'd never fit," Devon replied.

Andrei shot him a look. "What?"

"They'd never fit. Sascha's butt's too big."

Because Devon loved her ass, she couldn't find it in herself to be anything other than amused. "Thank you, Devon."

He smirked at her. "Your ass is many things, Sascha, but tiny enough to fit into Andrei's pants? Nope."

"Glad you've noticed," she purred, and his eyes flashed as he reached down to adjust himself.

Inwardly, she felt like celebrating.

Even though these past months had felt dark and dismal, she still had it in her to have one of her men adjusting himself after barely a few words.

"You know exactly what I mean," Andrei retorted, apparently not willing to be dissuaded from the topic at hand. "She knows far too much for me to just—"

"So, you're keeping her because you think she'd squeal?"

"No. Because training someone else would be a nuisance."

That answer satisfied her, and because it did look like she was jealous, she didn't prod the subject anymore. She knew she had no reason to be jealous. Andrei was like Devon—barely saw the woods for the trees when he was neck deep in a project, and he was rarely anything other than that. It was unusual for him not to be working on several deals at one time.

She trusted him.

She just didn't trust Jane. Not only because she laughed when Andrei wasn't even trying to be funny. Not just because the woman wanted a man who wasn't hers to have—there was no way someone who worked from Sascha's home could fail to see that she was with all five men under that roof. That meant Jane was trying to poach, and that pissed Sascha the hell off.

She hummed under her breath. "I'll be sure to encourage Matthew Dreyford's attentions when we're in Berlin."

Andrei scowled at her. "Sascha."

A smile curved her lips, but there was a sharp glint in her eyes. "Don't take me for granted just because I'm a sure thing." She shot him a kiss that was supposed to take the sting from her words, but from his uneasy frown, she knew the person who'd be feeling the sting was her.

Just on her ass.

Still, they couldn't boss her around the way they did, *dominate* her so totally without their dynamic changing in other ways too.

It was telling that Sawyer, Kurt, and Devon didn't leap into the argument either, which irritated her more, honestly. That meant her instincts were right.

Jane *was* over the top. They weren't the kind of men to try to appease her for the sake of it. They'd argue if they thought she was in the wrong.

"Do you have to go to Berlin?" Devon complained, breaking into her internal grumbling, then he shot Kurt a dirty look. "It's your fault."

"Sorry for being German," Kurt retorted, not hiding his laugh.

"You know I want to meet his parents before we go to the set," Sascha explained, hard-pressed not to laugh at Devon's scowl. "It will look odd enough with Sean visiting, never mind you too."

"Plus, Margritte doesn't even like you," Sawyer pointed out.

Kurt winced. "She says you're a loose cannon, Devon."

"She knows you quite well then," Sascha teased, making Devon pout. She reached for his hand and squeezed his fingers before nuzzling into his side.

It wasn't as complete as it ought to have been—without Sean there was a space, a hole that let in a draft almost. Even as she relaxed, for the first time in far too long, her smile coming as easily as her laughter at the bickering and conversations between her men, she wondered what was wrong with Sean.

---

SAWYER NARROWED his eyes at her as she moved toward his desk. "Why aren't ye sleeping?"

She smirked at him. "Why aren't you?" She pronounced 'you' like 'yoo' and he rolled his eyes at her, even as he grabbed her by the waist and dragged her over his lap. The side of his desk dug into her hip, but she ignored that.

Sascha liked to believe that her hips had so much damn padding because of all the narrow places she was squidged into when her men hauled her around.

"Working," he answered with a sigh, tipping his head back against the chair's headrest.

"You need to sleep. You've been working on and off all day." She reached up and traced her fingers over his brow, wondering how such a beautiful man could be beneath her at this very moment. She'd intended on heading to bed because Sean was definitely in need of her tonight, but having spied the light in here and seeing Sawyer's red head bent over his laptop from the doorway, she couldn't have stopped herself from wishing him goodnight properly.

"I'll be glad when this project is over with," he admitted softly, pressing his face to her throat. "I didn't realize it, but it's got Devon all worked up."

She frowned at that—Devon hadn't seemed any more manic than usual. "Why?"

He shrugged. "He likes all the data. More than usual."

She winced. "Oh."

No more explanation was required. Deep in his bones, Devon adored statistics. Sawyer was the statistician but for their resident mad genius, statistics were a hobby. For him, heaven came in data, reels and reels of it. There weren't fluffy white clouds around heaven's gates, but endless reams of paper loaded with statistics that would bore the average man senseless.

"Yeah. Oh." He blew out a breath. "Plus, I'm tired."

"Not like you to admit that," she murmured, reaching up to press a kiss to the corner of his mouth before she snuggled into him.

He reached up and ran a hand over her hair, tucking her into him as they just sat there, rocking back at his desk.

After a while of studying the positively 'posh' surroundings, she muttered, "This was probably a Duke's office or something."

He snorted. "Or something. The place is huge. Have you seen how many offices there are? And libraries? Jesus, why did they need so many libraries?"

"To show off their wealth?" she hazarded a guess.

"Could be," he admitted. "Books cost a fortune back in the day, after all."

She hummed, taking in the walls that were lined with embroidered silk of all things, then had panels with light fittings attached to them, which had been modernized from old candelabras. It was gothic and creepy all at the same time thanks to the shadows and play of light that fell oddly on the silk. Walls shouldn't gleam, Sascha thought drily, but these did.

The desk was huge, extra wide and covered with leather, and there was even a space built into it for an ink pot with a couple of quills jauntily plopped into it, which made her lips curve at how old and new married in here. It was like the house itself though. Or estate, she figured was the correct term.

Everywhere was modernized—electrics, WiFi, her bathroom even had a jacuzzi tub that had to have been installed within the past year—and yet history reigned. There were suits of armor everywhere, and pictures of dead dudes staring down at her, crinkling their noses in disapproval at having an American, or two if she included the Queen, wander their halls.

"The butler showed us around this afternoon but you missed out on that when you were nattering with the Queen."

She elbowed him in the side. "Shut up."

"Only if you make me," he teased, then sobering, he murmured, "Have the butler show you around too. You'll get lost otherwise. It's like a feckin' labyrinth this place."

She'd have preferred a guided tour from her Scot but knowing how busy he was, she didn't push it. It wasn't like they were on vacation. Sawyer, Devon, and Andrei were here to work. More's the pity. She'd have liked a chance to go all Lady Chatterley on this ducal estate. Talk about neat.

When she hummed her agreement, Sawyer sighed beneath her and she felt him relax a little more as his arms came around her, snuggling her deeper into his hold in a way that made her lips curve in a joyous smile.

There was something about this man that got to her every-fucking-time. There was a joy in the silence they shared, a joy because there was no pressure, no need to talk. Sometimes, it was just wonderful to feel connected to him because her Scot was so earthy, so vibrant with life, that he called to her in ways she couldn't begin to describe.

Rubbing a hand over his arm, her fingers trailing into a faint caress, she murmured, "You know what's wrong with Sean?"

"Think it's the case," he replied drowsily. "It's been going on too long now."

She thought back to the child killer who was haunting Britain and had been for the past several years. A shudder racked her, wriggling down her spine in a way that set her nerves on edge.

"Wonder if there were some updates. He's been moody since we arrived."

"Sean's always been a moody bastard. If you haven't figured that out by now, then you're not as bright as I took ye for, Sascha darling."

Her lips curved as she pulled back to stare up at him. "Jerk."

"Your jerk," he reasoned, making her snort.

"You're not saying it right," she teased. But the way he rolled his R's had her insides rolling in a similar pattern.

Yum.

"I'm saying it perfectly fine. You're the ones who fucked up the English language."

"I'll have you know that Americans speak the same English as Shakespeare."

He snorted. "You read any Shakespeare, lass? Because that makes no sense and so much sense it's crazy."

A laugh escaped her as she prodded him in the chest. "I've read plenty."

"Figures. You're too romantic for your own good."

Trust her Scot to consider Shakespeare romantic.

Rolling her eyes at him, she stilled when he asked, "You eaten three meals today? You had dinner with us but I didn't see you eat breakfast or lunch."

Fuck. She bit her bottom lip and peered at him from under her lashes.

Knowing what that meant, he growled under his breath. "Jesus, Sascha, how can it be so hard to fucking eat?"

"It isn't!" she argued, and that was actually the truth. "I genuinely forgot."

"Unlike all the other times where you genuinely remembered to forget to eat, you mean?" he grumbled.

She winced. "Honestly, there's a difference. I started eating more over Christmas. Can't you tell? My ass can. My jeans are tight."

He squinted at her. "You bullshitting?"

"Nope." She wriggled in his arms, and though—in a million years—she'd never imagined wanting to show a man in her life that she'd gained some fucking weight, she mumbled, "Let me up so I can show you."

He sighed, and she knew he was comfortable and cozy with her right where she was, but it was a testament to how important it was for him that she looked after herself that he helped her stand. The second she was on her feet, she lifted her shirt and showed him the button on her jeans, and it was, no shadow of a doubt, straining.

A grunt escaped him as he stared at it, then flickering a glance up at her, he reached over and curved his hands around her hips, before he trailed his fingers down over the fly and to the space between her legs. She bit her lip because even through the denim, that felt good. She rocked her pelvis up in response, making his mouth curve, his upper lip curling into a smirk that was well earned.

"You horny, lass?"

"You know I hate that word."

"You wet for me, then?" he countered with a sniff.

"Aye," she whispered, and she was. She didn't know if it was from that simple touch or from the threat of being spanked for not eating, but fuck if it wasn't the truth.

He narrowed his eyes at her. "I shouldn't reward you for bad behavior."

A snort escaped her. "I totally deserve some spankings, and I admit it. But this one? Nope. It's been a busy day, and coming across the fucking Queen *in flagrante delicto* was enough to make anyone forget about food. For a moment I thought I was about to be shoved in front of a firing squad!"

Sawyer wrinkled his nose. "I still cannae believe that you told her about us."

"I was trying to avoid the firing squad," she grumbled, poking his chest with her finger.

He huffed, then began to work on her fly. Her lips rolled inward to hide a smile as he unbuttoned the tight fastening, which had her groaning with no small amount of relief. He stripped the skinny jeans down her legs with her panties, so she was bare to him from the hips down once they were in a pile on the ground.

"Spread 'em," he grunted, and she shivered at his delicious words as well as the gorgeous tenor.

She obeyed because she wanted to, and there was a distinct difference to how sometimes, she chose to comply. Tonight? She wanted to be fucked.

Over this desk.

Ugh. Talk about a scene to add to her jill till.

Her lips curved at the thought, and he cocked a brow when he caught her smile. "What are you grinning at?" he demanded, his hands cupping her hips still but his thumbs hovering over her pussy lips, dragging her wet flesh apart slightly.

"I want this in my jill till."

"Your what?" he questioned, scowling at her.

She reached up and rubbed at the scowl. "My spank bank?"

He snorted. "Dinnae know you've got time to be touching this pussy, not when you have five of us dying to crawl inside it."

"Ew," she groused. "And I'll have you know I jill in the bath."

"Why the fuck didn't I know this, and why the fuck don't we have more baths together?"

She snickered. "I don't have that many. You know how I feel about wasting water."

He rolled his eyes, but there was amusement in their depths. He reached forward and pressed a kiss to the softness of her belly. "Aye, I know," he said gruffly. "Hop onto the desk," he added a second later, watching her with narrowed eyes as she perched on the side and hauled ass onto the surface.

He moved his computer at the same time, so she wriggled along, putting herself directly in front of him.

He eyed her as she fell back onto her elbows, watching him with a grin. "This might go to number one in *my* spank bank. Never going to forget you taunting me with your eyes atop my desk, lass."

"Good," she purred, making him growl.

That was all the incentive he needed. He grabbed her legs, parting them farther, and then he bent one and widened them so he could settle between her thighs. The move put him so close to her pussy that she wanted to scream because he just hovered there, his breath washing over her suddenly sensitive flesh.

She dipped her head back, needing to break the tension flowing through her veins by releasing the pressure on her neck, then she yelped when he bit her.

Fucking bit her.

"Ouch," she complained as she peered down at her abused pussy lip. "That fucking hurt!"

"Good. Eyes on me," he grumbled, and finally, *finally*, he made good on his silent promise.

Flattening his tongue, he slid the tensile muscle through her folds in a way that had her groaning, tensing, and relaxing all at the same time. She rocked her hips, only to have them grabbed and forced into stillness, and then she tensed her stomach muscles to try to deal with the pressure of the pleasure he was making her feel.

Already.

She'd never appreciated oral before her men. Other guys went too fast, they didn't savor the act. It was like a 'get out of jail free card.' 'Do this and she'll get wet then I can get my cock in faster.' But her men? Nope, they weren't like that. They treated her like she was a five-course banquet and she loved it.

The leather cushioned her elbows while being deliciously cool against her butt. She spread her legs wider, enjoying the ache in the tendons of her inner thighs as she did so. The way he fluttered his tongue around her clit before plunging into her, slurping her down in a way that, years before, would have made her cringe, now had her turning bright red with need.

Fuck.

Just, fuck.

She reached down with one hand and dragged her fingers through his hair. Gripping him tightly, semi-amused that he let her, she forced him into her cunt, forced him to fuck her, to suck her, to tease her and to taunt her. She wanted him. All of him. And this was just her appetizer.

She growled as he sucked down on her clit, then he nibbled and she went off like a light show.

"That was damn fast," he grumbled, and she knew it was because he'd been intent on torturing her for far longer than her body allowed.

"I'm on edge," she whimpered, her hips blindly rocking as she fucked the air, her nerve endings still on red alert as her empty cunt grasped at nothing and complained about not having one of their cocks deep inside her.

"Oh, Christ," he ground out, and she fluttered her eyelids up to look at him, saw he was watching her hips move and was loving it.

"I'm empty," she complained on a mewl. "Fill me, Sawyer."

He shuddered as he got to his feet, and before she knew it, his cock was out and a heavyweight against her folds.

Sascha hadn't come into the office on her way to bed for this, but fuck, she was glad she had now. His cock was thick and heavy and wide and... drool worthy. Seriously. Dick porn for her jill till as he rested it against her juicy flesh.

He rubbed it against her, rocking his hips back and forth, getting himself wet and keeping her riding the wave as each thrust nudged her clit in a way that promised more.

Greedy clit.

Ugh.

She didn't realize she'd said that until he slapped said clit with the back of his fingers. "Be thankful it's hungry for us, lass," he grated out, his eyes still on their sexes.

Sascha had never seen that look in his eye before, and having been on the receiving end of *many* looks, she wasn't sure what was different about now. Only that something *was* different.

"You on birth control, lass?"

The question came out of nowhere, and she froze as she looked up at him. "You've never asked me that before."

He shrugged. "We stick enough baby-making juice in you *to* ask, just never have."

Her cheeks flushed. "No."

That had his brows funneling in a frown. "That wise?"

She shook her head. "Nope."

A laugh escaped him. "You ready for the consequences?"

"Probably not. Nature will take its course."

First off, her men weren't getting any younger. More than that though, she'd wanted Camilla with every ounce of her being, and had Camilla joined them as she ought to have, the second she could, Sascha would have been ready for another baby.

She wanted three. It wasn't fair—each of her men wouldn't have a child of their own—but three was perfect. Just right. They could care for three, give them everything their children ever needed, and surround them in so much love that their kids would be spoiled on it.

Having seen the men with Tin? She'd never seen five guys more perfectly suited to being dads. They were patient when she was impatient. They were understanding and wise where she wasn't always herself.

Everything about them triggered her baby-making hormones, and she wanted more.

She wanted a big family, something she'd never had.

A shaky breath escaped her as he said, "I didn't think you were."

"Why ask?"

"I was curious. Wanted to know where your head was at."

He said 'head' like 'heed' and she grinned a little inwardly, loving his accent all the more.

This talk should have made her pussy dry up like the Sahara, but it didn't. She felt the loss of Camilla so fucking keenly some days that getting out of bed was a chore, but this? *This* conversation? It might terrify her, but she knew what she wanted.

"Andrei thought you might not want anymore," he rasped, grabbing his cock and sliding it down through her folds until he reached her gate. When he notched the tip inside, her eyes widened then shuttered as he surged in deep.

Several breaths escaped her as she tried to process just how big he was inside her, how thick and how deep, then she whispered, "Didn't at first. Then I did."

He snorted. "Ever verbose."

"I try." She winked at him even as she uttered a groan when he began to thrust.

He was as cocksure as ever, staring down at her with glittering eyes that made her body turn over inside, even as he dragged sensations from her that only her five had ever made her feel. She yelped when he grabbed her legs, pulled them against his chest, then hauled her closer to him and the edge of the desk. This move had her eyes closing as she winced at how deep he hit.

Fuck.

She sank back on the desk, unable to keep herself upright even as she reached between her legs and began to fondle her clit. When she felt his own fingers forge a path between her ass cheeks, she moaned when he stroked the pucker there, and grunted when he forced the tip in. Dry. It should have hurt, the bastard, but it didn't. It felt good. And it made her want to spread her legs wide for some reason, but he was intent on keeping them closed.

She shuddered as he nipped her calf, which was right beside his head, and then shuddered some more when he reached between her thighs. She half-expected him to slap her hand away, but he didn't. If anything, he pinched her pussy lips tighter around him and the move had her face contorting as the delicious squeeze made her body begin to tingle.

"You gonna come for me, lass?" he rasped, his dick sawing in and out of her.

"Aye," she whispered, and it wasn't even a joke!

A grunt escaped him and he moved faster, pinched harder, then he stunned the fuck out of her by biting down on her calf again, hard, and wiggling the tip of his finger in her butt.

She careened into the orgasm face first. She'd expected it, had anticipated it, but this? Oh fuck. It sent joy shuddering through her veins even as she cried out, hollering her joy and wonder at the release that made her euphoric.

The only thing that topped it was his own hoarse cry and the ragged thrusts as he fucked her body for his own pleasure, to reach his own end.

In the aftermath, the silence was broken by their panting breaths. He rubbed his brow against her calf, and she felt his sweat-slick skin touch hers as he began to pull out.

The second he did, his fingers were there, making her moan and her eyes flutter open in surprise. He shoved three inside her, making her jolt—not in discomfort, just surprise—and he thrust them a few times before drawling, "Think that made a baby?"

She gnawed on her bottom lip. "We're probably not ready for one."

"Probably not," he confirmed, but he carried on thrusting, making her face screw up as her sensitivity shot through the roof. When he spread those fingers, further plugging up his come, she moaned brokenly, and her hand grabbed his wrist to stop him.

He did, but his eyes were wicked as he stated, "My woman, Sascha."

"Of course," she replied, surprised at the statement. "*My man.*"

He smirked, then he stunned the fuck out of her by finally

leaving her pussy alone, pulling his fingers out, then reaching up and sucking each one clean.

Christ.

That was definitely going into the jill till.

---

SLEEP WAS IMPOSSIBLE.

It was more than impossible, in fact. It would have been easier to travel to a farm and count the sheep on the field there than it was to rest in the here and now.

The silence was damning.

In this strange bedroom, ornate as only the guest room of an ancient noble dwelling could be, Sean was adrift.

For the first time since Sascha had walked through the front doors of their Kensington villa, Sean was lost and he wasn't entirely sure what he could do to be found again.

The pillows felt too hot, and the duvet was choking him, but they also grounded him. Helped keep him in the present.

The threat was gone.

He'd discovered the truth.

But that hadn't stopped evil from infiltrating his house.

His throat closed as he heard the mechanism of the door handle turning. He didn't sit up. Didn't even move. He knew who it was.

She always knew when he needed her.

The soft, gentle padding footsteps came a second after the door was closed with a quiet snick. Then, he heard the rushing sounds as fabric tugged against fabric when she undressed. A sharp gasp escaped her, making his brow furrow as he wondered why she'd made that noise, then he almost smirked when her teeth started chattering and he imagined her darting across the room to get into bed with him.

The moment her cool body hit the sheets, he had no room to move. She was there, plastered against him like a second skin. She even pushed her nose between his shoulder blades, and her feet, like blocks of ice, shoved their way between his calves.

"That the way you say hello to your man?" Sean rasped, laughing even as he shivered—Christ, she was freezing.

"Yes," was her pert retort. "You're warmer than the sidewalk in Phoenix in high summer. If I can't steal your heat, then..." A puff of breath escaped her.

"Is this all I'm good for?" he demanded, amused by her logic.

"Well, I didn't want to say it, but yup."

He snorted. "My ego thanks you."

"So it should," she replied with a sigh. "You're toasty."

"You will be too," he assured her, rolling over onto his back so she could splay herself out with more comfort.

It took less than a second for her leg to come across his thighs, the soft heat of her pussy rubbing against his hip, and for her face to be smushed against the side of his chest when he raised his arm to curve it about her shoulders.

"Why are you so cold?"

"I went outside."

"Why the hell would you do that? It's snowing, Sascha."

She snickered. "You my daddy, Daddy?"

"You know I can be if the mood strikes me," he growled, pinching her butt and making her laugh again. "And why do you smell of sex?"

She ignored that question, choosing to answer his earlier one, and he had to wonder which one of his brothers had gotten lucky tonight. "There are dogs here."

"So? Vasily has dogs. You didn't wander out into the wintry night to watch them piss."

"I've been to Moscow before," she grumbled, slapping Sean on the side. "I've never been here. I wanted to see—"

"If the stars changed?"

"Wow, you're feeling sarcastic tonight, hmm?"

He grunted. "Edgy. I'm not good company tonight, sweetheart."

"I can tell. Could tell earlier. I can read you all like books. Well, except for Devon."

"No one can read Devon," Sean responded with a snort. "Not even Sawyer. He still amazes us all." It was no word of a lie. "You know the first time we met?"

"At college?" Her tone turned interested, and Sean knew why. They didn't really speak about the early days, but she soaked up each tale as though she were a neglected flower in desperate need of water.

"Yes. Andrei and I were in our second year, Sawyer and Devon were too—they started at a younger age than us but advanced quicker. Jacinta—" Sawyer's mother. "—had to wrangle some legalese to act as Devon's guardian. I'm not sure how she did it, actually."

"Probably strong-armed Devon's dad," Sascha replied drily. "Threatened him with a gun or something."

"Knowing Jacinta, maybe." Sean laughed a little. "I wish my mother had been like that."

"You never talk about your parents."

"Not much to say. They were overachieving parents who expected the same or more from their children." He sighed. "Anyway, there we were, all of us thinking we were far too old to be babysitting the likes of Devon and Sawyer—"

"How did you even get paired together?"

"Paired together?" His brow puckered.

"Yeah, like with dorm rooms?"

"Oh. This wasn't America," he teased. "We weren't in dorm rooms by this point, and Jacinta, knowing how Devon is, ensured that he and Sawyer could live off campus. That's where we came in.

"We'd advertised that there were two rooms left in the campus house we were renting. They applied, and paid more than the cover."

"You're pedantic over the dorm room and house thing."

He smirked at the ceiling. "It's all in the details."

"Why did they pay more than their rent?"

"Because Devon's Devon. They were bribing us." He shrugged. "It worked. They funded many a night in Morals."

"Morals?"

"A bar run by the Student Union." He laughed slightly. "It's a hell of a long time since I thought about any of this stuff."

"It's been a hell of a long time since we've been anything other than unhappy." She cleared her throat. "That's on me."

"What is? That you mourned the loss of our child? Jesus, Sascha, I'm lucky you—" He broke off, unable to continue with his train of thought.

"What is it, Sean? What's going on?" Her voice was soft, but for all its gentleness, there was power behind the words. Like a stiletto knife that slipped in between someone's ribs and pierced the heart. Thin and small, but deadly nonetheless. "You've been odd all afternoon. Then you missed dinner and have... what? Been lying here all night in the dark? What's going on?"

"I can't tell you," he admitted, tone husky.

"Because I don't have clearance?"

He could have lied, could have said that was the exact reason why he couldn't tell her, but that would have been a lie too far.

He released a shuddery breath. "No. Because I'm ashamed."

She went quiet then, and a part of him hoped she'd let it go, that she wouldn't press him but this was Sascha. She cared too much to ever let him get away with saying something like that. "Of what?"

"Of what I've done. Of what I've brought to us."

Her voice was strong, without hint of a quiver as she told him, "You know I love you, don't you?"

"You might not when I tell you what..." His eyes pricked with tears, and shame hit him with all the precision of that stiletto blade to the heart. How could he admit to what he'd done?

This year there had been two threats, *two* to this woman he loved, and he was the reason that danger had darkened their door.

"The child killer's been arrested."

"What?" she burst out, jerking upright at his words until he hauled her back down into his side. "You found out who did it?"

"Yes," he admitted on a low whisper.

"How?"

"Too many coincidences in one place."

"What does that mean? You always say that coincidences don't exist."

"They don't, and that's how I discovered the truth."

"Well, come on. Don't leave me in suspense. I like your rundowns. It's like being on Columbo."

He snorted. Trust Sascha to make him laugh when his entire world was going to shit.

"You know Jane?"

"Jane? As in, Andrei's PA?"

"Yes."

"What about her?" He didn't have to look at her to know she was confused as hell. Christ, *he* was confused and he'd figured it out.

"After the situation with Christopher Horowich, Vasily insisted upon procuring extra security for us. You know what we had before was pretty poor. We relied on anonymity and the police for extra security when a case spiraled into the news."

"Okay," she drawled. "But what does this have to do with your case—"

"I'm trying to explain," he whispered, and was relieved when she remained quiet. "He hired men to check into our history. Our staff. Everyone from the cleaners to our administrative staff. The other day, I received the report and noticed something strange.

"It was a coincidence, and like we just agreed, they don't exist. Birmingham, Salford, Dorset, and Notting Hill..." He sucked in a sharp breath, aware her patience was dying a quick death, yet equally as certain that he couldn't get this out quickly. He was still dealing with the fact that a monster had been under their roof for months.

How the fuck had they been so lax?

"Those four cities were where the boys were killed. Small neighborhoods within those cities, in fact. Such a small circumference in the scheme of things, but they stood out to me because of the timing."

"What timing?"

"Each boy was murdered when Jane was in that city, at that particular time."

Silence.

No words were forthcoming now.

He swallowed down his shame. "It was too weird to ignore. Twice? Sure. That could be explained away. But each occasion? No. I had Vasily's men look into her past and discovered far more than her resume and references could have ever explained." Clenching his eyes shut, he whispered, "Can you ever forgive me, Sascha?"

"Sean... I don't understand. You can't be trying to tell me that Andrei's PA is a serial killer. A *child* killer."

"I wish I wasn't. I wish I could tell you anything else, but I can't. She was behind the deaths of those four boys, and..."

"And what?" Her tone was too serene. Far too serene. The calm before the storm.

"She's been arrested." He reached up and rubbed at his eyes. "Today. That was the news I received on the plane."

"You mean to tell me that a serial killer has been under our roof, working with my husband, *associating* with my child, and...?" She scrambled out of bed and the light blared on the second her hand splattered against the fixing.

When he focused on her, her eyes were wild, but she was bleary because the tears in his eyes made everything a blur.

Shame like nothing he'd ever felt before swirled inside him, and when she stalked off, he didn't even have it in him to go after her.

He was a criminologist.

Their security had been woefully lacking, and if anyone knew just how morally corrupt humans could be, it was him.

There was no excuse.

No excuse, whatsoever.

# TWENTY-SEVEN

"DID SEAN TELL YOU YET?"

Andrei jerked in surprise at her words. His head tilted to the side as he studied her, sitting quietly in the corner of his bedroom, tucked into one of the armchairs with a throw over her.

She probably looked as freezing cold as she felt.

So frigid that she wanted him to wrap her up in his arms, but the cold went bone deep. She felt sure that if he touched her, she'd turn to ice.

"Tell me what?" he asked carefully, shrugging out of his sweater and dumping it on the dresser beside the door.

Before he could strip down however, Sascha gritted out, "About Jane."

He scowled at her and stacked his hands on his hips. "What about her now?"

"That she's a serial killer."

Laughter escaped him. "Sascha, I know you don't like her—"

She hissed. "I'm not joking, Andrei."

"What?" He scowled at her. "You can't be serious."

"Do I look like I'm amused? He just told me. The police apparently arrested her today."

"She's been charged? What the hell with?"

Her nostrils flared with irritation. "Aren't you listening to me?" she half-screamed. "The child killer case he's working on. She's behind it."

"No. No fucking way."

Before she could say another word, he reared back and stormed out the way he came, and she moved to follow him. She wanted answers, otherwise she'd stay where she was. Her legs were wobbly, and she felt as frail as a colt, but she staggered after him. Whatever Andrei had to ask, she wanted to hear the answers too. She just hadn't been capable of forming words, and knowing that her husband was as in the dark as she was soothed something inside her.

Whatever Sean had done, he'd told her first.

Told her they'd had a monster sharing the same air as them for the past...

God, when she thought about how long, she felt sick.

Curling into the throw she'd grabbed off the grand four-poster bed, she hurried after Andrei as quickly as she could. With her toes numb, it was harder than it ought to have been.

She heard the shouts before she reached the doorway, and her ever calm, ever cool husband was anything but.

A flurry of Russian hit her ears next, but Sean didn't speak the language, or at least, not fluently, so she knew Andrei was speaking out of anger. As well as the same cocktail she felt drunk on—fear, confusion, outrage.

"Andrei, stop it!" she barked after watching him wave his arms around for a good five minutes. She'd never thought that Russian could sound anything other than sexy, but hearing the words shaped like missiles, she knew too much of a good thing did exist.

He spun around on his heel and stared at her. "I need answers."

"You think I don't? Shouting at him in a language we don't understand isn't going to help," she hissed.

"What's going on?"

Kurt.

She turned to look at him and realized he'd been asleep—his hair all over the place, a mass of tumbled waves that her hands itched to touch.

She wanted to fall into the shelter he represented, move away from the taint that was spreading wider and wider.

"Sean told Sascha that Jane was the child killer in his case."

Kurt reared back, his sleepy eyes rounding in surprise. "*Nein. Dass ist nicht möglich.*"

Sean rasped, "*Da. Möglich ist. Es ist die Wahrheit. Ich wünsche dass ich lugen wäre.*"

Whatever the hell he'd said, it didn't bode well from the look Kurt aimed her way. He curved an arm around her shoulder, and pushed her toward the bed where Sean was sitting, his back to the headboard, his knees high, his arms over the joints where she could see he was wringing his hands.

Sean was the epitome of power. At least, in her mind. To see him so diminished hurt something inside her.

He was ashamed, and he wore it like a true sinner. Like he was the killer.

A breath whooshed from between her lips. "Explain," she demanded, her tone less frigid in the face of his shame.

"Was she targeting Tin?" Kurt asked, and though his voice was calm, she felt the way his body vibrated as he posed the question. It satisfied something inside her.

She wasn't alone in this.

"Maybe. It depends on her end game. He's too young to be of interest to her just yet."

Just yet.

Two words, two innocuous words, and yet they were some of the most terrifying terms she'd ever heard.

Nausea swirled inside her, making her fear she was about to puke on the very expensive rug beneath her feet.

This had to be one of the most surreal moments of her life.

Was it a dream?

She could only hope so, hell, *pray* so.

"What do you mean?"

Sean didn't look at her, just kept his eyes focused on his hands. "Four was her target demographic."

"You make it sound like an audience she was trying to hit," she hissed.

He didn't flinch at her words, instead, in a monotone that made her head ache, stated, "Four was an important number to her."

"Why?"

"She was four when her parents were killed in a car crash. Four when she was put into foster care where she was molested by her foster father. She had a child at nineteen, and that child died of meningitis—at four."

"And what? That twisted her to the point she started killing other kids?" Sascha screamed. "Who the fuck does that?"

"Someone who's psychologically and emotionally damaged," Kurt rasped, tightening his hold on her, but she didn't want to be held. She understood Andrei's need to throw his arms around. Except burning off the excess fury made her feel like an explosion was imminent. If she didn't keep these emotions contained, she was sure she'd burst.

"How do you know any of this?" Sascha addressed Sean. "I mean, you've been with us for the past few days, and the report came to you —" She curled her fingernails into her palms. "How long have you been keeping this from us?"

"I'm a profiler, Sascha. It's my job to figure out why people do the fucked-up shit they do." He blew out a breath. "I didn't want to say anything until the police investigated my findings. When they arrested her today, I knew that I was right. They had a case."

"This can't be real," she whispered. "I mean, if I suspend reality, I can almost come to terms with the fact she's a nutcase. It's not like I liked her. But she barely glanced at Tin. Never talked to him, hardly recognized his existence. And no, I'm not fucking complaining about that... just trying to make sense out of the impossible."

Sean grunted and the bones of his knuckles strained as he balled his hands into tight fists. "Without access to her, I have no true answers."

"Why the fuck haven't you flown back to deal with the investigation?" Andrei snarled.

"I've been thrown off the case," Sean admitted. "Too close to her."

"Who's on it in your stead?"

"Dr. Medcalfe."

Kurt gasped. "She hates you. She won't tell you shit."

"She might once she realizes what Jane did."

"What did she do?" Sascha inquired, panic soaring through her. Was she missing something?

"Infiltrated our home, of course," Sean stated grimly. "It's beyond personal now."

"It can't be her. It just can't be." Her voice was a whisper as her mind whirred. "You came to us in Glasgow after that boy was killed. She worked for us then."

"The boy was local to her. Notting Hill. She lives there." He blew out a shaky breath. "Medcalfe might take pity on me and let me see her report, but I have no answers, nothing save for what Vasily's men dug up. And half of that isn't permissible in court."

"None of it will be permissible in court," Andrei grated out. "You know they won't have discovered any of this information through any legal channels."

For the first time in their relationship, she was grateful as fuck that her grandfather-in-law was in the mafia.

Thanking God for the wily old bastard, she demanded, "Why was she working for Andrei?"

Sean shrugged. "From what I know of her, she's precise, incredibly so. To the point of OCD. She's calm, resolute, and neat as a pin. I have no doubt that she was there to make sure I wasn't close to determining exactly who the killer was."

"I-I thought it would be a man. They're always sick perverts who—"

"Not in this case. You said it yourself that day you saw the whiteboards in my office. The children were dressed, used as props even. *Preserved.*"

And that did it.

She couldn't hold it in anymore.

With the word 'preserved' ricocheting in her skull, she dashed to the bathroom and puked up everything she'd eaten at supper.

And when that still wasn't enough, she puked up the entirety of her stomach contents.

---

"WHAT HAPPENED LAST NIGHT?"

Sean cut Sawyer a glance. "You heard and didn't come in?"

"Devon finally cracked this matrix system that's been bugging him." He shrugged. "It was either disrupt him and potentially put a halt to something we've been working on for weeks, something that would speed up our stay here, or come and see what you guys were bickering about."

A huff escaped Sean at that trite declaration. "If only we *had* been bickering."

Sawyer scowled at him over the table.

They were seated in the small breakfast room, a room painted a bright sunny yellow, the color enhanced by the two walls of windows. Everything was antique. From the table itself to the chairs, the cutlery was silver and had small decorative touches on the stems that were worn with age but were still bright with luster. The plates were delicate bone china and were adorned with hand-painted flowers that made Sean, who'd grown up around 'delicate fripperies' as his mother had called crap like this, hope he wasn't about to turn into a klutz.

This place was light, airy... everything he wasn't.

"What is it? What's wrong?"

Of his brothers, Sawyer was the man who liked prevarication the least. So, he told him.

Everything.

Every fucking last thing. Even the shit he didn't understand himself, he laid it on the line and when he finished, when he could finally drag his shame-filled eyes to his brother, he saw Sawyer was eating his breakfast.

Eating.

His.

Breakfast.

"How can you eat?" Sean rasped.

Sawyer shrugged. "Not eaten since dinner and I've been up all night. I'm hungry."

"That's all you have to say?"

Sawyer dropped his knife, forked up a mushroom, and waving it at Sean, asked, "Did you invite Jane into our house?"

He frowned. "Of course not."

"Did Andrei? I mean, he hired her, but you know he only worked on recommendations..."

"Don't do this, Sawyer. Don't justify something that's impossible to justify."

Another shrug. "You're determined to be a martyr. I'm not going to try and talk you out of it. Sure, be pissed. I know I am. We were used—"

"To get to me."

Sawyer shook his head. "I don't think so. What was her endgame?"

"Fuck if I know, but why come into our world if she wasn't interested in cozying up to me? Trying to make sure I wasn't close to catching her?"

"Seems feckin' weird as shit to me," Sawyer stated after a few seconds. "And look at it this way, you could have been practicing as a shrink and could have enticed some loon into our world. Nowhere's safe unless you're locked up in a padded cell."

"You're making me feel a thousand times better," Sean drawled, having to hide a grin despite himself. "Padded cell? Fuck, Sawyer."

"What?" the braw Scot demanded. "It's the truth. Remember that time Devon had a stalker? The man never leaves his feckin' room and he got himself a stalker. Now, that has to be a record. But still, crazy attracts crazy and as normal as we are when it boils down to it, we're crazy.

"Devon's a mad genius, Kurt isn't far off with his fucking nutty writing habits. Then there's Andrei who comes from a background where murder is just fun and games, and there's me. There's a reason I understand Devon, Sean," he said pointedly, eying Sean until he had his full focus. "I'm halfway to madness myself and only you four fuckwits have kept me on the straight and narrow."

"Sascha did that—"

"Not until she came to us. Before that, it was you. All of you. I was a bad kid," Sawyer admitted. "Reckless because I was bored. Nobody understood how feckin' bored I was because, how could they? Then Devon came along, and feck," he sighed, "it was such a relief. Such a relief to speak to someone on my level. I felt like shite. My ma and da, they love me, I know they dae. They half-killed themselves to give me the best that they could, but it wasn't enough for my brain." He tapped his temple. "Until Devon, I was going mad. Who kens where I'd be if it weren't for him? And as for the rest of ye, well, you kept me sane when he drove me to the brink with all his shite."

When Sean made to speak, Sawyer shook his head and stated, "Now, sure, that bitch is mad. Sick and fucked in the head, but you can't help what she did. Do I like the fact she might have been sizing my boy up? Nope." The 'p' popped as he said the word. "Am I happy that all of us have been so fucking remiss in the security around the only two people who matter to us? I sure as shit am not. But we've been stupid. We *are* stupid. In things like life." He sighed. "I hate to say it, Sean, but we are. We weren't built for this world. None of us were."

"You can't say that, Sawyer. If anyone knows the fucked-up shit that can happen, it's me. I've worked around it long enough—"

"Sure, but it's a game, isn't it, lad? You do it for the puzzle. For the riddle." Sawyer cocked a brow at him. "Don't be lying to me about that. I know you too well for you to be bullshitting me."

Sean closed his eyes. "You know that's true."

"Exactly. You don't do it for the prestige or to help save people, even if the latter is more rewarding than the former. You do it to stop the boredom. And that's okay, mon. That's more than okay because it stops you from going nuts and, in the meantime, you put bad bastards away and you keep people safe from those who'd try to hurt them.

"But you're not perfect. We don't expect you to be. Sometimes, you're a man and you're stupid. Just like I am. Just like we all are. Do I hate myself for that? Aye. I dae. I fucking loathe that my head's so up with the goddamn fairies that I failed to protect the two people who have my heart. But that's who I am, who we are, and we need to address that."

"Vasily warned me about threats before," Andrei rasped, making Sean jerk as his brother slouched into the room, his eyes tired, his face worn as he slumped in his seat. "Said we weren't taking enough care."

"He's said the same to me," Sean admitted.

"So, we're stupid, but we're not fucking hopeless," Sawyer muttered as he grabbed his cup of tea and took a deep sip. "We do what rich folk do—we throw money at the situation."

Sean scowled. "How the hell can money help?"

"We get some fancy security company to do the things that we forget to do."

"Vasily's already on it. He's been having us watched for a while," Andrei confessed. "I called him last night, and even he was shocked about Jane."

"How did she slip through the net?" Sean questioned, shaking his head as he pushed away the toast that had been staring at him for the past ten minutes. "I don't get it."

"I hired her from an agency. They're supposed to run checks, but checks are only good for so much. The woman hadn't been caught so she wouldn't have a record, would she?"

Sawyer sighed. "So, there's no avoiding that. Jane wanted into our household, and there was no way of preventing it. If she had an arrest record, then it would have flashed up and been a marker. But it didn't. There was no red alert, Sean. How do we prevent anything like this from happening again?"

"Stop living like we're back in the campus house in Oxford," Andrei rasped. "We've been irresponsible."

"Aye, that we have, but that's nae exactly proactive," Sawyer chided, and Sean admitted he was stunned by how rationally his brother was taking this.

Sawyer had a redhead's natural temper, but it hadn't been detonated by their conversation and Sean wasn't exactly sure why.

"Proactive?" Andrei sneered. "Unless we live like Devon, we're never going to be completely safe. We're here in Veronia, for fuck's sake. There was civil unrest until recently, and our plans for the economy aren't going to be popular—"

"Aye, and I'm certain our security will be assured here. We need to get Vasily's recommendation and to get our own head of security. We need bodyguards and shit, and Sascha? She needs a team on her alone, not only because she's rich as Croesus, even if she still looks like she shops at Primark," he said with a huff, "but because she's worth her weight in gold to us."

"Platinum."

Sawyer cocked a brow at Andrei. "What?"

"Our *katyonok* is worth her weight in fucking platinum." Andrei rubbed his chin. "I want to kill Jane. I want to slice her in half for even—"

Sean raised a hand. "She's in custody."

He snorted. "You think Vasily couldn't get to her?"

"I think he could, and I think you're your grandfather's grandson." Sean cut his brother a look. "I felt the same about Horowich. He murdered our daughter. He hurt Sascha. And Jane is a sick bitch. She's killed and she's hurt the innocent, but jungle justice will get her—"

"With the pansy-ass prison system you Brits have, I doubt that," Andrei growled.

Sean narrowed his eyes at him. "So, what? You want to go vigilante on her too?"

"Am I missing something?" Sawyer demanded, cocking a brow at Sean. "What happened with Horowich? The fucker who Devon beat?"

Sean, for all the situation was anything *but* funny, had to stop his lips from twitching. "We handled the situation."

"I think I need to know how. Especially if it's going to blow back on us."

Sawyer's grated out words had Sean shrugging. "Vasily dealt with the threat."

"And what are we going to do when Vasily dies?" Sawyer gritted out. "The man won't live forever, even if he's trying to."

Andrei bit his cheek. "Let's be grateful he's still alive and kicking. Maybe by the time we lose him, we'll have grown the fuck up and won't need to rely on him for every goddamn thing—"

"Why are you arguing?"

The three of them swerved toward the door where Sascha stood, Tin sitting on her hip. Her eyes were red, the skin around them looked chapped, and the way she was clinging to Tin? Well, Sean wouldn't be surprised if their little boy soon made a mad dash for escape.

Tin was not a hugger.

He liked cuddles before bed but that was pretty much it.

In fact, there was a look of pleading on his face that was literally a 'save me, Papa.' Sean found himself fighting a laugh.

Sawyer, being Sawyer, grumbled, "Give the boy to me, lass."

Sascha scowled at him. "Tin's happy here, aren't you?"

Tin's sigh was long-suffering as he slipped his arms around her neck and mumbled, "*Da*."

"Now we know the boy wants saving," Sawyer retorted, getting to his feet and heading toward the two people who were the center of their world. "You know he only speaks Russian when he wants something."

Andrei snickered and blurted something in Russian that had Tin twisting around with a grin. Sascha pouted but handed Tin to Sawyer who immediately turned him upside down, dangling him by his ankles as he walked to the table where there was a booster seat set up for the toddler.

Tin giggled and squirmed, and each time Sawyer pretended to drop him, Sascha's lips pinched but Tin squealed with delight.

Sean stared at her as she studied father and son, then when she saw he was watching, her cheeks flexed and she stepped toward the hand he held out for her.

When their fingers connected, he swallowed, and it felt as though the chasm he'd felt certain his career and choices had created between them, was a little less *wide* than it had been this morning.

She settled beside him at the table and began serving herself some coffee from a silver service that sat at the center of the polished walnut slab.

As she doctored her coffee, her gaze remained fixed on Tin who, by now, was sitting while Sawyer sorted him out with a bib.

Andrei buttered toast and cut it into pieces then placed it in front of their son.

"*Dzhem*."

The command, while in a foreign tongue, was evident. Sascha tutted. "No jam."

"Why not?" Tin pouted, and he looked so like his mother that Sean's heart skipped a beat.

"Because sugar makes you loopy."

Tin giggled at that. "Loopy, loopy, loopy."

When Devon and Kurt sidled in a few minutes later, Tin was still repeating the words while the rest of them tried, and succeeded, in remaining patient.

Kids were, Sean had learned, the most complicated creatures on Earth. They were capable of pushing you past your limits, driving you to do things that you'd never imagined possible. They could bring the best out of you, and the worst, and for all that Tin drove him nuts some days, he couldn't imagine a world without him in it.

There were few days that passed where he didn't stand on one of Tin's toys and almost break a limb, but the joy Tin brought? Impossible to replicate or to replace.

Sean jolted when Sascha's hand squeezed his thigh.

"He's safe," she told him, her voice a rasp.

"I know he is." A shaky sigh escaped him. "Things might have been different though."

"My life might have been different if I hadn't decided to become a housekeeper... I wouldn't be with you. I wouldn't have Tin. That's how life works."

"You were mad at me last night."

"I was reacting," she stated firmly, her mouth pursing. "I'm not happy, Sean, not about what happened, that we let it happen... I'm scared and terrified and wondering what the fuck she did to my boy —" Said boy began giggling when Devon picked him up and put him on his lap, feeding him tidbits of his own breakfast as he discussed black holes with their two-year-old. "I have to believe that she did *nothing* because he wouldn't be like this, would he? If she'd hurt him, our little boy wouldn't be so fucking happy all the time."

"She didn't hurt him, *katyonok.* I kept her too busy for that," Andrei stated bitterly, listening in to their conversation with no shame. "And Tin would have said something. You know he tells us everything."

"How would he even know how to describe something like that though?" she whispered, sounding so frail that Sean wanted to strangle Jane again and again.

"I'm not certain it's much of a reprieve," he murmured, "but he was too young. Tin doesn't fit her profile."

A crack sounded then and Sascha released a groan. Coffee splashed everywhere as the bone china was crushed beneath her grip.

Sean, cursing under his breath, reached for his napkin, then grabbed her hand and pressed the snowy white linen to the cut that was bleeding profusely.

The white folds turned bright red, and he stared at the fabric, unable to look her in the eye. Unable to even raise his gaze to meet hers because he wasn't fucking worthy of sharing a glance with her, and that was the goddamn truth of it.

For the first time in his life, he wasn't in control of this situation.

He wasn't in control of his life.

And Sean, at that moment, could understand why Devon feared chaos because Sean was staring down into its pit, and he wasn't sure how to get himself out of it.

# TWENTY-EIGHT

"HER MAJESTY AWAITS you in the greenhouse."

Sascha cocked a brow at 'Ask Jeeves' and questioned, "The Queen's waiting for me in the greenhouse?"

"With Her Highness Princess Alice," the butler confirmed. "I believe she wishes to meet Master Tin."

For the first time in two days, Sascha found something to be amused about. Master Tin? It sounded so incredibly Dickensian, and yet it fit this place to a T.

This house, while in the twenty-first century for sure, was somehow in a time warp. One that made it A-Okay to eat on bone china that had been used three centuries ago, and to sleep on beds that had been used by nobility for generations. Of course, Sascha couldn't make sheets last more than a few years, but these ones seemed to have had ancient Dukes resting their patooties on them for a lifetime, she thought with an eye roll.

Her grandmother, the only grandparent she'd had, must have been right about the 'old days.' They made nothing like they used to.

Hiding another smile, she dropped her book onto the coffee table and called, "Tin? Would you like to go on a playdate?"

Tin, his eyes on an interactive sudoku puzzle, scowled at her. "Play?"

"Yep."

He tilted his head to the side, looking so damn regal that she laughed a little—he definitely got that from Andrei and not from her. Whether he was a prince in Bratva royalty or not, Andrei had been raised like a little lordling himself. "Who with?"

"You remember Perry? From the other day?"

He made a smacking noise with his lips. "I remember."

She snickered. "We're meeting her little girl."

Eyes flashing with interest, he scampered to his feet then dashed to her side and held out his hand in silent demand. She grabbed it, and together they followed Jeeves out into the hall and down an enormous corridor toward a side of the house she'd never even bothered exploring.

It wasn't her home, even though they'd been offered free reign of the building that was more like a palace than a grand estate, and she'd been more content with staying close to Tin—

Okay, that was bullshit.

She was clinging.

*Clinging* to her toddler.

Pathetic? Perhaps. But it wasn't every day a goddamn serial child killer penetrated your house, made a move into your life, and targeted you, was it?

Even if Tin wasn't old enough to fit Jane's profile, even if he'd have been safe for another year at least, that wasn't her idea of *safety*.

Mouth pursing with a mixture of anger, outrage, and downright fear, she was grateful for the distraction Perry presented. Truth was, she hadn't really expected to see the Queen again, but she was glad for it.

She knew no one was to blame for this situation except Jane, but God, it fucked with her head nonetheless.

They walked into a suite that was like their family room back home. All soft and squashy couches, lots of toys in a corner, a big TV, and shelves loaded down with a variety of books—some with ancient spines, others that were brand new. A few fat, plenty that were thin. An eclectic mix.

On an armchair in the corner, Perry was seated, her legs crossed at the ankle as she slouched back into the cushions. Alice, as far as Sascha could tell, was hiding?

Jeeves clucked his tongue, which had Perry darting upright as she stared over at them. She went from slouching comfortably to sitting with a back straighter than a ruler.

Sascha cut Jeeves a disapproving look—was that really necessary?

God, Sascha wasn't sure she could deal with all the BS that came with being a royal. Having to sit straight, drink coffee with your pinkie finger stuck out, and dealing with boring people as part of the job—nope. She'd prefer to keep house again.

"Thank you, Rodgers," Perry murmured, and the guy disappeared with a small bow. Sascha preferred the name Jeeves. With his wispy combover? Rodgers looked like the little illustration on the old school search engine.

The second the door closed behind him, Perry slouched back and Sascha teased, "*Vive la revolution*, hmm?"

Perry's nose crinkled. "I swear, the protocol is what sucks the most. I can deal with most things, but having to look perfect alllllll the time is just boring as heck."

Sascha waved at the sofa opposite her. "It okay if I sit?"

Perry snorted. "What do you think?"

"I don't know. I mean, it's not every day I'm invited for tea with a Queen."

"True." Perry's lips twitched. "Let's just forget about my status while we're alone, yeah?"

Sascha shrugged. "Fine by me."

"Alice, stop hiding for a second and come and meet our guests."

Sascha squeezed Tin's shoulder and called out to the seemingly empty room, "Alice, this is Valentin and I'm Sascha. We'd both love to meet you."

"She's shy," Perry whispered.

"Tin isn't," she replied with a laugh. "Don't worry. It's impossible to be shy around him."

A small face peeked out from behind a curtain, and Sascha smiled at the worried features. The little girl had a short mop of curls on her head, but when she alighted from the curtain, she wasn't wearing a girly dress, if anything, she was wearing something similar to Tin—blue shorts and a blue sweater. It wasn't that the outfit was distinctly boyish, but there was something different about it that told Sascha the clothes were for a boy.

She didn't say anything, just guided Tin over to Alice and crouched down as she initiated introductions. From the serious smile on her face, as well as the way she'd cupped her hand—fingers down, wrist tilted just so—Sascha sensed there was a regal handshake in the making. Tin, being Tin, just grabbed her hand and cried, "Play!"

Alice, jolting with surprise, let out a giggle and chased after him. Sascha smiled then moved closer to Perry, looking forward to a chat with a woman who was like her in so many ways, and yet living a life so completely *un*like hers.

"You want coffee?" Perry asked, tilting her head to the side. "Or cake?"

"Cake," Sascha admitted. "It's been one of those weeks." Then she waved a hand when Perry went to sit up. "I can serve us. Which do you want?"

"Double serving of cake. Being pregnant, it's the only time I can put weight on without the press going nuts."

That had Sascha scowling. "Well, that sucks."

Perry snorted. "Tell me about it. I don't really mind. I've never been skinny, but as the wedding approached I kind of dropped a lot of weight from nerves and after Alice, I reverted back to normal. It made tongues wag."

"Tongues always wag," Sascha grunted, serving them both double slices of a cake that reminded her of a Madeira cake but with frosting.

It was huge—stacked four layers high inside and loaded with what could only be buttercream.

Mouth drooling, she handed Perry the plate and a fork, and then retreated to her seat to gorge.

"I know why I'm stuffing my face, but what about you? You look like that cake is necessary," Perry stated softly.

"It is," Sascha said with a huff. "More necessary than oxygen, and it's probably a good thing. That whole weight loss through nerves crap? I've just gone through it myself." To the point where her husbands had started spanking her if she ever missed a goddamn meal. She couldn't huff about that too much, not when she enjoyed the spanking and she *hadn't* been looking after herself. "I could handle a few slices of this bad boy a day while I'm here."

"Want to talk about it?" Perry inquired, brows high.

Sascha stabbed the fork into her cake. "Miscarried." She didn't go into the ins and outs of what had happened.

Perry winced. "Sorry, Sascha."

Her mouth was a little less tight, her throat less thick as she shrugged. "Thank you. It's easing with time."

A snort escaped the Queen. "Bull. Happened to me eight months after Alice was born." Her mouth tightened. "No one understands. Not even the men who love you."

"They try—"

"Then we were both fortunate in having their support, but there's an expiration date on grief where it comes to miscarriage. My husband, *husbands*—" she amended with a whisper, "weren't like that, but the court?" She shook her head. "They weren't as generous. I even had one of my husband's councilors ask me if I could stop moping about the palace as it was bad for morale."

"That bastard," Sascha growled, spine straightening in outrage.

Perry's head bobbed in agreement then she shot Sascha a wink. "He wasn't a councilor for long. Don't worry."

"You told—"

"Edward. You don't need to call him the King. He has a big enough head as it is."

Sascha snickered. "Okay. *Edward*. You told him?"

"I sure as shit did. Even if I hadn't, he'd have figured something was wrong soon enough. After that dick's 'helpful' advice, I moped around the place more than ever," she admitted, then her brow puckered. "Do you ever feel pressure?"

"All the time—but from what specifically? I don't have a 'court' to pressurize me, but there's always something to spoil your day."

Perry shrugged and in a low voice, whispered, "To make sure they all have a child."

Sascha's eyes widened. "They pressure you for that?"

"No!" Perry cried, and the rejection was so swift that Sascha knew the Queen wasn't offloading any BS her way. "Not at all. It's self-imposed but—"

"But?"

"I just don't want them to miss out."

Sascha pondered it a second. "That would involve me having five kids, Perry, and I'm not about to do that," she teased.

"You're a brave woman. Three is enough for anyone," Perry said with a little laugh, but there was a twinkle in her eye that said *her* three were exactly enough for her.

Sascha snickered a little, but after taking another bite of cake, admitted, "I don't think that's an issue. At least, not with my guys. Tin is such a handful that when I *was* pregnant, I knew we were all concerned about what having another one of him around was going to be like." Guilt swarmed her at that.

"Why is he a handful?"

"My men are all geniuses. Devon is halfway to madness," she explained with a little chuckle. "It's my kind of madness, but it has to be said. He's nuts most of the time but boy, he's..." She thought about the word that best described her man. Her lips curved as she settled on, "Delightful. I never know what he's going to say or do. I never really understand him and yet, he's one of the purest spirits I've ever met. He's not innocent. By any means. But his soul is."

Perry smiled. "I'll look forward to meeting him."

Snorting, Sascha shook her head. "He'll probably offend you. Don't take it to heart."

A short laugh escaped the Queen. "How will he offend me?"

"Well, he's like an adult version of Tin. Blunt, honest to the nth degree. He can't help it."

"Ah, so you feared having another one of him and Tin around?"

"Yep," she said with a small smile. "It's crazy because Tin isn't Devon's biologically, and yet the two of them are like two peas in a pod." She cut a look at the two bright blond heads that were getting into mischief over in the corner where the stack of toys was situated. "It's weird but he's like them all."

"Nurture over nature," Perry said with a shrug. "A beautifully delicious quirk. Alice is like Xavier—so smart, so hungry for knowledge, but she can go from inquisitive to impish like George in the blink of an eye. And I swear, she can make half the court quiver in her wake when she decides to throw a tantrum—she's so damn regal like Edward, it's creepy sometimes." She rolled her eyes. "Not that that happens often, thank God."

"Just often enough to remind you of her father?"

Perry smirked. "Exactly."

Laughing, Sascha set down her now-empty plate with a sigh. Though it was rude, she settled back in a pose that mimicked Perry's —slouched, head cushioned and supported, legs crossed at the ankle.

"She's going through a phase that I'm fighting half the court over at the moment," Perry admitted, making Sascha quirk a brow at her.

"What kind of phase?"

"She's insisting she's a boy."

Sascha cut the little girl a look. "Ah." That explained the boyish cut to the clothes and the shorn mop of curls atop her head. "Is it a problem?"

"She won't wear dresses, so yup," Perry confessed with a sigh. "I don't want to confuse her, but she's just insisting—"

Sascha raised a hand when Perry seemed unable to continue with her statement. "I understand. They're stubborn little boogers sometimes. No making them do anything when they have their own mind."

There was relief and gratitude in Perry's eyes as she admitted, "One of my ladies-in-waiting is determined to make me feel like a real shit over the fact I'm letting her wear boy's clothes, but if that's what she wants, then why stop her? I'm sure it's only a phase, and forcing her to conform when she's so young just seems ridiculous."

"It is," Sascha said with a nod. "But it's causing arguments?"

"Not with my guys. They just think it's funny. But with the courtiers? Yeah."

"You haven't spoken of the tension it's causing?"

"No." Perry shook her head. "They're so busy and—"

"What? You aren't?" Sascha snorted. "You have to tell them, Perry. Look, you told Edward about the guy who said you needed to stop moping. Why haven't you explained about this?"

Perry sighed. "I'm not sure. I guess I'm feeling defensive and protective. She's little. What if Edward *insists* she starts dressing like a girl?"

Sascha frowned. "I don't get it, Perry. The dude's got eyes. He can see she's not wearing costume skirts and a false tiara. Nor is she waving around a plastic wand with a crown of braids on her head. I mean, I didn't see it at first, just thought her clothes were a little boyish, but Edward and the others have to have noticed."

Perry started gnawing on her bottom lip. "I want her to have some freedom before it's all taken from her." She closed her eyes then. "Did you know the DeSauviers make their kids go to boarding school at age six?"

Sascha's mouth dropped open. "No fucking way."

Perry's eyes closed in misery. "Yes way."

"You're going to fight that, aren't you?" Sascha demanded, sitting upright. There was no way in hell she'd be ready for Tin to be away from home most of the time in four years.

"I'm going to try. They're so stubborn sometimes," Perry whispered, like she was confessing a deadly sin. "I have to pick my fights, and that's going to be one of them, but even if I win, there's no guarantee that they won't want her to go away a few years after that. *Protocol*," she mimicked. "I fucking loathe it."

Sascha reached up and began to fiddle with her bottom lip. "You need to talk to them, Perry. This life we've chosen is complicated enough without taking communication out of the picture."

It was only as she *said* the words that she realized that was what she'd been doing herself.

For months.

She'd told her men the bare minimum, and instead, had been using her body, their dominance, as a means of communication, and that? Well, it was one of the least healthiest things she'd ever done in her life. And back in college? She'd tried ecstasy, for Christ's sake.

Staggered by the realization of what she'd been doing all this time, Sascha barely heard Perry when the other woman said, "I know you're right. It was so much easier before, and then? It wasn't exactly easy juggling three guys. Each one of them so different, yet, with their paths so ingrained in them..."

Sascha cleared her throat. "The boy thing—look, it might not be a phase, Perry. You know that, right?"

"I know. I've been reading about trans kids and stuff, but I've no idea how something like that would even be received here. It's not exactly embraced back home, is it? And here? They're a thousand times pricklier about tradition. I just... I don't care what she is as long as she's healthy and happy."

Sascha pondered that. "Okay, doing a U-turn here, but also, she might *not* be trans and it might just be a phase, but what isn't a phase is boarding school at six.

"If you can't talk to them about something as simple as Alice refusing to wear dresses, then how are you going to fight them on the boarding school shit?"

Perry's cheeks pinkened as she cleared her throat. "I'm sorry, Sascha, I-I just realized how inappropriate it is that we're talking about these things..."

Sascha snorted, well aware Perry was backpedaling now. But she wasn't about to allow that.

She hadn't been able to discuss her men, her life, her family, to anyone in forever. She hadn't been able to discuss just how fucking hard it was to make things work in a household where several men were in the picture—each with diverse beliefs and different backgrounds.

"Okay, so you told me something that's messing with your head. Time for me to spill, yeah?"

Perry's eyes rounded. "Sure."

Sascha grunted and then, to a woman who was pretty much a stranger, she blurted it all out.

The miscarriage. The stillbirth. The fact that she'd only been able to express herself when she was tied to a bed, her ass pink from being caned, her body aching from being fucked as one of her men controlled her pleasure. She told her about Jane, about her fears, about the danger Tin had been in and when she'd finished, Perry just stared at her and said, "I think we need more cake."

And like that, Sascha knew she'd made a friend for fucking life.

---

"YOU HAVE to tell me what's going on, Rick." Sean was well aware he was pleading, but fuck, he needed answers. More importantly, his woman needed answers.

"You're not on the case anymore, Sean."

"I know that," he growled. "But this bitch infiltrated my *home*, Rick."

A sigh came down the line and Sean knew the detective well

enough to know he'd be pinching the bridge of his nose with impatience.

"Look—" Sean started but he was cut off.

Rick grumbled, "I get it. I get it. But it's complicated. Fuck, when is this shit not? I wish you weren't involved so you could help, Sean. Dammit. This woman is messed up."

"Who've you got working the psych angle?"

"Eloise Rippon."

"Her?" Sean scowled at the desk he was seated at. "What the fuck are you using her for? I thought you were going with Medcalfe. I mean, she's crap, but Rippon has a screw loose."

"Because you're not allowed to work on the case, dipshit," Rick grated out. "You think all of our psych team is shit."

"That's because they are. They all think they're on some kind of police procedural show—" When Rick snorted, Sean hissed, "You're amused because it's true."

"Maybe. Okay, look, Jane was abused from a young age."

"Let me guess, *four*." It was Sean's turn to pinch the bridge of his nose.

"You got it." Rick sighed. "One abuser, and they sold her out. There's no condoning what she did—"

"But she's rightfully fucked in the head?" Sean clucked his tongue. "Survivors don't all feel the need to go around killing kids, Rick."

"I'm not saying that."

"No. And I'm not either, really. It was beyond wrong what she endured. But she didn't exactly right it by doing what she did, did she?" He ran a hand through his hair. Victim shaming wasn't about to go on the top of his to-do list for the day, but fuck.

There was no excuse for what Jane did, but only through learning of her past could they find some explanation for the acts Jane had committed.

"Her abuser died when she was seven and that was when the

abuse stopped. From what we can see of her records, she adjusted well. Surprisingly so…"

Sean shook his head, then realized Rick couldn't see him. "No. It fits the profile. Intelligent. Above average intelligence. These crimes were perpetrated over five years, Rick. That takes some balls but also brains."

A disgruntled hum sounded down the line. "Who's telling this story? Me or you?"

"You," Sean grunted.

"Anyway, she adjusted. Great grades, did very well at school through to university then she got pregnant. Single mother."

"Then her kid died, right? When he was four?" Sean remembered this part of the file Vasily had dredged up on Jane, and he reached up to rub the back of his neck. Most of this information had been procured illegally so he had to pretend he didn't know half the stuff Rick was telling him.

"Yeah," Rick barked. "Meningitis." He blew out a breath then. "Look, Sean, if you see her interviews, you can see she's adamant she's saving the kids."

"That's why she preserved them the way she did."

"Yeah. The sick bitch thought she was saving them from the world."

Nausea churned in his gut. "How did she select her victims?" He'd have hazarded a guess and said they looked like her deceased son, but all the victims had been as different as north and south. No similarities.

"She insists *they* selected *her*."

Sean's mouth twisted. "How did they do that then?"

"Happened to come across her at the park. Talked to her in a store. Something small. She'd follow the kid and the parent or parents' home, and begin stalking them."

Sean ran a hand through his hair. "What changed with me?"

"She was curious."

"Not interested in Tin?"

"Too young," Rick confirmed. "Like you thought. She was there for you but..." Another grunt. "She's fallen for Kirov."

For a second, his mouth gaped, then he bit off, "No fucking way."

"Yes way. Says she loves him and that they're due to run off and get married at any time. The woman's fucking crazy—she's talking about you and those guys you live with sharing Kirov's woman."

Sean winced at that. "Why the long spell between victims? Did she say?"

"She was methodical and each child had to fit her specifications."

"What? That they were four?"

"Four and ill. In some way."

"Angel of death?" Sean groaned. "Fuck no."

"Yeah. Messed up, right? You know all the victims were sick in some way."

"Not dying though, Christ. Pardeep had fucking psoriasis! It wasn't about to kill him! And Sammy had asthma. How was that terminal?"

"Don't shoot the messenger. This isn't my story; I'm just telling it."

Conceding that with a huff, Sean demanded, "Carry on."

"Yes, sir," Rick grumbled. "She moved around a lot because of her work. All temporary secretarial stuff. Things far below her intelligence level."

"She was bored?"

"I think so. Rippon says so. Says she wasn't challenged, and it made this plight of hers take over all the more.

"Anyway, she picked them that way. Random meetings, stalking the victim and their families until she figured out if they needed her help, and then she'd strike. When she did, she'd move on. You know how long it took us to uncover some of the bodies. And it crossed so many towns and cities that no one even pieced the puzzle together until you noticed the pattern."

The trouble with the murderer had been she'd carefully tended to her victims, but she'd placed them outside—in the woods, a forest, even close to a river. The elements and scavengers had undone their work, but they'd found evidence of cuddly toys and blankets that were used as comforters. Almost like the Egyptians had buried their dead with gold and beautiful items to help them enjoy the afterlife.

Sickness overcame him. The taint of Jane's stain was so pervasive that it seemed to overtake every single one of his senses.

The puzzle that Rick mentioned made his stomach churn even harder.

What the fuck was wrong with him that he could see a pattern in the games these sick bastards played?

Swallowing thickly, he whispered, "You'll keep me informed?"

"Sure. But..." Rick blew out a breath. "I wouldn't hold out hope for much more."

"Why?"

"She was Chatty Cathy at the start, but now? Not so much."

Sean dipped his chin. "Isn't she proud of what she did?"

"That's what had her talking at the start, but I think the repercussions are hitting home. She's realizing she and Kirov won't be a thing. That's hitting her hard."

He clenched his jaw. "She's insane, Rick."

"Yeah. I'm sure that will affect where she's imprisoned."

Sean gritted his teeth. "Keep in touch?"

"Same."

As he disconnected the call, Sean dipped his head and fell silent, letting his thoughts overwhelm him.

"Nothing much to say, Sean?" Kurt drawled, tapping his fingers on the armrest of his armchair. He'd been there for the entirety of that conversation, so he knew the score. Surely, he understood why Sean had nothing to say? Why all his words had dried up?

Swiping his hand over his face, he scrubbed it through his hair then changed the subject, "I wonder if coming to Germany with you guys is a bad idea."

He could feel Kurt's scowl from across the room. "Bullshit, Sean. Don't back away from her, from us over this crap. Anyway, Sascha will need you there. Especially after she meets my mother and father."

Sean sighed. "That supposed to make me feel better? Hannibal Lecter would have needed a hug after he'd met your mother."

Kurt snorted. "You're just full of compliments today."

"And you're not arguing with me because you know I'm speaking the truth." Bowing his head, he stared at the space between his feet on the floor. "Wish this would all just go away, Kurt."

"And it will. Soon."

"I'm going to stop this shit." He spoke more to the ground than to his friend.

"What shit in particular?"

"Working with the police. It's not worth this hassle."

"Jane wouldn't have stopped until someone caught her. You did. You saw the pattern, Sean."

"Only because it was obvious once I had the whole picture, Kurt," he snapped.

"Perhaps. But only you'd think that way."

"Is that supposed to make me feel better?" Christ, hadn't he just been wondering why he could understand the way these sick fucks worked?

"No. Not particularly. You don't have to appreciate your gifts to have to deal with them. Devon's a perfect example of that."

Sean snorted. "He loves his work."

"Sure he does, but I'm certain if he knew how much of his life it truly took up, he wouldn't be so happy."

Dipping his chin, Sean conceded, "It consumes him."

"Exactly. Eats him up, churns him out, won't let him sleep... At least your gifts enable you to function like a regular human being."

He sat back, slouching in the seat as he asked, "You have all the meetings arranged in Munich?"

"Of course. They've been settled for months."

Cutting his brother a look, he inquired, "How long have you been waiting to offload that script onto Sascha?"

Kurt's lips twitched. "That obvious?"

"Not to her, apparently."

Kurt had asked Sascha to work on the amendments to the script he had for his first movie adaptation.

Knowing how much Kurt loathed edits, Sean had been surprised he'd been this patient in withholding the request.

"She's good at it."

"She'd have to be for you to trust her with them."

Kurt beamed a grin at him. "You know me too well."

"Where your work is concerned, you're anal-retentive, Kurt."

"Perhaps, but she's almost as bad as I am. You know she found issues that even my fancy-schmancy editors didn't?"

"No, but I can imagine. She can be a nitpicker when she wants to be." He blew out a breath. "I don't know why you two don't just write something together. You're always hashing out ideas in the kitchen."

Kurt tilted his head to the side. "What would we write?"

Sean frowned then shrugged. "I don't know. It was only a thought."

He watched as, now contemplative, Kurt rapped his knuckles against the armrest once more. When his brother fell silent, Sean did too as he stared into the flickering flames of the open hearth.

It was bitterly cold, and though there was still light, the day not even having morphed into late afternoon, it felt grim outside these walls. As grim as his mood.

As the two of them sat there in silence, he didn't turn his head when the door to the library they were using opened. Staff were in and out all the time, and though the intrusion was irritating, it was damn nice to have people to pick up after him on this level—talk about five-star treatment.

When the figure came to a halt in front of him, he peered up, expecting the butler or a maid. But it wasn't either. It was Sascha.

Before he could say a word, she slipped her feet out of her shoes, then plopped herself on his lap.

Within seconds, she'd curved an arm around his neck and was

nuzzling into him. Her large tits were squashed against his pec, and her soft hair tickled his chin. With a soft sigh, he curved his arm around her, so grateful for her at that moment that he wanted nothing more than to just hide his face in her throat like Tin sometimes did.

"I'm sorry, baby," he whispered. "So fucking sorry."

She sighed. "Don't be. Not your fault. It's just fucked up and a lot to take in."

"You're telling me," he said drily, pressing his face into her hair. "I would never do anything to hurt you or Tin, honey. You know that, right?"

She tensed in his lap. "Sean, you say that like *you* were behind this. You weren't. Jesus. *She* was the reason I was mad. I didn't like her from the start, and I was jealous at how she was cozying up to Andrei, and then with this? With the threat to Tin?"

"I brought her into our lives."

"No. You didn't. She did. I was frightened, Sean. Frightened and irrational. I wasn't thinking right. Wasn't thinking with anything other than my instincts, and those were telling me that another of my children was in grave danger, and once again I couldn't protect them." She nuzzled into him. "You understand that, don't you?"

"Of course, I do," he rasped. "I just, I-I don't know what to do, Sascha. Don't know what to say to you to make things right."

"There's nothing you can say to make it right, Sean." When he tensed, she shook her head. "There's nothing because you haven't done anything wrong. It was a knee-jerk reaction, and I realized something today... these past few months? It's been one huge knee-jerk reaction after another.

"I've barely communicated with any of you. I'm here, and I'm present, but I'm not talking, and I know that has to change because it's not fair to any of you."

"You've been grieving," Kurt excused, his voice low, soft. Gentle. Everything Sean wasn't feeling.

Inside, he was a torrent of emotion. A veritable flood of feeling, and for a man who prided himself on his self-control, Sean understood how very out-of-control Sascha had been feeling of late.

"I know I have, honey, but that was no excuse to cut you out, and that's what I've been doing." She blew out a breath then turned her face into his chest again. "I'm sorry about that. I'm really, really sorry."

Sean sighed and repeated Kurt's words, "You were grieving. You're entitled to grieve how *you* need to grieve. If that means getting angry or quiet, that's your choice, sweetheart."

Silence fell between them with only the crackling flames in the hearth truly breaking up the sheer quiet in the library.

After a few moments, almost as though the continued silence was what triggered the question, Kurt asked, "Where's Tin?"

"Playing with Alice."

"Who's Alice?"

"The Princess," Sascha said with a small smile. "Perry's daughter."

Sean reached up and tapped her nose. "We're rubbing shoulders with royalty now, are we?"

Sascha laughed. "That should please your mother, Kurt."

"Nothing pleases mother, Sascha," Kurt replied drily. "You'll come to learn that soon enough."

Sean grunted. "How long are we there for?"

"Ten days." Kurt winced. "Longest ten days of my life."

"She needs to get to know Tin," Sascha chided, and though neither of them said anything, the look they shared spoke a thousand words...

Though Kurt claimed Tin was his biological son where his mother was concerned, Margritte wouldn't believe it until their boy had a DNA test.

Sean wouldn't be surprised if Margritte ignored them for the entirety of their stay anyway. It wasn't going to be the homecoming Sascha seemed to be expecting, but none of them had the heart to disappoint her.

Sometimes in this world, seeing truly was the only way to make someone believe, and where their parents were concerned? There was no salvaging those relationships. No matter how hard they tried.

Sean was the same with his folks. He and Kurt had the weakest relationships with their parents. He hadn't even called his on Christmas, for God's sake.

"Don't be disappointed if they don't welcome us with open arms, Sascha," he warned softly, unable to lie to her after what they'd been through these past few months.

"I don't really expect them to," was all she said, but Sean knew her. Knew how big her heart was, and knew that, deep down, Sascha would indeed expect a heartfelt homecoming for Kurt when that just wasn't about to go down.

# TWENTY-NINE

"ARE YOU SURE YOU WANT THIS?"

Sean stared down at Sascha's ripe curves and his cock began to pulse to his heartbeat.

Whatever he'd expected when she'd slipped into his room, almost parallel to what had occurred the other night, it hadn't been her asking him for release.

He'd never anticipated *that.*

Not when he'd thought, in her own way, she'd been telling him she didn't want this from him anymore. She'd called it a 'lack of communication,' but Sean had read between the lines and had apparently been wrong.

Fuck, that was happening more and more of late.

"Of course, I want this," she breathed, wriggling on his lap, her belly nudging his cock.

He stared down at her pale peach skin draped across his lap, the endless curves, the bright red hair that swept down her back, and shuddered.

To submit was to trust.

To be trusted was the only way to dominate.

He gripped one of her ass cheeks, parting the thick flesh to find her pussy. With his knuckles, he dragged them down the central line and gritted his teeth when he found her sopping wet.

He sagged back in the armchair, a mixture of defeat and success.

"Sean?" Sascha asked after a few minutes when he did nothing more than squeeze that ass cheek as though her butt was his stress ball.

"We can't do this if you don't trust me, Sascha," he rasped.

"And that's what I'm showing you. That I do trust you," she whispered, arching up, twisting, and propping her elbow on his leg. She was bright pink from hanging down the way she had, and she looked flustered as well as, he had to admit, horny.

"How can you?"

"Because you've done nothing wrong," she repeated.

"Why do I feel like I have then?"

"Because I reacted the other night in a way that detonated your Atlas complex." She blew out a breath as she shoved her hair out of the way, then she moved herself off his lap and sat on her knees between his feet.

There were rules to domination and submission. Hard limits and soft ones. Safe words and expectations.

He'd never been that strict with her. Not really. As he studied the way she knelt between his legs, he knew that back in the day, he'd have spanked a sub for not kneeling with her legs spread, pussy presented for him. And he'd probably have clamped her nipples for not cupping her elbows behind her back.

He'd been harder when he was younger. Meaner, he had to admit. Faintly sadistic in his tendencies as he meandered a path that later on, he realized, had taken him down a turn he regretted.

Andrei and Sawyer liked to play. That was their forte. They were kinky and Sascha's recent development had fallen into that. They liked tying her up, loved spanking her butt and marking her with their fingers and toys, but they weren't hardcore with it.

Sean had the power to be hardcore.

He knew that and he didn't like that about himself.

Never had, never would.

"What is it? What's wrong?" she murmured, breaking into his thoughts.

He parted his legs, pleased when she moved deeper in between them, her face coming to rest on his pajama-clad thigh. He reached for her then, his fingers coming to caress her hair with a care he'd never shown another woman. Because Sascha wasn't his sub, she was his. Plain and simple.

"Do you know why I stopped doing things like this?"

She blinked up at him, her bright green eyes like gentle sunlit pools. "Doing what? The dominating thing?"

His lips almost twitched at that as he shuttered his eyes and sank deeper into the armchair. Resting his head back, he stared at her forehead, not her eyes, not wanting to watch her flinch.

"I ignored a sub's safe word."

She stilled but didn't pull back. "Why?"

"Because I knew—" He blew out a breath. "I *believed* that she could take more. But that wasn't for me to decide, it was for her, and I ignored it."

She fell quiet a second, processing his words. After a while, she stated, "Did she leave you?"

He shook his head. "No. And it wasn't like that anyway. There's a club in Soho. Andrei, Sawyer, and I used to go there. It was a fetish place. Back in the day, it was dirty and grimy, I guess, but it was pretty much all there was at the time."

"Did you share women?"

He nodded. "Of course."

She rolled her eyes. "Of course," she muttered on a low grumble that had him faintly smiling.

"You know our history."

"Not complaining," she retorted, but he could see she was jealous and there was no need to be.

He hummed under his breath and began stroking her hair again.

"I took it too far, and though at the end she flew, it wasn't right. But I knew I'd do it again."

"Was she upset?"

"No. She was euphoric. You know what 'flying' is, right?"

"It's the rush of endorphins that comes from a gamut of pain or pleasure." She cocked a brow at him. "I can read too, you know?"

His lips twitched as he tapped her bottom lip. "Cheeky."

She winked. "Only for you."

He laughed softly, but his amusement died off as he said, "I tended to her, but all the while, I just knew I'd do it again. I was cocky back then. I'd just been offered my first book deal, and I was involved with the Huntington Case—I was getting famous for what I could do."

"That was the guy who murdered all those schoolteachers, right?"

He nodded. "It was." With his spare hand, he reached up and cupped the back of his neck, using it to prop himself up so he could better look at her. "It concerned me."

"That you were concerned at all tells me that *I* have no need to be concerned," she told him softly.

Sean hummed under his breath. "Perhaps."

"Go on, tell me what happened."

"Sometimes you open a door and it takes you down the rabbit hole. It's up to you to wander back up and shut that door, or fall even deeper." He cringed at his memories. "I went from sharing with Andrei to spanking a girlfriend as we fucked to getting off on whipping a sub in such a short space of time, Sascha, it frightened me."

"Are you a sadist?"

She asked the question so calmly that he didn't trust the velvet-lined question at all. "No. I have sadistic tendencies," he admitted. "I'm more into control now, but when I was younger, yes."

"What changed?"

"I made myself change."

"Why?"

"Because I didn't like that part of myself. It was too similar to what I was dealing with in the outside world."

She gaped at him. "You're not comparing yourself to those fucking sickos, are you?"

"In the nineties, anyone into BDSM was considered a 'fucking sicko,' Sascha. It's all a label. What people can't understand, they consider disturbing." He shrugged. "It's always concerned me how well I understand the patterns in these cases. Always made me wonder how close to insanity I am myself—"

Before he could do more than jerk, Sascha had jolted upright, and just as he expected her to bolt, she grabbed him by the shoulders and shook him. The move did delicious things to her tits, but he quickly glanced at her eyes, surprised to see the flickering fire of outrage buried in the depths.

"You take that back," she growled.

"Take what back—"

"That you think you're some kind of freak!"

He clenched his jaw. "Maybe I am. Maybe that's why I like what I do—"

"Fuck off, Sean. Just fuck off."

Growling, Sean grated out, "And where should I fuck off to, Sascha? Maybe I should move the fuck out and—"

Her hand retreated and his face whipped to the side as she slapped him. Once. She scrambled onto his lap, one knee either side of his thighs as she grabbed his jaw, pressed her forehead to his, and gritted out, "You want to leave me?"

He swallowed. "Never."

"Then what is this? Confession?" she rasped. "You. Are. Going. Nowhere, Sean. Do you hear me?"

Closing his eyes, he whispered, "It might be for the best."

"Why? Because you feel guilty about Jane? Or because you want out?"

"I don't want out," he ground out.

"That's what it sounds like to me," she retorted. "Look, Jane was a freak. She's done despicable shit, shit that no one can forgive her for. I don't care what the fuck led her to do what she did, *nothing* makes it right. *Nothing*. But that's not on you.

"The other night was a knee-jerk reaction. I apologized for that. You told me and I freaked out. You can understand that, surely? I don't believe you bring danger to our world. You haven't to this point, and this was an anomaly.

"We're working on making sure that it never happens again, but even putting security in place doesn't stop crazy. Look at this place. You've seen the guards stationed everywhere and it didn't stop a Queen from being assassinated!" she half-shrieked at him. "Am I mad that some bitch came into my home and got close to us? Yeah. I'm furious. I took that out on you, and I totally shouldn't have." Her bottom lip quivered. "Don't hate me for reacting, Sean. Don't leave me f—"

He reached up and grabbed a tight hold of her, and dragging her into his arms, he bit off, "I never want to leave you. Ever. Sascha, you're it for me. You're my fucking everything, and that's what kills me. She was attracted to us because she knew I was on the case."

"Why, though?"

"She came to snoop and then she fell for Andrei," he replied, his voice low as he made the admission, an admission that had her stiffening on his lap.

"I knew she had a thing for him," she barked but she didn't pull away, just sagged into his hold. "Fuck, Sean. This is so messed up, but..." She fell silent and after a deep inhalation stated, "That's life, darling. That's life."

He pressed his lips to hers and gently teased his tongue along the softly pursed clasp of her mouth. When she let him in, he sighed with relief and carefully explored her. Seeking her taste, her soft moans. He stole her breath, stole it intentionally, took it from her and made her breathe from him.

She shivered in his embrace, her arms sliding up and over his shoulders and around his neck. The proximity felt wonderful, especially after he'd felt certain she'd avoid him to hell and back.

"I love you," she whispered against his jaw, her body relaxing totally into his. "Nothing could change that."

He squeezed her. "I love you, too."

Her fingers began to trace shapes over his stubbled chin as they just sat there in a restful silence that somehow meant the world.

"Are you coming back to us?" Sean asked after a while, hoping she understood his inference.

Slowly, she nodded. "I'm coming back. To me, and then to you."

Another squeeze. "I'm glad. Maybe I can come back to myself as well."

"I've never seen you anything other than in control, Sean," she admitted.

"That's because it's how I prefer it. I hate being out of control. Hate it. But with all this, it knocked me sideways." Sean reached up and rubbed his temple. "I'm not entirely sure how to get back on track either."

"We take one day at a time. One step forward together." She shrugged. "Nothing more we can do."

He pondered that a second, knew she was right, and inquired, "And what about this? Do you really want *this*?"

"What? For you to spank me and shit?"

His lips curved. "And shit."

There was a gleam in her eye. "Rules are made to be broken."

"Brat."

"Always." Laughter tinkled from her, breaking and making his fucking heart. "Look, I'm not saying I want you to boss me around. I don't. But I kind of needed those rules, I'll admit. I didn't want to eat, and you guys made it so I had to. I needed you to handle that, and it makes me feel like I'm Tin's age to admit it, but it's the truth nonetheless.

"Do I feel like I need that at the moment? No. I don't..."

"This is a swift change of heart, Sascha," he cautioned. "In the space of a few months, you've gone from—"

She lifted a hand and pressed a finger to his mouth to hush him. "I've never miscarried before. Never been stalked before. Never had one of my men be under threat of jail before. Never been a party to kidnapping, never had a murderer work in my home... It's been a time of extremes, and I felt that. I felt the need for control, just as you do, and I do honestly believe that you need this from me.

"So, yeah, I want this. Not just because I feel like you need it, but because I enjoy it. I like the pleasure and the pain. I like how it makes me feel like I can... as you said, fly. I don't want to go to a club or a dungeon or anything like that. I don't want it to get extreme. But as it stands, it's sexy, *you're* sexy when you're in Dom mode, and I'm not about to say no to that when you make me as wet as you do."

It was his turn to laugh softly. "Ever eloquent, my darling," he rasped, the words smoky as he reached up and fisted her hair. Rolling it around his wrist, he tugged her head back until her eyes flickered wide in response to the bite of pain. "You're sure?" he asked, for what would be the final time.

"I'm positive," she hissed. "If things change, if *I* change, then I'll tell you. I have a mouth, Sean."

"And a very fine mouth it is, too," he purred, then he said, "You scared me, Sascha. That will never do. You need to be punished for that."

Another flicker in her eyes. A flash of desire, a flare of need.

"As you were," he told her, not releasing her hair as she maneuvered to drape across his lap again.

He eyed her, studying her ripe curves once more, but this time, it was as though he'd taken a deep breath after hours of shallow ones. On the brink of hyperventilation, his lungs relished the oxygen flooding them as he stared at his one and only.

She was his everything.

His world.

And it was time he showed her that.

---

FUCK!

Sascha gritted her teeth, gritted them then buried her face into the silky cotton pajama pants Sean wore. She was so tempted to bite them, to bite *him*, take a nice piece of his calf and grind down on it because fuck, this spanking?

The worst she'd ever taken.

He was intent on hitting the backs of her thighs, the tender areas that would make anyone flinch after a sharp slap to the ass, never mind an all-out spanking session.

How could a hand make her butt ache so much? A cane? A paddle? Sure. But a hand?

Yikes.

Her face was hot and flushed, sweaty as she tried to take each spank with composure. She was trying not to shriek, trying not to cry, and then, even as she processed that, she asked herself why.

Why the fuck was she trying not to shriek?

Why was she trying not to cry?

Sean hadn't asked her to do either, and he could be specific when he so chose.

She pressed her face into his leg, no intent to bite this time, and when his hand soared high and it connected with the fleshy curve of her butt? She released a yelp as all her nerve endings rebelled on her, almost as though if she hadn't decided to cry out, they'd made the decision for her.

Two more sharp spanks and the tears began to fall, and they weren't nice tears either. Not diamond globules that gathered in the corners of her eye, no crocodile tears.

They were raw.

They were gritty—they even stung her damn eyes.

*These* hurt her. Even as they poured from her, she felt them, felt the pain in her body diminish into nothing because it *was* nothing.

The spanking? Yeah, it hurt. But the pain inside? Deep, deep inside where nothing could get to it, where it could fester away and cause her untold agony? It was like this was the only way for anything to touch it. Only through *this*, could she get access to this one particular spot.

And it was a nasty spot.

All the negatives in her life, all the fear and confusion, the concern and anger, it gathered there. Like a goddamn boil in need of lancing. And each fucking spank was like a direct hit to the very core of her emotions.

He began to rub her butt, almost like he knew how she was feeling. But how could he? How could he understand what she was going through?

Her brow puckered as she inhaled some ragged breaths, tried to get her breathing back into some semblance of order before he began again—she knew him well enough to know that when he rubbed her butt, they were only halfway through whatever he intended on doing to her.

But her thoughts swirled. Sean said he felt out of control, was this how he regained it?

With each spank that sent her emotions careening, did he somehow feel fortified?

Did elation soar through him as she experienced something that allowed her to *feel*?

Wasn't that, in its own way, how he *felt* too?

Her brain was a big puddle of goo, and she wasn't in the right frame of mind to even be thinking about shit this heavy, but it was something she'd be pondering later on.

She'd never thought of him dominating her in this way. She'd only thought it was something he got off on, but had never thought about the hows and whys.

Even as she realized Sean was right, that Andrei and Sawyer enjoyed the kink but didn't *need* it, she saw the difference because *he* needed it. He needed this. He needed her to be free.

It was a revelation, and it made her feel so open, so raw, but equally, so needed.

He needed her, and that wasn't something she'd realized until now.

She jolted when another spank came, and a sharp yelp escaped her in turn. The door burst open then, though, and she scampered upright, her hands clinging to his calves as she stared at the opening to see who it was—when Sean made no move to cover her, she knew it wasn't a stranger but one of her men. And she was thankful for that insight because her eyes were blurry from tears and she couldn't seem to focus.

"Enough!"

Devon?

She blinked then reached up to rub her eyes. "Devon?" she questioned, blinking again as he slammed the door behind him and stormed into the room.

He rarely got mad. Hell, he never went above *agitated*, but here? He was mad. His hands formed into fists, and those fists were shaking as he came to a halt before Sean. She wasn't sure what he was doing, but a part of her feared he'd punch Sean! Then he crouched down and his hands came to cup her cheeks.

"Sascha? Why? Why are you letting him do this to you? Why are you letting him hurt you?" he asked, and there was such mournful worry in his voice that it hurt her.

Hurt.

Her.

She sucked in a shaky breath, then jerked a little when she felt Sean's hand on her thigh—stroking her. The move was gentle, caressing. He wasn't priming her, wasn't urging her one way or the other to say something in particular. If anything, it was just a gentle touch, a connection, a reminder that she was his and he was hers.

Just as Devon was.

"Devon, I need this," she whispered. When he flinched, she

reached for him but he staggered back. To Sean, she stated, "Help me up."

Within seconds, she was on her knees on the ground, and Sean was helping her stand. He didn't move from the armchair though, didn't say anything either. She shot him a look and likened him to a pasha watching his courtiers fight—neither amused or entertained, just watchful. Wary.

Devon was storming back to the door by now, but she grabbed him in time. It was kind of awkward, but that was what she and Devon did best—awkward—and she shoved him into the door and pressed him flush to the wooden panel.

"You're not going anywhere," she growled, and she was suddenly grateful it was Sean behind her, Sean and not Kurt or Sawyer because they'd have been giggling behind her like loons at her standing there, squishing Devon into the door, her ass bright pink, and her body totally out on display.

It was ridiculous, but fuck, it was her circus and she was the ringleader. She needed to own that shit, and own it she would.

"Sascha, I need to get out of here."

There was panic in his voice, a panic that scared her and stabilized her at the same time. That made her feel like shit to admit something like that, but also, it didn't.

Sean needed her, but so did Devon. All her men did, just in different ways, and that was one of the hardest parts of her life and one of the easiest too.

Men didn't want to need anything. Just because she lived in an unusual household with more men than some women had in a lifetime, didn't mean her men were totally different than the rest of the species.

Just because they wanted to share her didn't make them alien in other ways.

They shared because five of them could tag team her. One of them would always have time for her, for Tin, where singly, they just couldn't.

Devon didn't leave his office for days sometimes. If he was her lone partner? It would drive her insane. But with Kurt to tease her and Andrei to tie her up? Hell, it wasn't a problem what Devon did. She could leave him to be free, to let his mind soar, because she had enough on her hands with the others.

That was why it worked, and it worked so well.

She wasn't needy or clingy, but what was the point in being in a relationship if you were never going to see your boyfriend? Well, that was a question that never reared its head for her because she had five of them to love.

But her men?

Though their situation was useful for them, it didn't mean they'd suddenly grown ovaries and were in touch with their feelings. Of them all, Devon was the most open with his words and the most contained with his emotions.

To him, they were a whole other planet he had no intention of visiting, and that was saying something considering how repressed Sean was.

Jesus.

She pushed her forehead between his shoulder blades, rubbing back and forth as she tried to get her words together, tried to make him understand in a way that only he could.

Blowing out a breath, she whispered, "You know when you don't understand something, Devon?" He stiffened, so she knew he got her point. "When everything feels like it's tumbling down around you, when you want to scream as you see everything fall into madness. You want to shore it back up, want to rebuild everything, but you're only one person, and you can only do so much."

These were his words.

Verbatim.

One time he'd told her what made him break down.

For a man who understood so much, who was capable of so much, *not* understanding was his true chaos.

"This? It's my way of rebuilding," she ended softly.

"Why?" he rasped.

"Why do you shut down? Why do you freak out? It's a coping mechanism, but more than that, it feels good," she admitted.

"How can it? He's hitting you! I heard you. I. Heard. You!" he roared, and suddenly, he was no longer facing the door, but he was facing her. His hands were on her arms, holding her firmly but not tight enough to hurt. His beautiful face was red, bright red, a vein pulsing in his temple as he stared down at her, and she knew he wanted to shake her. Wanted to shake some sense into her.

"I want him to do this to me. It frees me, Devon. I need that," she murmured, staring deep into his eyes and wishing she could fall into them, fall into him, but that was the last thing he truly wanted from her. More than anything? He needed her to explain.

"How can you need it? You sounded just like *her*."

"I'm not your mother, Devon," Sascha whispered. "Sean isn't your dad. We've talked about this."

His teeth clenched and his jaw gritted down so hard that she knew he'd give himself a migraine if he didn't watch out.

"You sounded just like her," he repeated, but this time, his words were dull, pained, and fuck, she hated that.

For the first time in her relationship, she asked herself what she was doing.

This was breaking him.

Breaking. Him.

She saw that as clear as day. Her pain, the way Sean, Andrei, and Sawyer were treating her, it tormented him. But Sean needed this. And so did she.

She juggled five men with an ease that astonished her, mostly because they allowed it. They weren't all in her face every day, and they weren't making demands on her body, her time, every damn day. That was because they were busy, and they had their own shit to do as did she.

Their relationship had worked for so long until she'd introduced something that could damage it. That could damage Devon.

For a second, panic filled her, and she truly knew how Devon felt when he believed his world was caving in, because hers was.

Everything they'd built together, she was smashing to pieces. And Sean was helping her do that too, with *his* needs. But they were just as vital in the mix as Devon's.

She took a shaky step back from Devon, and the move had him whispering, "Sascha?"

Licking her lips, she retreated a few more steps, knowing the bed was close. When it hit the back of her legs, she released a shuddery breath and sank to the floor. Curving her arms around her knees, she huddled into herself and tried to process everything that was happening.

It felt too big.

Too much.

On top of everything with Horowich, Jane, and now this?

Existential crises were something she didn't need to be dealing with at the moment, and yet, the warring needs of two of her men tugged and pulled at her in a way that left her lost.

Adrift.

In a way she hadn't been since her men had come into her world.

# THIRTY

FROM WHERE HE WAS SITTING, Sean saw the scene for what it was.

A battlefield.

He hadn't anticipated this, just as he hadn't anticipated a lot these past few weeks. Fuck, this past year, he admitted to himself.

Life had a habit of doing that to you. Just as he'd believed he was at the top of his game, life had thrown him a curveball and suddenly, his pregnant wife had lost their baby, an accident became manslaughter, and then... Jane. There were no words to sum up the level of insanity she brought to their world with her doings.

But seeing Sascha fight for something she needed when those desires of hers hurt Devon?

There was no lying about this—Sean didn't know what she'd do.

She had a habit of letting Devon get his own way. None of them minded. They were just as bad. Devon needed things they didn't. Everything in its proper place, and only he could decide what was proper and what was a 'place.'

He wasn't like Andrei who was neat as a pin and liked things in order.

Devon preferred papers everywhere, dust on his desk, and utter bedlam in his office, so much so that Sean wasn't sure how Sawyer coped with all the mess. But that's what Sawyer did—*cope*. And that was what they all did.

They bent so Devon wouldn't break, and that was fine. That was their role in this world. To shield him, to protect that great mind of his because to be close to Devon was to realize how precious he was.

There were some men in this world that created for the sake of creating. Not the need for money or power. They wanted nothing other than to be free to go where their heart and their mind desired.

That was Devon.

He was an Einstein of his generation, a Tesla. The magic he made with his mind was for the good of the world, and the money that came with it? That was where Andrei came in. Devon had enough so that he would always be secure—Tesla had died in poverty, and they'd all made sure that would never happen to their brother. Come what may, Devon would always be protected.

He'd have food in his belly, a roof over his head, and there would always be someone to care for him.

That was what they'd all determined back when he was in his twenties and they hadn't been sure if—

Sean broke off from that train of thought when Sascha staggered back from Devon, not stopping until she was crouched on the ground, hugging herself.

Anger whirled inside him, but he tamped it down enough to say, "Devon, are you happy now?"

Devon's head whipped around to him. "Am I happy?"

"When you came in, Sascha was crying, and yes, her butt was hurting, but did you see her look like that?" Sean pointed at their woman. "Was she defeated? Was she beaten down? Was she caving in on herself as she was torn between right and wrong—right and wrong for her?"

Devon's mouth worked, and he shot a look at their woman, their *suffering* woman. His study wasn't something Sean would ever understand. Devon's mind worked like no other, so while Sean could see just how torn Sascha was, he didn't know if Devon could.

"Your mother was defeated. She was beaten down. She was caving in on herself because deciding to leave your father was more than she was capable of," Sean stated, hitting each word home with a hammer, and seeing each hit stagger Devon in a way that Sean hoped would make him see sense.

"I-I did that," Devon rasped, his hands shaking as he reached up and grabbed a hold of his head, his fingers tugging at his hair.

Sean reared up and stormed toward his brother. Before Devon could make another move, Sean slid his arms around Devon's waist, and hauled him against him in the tightest hug he could give him. He squeezed Devon, held him fiercely and didn't let up until Devon stopped shaking, until his hands dropped, until he was hugging Sean back.

They were both trembling, and Sean wasn't ashamed of that. He could feel wetness on his shoulder and knew Dev was crying—fucking crying. Shit, it about tore at Sean's insides to know that he'd made him cry, but Devon had to open his eyes, and Sean needed to make sure that when he did, Dev wasn't looking out at the world through the eyes of a child born in an abusive marriage.

Devon pressed his face to Sean's shoulder and whispered, "I hurt her."

"Yes. You did," he replied softly. "So did I. But her reactions to the way we did it are what differ."

"How can she like it, Sean?"

There was an agony in his voice that cut him to shreds. He wasn't talking to Devon at this moment in time, but the kid who'd found his mother bleeding out in the bath. The kid who checked in on Sascha when she was in the tub to make sure their woman was okay...

There were so many things wrong in Devon's past that there was no way to right them, not really, which was what hurt the most.

He sucked in a deep breath and explained, "She likes how it makes her feel. You don't have to understand it, Devon, to accept it.

We're not abusing her. She wants this, wants *me*, us, like this. The second she doesn't, that's when we stop. The onus is with her."

Devon cringed in his arms but after a few seconds, he nodded and began to pull away. When Sean turned to look at Sascha, he saw she was watching them both. Her eyelashes made the points of stars, and her eyes, while red, sparkled and shone with her tears.

"I love you both. So much," she whispered. "Don't make me choose, Devon. Please. Don't."

He stiffened, and Sean shot him a wary look, but when Dev released a sharp breath then headed over to her side, Sean relaxed.

"Can I watch?"

Sascha startled at that, then frowned as he sunk down beside her. She tilted her head to the side and asked, "What?"

Dev huffed. "Thought it was self-explanatory. Can I watch him do that to you?"

"Change the vocab, Dev," Sean grumbled.

The other man thought about his words for a second, then dipped his chin. "Can I see you get excited about what happens when you're both in this headspace?" He licked his lips. "Maybe if I see your pleasure, then I won't worry about your pain?"

Sascha sobbed and hurled herself into Devon's arms, and Sean? He just released a relieved breath and knew, even though the evening hadn't started off this way, that they'd turned so many corners tonight that they were headed in a completely different direction than where they'd started.

So long as the destination was brighter than it had been of late, Sean didn't care where it took them, only that it was away from the shadows of the recent past.

---

"MAYBE TOMORROW, DEVON," Sean rasped. "It's been a very long day."

Sascha scrubbed at the tear tracks on her cheeks and shook her head. "No." Then, louder, more strident, she stated, "No, Sean."

She peered up at him from within the confines of Devon's loving embrace and saw him frown at her then at Dev. He reached up and rubbed at his eyes, looking so gorgeous as he did so that she could have bitten him. Yep, *bitten* him.

Jesus.

In a pair of pajama pants, no man should look *this* good, and yet here he was. In the flesh. She knew he worked out, knew he and Sawyer went to the gym together and often drooled when the pair of them came back all wet after a shower. But staring at him, seeing him like this? She truly appreciated his efforts.

"I wasn't even going to do that much tonight," Sean admitted, breaking into her lustful thoughts. "It's been a hell of a day."

She gnawed on her bottom lip then nudged Devon in the side. He shot her a look. "What?"

Wriggling in place and feeling like Tin when he was working up the courage to ask for candy, she nudged him again.

"Sascha, what?" he demanded this time, grabbing her hand and lengthening her arm to avoid being nudged. "I'm getting the hint, Sascha, I just don't know what the hint is."

Sean snorted. "Devon, you're so blind sometimes."

Sascha cleared her throat. "Well, I mean... we've never. You know."

"No. I don't." He frowned. "Never what?"

"You, Sean, and me."

His eyes widened. "Well, no. Sean doesn't do that."

"Why doesn't Sean do that?" Sascha asked Devon, and the question was aimed at Sean, but it was easier to ask Dev.

"Because Sean's a possessive arsehole who doesn't like sharing," was the man's retort.

Devon snickered, shooting Sean a look. "Don't know what you're missing out on. She has the best arse in the world."

Her cheeks were pink as she primly said, "Well, I think I should have heard that compliment first."

He winked at her. "You know I love your butt."

"Well, yes," she said with a sniff, "but..."

"No buts, unless it's *the* butt," he quipped with a quick grin. Then he cut Sean a look. "I'm game."

"When aren't you?" Sean huffed. "Dammit, this conversation has derailed." He rubbed his chin. "Sascha, are you sure—"

"Of course." And she was. Her blood was on fire at the thought of being shared by Sean and Devon.

Sean only ever let Kurt get involved in the bedroom. Mostly because Kurt liked watching and Sean liked being watched—he'd probably never admit to that though. They didn't cross swords, and there were never any sloppy seconds, a prospect that had her almost drooling.

God, she was turning herself on here without even trying.

Sean closed his eyes, blew out a breath, then stated, "Stand up."

On shaky legs, she did as she was told, using Devon as a prop. He helped her up too until she was toddling over to her man, a man that looked, without a doubt, conflicted, but his eyes burned with a fire she understood — a fire she liked to feel flicker against her skin.

Gulping, she came to a halt in front of him. Her body bare for his gaze, his delight.

"Bend over and touch your toes."

Her cheeks flushed with embarrassment, but he reached up and tapped her cheek. "Don't question, just do," he rasped.

Her insides flip-flopped around at his stern tone, at his lack of give, and though something inside her rebelled at his sternness, something more powerful urged her to relent. To concede to this strong man who knew her better than she knew herself sometimes.

She turned around, faced Devon, and saw he was studying her like she was a mathematical equation he'd yet to solve.

Her cheeks were pink but she folded over so that her eyes were on her shins, her hands draping gracefully over her feet.

A shudder wracked her as his hands dug into her hips, and he said, "Devon, she doesn't always want to obey, but she usually does."

"Why?" Dev asked.

"Come here," Sean invited, and she heard Dev shuffle around as he got to his feet and moved to their side.

That both of them were staring at her like this, all her flaws on display, her ass as wide as it was going to get, her thighs thick and round under their perusal, her belly squidgy and not as taut as it should be, made her both hot and cold. Cold because she was embarrassed even though she knew they loved her, warts and all—thank God she really didn't have any warts though, because that might have been the final straw for her ego at that moment—but hot too, because they were studying her. Clinically.

Sean was explaining. Instructing Devon, and that had her blood racing, surging through her veins so fast it was a wonder she didn't feel faint from high blood pressure.

Devon thrust two fingers into her pussy, making her jerk and tumble forward. Only Sean's hands on her hips kept her upright, in place, and she shuddered as Devon noted, "She's sopping."

Sean hummed. "Always."

Devon finger-fucked her as they talked, like she wasn't even there, like he didn't even realize he was doing it. "But why? She didn't want to obey you."

"No, but she knew I'd make it worth her while, and she also knew if she didn't, I'd make her regret it."

Those words had Devon stilling, just as her body was starting to creep up toward a small peak.

"That doesn't sound good, Sean," he responded. "Regret it? How?"

Sean hummed. "Take your fingers out."

A mewl escaped her now that she was empty.

"She wants your fingers, Devon. But why give them to her if she doesn't behave?"

There was the sound of a tongue clucking, like suddenly everything that was confusing in the entire universe made sense.

"I do that too," Devon admitted, and there was a note of caution in his voice that surprised her. Well, sort of. He *did* do that. He did deny her until she did as he wanted in the sack, and Sascha wondered if that was as much of a revelation for him as it was to her.

He'd been controlling her orgasms for years, but they'd never put a label on it.

Sean, inadvertently, had.

She purred when Dev's fingers returned to her cunt, but this time, he reached down and rubbed her clit.

Sean sighed, but his fingers gripped her hips tighter as he moved into her so that she felt his cock rub her ass, the soft cotton pajama bottoms slid against her sensitized skin in a way that had her clenching her jaw.

"Why do you tie her up?"

"Because I like it," Sean admitted. "I like seeing her that way, spread out for my pleasure. Sawyer and Andrei are the same. You know how she is — always moving. Sometimes it's nice to make her still. It makes her pussy like a vise when she comes because she isn't used to it, she's used to freedom."

Devon sighed. "You can't tell me this is all for her, Sean."

"No. Maybe not. I'm not that ambivalent or generous," Sean joked, but his voice had deepened. "I like seeing rope against her creamy flesh, and I like spanking her. I love watching her butt jiggle and grow pink under my palm, and that's for me. It's my own personal porn. But knowing that she gets off on it? *That's* what detonates me every time.

"She wants this, Devon. Feel how wet she is. She isn't running screaming for the hills, is she?"

"No," Devon agreed reluctantly.

"Sascha?"

She wasn't pissed that they were talking about her and around her rather than, up until to now, to her, but their conversation was, she'd admit, making her even wetter.

Sean's own personal porn?

Dammit, wasn't that the most empowering thing she'd heard all year?

"Yes," she whispered, then jerked when his hand came down on her ass. "Yes, sir?"

He hummed even as he rubbed where he'd just hit. "Did you eat today?"

She released a thankful sigh at the question because she had a *good* answer for him today. "I did."

"All three meals?"

"Yes. And a snack." And didn't her jeans fucking know it. But the kitchens here were heaven. Seriously. What they made would have Michelin-star chefs weeping in dismay.

Sean's delight was evident as he praised, "Well done, darling," and like that, he was crouching down on his knees and before she knew it, her clit was literally in his mouth.

It happened in a flash.

From nothing to every-fucking-thing.

He'd pulled her lips apart, spread them wide and even as Devon's fingers were close to touching his head—she could see through the space between her legs—his mouth attacked.

She immediately rocked onto her tiptoes and the move destabilized her, but she didn't care. A forearm shot out and tunneled between her belly and thighs to hold her still, to keep her in place. Devon.

There was no moving, no avoiding Sean's attack. He slurped at her clit like he was a kid intent on decimating his ever-lasting gobstopper, and God help her, she wanted to be decimated.

It should have been embarrassing how fast she came, but with Sean sucking on her clit like there was no tomorrow and Devon's fingers thrusting into her, dragging down against that sensitive patch deep inside her cunt where her G-spot lay?

Hell no, there was no avoiding this.

She exploded. Burst into a million pieces, only for those pieces to be reformed, forged anew into a Sascha-shaped blob. Her cries were both agonized and delighted because the two of them didn't stop, made no move to leave her alone to come down.

They carried on.

Dragging her higher and higher, taking her to the next level, a level that only existed when Sean, Andrei, or Sawyer were doing something deliciously wicked to her.

Her second orgasm had her knees crumbling and she knew that was the only reason they stopped. When Sean helped prop her upright, he ceased slurping her juices down like they were a shot of tequila—and she knew that was a gross visual, but holy fuck, in the flesh? There was nothing hotter—and he got to his feet. Devon's fingers made a retreat too and when Sean helped her straighten, he nipped at her ass on his way up.

Her face was so beyond red that it might as well have been steaming. She groaned as she was hauled back against a strong, lean form, and moaned harder when Devon's hands came up to cup her tits—she'd recognize those fingers anywhere.

How he earned calluses when he pushed nothing more than paper, she'd never know, but Lord help her, she'd thank God every day for them.

He tweaked her nipples, pulling at them, tugging until the muscles of her belly rolled and she arched up on tiptoe.

"Pinch down, Devon," Sean instructed, and he obeyed, and somehow that made it all the hotter.

This was the sexiest class she'd ever been in.

Bar none.

A squeak escaped her and she shuddered as she stumbled back into Devon's strength when he pinched down. Hard.

Fuck, that stung.

"W-Why?" she whimpered.

"Did I say you could come?"

Sean's tone was cool, and it lashed at her like a whip. Her breath stuttered and she realized she'd walked into his trap.

Two orgasms.

Both not permitted.

Fuck.

She gulped, her eyes reaching his, but he was stepping away, heading for one of the many closets in his room.

Devon nuzzled his nose into her jaw and he whispered, "Sascha?"

A whimper escaped her. "Y-Yes, love?"

"You have the best pussy in the world."

She couldn't withhold the snort. "Thank you, honey."

"Seriously," he told her. "It's all wet and juicy—"

*Weren't all pussies?* Sascha found herself asking inwardly. At least, with the right men?

When he groaned, his own words turning him on, her eyes about rolled back in her head because sweet fuck, what this man could do to her.

She wasn't entirely sure why all five of her guys found her so hot. She didn't have confidence issues, but she wasn't a skinny minny no matter how hard they warbled on at her about losing weight, and her ass wasn't tight and firm, her tits were kinda saggy and, shit, not one bit of her was perfect, but the way they acted? It was like they had a Sports Illustrated model in their bed.

Not that was she was complaining, of course.

But still, it made her wish she could see herself through their eyes, because sheesh, she really must be banging the way they went on about her body.

Dev grabbed a deeper hold on her tits and murmured, "I never want to hurt you, Sascha."

"This is a different hurt," she assured him. "You like fucking me, Dev?"

He stilled. "Is this a trick question?"

She snickered. "Nope. Do you like fucking me?" Her attention split between him and Sean when she heard a zipper being opened.

Distracted, she forced herself to focus when Dev murmured, "Of course I do."

"And when you're really frustrated, and you pound into me?"

He grunted, and his fingers tightened around her flesh. "Yeah. Hard and fast, baby."

Her already-wet pussy got a little bit wetter. "Do you think that doesn't hurt after?"

Devon stilled behind her again. "That's different."

"Is it?" She rolled her head on his shoulder so she could look at him. "I'm not complaining. It's a good hurt, especially as many times as you make me come, but I'm still sore the next day."

He was frowning, and she didn't want him to, but these things were food for thought where he was concerned.

Devon was so certain she was being abused when she wasn't, and he only believed that in the first place because of his past. But this wasn't his past. It was his present, and his future, and he needed to accept that sometimes, and not every time, she liked a bit of pain with her pleasure.

It was like adding salt to a dessert—it made it all the sweeter.

Of course, they had to be her famous last words. Sean returned with something that looked like it belonged in someone from the Spanish Inquisition's arsenal.

"What's that?" Devon asked, and she was grateful because it saved her from having to.

"A Wartenburg wheel." Sean pursed his lips. "Safe word time, Sascha."

She stiffened. "Really?"

He shrugged. "It can hurt. Just say 'red' if you want me to stop."

Biting her bottom lip, she nodded and watched on as he spun the small device on his fingertip. It was a small tool. About eight inches in length, more handle than anything, but a wheel hung suspended between two points at the tip, and the wheel was covered in spikes.

"Hold out her tits, Dev," came the next instruction and Devon complied.

Sean began to drag the spikes along her skin. "It can tickle if we move it gently. Or it can bite if we dig deep." He gave her examples of each. "Then it can scratch if I want it to."

She absorbed each different sensation, and found it distinctly odd. It wasn't nice or nasty. Neither pleasant nor unpleasant. But against her sensitive skin, it made her feel on edge. Antsy.

Sean began to run the wheel over her tits, back and forth, digging a little harder down on her nipple, which made her yelp before he instantly retreated and dove around the dips and troughs of her flesh.

"Part your legs, Sascha," he ordered, and imagining this odd sensation on her pussy had her tensing but complying. He didn't immediately go south though. Instead, he rolled the wheel along her waist, down over to her thigh and to the side of her butt where she could still feel the remnants of her spanking.

Then, it was there.

Moving over her folds, sending electrical sparks along her nerve endings. Again, there was no pain, but no pleasure either, and again, it made her feel antsy.

She started to pant.

And she didn't even know why!

"Wider apart," Sean instructed.

This time, she felt him tap the wheel against her clit and the cold metal had her biting her bottom lip. The spiky wheel, while not sharp enough to draw blood, sent more electrical impulses shooting through her system as they tapped her clit hood.

For whatever reason, that made her wonder what it would feel like to get her clit pierced, and in the back of her mind, she thought about that.

Thought about looking it up on Google in the morning.

A shaky sigh escaped her when Sean, in a smooth move, rolled to his feet, adjusting his hold on the wheel as he slid it over her body.

To Devon, he murmured, "Take her to the bed, Dev. On your belly, Sascha."

She shivered, wondering what he was up to now. It was odd to think that she trusted him implicitly while not trusting what his next move would be. The former spoke of how safe she felt, with the latter describing how on edge she was.

Positioned on her belly, she wasn't surprised when she felt a cock hit the seam of her ass. She closed her eyes when it tunneled between her lips and slipped into her.

The sensation of fullness was a delight, and that was when it started.

The wheel.

On her back.

Down her spine.

On the fleshy parts and the bony, the claws digging deep here and there, scratching as well as tickling. Never the same thing in the same place. Always changing, always something different so her nerves couldn't settle.

Her body shuddered. One big shudder. She felt so unsexy, unsure that she looked as though she was jerking and jiggling like a fly had landed on her back and she was trying to get it off, but the slow slide of the cock inside her, the relentlessly slow thrust had her on edge in a way that didn't compute.

"What are you doing to her?" Devon rasped, his voice deep, confused, but also turned on.

"Messing with her senses," Sean murmured, sounding so in control that she wanted to scream.

Her hands gripped the bedding, fisting it tightly as she tugged the sheets from the bottom of the bed. A scream escaped her as he dug the claws in deep on her sore ass cheeks and tears finally began to prick her eyes as her hips jerked, the pleasure of his cock and the discomfort from the wheel, making her feel beyond discordant.

The men talked but she wasn't listening, instead, she focused on her sore ass, the reddened and sensitive skin that was being tormented by such a small device. What didn't hurt that much on regular flesh was three times as uncomfortable on a sore butt, and of her own accord, her hips began to dance, her legs swaying as she tried to evade the relentless wheel.

And what made it worse?

Sean wasn't even concentrating on fucking her.

He might as well have shoved a dildo in her cunt for the amount of attention he was giving her.

Frustration surged inside her and with it, more tears. She. Needed. More. They weren't going to give it to her though.

She'd come twice.

Without permission.

Her heart began to race as she thought about enduring more of this, continuing and suffering until she thought she'd go insane. Her lungs began to burn, her body began to shake, and almost as though that was what he'd been waiting for, the wheel was discarded and she was drawn up off the bed. Her back collided with his front, and then Sean's hand was on her throat.

"Breathe," he told her, like she needed the *obvious* instruction.

Or maybe she did.

"In," he soothed, inhaling deeply. "Out," he continued, exhaling slowly. Repeating it over and over until her heart wasn't stuttering in her chest anymore, and that was when he moved.

His hand cupped her throat tightly, the other moved down to hold her between her legs, and then he finally fucked her.

Hard.

*Fast.*

The thrusts were shallow from their position, and yet his cock dragged against the front of her pussy in a way that had her eyes widening in both distress and delight.

When they did, she saw that Devon was watching with interest. He wasn't even holding his cock in his fist, even if she could see his erection. He was watching as though he were in class, his stance and his interest so clinical that it was almost a slap in the face and yet, it made things a thousand times hotter.

"Don't come," Sean growled in her ear, even as she felt her orgasm surging forth.

"No!" she whined with a mewl.

"Yes," Sean ground out, and when he came, each thrust harder and faster than before, she sobbed in distress as her aching pussy begged for release.

He stayed inside her, a hot presence in her starving cunt, and his fingers flexed around her throat as he whispered in her ear, "Who do you belong to?"

"Y-You. Devon." She sucked down a breath, starved for oxygen again. "Sawyer, K-Kurt, Andrei."

"Do you need our cocks?"

Her eyes flared. "O-Of course."

"And our hearts?"

This time, the tears that pricked her eyes began to fall. "More than anything."

"You're ours," he rasped.

"I'm yours," she confirmed on a sob.

Her words had him thrusting his softening cock inside her, then he kissed the side of her cheek and pulled out. She felt his loss keenly, but was overjoyed when he turned her in his arms and slid her into his embrace.

God, that felt good.

His hands were everywhere the wheel had been, but his touch soothed every jarred nerve ending. She shivered and moaned as he touched her, as he caressed her, then he tipped her back onto the bed, climbing beside her in an instant.

He positioned her so that she was between his legs, her body resting over his, his arms around her, his chin on top of her head. He surrounded her, nearly all of her back and sides were touching him, and what he couldn't touch with his front, his hands did.

He stroked her, soothed her, gentled her, and she tumbled deep into sleep. Her last thought was that even when she'd expected to be shared, Sean wouldn't do that. This had been his claiming. Not Devon's, and she knew she wouldn't have changed it for anything.

# THIRTY-ONE

"SASCHA?"

Turning away from the screenplay in her hand, Sascha tilted her head and sought the female voice who'd called her out. Smiling, she murmured, "Perry! I didn't expect to see you."

Perry shrugged. "It's addictive."

"What is?"

"Speaking to someone who knows the score and is living it herself." Perry grinned. "I'm not sure what's going to happen when you go back to England."

Sascha could empathize. On just the few occasions they'd spoken, she'd come to see how remarkably freeing it was to hang out with Perry. She didn't have to watch her words, could mention three of her men in the same sentence without having to qualify the fact that they were just 'friends.' Jesus, that alone made her want this friendship to grow and grow.

"Skype?" Sascha reasoned.

"True. Not the same though."

Sascha's lips curved, and she had to admit that she was glad Perry felt the same way. Sure, their friendship wasn't years in the making, but that didn't mean it couldn't deepen over time. Being with someone who understood the nuances of a complicated relationship like hers might be the reason why they'd initially become friends, but that could morph into more, and Sascha hoped it did.

"I didn't just come to stalk you though. I came because I wondered if you'd like to go to this little coffee shop in Madela... they let me have this private room so there are none of the paps around to hover."

Sascha tilted her head to the side, noticing something for the first time... "How the hell did I only just see that you're a blonde now?"

Perry snickered. "It's a wig, and that script looks like it might be interesting?"

She waved it in the air. "It's Kurt's screenplay. I'm just giving it a final read through before I finalize it for production.'

"He lets you do that?"

"He asked me to." Sascha shrugged. "He hates edits. Hates them with a passion, so he asked me to take over. It's a pleasure really." She tilted her head again. "The wig's so you're incognito?"

Perry's nose wrinkled. "Yeah."

"Why? I mean, if the cafe lets you in privately, why all the hiding?"

"Because I want you to meet George."

Sascha's mouth rounded. "Wouldn't that be wiser for me to meet him here?"

"Maybe but..." She sighed then reached up to pinch the bridge of her nose. "It's either go there or go to the palace."

"Why?"

"Edward thought some of the courtiers were onto us, so he set up this whole charade."

"What kind of charade?" Sascha asked slowly, seeing the discomfort and distaste etched in both Perry's features as well as her eyes.

Perry was hurting. A fact that didn't sit well with Sascha at all.

"Xavier and George usually butt heads over something, but it's always harmless. A few arguments, then they fuck me, and boom, all's well again."

"Okay, so what did Edward set up?"

"He made them have a real blowout argument, and now they're not talking in public."

"But they're good in private?"

Perry dipped her chin. "Of course. It's only for appearances, but it's hard because I come here a lot, for..." She cleared her throat. "You know. And George can't come here for a while. Masonbrook is where I have to be on show all the time, but here? I can relax."

"You're the mistress of the estate, aren't you?" Her brow puckered. "The staff know?"

She licked her lips. "They know. But they've been with the family for years so there's no fear, and Edward would string them up with the NDAs they've all signed, so there's no need to worry."

"So here's home, and you can't be here with all your men because of a stupid fight?"

Perry's lips wobbled, and Sascha jumped up from her seat in front of the fire and moved to the sofa where Perry had perched herself earlier. She curved an arm around her shoulder and said, "Hey, it's okay."

"No, it's not. I'm a real watering pot at the moment." She patted her stomach. "These babies are determined to make me a wimp."

Sascha snorted. "We're entitled to be wusses when we're knocked up." When Perry snickered, Sascha grinned but said, "Look, how about this... you haven't met all my men yet. How about I introduce you? Then we head to Masonbrook—" Yikes, she was about to go into a freakin' palace. "—and I can meet George and we can have tea there?"

Perry gnawed on her bottom lip. "Raincheck on the cafe?"

"Sure."

"I'd like you to meet Cass, as well. She's my head lady-in-waiting, but she's been taking some time off recently. Her mother-in-law is sick and needed some help with social events."

Sascha blinked. "What kind of social events?"

Perry rolled her eyes and patted Sascha's knee. "It's a whole other world, Sascha. They're all on boards or foundations, and they host balls and crap. Cass has had to take over her mother-in-law's events and handle them as her own."

Was it rotten that Sascha would prefer to stick pins in her eyes than handle that kind of crap?

Ugh.

It was mean to just throw money at the situation, but she let Andrei handle her funds and let him do what he deemed best. She had enough on her plate with five guys and a son.

Never mind the journalist from hell on her tail and the serial killer secretary in one of her men's offices.

Grimacing at the thought, she got to her feet and hauled Perry onto hers. "Come on, let's get you introduced... We should have done this before. It was rude of me not to."

"No. It's okay. With guests, they rarely know I'm here anyway. I just come in, do my stuff, then get out again."

"You're hanging around more because of me?"

Perry grinned. "Hell yeah. I told you—you knowing the truth is addictive as hell."

Because she agreed, she just grinned back and began to lead Perry down the hall to the different offices each of her men had staked a claim on.

"Do you actually know what they're doing here?" Perry questioned her curiously, as they moved down the long-ass corridors. This place was *massive*. It was no wonder Perry could slip in and out without anyone knowing, because just heading from one room to another could take a handful of minutes.

"Nope, and I prefer it that way. Devon tells me stuff, but it usually goes over my head."

Perry snorted. "I'm the same way with Edward. Although this is Xavier's pet project. It's unusual though, because George is the one who ordinarily handles finance matters."

"Is that what the staged argument was about?" she asked quietly.

"Yeah." Perry blew out a breath. "I'll be glad when all of this is handled because it sucks. I hate the pretense on a regular day, but this added shit? It drives me crazy."

Sascha nodded, then tapped on Sawyer's office door.

"Aye?"

Perry grabbed her hand. "He's Scottish?"

She smirked at her. "Yup."

"Does he wear a kilt?"

Outright chuckling, Sascha shook her head. "Not that I've ever seen."

"Are you just going to stand there giggling outside my door?" Sawyer grumbled, and when they laughed at one another, she opened the door and headed in, not surprised to see Devon was in here too. He'd been given his own office space, but Devon and Sawyer were like bees around honey. Or flies around shit... the analogy depended on her mood.

In this instance, it was bees and honey because Sawyer had given her some delicious orgasms on that desk a few days ago, and even though, last night, Sean hadn't let Devon touch her that much, she was still pleasantly sated from her sexcapades.

"Sawyer, Devon, I'd like to introduce you to a new friend of mine."

Sawyer blinked at her, then at the woman behind her. Devon frowned and blurted out, "Who is it?"

"Is my disguise that good?" Perry teased, knocking Sascha in the side with a laugh.

"Yeah, it is, but Devon and Sawyer probably wouldn't recognize their Queen either," Sascha joked. "It's Perry, guys. Perry DeSauvier."

Devon blinked. "Where's your crown?"

Sascha rolled her eyes and Sawyer grunted, but Perry just laughed. "I don't wear it every day."

Devon frowned. "Why not?"

"Because it's too heavy."

"Really? That's very inefficient. If you wore your crown then everyone would know who you were without you having to introduce yourself—see, far more efficient."

"She doesn't want everyone to know who she is, Devon," Sascha explained.

"Why not? She's a Queen. That's her job."

"Just like it's your job to be a pain in my butt?"

He shot her a smile that made her pussy melt. "I can definitely be that for you, Sascha."

Sawyer cleared his throat. "Let's keep the conversation PG, Devon." He got to his feet. "It's a pleasure to meet you—"

Perry smiled. "Perry. Call me by my given name. No need for formalities when I'm here."

Sawyer dipped his chin and Devon just stayed where he was, his legs over the armrest of his armchair as he stared at them both. Sascha knew, point blank, that he was thinking of her with a crown on her head as he fucked her in the ass.

Don't ask her how she knew that, but know it she did.

"It's a pleasure to meet you both," Perry said softly. "Sascha's told me a lot about you."

"All of it bad," she confirmed, making Sawyer snort and Devon rub his chin. "I wanted to introduce her before I go out."

"Go out? Where are you going?" Sawyer inquired, scowling at her.

"To Masonbrook," Perry inserted. "It's the royal seat, but it's where I live. With my husband."

Devon hummed. "What about your other husbands? Xavier said he lived here."

Sascha cocked a brow at that. "When did you meet Xavier? You never told me."

"Sascha, I can't tell you everything," Devon retorted with a sigh. "You'd get bored."

Her lips twitched. "I'm sure I would. I don't need to know how many times you used the bathroom, Devon, just, you know, when you meet with a Duke! Shit like that."

That had him frowning at her. "I never talk about the bathroom with you."

"I was making a point."

"I see what you mean when you say he's literal," Perry said with a laugh.

"Beyond literal," Sascha retorted, folding her arms across her chest. "Anyway, I'm going to meet George. I've already met Xavier."

Perry shook her head. "Hardly. You barely met Edward either, but you're here for a while, aren't you? There's plenty of time."

Sascha smiled. "True." Thrilled at the prospect of growing closer to Perry, and doubly thrilled that she could do what she was about to do... Sascha headed over to Devon, dipped down and pressed a kiss to his lips. Then she trailed her mouth along his jaw and whispered in his ear, "I'll buy a tiara."

"And lube?" he asked, his eyes flaring wide with hunger.

"Andrei usually has some."

Devon hummed. "Good. Get some more to be safe though."

She hid her smile, then trod over to Sawyer. His kiss was a little less innocent, and he growled in her ear, "Behave, and don't do anything that necessitates a firing squad. They still do that here."

She remembered. The whole world did. That was how the enemies of Veronia had been punished—death by firing squad.

"I'll be good."

"Sascha, you're many things, but good isn't one of them."

Snickering, she reached for her cell phone when it buzzed. Eying the screen, she cocked a brow and answered, "Kurt? What is it?"

"Sascha, where are you? This house is too damn big. I can't find anyone."

She blinked at the curious note in his voice. "What's wrong? I'm with Sawyer and Devon in their office on the ground floor."

"East wing," Sawyer prompted, brow furrowed at her as she repeated that to Kurt.

"I'm on my way."

"Tell me, Kurt. What's wrong?"

Kurt was the most even-tempered of her men but he sounded rattled, on edge, and that made her nervous.

He cleared his throat. "My father just called."

"Your father?" She knew Rudi never called Kurt. He barely spoke to either of his parents, in fact.

"His father?" Sawyer repeated, eyes wide in surprise.

"Mother died last night," was Kurt's reply. "Heart attack. I... She's being buried in two days' time."

Heart in her throat, she whispered, "Are you okay?"

Kurt grunted. "Of course."

When he cut the call, she winced and stared down at her phone. Sawyer's hand reached out to cup her wrist. "Margritte's passed?"

She nodded, the gesture was jerky. He sighed and said, "Christ."

That about summed it up.

---

THOUGH SEAN SPOKE GERMAN, there was no need to understand the language to recognize the sorrowful words that were spoken as Margritte Keller was laid to rest.

Well, as much rest as she'd ever allow.

On the rare occasions they'd met, Sean knew she was the least restful woman he'd ever encountered, and the least pleasant.

They'd all disliked her. Not just because of her manner, but for the way she'd treated Kurt. Not only had she forced him into a miserable marriage, but she'd practically disowned him when he'd divorced his ex-wife too. All because she'd feared her straight son was gay, since that was the only reason he could possibly want to share a house with men that were like brothers to him...

Rolling his eyes at the thought, he felt Sascha's grip on his hand tighten. She stood between him and Kurt. One hand on Tin's shoulder, the other in his, while Kurt's arm was around her waist. Behind them, Devon, Andrei, and Sawyer stood, silent sentinels at the society-packed funeral.

He wasn't a part of this world, but he knew Margritte had been infamous among this set. The Elizabeth Taylor, almost, of Germany thanks to her past and the family's fame.

Rudi, Kurt's father, was the one who seemed the least affected, and maybe he was. Hell knew what Margritte had been like to live with. Maybe the man didn't have PTSD at all, just selected muteness. With a woman like Margritte at his side, Sean knew *he'd* pretend to be deaf as well.

Thankfully, because it was colder than a witch's tit outside, the service didn't go on too long. They hung around longer than most as Kurt shook hands with people who gave him their condolences and he 'hosted' the event more than his father did, whose gaze alternated between looking at the pit where his wife was now buried and staring out onto the misty graveyard.

It was creepy here, creepy and cold. He couldn't blame Sascha for snuggling into him and Kurt, and he didn't even give a fuck about the ramifications of it either. People could think what they wanted. This was a funeral, and there wasn't a more natural time for anyone to need comfort and succor, so they could go screw themselves.

When they began to wend their way through the cemetery, their destination the front parking lot where their car was waiting on them, they did so in silence. The hem of Sean's trousers were wet from the slick grass, and Sascha and Tin were routinely shivering.

This was Tin's first brush with death, but as far as he could tell, their son wasn't overly affected. More than anything, he was confused. He didn't understand why they were standing outside in the cold, didn't understand why they'd traveled to Germany so suddenly, and didn't understand why he had to be quiet and why he couldn't play.

Truth was, Sean didn't want to explain the truth to him yet.

He was happy for Tin to be in the dark, and considering most discussions of a 'heavy' nature were something the others left to him and Sascha where Tin was concerned, he was relieved that it wasn't on the top of their to-do list, because they could have forced the issue when he didn't want that.

Tin wasn't even three yet. It was too soon to learn about death, especially when it was around a woman who hadn't given a fuck about him and who he didn't even know that well.

Kurt's arm was tight around Sascha's waist as he hauled her into his side before they separated so they could climb into the limo. Rudi being Rudi, aka weird, didn't join them. He'd had the family chauffeur bring him separately, and now they were alone in the back of their limo, Sean was glad for it.

When they were on the return journey to the family mausoleum—i.e. Kurt's childhood home—he blew out a breath and reached up to rub the back of his neck as the relief of being out of the spotlight hit him.

"You doing okay, sweetheart?" Sascha asked Kurt softly.

He shrugged, turned to her and reaching for her chin, tipped her head so he could kiss her. After he'd thoroughly flustered her, a sight that made Sean's lips twitch, he pulled back and murmured, "I am now."

She winced. "You know I didn't mean it like that."

"I do, and I'm okay, Sascha. I promise. My..." He didn't say the word, just cast a look at Tin. "We had a difficult relationship. I just never expected her to be the first to go. Not when Rudi is so fragile."

That was the one word that summed Rudi up. He was like porcelain. That, or bone china. He looked like a good wind could and would knock him over. He coughed pretty much constantly, thanks to some kind of gas the Stasi had exposed him to during his time in one of their torture chambers, and his skin had a strange gray pallor that reminded Sean of a corpse—not the best of looks.

Considering Margritte could be considered hale and hearty for a woman of her advanced years, of the two of them, it was definitely a surprise that Rudi had outlasted his spouse.

And Sean didn't give a fuck about how rotten that sounded. How cold. Margritte made snow look warm and cozy, so she'd approve of his chilly outlook on her nature, he was sure.

Kurt raised an arm and curved it about Sascha's shoulders, then he eyed Tin who'd caved in and had his head buried in Andrei's lap, his daddy's hands stroking his hair softly as he slept. The drive home would take ninety minutes because Margritte just had to be buried at this particular cemetery, and after the long day and the time spent outside, Sean hoped that a nap would prep Tin for the next part of this torment—the wake.

"I rearranged the schedule with the production company," Kurt announced a few moments later after they all watched Tin sleep.

Sean tipped his chin. "Why?"

"Because, now I'm here, I don't intend to stay all that long. Rudi's away with the fairies and he doesn't need me here. Nor does he want me. I'd prefer to get the business out of the way then return to Veronia, that way I can work on my next project without further interruption."

Sascha stilled in his hold, then she turned her head and murmured, "You don't have to like her to grieve her, Kurt."

The other man swallowed at Sascha's soft words, and though Sean half-expected Kurt to shrug her off, Kurt didn't. Instead, he murmured, "I know, Sascha, but I don't have that much to grieve about. She pushed me until I didn't even bother pulling back. I just drifted away. I don't know her, didn't know her at all these past few years, and to be honest, I never anticipated our visit to even go that well." He blew out a breath. "I rented us rooms at the nearest hotel—"

"But we were supposed to stay with your parents!" Sascha argued.

"I know we were," Kurt confirmed, "but that was never going to happen."

"He's right, Sascha," Sean interrupted. "It was a pipe dream hoping that she'd even let us in through the door. When she saw Tin, then the three of us? It never would have worked unless she thought Tin looked like Kurt, which he doesn't."

Andrei cleared his throat. "She was an old bitch, and she doesn't deserve an ounce of Kurt's energy, Sascha."

"Andrei!" Sascha chided. "That's hurtful."

He snorted. "You didn't meet her. If you had, you'd know what hurtful is."

"He's right," Kurt said sadly. "I wish he wasn't, and I wish there was something to defend, but *Liebchen*, there isn't. There's nothing to defend, no memory to protect." He reached up and rubbed a hand over his face. "Maybe this is for the best. It's closure, at least."

Sascha frowned at him but didn't counter his words. Sean did though. "When are you meeting the production team?"

"Two days from now. There's a business meeting, and then, it's quite good timing actually, on Wednesday, there's a party. My publicist didn't bother scheduling me there because she knew I wouldn't go, but now I'm here, there's no reason to avoid it." He tugged at Sascha's waist. "Do you have something to wear?"

"No, but I can find something," she teased. "There are shops in Germany I assume?"

"Smartass," he mocked, but he pressed a kiss to the side of her head.

"Is it wise for me to go? Dreyford was weird last time, and I wanted to bitch slap Jennifer Houghton."

Sean's brows furrowed at that. "They're the main actors in the film, aren't they?"

Sascha's lips curved. "Trust you not to know who they are really."

He rolled his eyes. "You know Hollywood means shit to me."

"Oh, I do, and I'm not making fun." But she was smiling, and he wasn't about to chide her on that. He loved her smile, and he especially loved that it was shining more and more often for them all.

Jane and her presence in their world could have been the straw that broke the camel's back, but it hadn't been. Somehow, they'd come through the bitch's invasion in their life, and their first few forays out of the quagmire of grief that had settled around them seemed to have drawn them closer together.

Eight months ago, Devon and Sawyer would never have attended Margritte's funeral. Andrei probably wouldn't have either. But now? After losing Camilla, after the stress of learning about Horowich's perfidy, the drama of Devon's arrest, and then the cluster fuck with Jane? Yes, they'd come together, morphing into a tighter, closer unit.

Sean couldn't find it in himself to be anything other than thankful about that. When their entire world might have disintegrated to dust, here they were, still together and stronger than ever.

These past six months had been a sharp learning curve for them all. Sean knew he'd made mistakes, done things he was ashamed of, things he'd never be able to forgive himself for, but these men did. His woman did. They accepted that he wasn't perfect, loved him for his imperfections.

The end didn't justify the means, but he was damn content to have his brothers, son, and the love of his life with him today and for the rest of his days. As long as they were at his side, he could learn to accept his flaws, start the journey to self-forgiveness.

Rome wasn't built in a day, but with his family at his back, he had all the time in the world to be a better man. The man they needed him to be.

# THIRTY-TWO

THE DRESS WAS TIGHT. It clung to her every curve and then some. So much so she felt uncomfortable. The zipper felt on the brink of bursting, but it was technically the right size for her, with the fit being just a little too snug.

When had her tits grown? And her ass? Jesus. She'd obviously packed away more food than she'd thought back at the ducal estate in Veronia.

As she stared at the navy body con dress that she'd teamed with a pair of strappy heels, she wondered if it was too much, and then she thought back to the few times she'd seen that bitch Jennifer Houghton this week. The woman made 'barely there' look overdressed, and every time she saw Kurt, she was practically drooling over him.

The time to be amused over this was way in the past, and it wasn't like she could even be jealous about Kurt's reaction. He didn't even notice her, and if he did, he was frowning at her with distaste. He didn't encourage her, didn't lead her on, but Jennifer was determined to get in his face, determined to be *his* leading lady.

Ha.

Sascha thought not.

She dipped her hands into her dress and jiggled her tits, repositioning them in the sweetheart neckline. A groan sounded behind her. "I'll give you a thousand pounds to do that again."

She turned around to grin at Sawyer. "Only a thousand?"

"Two?" he doubled, strolling into the bedroom with an ease that made her pussy melt. He wore a tuxedo, one that was tailored to the long lines of his body, and fuck, he was a dream in the flesh.

The white crispness of his shirt made his red hair seem all the more vibrant and, for once, he'd shaved, so when she reached up to rub his jaw, it was like touching silk.

"You shaved."

He cocked a brow. "I can, I just don't."

"You're telling me. I'm the one with stubble rash everywhere."

His lips cocked up in a smirk. "That a complaint, lass?"

"Only when you rub my pussy raw."

He repeated drolly, "That a complaint, lass?"

She huffed and pushed off him, but he didn't move an inch. Ignoring him, she turned around and stared at her reflection in the mirror. "Too much?" she asked.

"For war?" He shook his head, his eyes narrowed on her. "Nope."

"War?"

He snorted. "I've seen the way you watch that actress. Have a care, lass. Your claws are showing."

She stuck out her tongue at him. "Don't be a spoilsport."

It was his turn to ignore her, and he reached around, held her tits over her dress and jiggled them himself. "You look like fucking sin rolled up in fur," he drawled. "I'm going to fuck you in this dress tonight."

"Promises promises," she whispered breathily.

"And you'll have to get in line," Kurt grated out as he too made an appearance in the room. "This is my night, Sawyer," he grumbled, and the Scot pulled a face at him.

"Hey, I'm always down for taking both of you on," she said with a grin, staring at their faces in the mirror's reflection.

When the two of them growled, she giggled, then she finished gawking at herself and sucked down a deep breath.

The navy fabric clung to her in all the wrong places, but the guys' reaction was positive so she couldn't complain. Her tits looked huge and they were almost spilling out of the neckline, but between her cleavage was a heavy sapphire necklace, which nestled within the curves of her snowy flesh. She had matching earrings and a cuff on her forearm that came from the same set.

It seemed incredible to her that she owned these pieces, and they were hers. Not gifts from her men. The estate she'd inherited from her father—her biological one not her adoptive one—came complete with ancestral jewels that required storage in a safety deposit box.

She didn't often travel with them, but when you went to a kingdom at the invitation of a Duke? With the knowledge that at some point you'd meet with a King and a Queen? When was there a better time to take out ancestral jewelry?

Turning on her heel, she reached for the wrap that Kurt held out for her. It was a heavy silk pashmina that she curved about her form before Sawyer tucked her into a coat that half belonged in a 1940s film. It was pure glamor.

When she was nestled in its folds, she arranged her long curls about her shoulders and said, "I'm good to go."

"You're more than good, and I wish we didn't have to go anywhere," Sawyer grumbled as he planted his hand on her ass.

Amused, turned on, and feeling a little buzzed from their reaction to her dress, she strode out of the room with her head held high. As she did, she saw Devon and Tin waiting for her, and her heart nearly fucking melted at the sight of the pair of them. Andrei slouched out of his room then in a pair of jeans that should be illegal.

Fuck, she wanted them all.

So. Badly.

Pussy and heart melting at her family, she murmured, "Hey, baby."

Tin squinted at her. "Mommy's boobies are mine."

Devon grinned. "Boy after my own heart."

The others snorted, and she just grinned as she bent down and scooped Tin up. His hand clapped against her breasts and she tutted. "Tin, they're not exclusively yours anymore."

Another squint. "Not mine, then whose?"

"Mine," she retorted, amused even more when he huffed and shook his head like she didn't have a clue what she was talking about. He turned around and stared at Devon who just sighed.

"She's not wrong, champ."

"I'm just not right, huh?" she challenged, smirking when he winked at her.

"You are a sight for sore eyes," Andrei rasped, and she could see the fire in his gaze that backed up his words.

His cock was thick and hard against his fly, and she felt her mouth water at the sight.

"Thank you, darling," she told him huskily.

Devon stepped forward, sandwiching Tin between them as he kissed her. It wasn't soft, but it wasn't hard. What it was, was thorough.

She groaned and grumbled when he pulled back. Thankful she hadn't painted her lips yet, knowing kisses were going to happen, she sighed as he grabbed Tin and hugged him to his hip.

If there was ever a sight to make any woman's ovaries quiver, it was that.

"The car's here," Sean called out, and she turned and saw him standing in the doorway, his phone in his hand. When he saw her, he gritted his teeth, his eyes aflame as were Andrei's, then he cut a look at Tin, cleared his throat and stepped back.

Amused and feeling hornier than ever, she cleared her throat and said, "Tin, I'll see you in the morning. Daddies, behave."

Devon and Andrei rolled their eyes. "I think we can manage."

"You two can make or break economies." She winked at Andrei. "God only knows what happens when I'm not here to check up on you."

He snorted, then stepped over to kiss her goodnight. "I want to fuck you."

She cocked a brow at him. "Get in line."

He grunted, slipped her his tongue this time, then pulled back with a growled, "Go on. The sooner you get back, the sooner I can get you out of this dress."

Amused, she bit her bottom lip then strode out of the lounge of their hotel suite and into the hall. Sean was waiting there for her in his tux and camel-colored overcoat. He looked divine, like James Bond or something, and being surrounded by three hunks in tuxes definitely put her in a good mood.

The drive to the event happened mostly in silence. She knew why. They were all putting their game faces on. This was a party for the Press, and Kurt was now the guest of honor alongside Dreyford and the director, David Masterson. They were attending as his support system but intended to mostly stay in the background. Well, Sawyer and Sean did.

Considering they hated these kinds of parties, it was only natural that they needed these quiet moments to prepare themselves for what was to come.

It didn't help that she'd see that bitch soon, either.

As they pulled up outside the large hotel where the event was being held, she saw there was a red carpet and a line of Press that weren't allowed inside.

Kurt was big news in Germany, and his mother's death was equally as big. They hung back as he strode down the red carpet after a valet opened their door, and when he was done, the driver took off and deposited the three of them at the back entrance where Kurt had made arrangements for them earlier that day.

They didn't want the spotlight, and walking in via that red carpet only invited it.

Sneaking inside was more fun than the party would probably be. She enjoyed the subterfuge of sneaking into the party through the kitchen, with a bunch of hotel security keeping them separate from the kitchen staff.

Entering the event, she passed her coat over, as did her men, to the guards, and then she turned to face the crowd. When she did, she winced, seeing that it was going to be as boring as she feared. The lights were dim and candles glowed, but that was about as intimate as it got. The cavernous space contained over five hundred people. Gilt-edged moldings ran around the perimeter of the ceiling, with antique paneling decorating each wall and beautiful parquetry that was being destroyed by the female guests' high heels. The hall was blood red in color which made the shadows gloomier, and when she caught sight of Kurt and saw Jennifer-fucking-Houghton on his arm, she saw red, the same color as the damn walls, as anger overwhelmed her until she forced herself to calm down.

She wasn't sure why she kept getting so jealous recently. First with Jane and then with this bitch? It wasn't like her, but she figured it was to do with her emotions being all over the place, her hormones too. Plus, there was the vague insecurity of knowing that to the public, her men weren't taken and were very much available on the 'market.'

Still, there was nothing to be done. Nothing she *could* do about that, so there was very little point in fretting. What she did instead was grab a champagne flute the second a waiter passed her and chugged it down.

The bubbles made her want to sneeze, and Sawyer's chuckle had a similar effect on her eardrums—except she wanted to slap him rather than sneeze. "He doesn't even like her."

"Like who?" she countered, making Sean snort.

"You're far too transparent for all that," he chided, making her narrow her eyes at him in warning.

He just cocked a brow at her, a warning in and of itself that reminded her if she snarked at him too much, she'd end up over his knee, but fuck if that didn't seem like a nice place to be right this second.

Grunting, she reached for another flute but she took her time with that, and murmured, "I'm hungry."

Sawyer chuckled. "Our rules worked, at least." He rubbed her stomach. "Your appetite seems to have returned."

She narrowed her eyes at him. "Is that a complaint?" she demanded, throwing his earlier words back at him.

He growled and dropped his mouth to her ear. After he sucked on the lobe, sending shivers down her spine, he grated out, "It's the exact opposite. I like to have something to hold on to when I'm fucking you, lass. Don't rob a man of his curves."

She rolled her lips inward to hide her smile and decided then and there to stop being a stuck-up bitch. It wasn't Sean and Sawyer's fault that she was over here in this corner. They were too. Kurt wanted them there for support, and that was what they'd do. What they'd be.

He'd had it rough these past few days. His mother had died, and even if he insisted that he wasn't upset, she knew he had to be feeling *something*. Whether it was regret for how their relationship should have been, or anger for how little they'd known each other, she didn't believe he was simply 'okay.'

Relieved when a waitress appeared with a tray of canapés that wouldn't fill a canary, she sighed and picked up three, ignoring the surprised look on the woman's face at her 'greed,' she watched as Sawyer and Sean took some too, only they didn't eat theirs. They handed her them after she'd finished her own.

Beaming at them in thanks, they grinned back at her and returned to their champagne. After a while of staring out into the crowd, she grew bored enough to ask, "Should we dance?"

Sawyer grabbed her hand and murmured, "Thought you'd never ask."

Surprised he was the one to grab her, having expected Sean would want a turn first, she tumbled into his arms.

"Thought you hated dancing."

"I do, but it's the only way I can have my cock against your belly so I'll take it."

She snickered and murmured, "Do I look so different tonight?"

"You look hot as fuck," he told her, then he reached up and cupped her chin. "But it's your eyes that are different."

She frowned. "What do you mean?"

"You're coming back to us, love," he answered softly, staring down into her gaze with a tenderness that made her mush.

Sascha wanted to lie but couldn't. She couldn't say that she didn't have a damn clue what he was talking about, because she did. Even though they'd always had her back, she'd been feeling lost until recently. Now? They'd found her, or she'd found them. She wasn't sure which and she wasn't about to argue.

Releasing a sigh, she pressed her face into him and let him use this slow dance as an excuse to rub his cock against her belly. The move made her wet, but that was her usual state of being around her men.

With a grunt, his hand slipped down to her ass and he drew her closer into his embrace.

"Sawyer," she warned. "Not in public."

He ignored her, of course, and she didn't mind because the place was teeming. No one could see. Not really.

The evening carried on in that vein.

First Sawyer, then Sean. The two of them danced her until her feet started to hurt, but being in their arms, standing so close to them? God, it felt good.

It was both innocent and enticing, and the mixture of the two stirred her blood something fierce.

The night wore on and the atmosphere changed with it as people grew drunk. A DJ appeared and the beat changed, the room darkened and she preferred the shadows because it meant when Sean and Sawyer held her close, they could get a little more creative with their hold on her.

Her dress was fastened with a large zipper that ran down the central seam of her dress. Sean, on the premise of leaning down to fasten his shoe, reached for the zipper and dragged it up so that when he hauled her into his arms next, she could spread her legs with a little more ease.

He pushed his knee between hers and she moaned, hiding her face, as her pussy rubbed against his inner thigh.

She felt hot and needy, wanting them both, yet loving how public this was and yet how safe too.

As Sean spun her out of his arms, it was then that she saw Kurt. With Jennifer Houghton. Again.

The way the two of her men had ramped her up, it wasn't a surprise that her mood dropped from the soaring heights they'd taken her to when she saw her lover and that bitch dancing.

Kurt stood stiffly. His shoulders ramrod straight and his face—well, it didn't look aroused, just pained. If anyone knew the difference, it was Sascha. But it was Jennifer that pissed her off. She had her hands on Kurt's ass. Underneath his tux jacket.

It was like a red rag to a bull, and even as she stormed over to them, she felt Sawyer collect her in his arms and keep her there, making her dance as he tried to draw her away from Kurt and that bitch.

It worked.

But she fumed.

Keeping her eye on her man, she watched as he danced with three more women until Jennifer threw herself at him again. This time, she'd done something to her dress. The sweetheart neckline looked perilously close to falling down and her tits were on the brink of spilling out. Whether she was drunk or not, Sascha wasn't sure, but she watched as Jennifer reached up and slipped her fingers through Kurt's as she lifted their arms before twirling around in a move that Sascha had pulled on the dance floor herself.

But this time, Jennifer's tits fell out of her dress and she pushed herself into Kurt all on the premise of shielding herself.

She saw Kurt's surprise, wasn't even concerned about him, but the primal urge to make a claim on him, to stamp on *her* territory roared through her veins.

Slipping out of Sean's arms, she stormed over to her lover and dragged Jennifer away from him with her hair.

"Cover yourself," she spat, hissing the words at the woman who yelped as Sascha tightened her fist about Jennifer's hair.

"Who the hell are you?" Jennifer cried, her words too low to be heard over the music, but the way she moved as she covered her tits drew a few eyes their way.

"I'm Kurt's woman," she snarled. "If I see you drooling over him, flaunting yourself at him *again*, I'll make you grateful to get a bit part in a Z-list zombie movie."

"Who the fuck are y—" Jennifer's mouth dropped as a strobe light flashed over them, exposing Sascha's face. Jennifer blanched and Sascha, for the first time in her life, was grateful to be Sascha Dubois, 'The Right Honorable,' billionaire heiress.

If she wanted to, she could destroy this tart's career, and there was nothing more satisfying than Jennifer knowing it.

Jennifer reached down and rearranged her neckline before storming off, her head arched with her nose in the air.

Kurt's hands appeared on her hips and he laughed in her ear. "That shouldn't have been as hot as it was," he mocked.

She stiffened. "You liked her drooling all over you?"

He snorted. "No. I liked you dragging her off by her hair. How very cavewoman of you."

Sascha grumbled, "When she did that with her tits, it was the final straw."

Kurt rubbed his nose along her hairline. "I only want you, Sascha."

That had her huffing. "I know *that*, Kurt."

"Then what's the problem?"

She shrugged. "The rest of the world doesn't know it too."

When he hummed, she rested against him, understanding that he had no words for her, no words that would make this better. They were in the same boat, after all. None of them could claim the other, and in this, they were all stunted. All unable to make any formal declarations, and though Sascha never felt the lack of a wedding ring, she did sometimes. At moments like this in particular.

With a sigh, she pressed her face into Kurt's shoulder and for the first time that evening, danced with him.

It felt good.

Wonderful, in fact.

She sighed, finally able to be calm—even as stupidly irrational as it was.

Kurt danced with her four more times until he murmured in her ear, "I think we can get out of here now."

Nodding, she replied, "Okay."

He guided her toward Sean and Sawyer, then squeezed her hand and retreated with only a glance.

Sawyer curved his arm around her waist as he guided her toward the kitchen like the dirty little secret she was, and they headed out toward the exit where they'd arrived earlier.

Their car waited for them—either the chauffeur had been parked there all evening, or Sean had called him and put him on alert.

The driver stood there with their coats and after they wrapped up in them, they headed into the limo's cab.

She pressed her face into Sawyer's side when he'd curved his arm about her shoulder, and stiffened when he asked, "It's not like you to be jealous."

"Didn't you see her flash him?" she growled.

"Aye, I did, but you know he's not interested."

"It was beyond a joke! Who does that? For God's sake, we were at a press party!"

Sean hummed under his breath. "That's not the underlying issue, though, is it?"

She tensed, then firmed her jaw. "I don't want to talk about this."

"No? Well, tough, because we do," Sean retorted, but before he could, she had a reprieve as the car pulled up at the front of the hotel.

A valet opened the door for Kurt to climb inside, and the minute he was in, they drove off, back to their hotel.

She could feel her men's disapproval and disappointment and it pissed her off all the more.

Why didn't they get it?

If a guy came onto her, right in front of their faces, if he'd shoved his hands down her dress or cupped her ass, they'd have done more than pull the bitch off by her hair. They'd have gotten into a fucking fistfight.

She said as much, snarling, "If any man put his hands on me, I don't think you'd be smiling. Not unless you'd caved in his front teeth. And the only reason they don't is because I don't put myself out there. I don't *let* that happen to me."

"You think I let her do that? Did I look like I was having a good time?" Kurt retorted, for the first time sounding aggravated.

"Did you push her away? No." She reached up and tugged off her earrings and dumped them in her purse, grateful for the lack of the pinch on her earlobe.

"I was just trying to be polite."

"She had her hands on your ass, and she flashed you, Kurt. How polite do you think you need to be in that situation?" She shot him a dark smile. "Maybe I'll go dancing tomorrow and flash my tits at some random guy... that'll help you understand how *I* feel."

Sawyer growled under his breath. "What the hell's going on with you, Sascha?"

"If you can't get it, then you're all fucking stupid. Geniuses, my ass," she snapped. "I get that you're all too big for this world, too smart for the regular shit that goes on, but if you don't get that some slut wanted her hands on *my* man just to fuck her way into a bigger role in his film, then you're seriously too stupid to live.

"And don't you dare try to put this on me as if I'm being jealous. Wasn't I right about Jane? I heard you talking to that detective you work with, Sean. I'll admit to listening to your conversation because I know how it works—you'll only tell me as much as you think I need to know. And what you'd always keep me in the dark about is the fact she initially hung around to figure out what you knew, but stuck with us because she'd fallen for Andrei.

"I'm not blind, nor am I deaf or dumb. You five are some of the hottest men I've ever come across. You're intelligent, *sometimes*, and you're rich. You're all powerful too. You're like the trifecta of what every woman wants, and there are five of you. So every woman out there who knows of you thinks she has five chances to hook a rich motherfucking Adonis, because she doesn't know you're tied to me.

"And guess what, I'm okay with that. I get it. I do. We can't say shit without drawing a whole heap of crap on our heads, but if you could try to understand the situation from my point of view, I'd appreciate it."

Silence fell after the storm of her words, and Sawyer broke it with, "Is that true, Sean? About Jane and Andrei?"

Sean sighed and reached up to pinch the bridge of his nose. "Unfortunately, she's right. I don't appreciate you eavesdropping—"

"Don't even go there," she snapped. "I could give a fuck about your usual conversations, but when I heard you talking about Jane? I listened in."

Sawyer reached for her hand and squeezed her fingers. "What will make you feel better?"

She tensed, her teeth clenching as she heard the conciliatory tone and knew he wanted to help, but the fuck of it all was they could do nothing.

Change nothing.

Gulping down a deep breath, she whispered, "Thank you, Sawyer, but there's nothing *to* do. Not really. Just don't dismiss my feelings as irrational jealousy, okay? I'm not a lunatic. I don't see shit for the fun of it. Jennifer Houghton made a fool out of herself tonight, but I did too because Kurt didn't listen to me the last time we met up. And when we did meet up, Dreyford was coming onto me so hard, but what did I do this evening? I stayed the hell away from him because I knew he'd pull something too.

"Just treat me with consideration, the same as I do you," she said softly, then she pulled away from him and slipped over to the other side of the limo so she could stare out at the roads.

It was an uneasy quiet that settled among them, but she was okay with that. It wasn't how she'd anticipated the evening ending, but neither had she thought she'd see another woman's tits—who even did that? How desperate did Jennifer have to be for her few scenes to be doubled thanks to the casting couch?

She gritted her teeth in agitation, and when they pulled up at their hotel, she didn't wait for them or for the driver to help her out. She climbed out and strode through the reception to the elevator. Ignoring them as she waited for them to climb on board with her, she pulled her hand from Kurt's when he tried to hold hers.

Grateful that the elevator was fast and that it took them directly to their penthouse suite, thanks to the card Sean inserted into the fancy dashboard, she slipped out of her heels and was on the brink of storming over to her room when Andrei called out, "What the hell happened tonight?"

She put the brakes on and turned to him. "What?"

He frowned and held out his phone. Half-expecting to see a picture of her dragging Jennifer Houghton off Kurt's chest, as well as another glimpse of her tits, she froze when she saw the intimate pictures as she scrolled down the feed.

It was tonight's event, sure, but there were images of Sawyer kissing her throat, Sean's hands on her ass, and then Kurt nuzzling into her right at the end.

Fuck.

When she scrolled back to the top to read the captions, she blanched.

*US billionairess dirty dances with no less than three bachelors.*

It could have been innocent. Could have been shrugged off as nothing but a very drunk woman having a *very* good time with three men on the dance floor.

But the article?

Andrei ran a hand through his hair. "Horowich must have had a partner," he stated grimly, and as she stared down at the intimate details of her life that were revealed for the world's consumption, she knew that the pictures were the Pandora's box that would bring chaos to her world.

The article was too thorough for a rush job, indicating that, as Andrei had said, someone, be it Horowich or indeed a partner, had been investigating her for a long time for such a detailed and thorough accounting. But the pictures were the evidence that some sleazeball editor had needed to make her and her love life front-page news.

There were no other words she could utter, nothing else she could say than, "We're screwed."

# THEIRS

And, if you'd like to read more about Perry, Alice's mother, and her men, then be sure to check out the THEIRS collection.
It's available on KU!
**THEIRS**: www.books2read.com/TheirsVeronia

# AFTERWORD

Want more from the Quintessence family?

COMING DECEMBER 12th 2021!

A Christmas Second Gen - Quintessence Story :O

www.books2read.com/QuintessenceTinAndAlice

**How are you feeling?**

Happy?

Sad?

Teary?

Please, talk to me. Let me know what you thought.

Join me in my Diva reader group: www.facebook.com/groups/SerenaAkeroydsDivas

Email me: Serena@serenaakeroyd.com

Or follow me on FB and message me there: www.facebook.com/SerenaAkeroyd

I want to hear from you!

PLEASSSEEE.

Love you all, hope to hear from you, and, if you're feeling in a generous mood, could you leave a review? <3 They mean everything to authors, and they can make or break whether or not someone buys a book. Just a few words, that's all it takes. <3

Thank you for reading this, thank you for loving Quintessence, and thank you for being YOU!

Love

Serena

xoxo

# FREE BOOK!

Don't forget to grab your free e-Book!
Secrets & Lies is now free!

Meg's love life was missing a spark until she discovered her need to be dominated. When her fiancé shared the same kink, she thought all her birthdays had come at once, and then she came to learn their relationship was one big fat lie.

Gabe has loved Meg for years, watching her from afar, and always wishing he'd been the one to date her first and not his brother. When he has the chance to have Meg in his bed—even better, tied to it—it's an opportunity he can't refuse.

*With disastrous consequences.*

Can Gabe make Meg realize she's the one woman he's always wanted? But once secrets and lies have wormed their way into a relationship, is it impossible to establish the firm base of trust needed between lovers, and more importantly, between sub and Sir...?

This story features orgasm control in a BDSM setting.
Secrets & Lies is now free!

## CONNECT WITH SERENA

For the latest updates, be sure to check out my website! But if you'd like to hang out with me and get to know me better, then I'd love to see you in my Diva reader's group where you can find out all the gossip on new releases as and when they happen. You can join here: www.facebook.com/groups/SerenaAkeroydsDivas. Or you can always PM or email me. I love to hear from you guys: serenaakeroyd@gmail.com.

# ABOUT THE AUTHOR

I'm a romance novelaholic and I won't touch a book unless I know there's a happy ending. This addiction is what made me craft stories that suit my voracious need for raunchy romance. I love twists and unexpected turns, and my novels all contain sexy guys, dark humor, and hot AF love scenes.

I write MF, menage, and reverse harem (also known as why choose romance,) in both contemporary and paranormal. Some of my stories are darker than others, but I can promise you one thing, you will always get the happy ending your heart needs!

www.ingramcontent.com/pod-product-compliance
Lightning Source LLC
Chambersburg PA
CBHW020718310726
48979CB00004B/963
* 9 7 8 1 9 1 5 0 6 2 8 9 5 *